The Pasha's Tale

The Ottoman Cycle, book 4

by S.J.A. Turney

For Nick and Sami

(Even though Nicolo's already left the series!)

I would like to thank everyone who has been instrumental in this book seeing the light of day in its final form, as well as all those people who have continually supported me during its creation: Robin, Alun, Barry, Leni, Nick, Prue and of course Jenny and Tracey and once again my little imps Marcus and Callie who keep me entertained throughout, driving me to wonderful distraction. Also a big thanks to Christian Cameron, a fellow traveller in medieval Istanbul, whose encouragement drives me on.

Cover image by Lucy Sangster of Use or Ornament.
Cover design by Dave Slaney.
Many thanks to both.

Also by S. J. A. Turney:

The Marius' Mules Series

Marius' Mules I: The Invasion of Gaul (2009)
Marius' Mules II: The Belgae (2010)
Marius' Mules III: Gallia Invicta (2011)
Marius' Mules IV: Conspiracy of Eagles (2012)
Marius' Mules V: Hades Gate (2013)
Marius' Mules VI: Caesar's Vow (2014)
Marius' Mules: Prelude to War (2014)
Marius' Mules VII: The Great Revolt (2014)

Tales of the Empire

Interregnum (2009)
Ironroot (2010)
Dark Empress (2011)

The Ottoman Cycle

The Thief's Tale (2013)
The Priest's Tale (2013)
The Assassin's Tale (2014)

The Praetorian Series

The Great Game (2015)

Short story compilations & contributions:

Tales of Ancient Rome vol. 1 - S.J.A. Turney (2011)
Tortured Hearts vol 1 - Various (2012)
Tortured Hearts vol 2 - Various (2012)
Temporal Tales - Various (2013)
Historical Tales – Various (2013)
Deva Tales (2015)

For more information visit http://www.sjaturney.co.uk/
or http://www.facebook.com/SJATurney
or follow Simon on Twitter @SJATurney

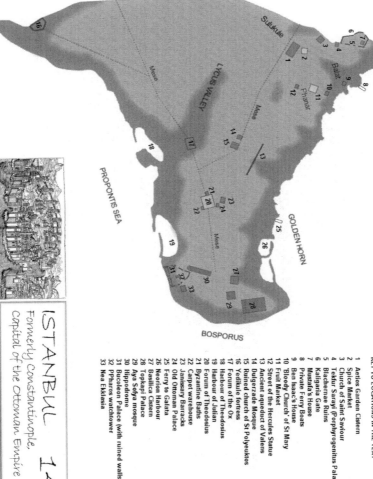

ISTANBUL 1495
Formerly Constantinople,
Capital of the Ottoman Empire

KEY TO LOCATIONS IN THE TEXT

1 Aetios Garden Cistern
2 Spice Market
3 Church of Saint Saviour
4 Tekfur Sarayi (Porphyrogenitus Palace)
5 Blachernae Ruins
6 Kaligaria Gate
7 Mustafa's House
8 Private Ferry Boats
9 Ben Isaac's House
10 'Bloody Church' of St Mary
11 Fruit Market
12 Street of the Hercules Statue
13 Ancient aqueduct of Valens
14 Bulgerzade Mosque
15 Ruined church of St Polyeuktos
16 Yedikule fortress
17 Forum of the Ox
18 Harbour of Theodosius
19 Harbour of Julian
20 Forum of Theodosius
21 Byzantine Baths
22 Carpet warehouse
23 Janissary Barracks
24 Old Ottoman Palace
25 Ferry to Galata
26 Neorion Harbour
27 Basilica Cistern
28 Topkapi Palace
29 Aya Sofya mosque
30 Hippodrome
31 Bucoleon Palace (with ruined walls shown)
32 PPharos watchtower
33 Nea Ekklasia

SULUKULE
Balat
Phanar
LYCUS VALLEY
Mese
Mese
Mese
PROPONTIS SEA
GOLDEN HORN
BOSPORUS

Prologos

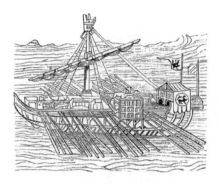

Of the kingmaker and the kingbreaker

February 27th 1495, off the coast of Sicily.

SKIOUROS shuddered and pulled the rough wool cloak tighter about his shoulders, noting sourly how Parmenio seemed to be taking the night chill easily in his stride, in the manner of a veteran sailor who had experienced far worse and still labelled it *summer*.

'Why are we moving so slowly?' he complained.

Parmenio gave him a look with which he was becoming more than familiar – the one sailors give the uninitiated when they ask a question to which the answer may as well be plastered across the heavens in letters made of brilliant stars.

'Sailing south in the Tyrrhenian in winter is a troublesome business, Skiouros. The currents and winds are all against you, so you must rely on God's own breath in the sails or the base muscle of your oarsmen. Not to mention that the political situation in the peninsula is complex and dangerous at the moment; even between the Italian states themselves, let alone with the sultan's empire. Kemal Reis has no interest in landing us in trouble somewhere along the coast.'

His Greek companion simply grunted and pulled the ineffectual wool tighter against the icy wind.

'Besides,' Parmenio went on undeterred, 'the Kingdom of Sicily is so very Spanish, and you know how the great Kemal feels about Spaniards after his last few years. And *I* know how *you* feel about them. One will get you ten that Fernando and Isabella's priests are already sniffing around the island like a dog under a feast table.'

Skiouros nodded acidly. His feelings about God and the churches of man had taken something of a knock over four years of vagrancy. His eyes had been opened to possibilities by the nomads of Africa who saw no ill in combining their ancient spirits with the teachings of Mohammed, and by the tribes of the New World, who had expressed an open interest in the Catholic faith of the crews, and yet had managed to successfully meld them with their own beliefs. Yet the one thing that had struck him time and again was the foulness of fanaticism whatever its base. Etci Hasan, the Ottoman pirate captain, had felt such soul-burning hatred for Christians that it had turned him from a devout path and sent him down the track of the cold, hard, unbending killer. And the Catholics of Rome had been set upon a different course, revelling in corruption and murder, all ostensibly for the greater glory of God. Yet despite all of that, what chilled Skiouros to the bone – far more than the icy wind of the Tyrrhenian in February – was the thought of those black robed zealots back in Spain who had been hungry to peel the flesh from a man and burn his pink-white remains merely for questioning the word of the priesthood.

He could hardly wait to be back in the old Byzantine lands, in a world where the Christians were of the good Greek Church and were pious rather than avaricious, and the followers of Mohammed were more tolerant and sincere.

That last thought jarred him and he tried not to picture the fanatic Hamza Bin Murad in too much detail, or his great uncle Stephanos who had lost an eye when Byzantium fell to Mehmed and had never been able to speak the word *Turk* without spitting bile. Yet despite occasional fanatics in the east, Bayezid the Just – a sultan with true vision – worked ceaselessly to bring order and understanding to the world. So long as there was always a *Bayezid* on the throne...

He shook such morose thoughts from his mind. Soon enough he would be back in his homeland and all would be right. And he had absolutely no wish to land in Italia, where men dripped jewels while they drew blood from the innocent, or on Sicilia where the black priests of Fernando and Isabella would be torturing farmers for imagined slights. Kemal Reis clearly knew exactly what he was doing. Kemal. Another man like Bayezid. Another with vision. If only he would lower himself to conversing with his passengers instead of just favouring Skiouros and his friend with a look of faintly distrustful regret.

Again he was forced to shrug off gloomy feelings. Perhaps it was just the weather and the confinement on board that was to blame for the atmosphere.

Back to Istanbul – to *Byzantium*. To the ancient and sacred city of Constantine.

His heart jumped just a little as it did every time he thought of home.

A faint spicy aroma tinged with the sharp tang of burned hemp announced the return of Dragi, and the Romani sailor dropped to a crouch near the other two.

'Kemal Reis is aiming for landfall at Crete in mid-March,' he announced quietly.

'So long?'

Dragi turned a knowing smile on Skiouros. 'Even mid-March is reaching for speeds that might be unwise, my friend. Had we no pressing matters, we would take far longer. The waters around Sicily, Malta, Tunis and southern Italy are hazardous for a good Ottoman captain, especially one who has made his reputation in the manner of Kemal, rescuing the worthy and raiding the unworthy. The eastern sea is prey to the Knights Hospitaller, who do not baulk at sinking and enslaving their own peoples, let alone the Turk. And beyond the heel of Italy, too far south would send us into the waiting arms of the Mamluk sultans of Egypt, while too far north will throw us into the lap of the Republic of Venice.'

'I thought the empire had a peace treaty with Venice?' Parmenio frowned. 'After all, Venice owns Crete, and we're bound *there* happily enough.'

'Oh it does, and we shall be safe on Venetian Crete, my Greek friend, but tensions are still high and trust hard to come by. Do not forget that Bayezid's armies are in Croatia and southern Hungary, within spitting distance of the Venetian Doge's realm. A lone Ottoman kadirga roaming the Venetian-patrolled Adriatic region might just disappear without trace, regardless of treaties. Slow and careful, my friends. Anyway, do you not enjoy your time aboard Kemal's vessel? For a captain of his rank, this is a well-appointed vessel, and well-supplied, too.'

'Not with wine,' grumbled Parmenio, and Skiouros smiled. In their two days aboard, the Genoese former captain had complained about the abstinent habits of the Muslim crewmen on fairly numerous occasions.

'If you've not found a drinking companion, where do you keep sloping off to in the evenings?' grinned Skiouros.

Parmenio ignored him, and wagged a finger at Dragi. 'And since we're the guests of this ship's second in command, it would be nice to eat something faintly recognisable for a change!'

Skiouros tried not to think too hard on the different meals he had suffered his way through these past few days aboard. The choice of *grey meat* or *greyer meat* had been a tough one. And the fact that the vegetables were almost the same colour and consistency as the meat had troubled him even more.

'Anyway,' Dragi smiled, and Skiouros noted – not for the first time – a strange hardness buried in the folds of the upturned lips, 'the time has come for our most important tale.'

'The *king-maker and king-breaker* at last?' Skiouros asked, shivering and rubbing his hands together. The Romani nodded, and the young Greek leaned forwards, clutching his cloak tight. Despite Dragi's mention of the tale that first night, he had held off, instead spending the previous day reeling off odd stories of his peoples' devising that would have seen him broken and peeled had he spoken of them in front of a Spanish priest. The Romani was strange, and on occasion irritating, with his onion-like layers of personality and meaning, and Skiouros would have walked away before now, had he not owed the man such a great debt.

Dragi licked his lips and began.

'Once, when the world was simpler and wisdom was prized, there lived two brothers. One was a holy man. An imam of sorts. You would probably think of him as a hermit, like your saints of old. A wise and pious man who sought peace and understanding, whose insight was craved by the faithful. He had become so famous for his interpretation of the will of God, in fact, that his name was spoken of alongside those of the prophets.'

'Holy. Got it.'

Dragi flashed an irritated glance at Skiouros, and the Greek smiled.

'The other brother was a teacher,' the Romani continued. 'He valued knowledge and intellect more than the divine, though he was equally sought-after and respected for his mind. He had taught most of the gifted thinkers of the world, such was his own intellect.'

He leaned back and paused for a moment, watching half a dozen of the Turkish sailors down by the prow playing some game, laughing and pushing each other about amiably.

'The brothers did not always see eye-to-eye, of course. You can imagine. In fact, they argued about everything. When the holy man gloried in the pure green of the clear waters, claiming they were the same shade as the eyes of God, the teacher would snort and explain how that green could be formed from a drab blue and a sickly yellow, and that it was no more divine than was the goat's-meat broth that they both drank.'

'I understand the situation,' Skiouros murmured with feeling, his mind filling with saddening images of Lykaion in their earlier days of argumentative separation in the great city.

'Do not misunderstand,' Dragi noted carefully. 'The brothers were the best of friends, and they each respected and valued their sibling's talents. But it is in the nature of the intelligent to question and debate, and they were the brightest of the bright, so they questioned and debated everything that passed between them.'

The Romani flexed his fingers. 'Then there came a time when the sultan of their realm passed on and went before God, leaving his two eldest sons grieving and regarding one another in anticipation. For while the sultan had several other children by his concubines, only two would struggle for the throne, as they two had both led armies and held governorships in the traditional manner.'

'Wouldn't the succession fall to the elder?' asked Parmenio curiously.

'Not in the world from which they – from which *I* – hail, my friend. There is no line of heredity. There is no clear heir in the court of the Osman sultans. Succession is a matter of strength and luck.'

The former captain frowned. 'That sounds messy.'

'Perhaps. Sometimes it is, but think of it as being tested for your fitness for the role ahead. A man who can win the war of succession is likely strong enough to take the reins of the empire thereafter.' Dragi shook his head and rolled his eyes. 'You are interrupting an important tale.'

Parmenio shrugged apologetically and the Romani went on.

'The heirs had both tried to reach the capital first to claim their throne in the old way, but had arrived together, rendering the succession still moot. And so both men warred for a year, taking and retaking territory and causing endless destruction in the land. In the end, their courtiers begged them to halt the damage and to find a new solution. And so it was that they turned to the wise brothers in their mountain fastnesses, for the pair were respected above all, and their decision would be indisputable.'

He sighed and took a swig from a mug of warmed fruit drink, his breath clouding in the cold.

'The heirs disbanded their armies to allow the land to recover and went to the cities of their former governorships to await the brothers' decision. And the argument began. For the holy man could see the greater value in the heir that had clearly fought with the grace of the Qur'an in his heart and with God at his shoulder, while the teacher could see that the other heir had been careful and wise in his dealings with men and with nations. And the pious one saw wickedness in the heart of the second, while the learned one could see a dangerous impetuousness in the first.'

Dragi gave them a meaningful look. 'As one sought to make a king, so the other sought to break him. And so they debated and argued and deliberated for endless days, while the world waited outside, its breath held, for the result of their discussion. Then, suddenly, as the cock crowed one morning, the teacher looked at his brother and shook his head in amazement.'

'"Do you realise," said the teacher, "that we have argued for a year and a day. We have argued for longer than the heirs fought, and still we are at an impasse. We are apparently too wise to decide between two such viable candidates." And the holy man was struck by the wisdom of this insight. Smiling and shaking hands, the two men went to their door, preparing to pass the task onto someone less burdened with wit.'

He stopped and tilted his face up to the sky so that the cold starlight bathed his face.

'And?' urged Parmenio after a pregnant pause.

'And they discovered that they were too late. They had argued – the king-maker and the king-breaker – for so long while the two heirs waited patiently, that one of the sultan's lesser children, sick of the indecision, had raised an army, stormed the palace, executed both heirs and had instituted a reign of harsh terror upon the land. The world experienced a darkness of fear and blood that lasted for a year and two days, and from that time on, only decisiveness and strength has been prized in successions, for excessive prudence had shown itself to be weak.'

'Well *that's* a depressing tale,' snorted Parmenio, leaning back.

'So,' Skiouros mused, 'in your tale, both men went out to make a king, but together they failed. Who is the king-maker and who is the king-breaker? Where do wisdom and piety lie in that system?'

Dragi sighed. 'It is unimportant who is who. Do not fixate on unnecessary nuances of the tale such as its popular name, when it is the underlying moral that is important. The tale carries a warning,' he noted. 'Indecision and vacillating achieve nothing. A man should not seek to discover every angle of every facet of a thing, for by the time he has uncovered the deepest meanings, that thing may be gone. Decisiveness and a willingness to act promptly for the good are of prime importance. If the king-maker and the king-breaker had been kept apart and asked independently to advise a third, then the matter might have been resolved without such a terrible end.'

Skiouros frowned and pursed his lips.

'You seem to be advocating taking things at face value and taking uninformed action?'

'Not so, but a truly wise man can absorb the principle facts about a thing in a short time, while continued deliberation will only serve to cloud his mind and make him uncertain.'

The young Greek huffed into his hands. 'You may take the moral of your tale to be a warning to act decisively. To me it sounds more like a caution against outside interference. The king-maker and the king-breaker should have kept their noses firmly out of the business and let the princes get on with it.' He noted a darkening of Dragi's expression and pressed on. 'Anyway, I am not sure why you attach such significance to this tale and why you were so set on its telling to us in the first place?'

'That,' Dragi said with an infuriating half-smile, 'is yet to be revealed. The time is not quite right, for other pieces must fall into place before its significance can become clear. I tell you this now in preparation. By the end of May, you will see everything clearly, and you will understand why I have chosen to reveal what I know slowly. If I tell you all I know straight away, you will feel the need to over-analyse like the two wise brothers, and we cannot afford such a thing – especially without the benefit of *first-hand* knowledge.'

'You may be the most infuriating man I've ever met, Dragi.'

'Then you have lived a sheltered life, Skiouros the Greek. Keep faith with me until the end of May and all will be revealed and resolved.'

The three men sat silent, shivering in the icy air, and Skiouros found himself gazing at the dark bulk of Sicily off the larboard bow, for behind that island, far away, lay the island of Crete, that the Venetians called Candia, where an exiled Spanish swordsman and a reliquary containing Lykaion's head awaited. And past that, up to the left, far beyond the distant line that was the Italian coast, sat Istanbul, which had been Constantinople.

Crete by the middle of next month, and Istanbul soon after.

Skiouros was going home. What to, he couldn't imagine from the tantalising esoteric hints Dragi kept throwing at him, but whatever awaited him, it would be good to be back.

Chapter one – Of familiar lands and unwelcome faces

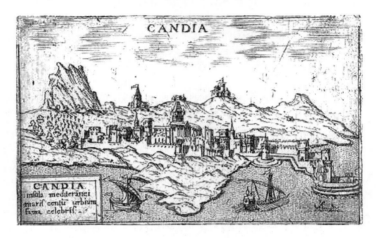

Heraklion, Crete, March 19th

THERE was something indefinably warmer and more welcoming about the waters around Crete. The Ottoman galley was in truth no more than a couple of hundred miles more southerly than it had been at Sicily, and they were a mere three weeks later in the year, and yet the difference in weather was palpable. Almost overnight, as the kadirga of Kemal Reis had come within sight of the Cretan shore, the temperature had seemed to rise. Men stopped wearing cloaks and breath stopped frosting except in that chilled, gloomy hour when the sun was still just a gleam in the eye of God. The water was a more pleasant blue-green and the world just seemed more acceptable.

The morning sun glowed off in the direction of Rhodos – the home fortress of the Knights Hospitaller – still shining just above the horizon, and yet already Heraklion was clearly a hive of activity as the ship's oars rose and dipped in perfect unison, sliding the elegant Ottoman galley through the waters of the harbour and towards the very jetty upon which Skiouros had alighted four years ago, following his desperate departure from Istanbul. Then he had come disguised as a priest and running from his past. Now he came as a seasoned traveller, welcomed aboard a vessel of the Ottoman navy at the behest of its pilot, and returning to his homeland with a straight back and a calm heart.

Full circle.

At a command from Dragi – Skiouros still could not comprehend how the Romani beggar had risen to become Kemal Reis' second in that time he had been away evading the dreadful pirate Hasan – the oars rose and were shipped. The man at the steering oar expertly guided the wide, low vessel in alongside the jetty using just gentle momentum to settle it by the creaking wood. Instantly, men leapt ashore and hurriedly hauled ropes taut, tying them off to the mooring posts both fore and aft. Parmenio nodded at the professionalism of it all, finding only two faults with the whole process and leaning close to Skiouros to murmur them out of earshot of the Turkish sailors.

The flags snapped in the temperate breeze, making the muscles of the golden Venetian lions upon them bunch and stretch on their red backgrounds – a permanent, glittering reminder to the people of this wondrous ancient island that while they may speak primarily Greek – and many might still owe their allegiance to the Patriarch of Constantinople – the government, taxes, churches and all facets of power belonged to Catholic Venice.

While he felt for the locals, as a boy who had grown to manhood in a once-Greek land now dominated by the Turk, he noted that Parmenio's expression was darker still. As a Genoese, the former captain probably held less love of Venice than anyone else present.

And they would be here for some time. It had come as something of a surprise to Skiouros to learn that. He had expected a quick layover for resupply and the few small pieces of work the kadirga could do with. He had *not* expected weeks. But as they had left the waters off Napoli at the start of their journey, the other two kadirga in Kemal's fleet had been despatched by the Turkish *Reis* to gather the last of the refugees from Spain, who were apparently waiting somewhere on the northern coast of Africa. Kemal's ship would wait at Heraklion for the other two to rejoin them, and then those refugees – mostly Jews and almost entirely learned men – would accompany them to Istanbul to settle there under the open acceptance of the great Bayezid the Second, while the commander and his three ships would be given new orders.

Skiouros wasn't sure how he felt about the possibility of spending weeks on the island. Crete had been something of a second home to him for a while after his flight from the great city, but now he was itching to return to the land of his youth – not to lounge about, idling in this place. Still, it would be interesting to visit some of his old haunts. And he was more determined than ever to seek out his former sword-master. What he would do with Don Diego de Teba when he found him, he had no idea. But somehow he felt that things were unfinished there, especially with what he had learned of the Don's lands and family during his stay in Spain.

And there was Lykaion...

That last troubled him a little. What he was going to do about his brother's casket, which remained in the church of Saint Titus, he did not know. It was venerated by priests who coveted it, believing it to contain a sacred relic – the head of Saint Theodoros – and how he would retrieve it, he could not yet imagine. But he had achieved the unachievable so often in so few years that this was no more daunting than any other task, really.

As the sailors went about the busy tasks of finalising the ship's berthing, Skiouros looked about himself. The great heavy harbour tower, of Byzantine construction so familiar from his homeland, began a line of fortifications that had been upgraded in the past half century by the Venetian authorities, turning an ancient system of walls into a modern series of bastions and thick, cannon-proof defences.

Those heavy fortifications sealed in a city that was as much Venetian as Greek – and even early Arab in places. A cultural melting pot that was slowly and steadily becoming more Italianate as the Republic of Venice continued to settle its own people here. His gaze moved across the roofs of the city and back down to the dockside, and his heart lurched.

Perhaps *that* was why Parmenio's expression was so dark?

Beyond the end of the jetty, between the new arrivals and the great *Arsenals* of the Venetian fleet, a group of black-robed priests stood beneath a cross the height of two men, the joint between the horizontal and vertical beams reinforced with steel that flashed and gleamed in the morning sun like the eye of God roving across the port, seeking out sin.

What were *they* doing here?

Finally the sailors seemed happy with the securing of the ship and a boarding ramp was run out to the damp jetty's boards. The officers and passengers of the kadirga were helped across to the timbers of the jetty where a diminutive man in red and gold livery stood with a ledger, accompanied by half a dozen guards in the uniform of the Duchy of Candia, as the island was known to Venice. Kemal Reis, stroking his voluminous white beard and narrowing his

11

eyes suspiciously, stepped close to the passengers and addressed Dragi in his native tongue, quietly, such that no one else could hear, even Skiouros so close by. The Romani second in command stepped forward, clearing his throat, and then launching into passable Italian.

'My captain, the admirable and honourable Kemal Reis, valued representative of Sultan Bayezid the Second and the Ottoman court and a recognised friend of the great lion of Venice, asks the reason for the presence of armed men at his disembarkation. Are we not allies, bound by treaty?'

The short, heavily-brocaded official looked distinctly uncomfortable and used a hooked finger to loosen the tight collar of his doublet.

'My apologies if the noble Reis sees this as an insult or a threat. I can assure you that was never our intention. The city guard are here to escort your captain and to protect his ship, nothing more.'

There was a pause as Dragi relayed this to the captain, who looked less than convinced by the response.

'The great Kemal Reis would like to know from what he might be expected to seek protection in an allied city.'

The official's discomfort was becoming too much for him and beads of sweat started to run down from his hairline. Skiouros noticed the man's eyes flash for a second to the group of black-robed priests and he could quite understand the man's fears with the heresy-hunting Dominicans and the heathen Turk sharing his wharf.

'Respectfully, sir,' the man went on, 'the Republic has recently signed treaties with Spain and the Kingdom of Sicily, supporting their war against the French invaders in Napoli. And while our treaty with the sultan remains firmly in place, the whole Mediterranean world is aware of the strained relationship between their Catholic Majesties Fernando and Isabella and those of an… Islamic nature. Moreover, the name Kemal Reis is synonymous with…' he paused and the discomfort shifted up yet another notch. He wanted to say *piracy*, Skiouros realised. 'Coastal raids upon Spanish lands,' he settled for, weakly.

Kemal nodded a slow and forced understanding as this was relayed to him, and his response was measured in its nature.

'Kemal Reis thanks you for such thoughtful provision and entirely understands the difficulty of maintaining alliances with two nations who distrust one another. It is the captain's intention to remain in port until the other two vessels in our fleet rejoin us, and he would be pleased to accept the security of a port guard on his ship during that time. Our passengers will see to their own safety and quarters once they have disembarked, but the crew will continue to stay aboard the kadirga. The great Reis hopes that he might use his time in port to speak to the authorities in the city and secure an ever greater understanding between our nations.'

The little man, seemingly relieved, nodded emphatically. 'I am sure the Duke and his court will be most grateful for such an opportunity, and accommodation for the Reis and his officers will be secured within the *Palazzo Ducale* at the Lion Square. And please, leave the low business of port bureaucracy to a lesser and I will see that all runs smoothly. As a gesture to our Ottoman friends, I am willing to waive all berthing fees and other sundry costs for the duration of your stay.'

Diplomatic, smiled Skiouros to himself.

As Kemal followed the eager, gesturing official, and half a dozen of his own men fell in with him in front of the city guard, Skiouros collared Dragi, who trailed along behind.

'Weeks? In port with *this* lot?' he gestured to the priests on the quayside.

Dragi nodded. 'All will be well. By mid-May, my Reis will be in Istanbul. There is a festival planned that he cannot miss, and it will take several weeks to journey there.'

Skiouros blinked. 'That's *two months*, Dragi.'

'All will be well,' the Romani repeated with a reassuring smile. 'I must accompany the Reis to the palace, as his second, so I cannot go with you, but remember what I said about staying in contact. Be ready for word from me at any time, and be sure that I will receive any message from you speedily. And be careful,' he added, and hurried to rejoin Kemal as they left the jetty under escort and made their way into the city proper. More city guards tromped along the timbers, coming to form a protective barrier for the Ottoman ship, though Skiouros still couldn't quite shake the impression that they were more prison guards than defenders. He and Parmenio hurried along the jetty behind them and realised that the organisation of the wharves meant that they would have to pass close to that towering crucifix.

He watched with a tight chest as the eight Turks were led under guard past the black-robed men, and the priests immediately dropped whatever they were doing and turned to harangue the new arrivals. Skiouros was far from surprised to hear the shouts issue in a thick Spanish accent, though he was taken aback by the bile, venom

13

and vehemence in their cries, given the fact that it was their hosts who were escorting the Turks.

The new arrivals were *agents of the Devil*. No. The bearded one was the Devil *himself*, taken human form. Could the people of good, Catholic Candia not understand that the turban was a fiendish device designed to hide the horns of demons from good Christians? Could they not see that the cursed Turk were the enemies of Christ? That they chose not to drink alcohol so that no sacred communion wine might pass their lips? See how that Turk had a hooked nose almost as pronounced as the Jew? Because the devil was imperfect and so he could not perfectly recreate a human visage!

The insults and denouncements went on and Skiouros felt his blood first run cold at the presence of such blind hatred this far east – so close to his homeland – and then felt it slowly rise and come to the boil at the very idea that this kind of intolerance and stupidity could begin to encroach upon his own beloved world.

'Don't react to them,' Parmenio hissed at his shoulder, and Skiouros realised with a start that he had his hand on the hilt of the sword at his waist rather provocatively. Carefully, he removed it. The black-clad priests had not yet noticed he and Parmenio, for they were still busy denouncing the bearded devil who had passed and was now on his way to the island's authorities.

'I can't believe they're this far east. I thought we'd left that sort back in Spain, or at least in Rome. How long before they're knocking on the sultan's own high gate with their crosses?'

Parmenio shrugged. 'I can't see this lot in Istanbul. But wherever their Catholic Majesties of Castille and Aragon get their claws into, they pop up,' he replied. 'Just hope this alliance is temporary and that they don't get to set up here permanently. I heard horror stories when we were back in Italia. Once they insinuate themselves, the Inquisition is near impossible to remove. As soon as they get to read their *Edict of Grace* in the churches here, the troubles will start for real and then no one will be safe.'

'Curse the whole damn lot of them,' Skiouros snapped, glaring at the black figures. One of the priests turned at the words, narrowing his eyes at the pair, seemingly trying to weigh them up. They wore no turban, of course, but that did not make them friends in the eyes of these men – especially with Skiouros' clear eastern Mediterranean skin-tone and appearance.

Parmenio was shoving him now, moving him on past the priests and into the press of people.

'What now?' the former captain asked.

'Dragi said that he would be closeted away with Kemal for most of our stay, but he would leave messages at the Taverna di San Marco on the main port street if he needed to speak to us, and we could do the same for him. Other than that our days are our own, I suppose, until we're ready to embark once again. I suspect we might need to take on a job in order to survive for weeks.'

'Probably a good idea for us to stay at the tavern Dragi mentioned,' Parmenio replied. 'I rarely left the port and warehouse district when I was trading here. You know the tavern? Do they have rooms?'

'I know it well. And yes they have rooms, but we have pitiful few coins, my friend.'

Parmenio gave him a wicked smile and hoisted up a purse that fair bulged with coin. As Skiouros stared, he opened the top and tipped a few out onto his palm. 'I think we'll manage.'

'How did you get all *that*?'

'Sailors like to play games. Few of them can play dice like a Genoese, though. You asked me where I kept going on board? A few games each evening, and a man can amass quite a pile without it seeming too much like he's fleecing his shipmates.'

Skiouros boggled, and the captain chuckled in response. 'Nicolo was a past master at it. Used to do it to me without even me realising it.'

'Can we spend *those* here?' the Greek enquired, picking up a Mamluk coin with a lion on the obverse face and Arabic script filling the reverse. His eyes shot back to the black-robed figures nearby.

'The Inquisition doesn't rule here, Skiouros. At least not yet. And I've still to encounter a port where gold is turned away just over a little writing. A place like this would accept coin from the devil himself if it shone with the right colour. Come on.'

Chapter two – Of teachers and rogues

Heraklion, Crete, March 28th

MORE than a week had passed and the chill in the air had dissipated, leaving the island wallowing in early spring, temperatures gradually rising over the days as the flowers burst into multichrome life. Traditionally it was a time of optimism and good nature among the islanders, and this year was no exception but for the few who had cause to resent the presence of the Spanish priests. Those Dominican clerics daily traipsed through the streets of the city – a black stain on the brightly-coloured spring – chanting their liturgy of hate behind their great cross and casting hateful looks at those islanders whose ancient heritage had left them with dark skin tones or a Levantine facial cast.

For more than a week Skiouros and Parmenio had stayed quiet and unobtrusive in the tavern on the great street that led from the port up to the basilica and the city's centre. Scant information had come down from the palace, and in this limbo of inaction ennui was quick to set in. Barring the Inquisition, nothing here had changed since Skiouros had last visited, and somehow it had become easy to sink back into that lifestyle, though both he and Parmenio were ever aware of the dwindling coin in the latter's purse and the fact that they would soon need to acquire more funds somehow.

Perhaps Dragi would be able to help? Maybe it was time to leave a message for him?

They had not seen their friend since their arrival, the Romani sailor closeted away in the Ducal Palace with Kemal Reis, involved in complex trade and treaty negotiations, but the man had left them a message a few days ago, telling them not to expect departure until mid or late April. Rather than suffer so many weeks of languor, the pair had decided upon a course of action.

Skiouros took a pull of his cup of wine and smiled to himself as he realised he was sitting at the very table at which he had first spoken to their Romani friend. He'd not known who he was at the time, of course. The man had just been some itinerant Romani vagrant with an outspoken manner and a strange – ridiculous even – accent, which Skiouros now knew to have been affected for the benefit of performance. Dragi was a consummate assumer of roles, and had a personality and tone that seemed to fluctuate to fit the situation. Skiouros was pretty sure that if he lived to be a hundred, he would still never really know the man.

Parmenio, sitting opposite, nodded slightly towards the street. 'Hello. Here we go.'

The two men kept their gazes casually out on the street as a shabby man with a slight limp strode past the table in the open-fronted tavern and on up the street, a small, folded piece of paper fluttering to the table-top in his wake and settling between the two wine cups in the bowl of olives.

'I wasn't made for all this clandestine stuff,' Parmenio grumbled, prodding at his midriff – still surprisingly ample considering the privations of a sea voyage – as a hungry murmur issued from it.

Skiouros nodded sympathetically. Of course, *clandestine stuff* was very much what he was made for, but he'd believed that part of his life to be behind him now, for all that Dragi had hinted at further, darker enemies lying in wait in his future. He was just a traveller returning home. And planning to steal a holy relic from a church. And track down a fugitive...

He opened the piece of paper and scanned the four words upon it.

Michele Testabianca – Lanterna Azzurro.

'Do you know it?' Parmenio enquired, indicating the paper.

Skiouros nodded. 'The Blue Lantern, in the back streets towards the Rethymno gate. Never been in, but I've been past it occasionally and avoided a couple of fights outside it. Come on.'

The pair rose, threw down the last of their drinks and gathered their bags, stepping out into the street and heading southwest, deeper into the city.

Clandestine. A good word for it. Surprisingly so.

He and Parmenio had spent a few days in the city after they docked just getting their land legs once more. Skiouros had shown his friend around the parts of the city that he had known well during his sojourn here a few years back, for Parmenio had a sketchy knowledge of the city at best, his own experience largely limited to the port.

And then, upon discovering that they would still languish here until at least mid-April, Skiouros had decided that the time had come to try and find Diego. When they finally came to retrieve Lykaion's head the assistance of the aloof, talented Spaniard could only be of help. Full of confidence and optimism, Skiouros had strolled into the tavern near the market where he had first met the swordsman and which remained a favourite of expatriates from Iberia. Wandering up to the counter with Parmenio in tow, he had smiled at the portly, grease-stained innkeeper and had asked after the whereabouts of the fencing master Don Diego de Teba.

He had been shocked at the sudden change in the owner's demeanour. The man reacted as though he'd been asked to kiss the devil's backside, recoiling and pointing past Skiouros, his eyes flashing. 'Get out of my tavern!' he'd snarled. Taken aback by the vehemence, Skiouros had done just that and, as he and Parmenio had stood in the alley next to the tavern, an old soak had tumbled out of the side door and accosted them.

'Shhh,' the man had said, crumbs and froth dripping from his face. 'Askin' after Teba can bring a man a heap o' trouble.'

'But why?' Skiouros had managed.

'Runaway, he is. Wanted by the guard. Every few days they rough up a few of us trying to find out where he is. You din't know?'

Parmenio had shrugged. 'We've only been on the island a couple of days. Just got in from Napoli.'

The man had nodded his understanding.

'I knew him a few years back,' Skiouros added. 'He was my sword instructor.'

Again that nod, and more crumbs. 'There are those as claim to know where he is, though they be secretive and dangerous folk.'

Skiouros had nodded and the pause stretched out expectantly, until the man widened his eyes and waggled his brows meaningfully.

'Oh,' Skiouros said suddenly, 'of course.' He'd gestured to
Parmenio, who sighed and fished out his purse, selecting four
gleaming coins, glancing briefly at the man and then sliding one
back in before dropping the three into the hungry palm. The sot
narrowed his eyes at Parmenio, but nodded.

'Might take some days. Where you staying?'

Skiouros had replied easily and the man told him to sit tight
at the tavern.

There had followed a week of tense waiting. Every few days
the old man had wandered up to their table to let them know he'd
had no luck yet and to fleece them of a new coin. Parmenio had been
full of doubt. *He's just playing us. He's draining our purse faster
than the rent. Is this swordsman really worth all this fuss?*

The truth was that Skiouros was experiencing the same
doubts. But then, they had weeks to kill on Crete before departure
and little else to fill the time. And while he was not at all sure what
to make of this turn of events, he remembered the Spaniard's skill as
a match for Orsini – may God have mercy on the nobleman's soul. If
they were to attempt to retrieve a holy relic from the church, a master
swordsman might just mean the difference between success and
failure. Besides, Skiouros was still intrigued by the man, and felt for
a fellow exile down on his luck.

And then yesterday, just when the pair had made the decision
that they were being cheated and to cut the old man loose, he had
dropped by for yet another coin, but had claimed to have found his
lead at last. They should sit tight one more day, he'd said, and then
they would have what they wanted.

Skiouros smiled as he made his way through the streets. It
would be more than interesting to meet the Spaniard again and find
out what had brought him to this situation. Half an hour later, he and
Parmenio had passed through the city centre and made their way out
towards the gate from which the road led along the coast west to
Rethymno. Turning off the main street, they took a narrow alley to
the right that sloped down towards the sea and lay deep in shade,
three storeys of building to either side of a lane too narrow for a man
to lie across. The white paint to reflect the heat was chipped and
peeling all over this neighbourhood, but soon they emerged into a
small square with a wilted-looking maple dominating the centre and

overhanging a marble fountain formed from re-used ancient stonework.

The Lanterna Azzurro tavern occupied a wedge-shaped building between two streets that led off down to the north. If any single word could describe it, that word would be *seedy*. Skiouros had been past the place once or twice in his time, but had never had cause – nor the desire – to enter. He could easily imagine shady deals being made inside and occasionally bodies being carried back out. It occurred to him that he was about to experience the former. Hopefully he wouldn't be experiencing the latter too.

Parmenio held his shoulder for a moment.

'Are you sure this Spaniard is worth this?'

'No,' Skiouros smiled, and pushed open the door.

The *Blue Lantern* smelled like feet. Bad feet. *Sick* feet. The hazy atmosphere enveloped them in a reeking fug. Behind Skiouros, his friend made a gagging sound and pulled a stained kerchief up to cover his mouth and nose. He looked around. The source of the interesting atmosphere quickly became apparent: miscellaneous reeking meats were being smoked in a kitchenette that was only separated from the bar by a wide arch. Three men crouched over a table playing dice by the light of a stinking, dribbling, dysentery-brown and poor quality tallow candle. An old man sat over a commode in one corner, flies buzzing around the bucket beneath the wooden seat as he groaned and strained in full view of the clientele.

Skiouros sauntered over to the bar, affecting a somewhat-false air of confidence, and nodded to the scarred barkeep. 'I'm looking for Michele. Michele Testabianca?' he asked in his best Italian.

The barkeep frowned at him suspiciously, but a swarthy-skinned, neatly-shorn and bearded man supping wine at the far end turned to them, hazel eyes gleaming unpleasantly in the dim light. The slight smile on the man's face didn't quite touch his eyes.

'Who wants him?' he replied in Venetian-accented Italian.

'I'm looking for an old friend,' Skiouros answered truthfully.

'Anyone important?'

'I am led to believe so.' Skiouros glanced around and lowered his voice. 'The fugitive De Teba.'

The man simply raised an eyebrow. 'Who are you?'

'Just an old friend.'

'Let me see that sword.'

Skiouros frowned, drew his blade and held it out, hilt first. The bearded drinker looked down at it for a moment. 'Not a soldier's sword, that one.'

'Appropriately so, since I'm no soldier.'

The man nodded and turned back to the bar. 'Drink gets more expensive every year.'

Skiouros slid his blade back into the sheath. 'True.' Gesturing to Parmenio, he waited for the purse to open and then slid a coin onto the bar, ignoring his friend's sour expression as he shook the purse meaningfully and then shut it.

'Mamluk gold, eh? You're *certainly* no soldier of Venice or Castille, then.'

'No.'

'That one will see me through a night's warm oblivion. But what am I to do for the rest of the week?'

With narrowed eyes, Skiouros slid five more onto the bar. The man stacked the six coins, tapped a finger on the bar and turned a questioning gaze on Skiouros, who smiled. 'And on the seventh day, Michele Testabianca rested.'

The man at the bar chuckled and reached out to collect the coins, but Parmenio's large hand slapped down on top of his. The room suddenly felt tense and dangerous.

'Where is our man,' the Genoese sailor asked.

Testabianca shrugged. 'Take the road out of the Rethymno gate and after about a mile and a half, you'll reach a shrine by the roadside. Turn left there onto the trade road that crosses the island. The great market town of Moires is about twenty-five miles along that road, but five miles or so before that is the village of Agioi Deka. Near there is a ruined church dedicated to Saint Titus. Last I heard, your friend was using the church as a base. For your ongoing health, I recommend keeping this information to yourself.'

Skiouros nodded his thanks and stepped back from the bar. The strange atmosphere in the place was in no way lessened by the occupants who watched with guarded expressions as he and Parmenio left. As they emerged into the fresh air, Parmenio eyed a huddled shape on the ground opposite which could as easily be a corpse as a drunken vagrant, cleared his throat and turned a wary look on his friend.

'You realise we could be walking straight into some nest of Cretan villains on the word of a man we don't know and who,

21

frankly, I cannot consider an openly trustworthy character? I'll ask you once again: is your Spaniard worth this danger?'

Skiouros gave him a strange smile. 'You might imagine Testabianca to be lying, but I don't. Believe me, I've spent much of my life in dealings with men like him and if he were lying, I'd have known.' He sucked in air through his teeth. 'On the other hand, let's be on our guard, eh? He may not have been lying about the details but there was something he *wasn't* telling us, too.'

Parmenio's expression confirmed how little this information consoled him.

'I'm a sailor, not a walker, Skiouros. Twenty miles is a long way for a man used to a world only fifty feet long and twenty wide.'

Skiouros nodded. 'He said we take the trade road to Moires. I remember hearing about it before. There's supposed to be a lot of traffic on that route. A couple of coins apiece and we can probably hitch a ride on a marketer's cart.'

'Oh good. Off into the unknown with a lighter purse, a sore backside and a splinter or two.'

March 28th, on the trade road.

Skiouros and Parmenio dragged their heels as the sun's last rays sank behind the hills to the west of the valley along which they trod wearily. Despite the renowned busyness of the road, they had tried to hitch a lift with the few carters they had encountered in the three hours since they'd left the city, and had failed each time. Two carters had informed them flatly that there was not room and they would not shift their cargo about for the kind of money the pair were offering. The third had given them a suspicious look and put his hand on the hilt of a knife at his belt before leading his cart away, watching them intently as he did so.

Then one of the locals they passed had told them that many carters used Voutes as a stop along the road, and they might well find a ride there, and so they had pressed on, intending to spend the night in this Voutes – a hamlet some seven miles up into the hills that formed the backbone of Crete. Ahead, they could see the village, all white houses and an ancient brown church, clinging to the ridge that separated this valley from the next. It was a welcome sight. Skiouros felt his tired spirits lift a little, and turned to Parmenio. 'How many coins do we have left?'

'Not enough. We can afford a snack and a barn maybe, as well as a cart-ride if we can find one.'

Skiouros nodded glumly.

'Remove those swords very carefully, drop them to the ground, and kick them away.'

The pair stopped dead at the words, spoken in thick Cretan Greek by some unseen tongue. Skiouros' hand went to the hilt of his sword.

'Slowly,' urged the voice again.

'We have very little to rob,' Skiouros said quietly and with genuine feeling as he gently eased his sword from its sheath, Parmenio mirroring the action next to him. He hadn't yet decided whether the blade would fall or be brandished in defence, though he was already favouring the former. The disembodied voice held the confidence of a man with a small army at his back and fighting would probably be tantamount to suicide.

'Then this should be quick,' the voice replied, 'though the swords alone will earn a pretty ducat or ten.' As Skiouros' blade cleared the mouth of the scabbard he hesitated, and a shadowy figure separated from the darkness beneath a juniper, a naked blade in each hand. Just as Skiouros expected, half a dozen others simultaneously emerged from the bushes and trees around them. Perhaps this was why the carters were less than pleased to see two armed men on the road?

'If you leave us the swords, we will give you what else we have without a fight.'

The man coughed out a dark laugh.

'Drop the blade or I will find somewhere new to sheathe it.'

Still Skiouros hesitated, and next to him he could see Parmenio in a similar state, waiting to see what his friend decided. The Genoese captain's knuckles were white on his sword hilt.

'What guarantee do we have that you will not simply kill us anyway?'

'None,' admitted the bandit leader, and the silence became a little more oppressive.

'Last chance, little man. Cast your blade away or you'll regret it.'

Skiouros felt helplessness tighten its grip on him as his fingers sweated into his hilt. Taking a deep breath, he lifted the sword defensively. The bandit took three steps forward, emerging from the gloom. He was ugly and unkempt, but clearly confident and strong. The man gestured to left and right with his blades, and the circle began to close around them. Parmenio hefted his sword ready, and cast a nervous glance at Skiouros.

'Any last-minute bright ideas?'

Both men tensed, and Skiouros almost lost control of his bowel at the sudden, heart-stopping sound of a crossbow string twanging taut. The bandit leader was suddenly thrown forward, hurled to the dusty ground at the pair's feet, his swords clattering out to the sides as he bit down on the earth, three inches of a crossbow bolt standing proud from his spine.

'Shiiiiiiiit!' breathed Parmenio, staring at the twitching body. The circle of thieves had stopped advancing and, as two more of them doubled over and collapsed on the ground to the soundtrack of a thwack and a whooshing thud, the rest began to melt away again into the shadows. Two of them managed to disappear into the undergrowth, but two more suddenly found themselves facing new figures closing in around them, crossbows now thrown over their shoulders and swords drawn. The panicked, desperate bandits were quickly and efficiently dispatched by the new arrivals. Skiouros and Parmenio watched in a strange mix of relief and bafflement as their rescuers finished off those on the ground, and four of them were sent off to hunt down the pair who'd escaped.

A man with the distinct air of a leader stepped towards them, wiping clean a bloody utilitarian sword and then sheathing it.

'Scum,' he noted, nudging the body of the bandit chief with his boot. 'This lot have been causing trouble for some time. It's rare a merchant travels without a weapon these days, and often they move in groups or hire guards. Perhaps things can return to normal now. Where are you bound?'

Parmenio opened his mouth to reply, but Skiouros shot him a concealed warning look as he spoke over the top. 'To Voutes tonight. Then on to Moires to visit the holy men of Agios Andonis.'

'Pilgrims? And not local,' the man said, cocking his ear at Skiouros' accent. The young Greek shook his head. Though these men wore travelling clothes with no insignia, he had seen enough soldiers and guards in his time to recognise the type.

'No. I'm from the Morea, but Venetian lands are more comfortable than Ottoman ones,' he answered calmly. 'Lucky for us the trade road has protectors, eh?'

'Extremely.' The man straightened. 'I would suggest you move on to Voutes as quickly as possible. There may be more of them out there yet. Find other travellers and join them. Safety in numbers, remember.'

Skiouros nodded as he sheathed his sword. 'Again, my thanks,' he said, and moved to the side, with Parmenio replacing his own blade and following suit. As the two men strode on up the dusty path towards the village ahead, the leader watched them with interest until they passed around the next bend.

'You didn't trust them?' Parmenio murmured, glancing back over his shoulder.

'Not particularly. Remember where we're going. It pays to be careful. Convenient that they happened upon their prey just as we came along. *Too* convenient for my liking.'

'What was that dung you were talking about holy men?'

Skiouros shrugged. 'They're real. Heard about them last time I was here. Hermits from Moires.'

Parmenio sighed. 'Let's get to Voutes and have a drink and a bite to eat, and look for a carter who'll take us.

March 30th, Agioi Deka.

Skiouros and Parmenio stumped along the dusty road beneath brown, dry hills that rose to the north and endless olive groves marching off to the south like a twisted green army in the dirt. They had said farewell to the carter and his wife, who had transported them in relative comfort from Voutes, across the backbone of Crete and down to the southern lands, departing at the village of Agioi Deka half a mile back, where the couple would be staying the night before moving on to the great market of Moires. Despite the lateness of the day, with the sun now hovering like the sword of Damokles over the low hills that separated this place from the town ahead, the pair had decided to press on, since they were so close.

An ancient city had once stood here, as was attested by the crumbled walls that rose above the olive trees, the shattered aqueduct that they passed, perfectly-worked fluted columns lying ignored in hedgerows, and once-crucial civic fountain basins now used as agricultural water troughs. For more than half a mile they had passed these sad reminders of long-lost glory in the warm glow of evening, but soon, between the gnarled dry trees, they had caught sight of the monument that had to be their destination.

The ruined church stood beside a small stand of poplars and more of the ubiquitous olive trees. Formed of smooth limestone ashlar blocks it almost glowed in the setting sunlight, standing out

25

clear among the undergrowth. Perhaps half the church remained standing – the eastern half close to the travellers – and other ancient civic ruins surrounding it spoke volumes as to its great age. Beyond, on the hillside, stood the ancient arc of a theatre, and the crumbled walls of a fortress crowned the summit.

Skiouros shaded his eyes against the golden orb ahead and peered at the ruins. It seemed such an odd place to find the swordsman. Diego de Teba had been the very epitome of the gentleman tutor, paying more heed to his dress and manners than to the baser side of wielding a blade. This place would have been so much more suitable to that group of bandits they had met on the road than to a nobleman, however *exiled* he might be. What had he done to fall foul of the authorities and end up in such a place? Skiouros had not wanted to enquire back in the city, for fear of provoking some kind of reaction, but the question nagged at him.

Parmenio seemed to have been experiencing similar thoughts.

'What a shit hole. Not a place to seek a reputable teacher. Are you still sure you want to find this Diego fellow?'

Skiouros huffed. He might have been tempted to complain about his friend's repeated grumbling on the subject, but in truth the man was right to question, given what they were going through, and Skiouros did indeed doubt the wisdom of this journey. With a sigh, he took from his pack one of the apples they had purchased from the carter along with other sundry morsels, and crunched into the sweet, juicy flesh.

'No point in backing out now,' he mumbled through his mouthful.

Ignoring the look on his friend's face, Skiouros left the road and angled off between twisted trunks and towards the ruined church. Instinctively, his hand went to the hilt of the sword at his waist as he closed on the building, and Parmenio did the same. Carefully, Skiouros dropped the chewed apple core into soft grass as they advanced.

Some twenty yards from the church they paused and fell silent, listening carefully. Above the gentle sounds of nature and the trickle of water somewhere nearby, there was a faint scrabbling noise from the church and that tiny skittering of grit falling down stonework. Skiouros felt his heart beat faster and motioned to Parmenio to move quietly. Slowly, silently, they closed on the church and rounded the corner of a high side-aisle into the *naos*, only the eastern end of which still stood, covered with a perfect arched roof. Though there was no sign of life in the centre, a low, dark doorway led to one of the side-aisles, and Skiouros nodded at Parmenio before taking the lead and stepping towards the doorway.

'Slowly draw your blade and toss it away,' said a rough voice from behind them, almost a heart-stopping repeat of their encounter on the trade road. Skiouros spun round in surprise to see the dusty and dark figure of Don Diego de Teba immediately behind Parmenio, his fine sword at the Genoese sailor's throat, the razor edge tickling his throat apple.

'We're not here for trouble,' Skiouros said carefully.

'Then lose the sword,' Diego said, his blade drawing just a tiny bead of crimson from Parmenio's neck.

'One of the first things you taught me, de Teba, was that only a fool voluntarily disarms himself.'

The words had the desired effect, and the blade moved a fraction from the skin, allowing Parmenio to swallow at last. 'Who are you?' the Spaniard demanded quietly.

Skiouros smiled and spread his arms, sword still in hand. 'Have I changed so much in three or four years?'

'I taught you?'

Skiouros felt slightly crestfallen. 'Well, yes.'

'You'll have to give me a clue, young man. I've trained a lot of people.'

'I think I broke your toe when I stamped on it,' Skiouros said quietly, and Diego's face darkened with recognition.

'The Greek boy. Skirris, is it?'

'Skiouros, but yes.' The man's blade was still hovering close to his friend's neck and showed no sign of further movement. 'Is this necessary?'

'Until you tell me why you're here, yes.'

'I've come seeking you.'

'Why?'

Skiouros frowned. 'That is actually a surprisingly good question. A landslide of reasons, I think. I was in your homeland a year or so after I last saw you. I hear that Teba is now the haunt of bandits and thieves. It's something of a disappointment to come back to Crete to find that you seem to have followed that same path.'

'I am no bandit. What do you want?'

'To be honest, I have a task ahead of me for which I think I might need your help, but what's *certain* right now is that we mean you no harm. Could you kindly lift the blade and let my friend go?'

There was a pause and finally de Teba removed the weapon from Parmenio's throat and stepped aside. With a gesture to Skiouros, he strode off towards the arched apse of the church. Parmenio flashed Skiouros a dark look and they followed on as de Teba carefully cleaned off the tiny red mark from his blade and then slid it back into the scabbard.

'How did this come about?' Skiouros asked, indicating the church with a sweep of his arm.

The Spaniard's brow furrowed for a moment, and then he sank to a stone block that, covered with a folded cloak, formed a seat. 'I had an unfortunate disagreement with an employer. He took my refusal to obey his order blindly rather to heart, and was foolish enough to draw a blade on me in anger.'

'You killed him?'

De Teba shook his head. 'If I had, things might have been easier. He will take many years to retrain left-handed, though. And he will probably require help at his toilet in the coming years.'

Skiouros shook his head. 'Who *was* this man?'

'His name is Antonio Rizzi. He is ostensibly a nobleman and a distant cousin of the Duke of Candia. In reality he is a highborn criminal with no ethics or morals – a rich, landed thug, who is quite possibly also completely insane. I was working as one of his bodyguards, but there are some depths to which I will not stoop even in the most desperate of circumstances.'

'How did you end up as a bodyguard? Surely teaching the sword is more lucrative? Certainly it's *safer.*'

De Teba snorted. 'It's also a little dangerous to be so publically advertised when the Dominicans are busy looking around for anyone they consider worth burning. There is that in my lineage for which they would single me out. It seemed prudent to seek a position with some protection. Rizzi was well-placed enough that I needn't fear the inquisition while in his employ. In retrospect, it seems that I avoided the black wolves by seeking refuge in the cave of a mad bear. And so I find myself a fugitive. I would be interested to know how *you* located me, though.'

Skiouros shrugged. 'It wasn't easy. Took us more than a week and quite a bit of coin. But there are taverns in Heraklion where you can learn anything if you know who to ask.'

De Teba nodded his understanding, and then his eyes narrowed suspiciously. '*What* tavern?'

'The Lanterna Azzurro.'

The Spaniard straightened in his seat, his face becoming suddenly very serious.

'Have you nothing but cloth between your ears, Skiouros the Greek?'

Parmenio grinned as he rubbed his sore throat. 'I think I'm going to like you.'

'Have you any idea how many eyes will have followed you in and out of that place?' de Teba snapped.

'I'm guessing it's not an odd number,' Parmenio grinned, drawing a sharp look from the Spaniard.

'We thought...' Skiouros began, but de Teba cut him off sharply. 'No you didn't. Be quiet.'

Skiouros began to object, but the Spaniard put a finger to his lips and glared him into silence. The sound of birds chirruping and flapping their way from tree to tree in the late golden sun filled the silence, but Skiouros' sharp ears, alerted to danger by de Teba's manner, could just pick out a scuffing, scrabbling noise that could so easily be wildlife in the undergrowth and yet so clearly wasn't.

As quietly as he could, Skiouros drew his sword, the blade leaving the sheath with a faint hiss. De Teba rose from his stone block seat and crept past the others, though another arch, into the darkened side-aisle, where a deep, wide window looked back east along the road toward Agioi Deka. For a moment, he peered out through the lowest corner of the dark aperture before dropping back and returning to the others, holding up a hand and flashing five fingers and then three at them.

Skiouros felt a moment of panic. Eight men. And from what de Teba was suggesting, it seemed unrealistic to think they might be anything except men of the Duke of Candia's guard. His helpful mind's eye supplied him with a memory of that group of not-quite-soldiers who had saved their life on the trade road and then asked a few pertinent questions. *Idiot!* Not only did Skiouros not relish the thought of taking on eight men with only three – even if one of them was Diego de Teba – but he could finally, after years, count himself a law-abiding citizen, and the idea of having to fight and kill men of the guard did not sit well with him.

Fortunately, the fact that de Teba had not unsheathed his blade suggested that there would be no violence. Skiouros felt a further quickening of his blood as the Spaniard grabbed his cloak and dashed off between the shattered piers that had once supported columned arches in the church, past a cypress and out of sight. Without pause, the two friends scooped up their packs and scurried off after him.

Trying to remain as quiet as possible, they rounded the bole of the tree to see that de Teba was already disappearing through a thick carpet of white and purple flowers dominated by drooping ancient trees. Hurrying to catch up, the two men found themselves at the bank of a narrow stream running deeper than usual with meltwater from the early spring. The babbling and stuttering of the water masked the sound of their movements and the low undergrowth hid any potential footprints as they reached the water and caught up with the Spaniard, who had slowed for them now that he was out of sight of the church.

They could hear challenging voices back at the ruins, along with a shout of consternation and then a flurry of argument, one familiar, commanding voice clearly irritated. There was still almost an hour of daylight, and it would not take long for the men to find the stream and figure out to where their prey had disappeared.

De Teba was already moving at speed by the edge of the stream, along the mud and grass, ducked to remain low and out of sight of the hunters. The friends ran on after him, turning first right and then left, following the stream bed and the trees and plants that cut a green line through the dry brown landscape. The hill with the fortress ruins atop slid by on their left and soon they were rounding it as the Spaniard climbed the far bank at last and scurried off along a narrow tributary towards the shattered remains of an aqueduct bridge which rose like grey fangs from the brown brush. De Teba waited for the others to join him and spoke in low tones.

'They will probably search south towards Mitropoli, or follow the river north as far as Psalida before they realise we've slipped away. Around a mile and a half this way is the village of Plouti. The smith there owes me a favour, so I can stay for the night and then move on in the morning. Now you've helped them find me, Agioi Deka's unsafe anyway.'

'Can we move back to Heraklion from there?' Skiouros enquired.

De Teba shot him a surprised expression. 'I was thinking of moving on to Zaros, rather than walking north and putting my head between the lion's jaws while you tickle its privates. What *you* decide is your own affair.'

'Where's better for you to hide than right under their noses?'

He was rewarded with a scathing look. 'Just about anywhere, I'd say.'

Skiouros sighed. 'Then what's your plan, Diego? To keep flitting from hideout to hideout until eventually something goes wrong and you land up in the duke's jail?'

'More or less. You have a better idea?'

'Yes. Come to Heraklion with us. We'll slip in quietly and stay low and out of sight. You can help me with my little problem and in return I'll see to it that you leave Crete for somewhere safer.'

The Spaniard's eyebrow arched. 'You have a ship?'

'Our friends do. A Turkish galley bound for Istanbul.'

'Into the hands of the Turk? You think that's *safer* than here?'

'Are the Turks actively *hunting* you?'

De Teba tapped his lip thoughtfully. 'Point conceded. Can your Turkish friends help keep us hidden in Heraklion? I'm somewhat well-known, remember, and every man in red and gold there will be on the lookout for me.'

Skiouros grinned. 'We'll be fine. I have some experience of remaining out of sight of the authorities. You're in good hands.'

The Spaniard nodded slowly and heaved in a breath. 'Alright, then. My friend in Plouti will be able to give us supplies and help us on our way. He might even spare a pack donkey. We'll use the back roads up through Gergeri and cross the Rouvas pass. No one will be watching the mountain roads.' He cast a resigned look at Skiouros. 'Am I going to regret this?'

'Probably,' smiled Parmenio flippantly.

Chapter three – Of relics old and new

Heraklion, April 23rd

SKIOUROS leaned over the low balustrade that ran along the flat roof of the decorative new Venetian building. Beside him, Parmenio huffed angrily.

'What now?'

For the best part of a month the pair of them, along with Diego, had languished in a dingy, small room of a tavern in the city's back streets, planning this day from every angle they could think of. They had made it back over the mountains to Heraklion with relative ease, moving slowly so as to attract no unwanted attention, and had timed their re-entry to the capital city to fall upon market day when the guards would be over-busy, harassed and at their least observant. Once they had slipped unnoticed back into Heraklion, they had hurried through rarely visited alleyways to a bar of which Skiouros knew, where he felt certain they would be safe from the authorities.

Zion's Gate was a tavern, coffee house and social meeting place for the Jews of the city and as such was shunned by the Catholic authorities, considered unimportant and unpleasantly heretical. If the inquisition gained a hold here, the place would become unsafe, but for now it was one of few places in the city the Duke of Candia's guard would not suspect.

It was clean and well-looked after, and the interior was well-appointed, though with only small, slit-like windows, maintaining a bland, poor exterior for the comfort of the Christian authorities. And it had served them well as a base, keeping de Teba out of sight.

For over a week, the three of them had drawn maps of the church of Agios Titos in Heraklion, along with its square and surrounding buildings. Skiouros and Parmenio had made repeated visits and forays to check every detail, prompted by the questions of Don Diego, who was forced to remain in the safety of the Zion's Gate, well looked after by the local Jews who also held no love for the crazed *Cavaliere* de Rizzi, who yet maintained his fevered hunt for an errant guard.

Slowly, over the week, they had built up a collection of hand-drawn maps, carefully tweaked time and again, and covered in notes. The chosen date had been the child of both planning and fortune. By chance they had received a message from Dragi that the other two Turkish vessels would put into port some time within the week, and consequently Kemal Reis had decided they would set sail on April 24th, barring unforeseen circumstances. The three conspirators had already decided that it would be prudent to leave their larceny until the last possible opportunity, in order to be away from the island before the inevitable backlash over the disappearance of a relic. And the realisation that the preceding day – April 23rd – was the holy day of Saint George, venerated by both Catholics and Orthodox, and patron saint of Crete, had confirmed their decision. The day would be chaotic and the clergy would already be busier than at almost any other time of the year. This *had* to be their day. Of course, Skiouros knew of the additional complication this decision brought upon them, but exchanging one new complication for the solution to numerous others was worthwhile, especially with Diego now involved. By necessity, though, he kept that complication to himself.

As for the plan itself...

As was the case with so many Byzantine churches, Saint Titus' basilica had begun as a simple domed cross-in-square affair, and had grown and expanded over the centuries to acquire side chapels, narthex entrance halls, a sacristy and a baptistery and various other additions. Now it hunched, sprawled in the centre of the paved square as though it had fallen from the sky with a splat.

Skiouros and Parmenio had been inside a number of times over the last couple of weeks, and had committed to memory every inch of the building to which they had access. The main stumbling block had been the location of the relic. For some unknown reason,

33

the Church authorities seemed to be more nervous of their relics' security than was commonly the case and consequently the holy items were not on public display in the church's main naos, at the altar. Now, the relics were kept in a side-chapel which was open to members of the public only by appointment and with the consent of the priests. Members of the public were permitted to worship the relics only at the entrance to that side-chapel, the business-end of the structure remaining concealed by a rich, brocaded curtain displaying a gaudy image of Saint Titus receiving his instructions from Saint Paul. What lay behind that curtain only God, the priests, and Lykaion's mouldering head knew.

Therein lay Skiouros' other worry. Over the years he had become so used to hearing his brother's shade speaking in the silence of his head that he had considered it almost normal, and yet recently there had been nothing. Somehow, he had expected to hear *something* now he was back on Crete, so close he could almost touch his brother's earthly remains. Yet nothing came.

It led him to wonder, deep down, whether perhaps something had happened, and whether Lykaion was in fact still there. Had the priests sent the casket on to Venezia for safety? Had they somehow discovered the substitution and burned the worthless contents of the holy container? He dared not voice these concerns to the others, of course. Parmenio was already deeply unhappy at what they were doing and was only part of it because of his close ties with Skiouros, and Diego, while he felt less troubled at the nature of their mission, would still have had nothing to do with it had it not essentially been buying him passage from this dangerous place.

With input from the other two, Skiouros had planned as best he could, drawing together a flexible, open strategy that allowed for the many unpredictable variables involved. He had been coy, keeping certain portions of the plan to himself, since he knew there would be objections. That was to be expected and was unavoidable, but they must not prevent the plan from going ahead, and so he had kept his secrets from his friends, despite their clear unhappiness over the matter. The critical factor had, of course, been the escape.

Skiouros and Parmenio's investigations had provided a good, accurate plan of the city's tangled street network from the square to the port. The three conspirators had worked over the map for seven straight nights, memorizing all the best routes, the house-bound Diego remembering them principally from the map and from the landmarks described by his companions, who walked those routes every day for familiarity. If anything went wrong, the three would all make for the port and meet up at a Greek spice-merchant's warehouse with a clear view of the three Ottoman kadirga moored nearby. They should be safe from the inquisition there, as any priest worth his cross would be at one of the houses of God on such a sacred day.

The timing had been easy to decide upon. The normal order of service for the church of Agios Titos had been amended for this great feast day, and the services of *Sext* and *None* had been removed, replaced by one great mass and associated rituals from noon until the middle of the afternoon. Thus the perfect time for their task was immediately following the great mass. Beforehand, the church would be busy and filled with priests, and during it, there was no chance. But afterwards, the church would empty quickly and the rest of the day's festivities would continue, drawing attention from the church interior. In theory, only a skeleton staff would stay on, the rest of the priests and monks moving up to the small church of Agios Georgios, where the statue of the saint would be blessed and garlanded before being paraded about the city until the sun set.

Yes. The timing and the escape were as well planned as they could be. And little could be anticipated of what they would do if they *reached* the side-chapel, for none of them had seen past the curtain.

And then there was Skiouros' little secret, of course: how they would get in to begin with...

He looked along the balustrade at Parmenio, who was becoming twitchy.

'We go ahead as planned.'

Parmenio's brow furrowed and he looked back down into the square. The last of the public who had attended the great mass were dispersing into side streets, each to his own personal celebrations of the patron saint's day. Many of the church's priests had departed in a small knot towards the church of Saint George. Agios Titos would be pretty empty.

But the square around it was not.

'We have to get word to Diego before it's too late,' Parmenio hissed.

Skiouros looked down at the soldiers in the square. They had escorted the grand parade to this church – the most important in the city – and had stood outside throughout the mass while the banners and pennants of Candia had been taken inside. But parading in the Cretan sun, even in April, in full dress for many hours was an exhausting business, and a second unit of the Ducal Guard had arrived during the service to take on the duty from this point. Once the service was complete, the replacement force had accompanied the banners onwards, but the earlier escort had been dismissed by their officer and his adjutant and now lounged in small groups around the square as festive innkeepers from the surrounding taverns moved among them with free jugs of wine and loaves of bread.

'How long will they stay here?' Parmenio asked nervously.

'Until the innkeepers stop giving them free drink. Happens every year.'

'And when will *that* be?'

'When it gets dark and the people start to flood their taverns again.'

'So you knew there would be soldiers in the square all along?'

Skiouros nodded. He wasn't proud of the way his mind worked sometimes, but the fact remained that it was sharp, even if he occasionally cut friends with it.

'And *that* was why you wanted Diego? *That's* why you kept this a secret?'

Again, the Greek nodded with a shiver of self-loathing.

'You bastard.'

All Skiouros could do was nod again. An ordinary day would have offered them no chance at their prize, and earlier on this festival day would have been no easier. No matter how much he'd thought on matters, he had always known that the weary soldiery of the Ducal Guard would stand between them and the church. And while the pair of them could enter the church easily enough, even if they managed to escape past the reclining soldiers on the way out, their faces would be remembered, and there was little chance of managing to make it to sea the next day without being brought up on charges.

Unless they could somehow make the soldiers disappear.

And what could be more important to a unit of tired soldiers than free wine and bread?

His eyes lifted slightly as, just on cue, a cloaked and cowled figure emerged from a side street and began to make its way across the square, slowly, between the small groups of relaxing guardsmen.

'You can't do it, Skiouros. They'll kill him. They'll crucify the poor bastard.'

Skiouros shrugged. 'What's done is done. He's fast and he knows the back streets. I have every confidence in him. If there had been any other way...'

Parmenio glared at him angrily and then turned back down to the square below. A young boy – probably a homeless wretch by the look of him – was converging with the cloaked figure.

'Stop!' yelled the boy.

The cloaked figure came to a halt, the covered head snapping this way and that as this new entertainment caught the interest of a dozen of the closest guards. The officer busy laughing with his adjutant turned to look.

'Diego de Teba!' the young boy bellowed at the top of his voice, and the square fell strangely silent and motionless for a heartbeat.

Then, suddenly, Diego was running. Some of the nearest and sharpest of the soldiers were already leaping to their feet despite their exhaustion, and the officer was bellowing commands. Across the square the guards unhappily lowered their cups and jars to the paving and rose straight into a run, making for the cloaked fugitive as the officer urged them on.

A man – very fast for a soldier who had been stomping around the city in the sunshine all day – managed to reach Diego before he left the square and grasped for him. Though he missed the fugitive himself, he caught the cloak and ripped it away to reveal the Spaniard, his eyes wild but already calculating as he left the square.

Two heartbeats later the officer and his adjutant were running for that side street, every one of their tired men converging on the much-sought prey. By the time Parmenio had called Skiouros a bastard for the seventh time, the only occupants of the square were three rather surprised-looking innkeepers gathering up the abandoned wine jugs.

'If Diego dies because of this, you know I'll hold it against you 'til the end of days.'

Skiouros simply nodded again. Just the latest in a long line of sacrifices he had made. Should he worry that he was becoming so accustomed to losing friends that he was becoming numb to the prospect?

'He'll be waiting for us at the spice warehouse, mark my words.'

Parmenio answered with an ambiguous silence, and Skiouros threw up a quick prayer to God – and to his Muslim prophet just in case – that Diego was as good as he thought. And with that he pushed what was already done from his mind and made for the open doorway that led back down from the roof. Behind him, Parmenio cast him a black look, swept up the bulky oiled-cloth bag meant for their grisly prize and scurried on after.

All the various office doorways in this Venetian trade building stood closed and silent, their occupants uniformly out in the city, honouring the feast-day's patron by drinking until they couldn't recognise Saint George from a hole in the ground. A few of the poorly-paid youths who ran the baser sides of the business moved about on the lower floors, but none of them blinked at the pair descending from the higher levels and in moments the two were out and striding across the paving, past the last two innkeepers who were exchanging muttered comments about the guards.

A commotion audible from several streets away confirmed that Diego was still moving, occasional angry shouts in Italian rising above the din, and Skiouros was sure that more than once he heard the muffled clash of steel.

Run, Diego.

A large number of pigeons had descended to the pavement in the wake of the soldiers, gathering up the crumbs from the various small loaves that had accompanied the wine, and Skiouros couldn't help but smile as he remembered the flurries of pigeons that used to gather in exactly the same manner on the ancient square outside the church of Saint Nikolas back in the Greek Enclave of Istanbul. As used to humans here as those back in the great city, the pigeons continued their hungry work as Skiouros and Parmenio moved through them towards the church, a few flapping out of the way as the men passed, only to settle back down a few feet further away.

The pair approached the great church, the afternoon's golden sunshine at their back, casting spindly shades across the paving, the fluttering shadows of the pigeons pock-marking the triple-arched church front. The central arch contained the plain, unadorned door of the building, the left arch empty and the right occupied by a beggar rocking slowly back and forth in the brilliant glow. As he neared the door, Skiouros narrowed his eyes, trying to shut out most of the bright light and moments later, he passed across the threshold and into the dim interior of the church, his vision adjusting all the quicker because of his preparedness.

As was so common – and so breathtakingly comforting to the Greek – the interior of this former Byzantine structure belied its frontage. Unlike those glittering churches of Catholic Rome, the buildings of the Greek Church presented a sober exterior, with no delicately-carved saints looking on and no gilded roofs or delicate tracery. The only external decoration one found in these ancient churches was a skilfully balanced architecture, perhaps with patterns picked out in different brickwork. Their decoration was in their design and their domes, their arches and columns. Glory for God and not for man. The rich internal decoration of these places lay in their masterful painted walls and the mosaics that covered the domes, each telling tales of the Lord and his servants.

Passing into the shadow, from the square, the two men slipped through the empty exo-narthex and inner narthex and approached the doorway that opened into the naos where the main business of religion went on.

The church was not empty, which surprised Skiouros, and he was grateful that the door had stood open and he had not disturbed the half-dozen or so locals kneeling towards the front of the church, deep in prayer. Quickly he gestured over his shoulder to Parmenio and slipped to his right, out of the doorway, and a moment later, the pair were in the gloom at the edge of the large nave, pausing quickly to take stock. Apart from the few locals, the church seemed to be quiet. No priests were visible, though the doorway to the sacristy stood open, so they were around and would likely reappear shortly.

Skulking in the shadows, Skiouros and Parmenio moved around the edge of the church, beneath the colonnaded aisle until they reached the doorway that led to the side chapel containing the church's relics. A centuries-old mosaic showing Saint Titus arriving in Crete with the apostle Paul filled the arch above the doorway, the writing below it in an archaic form of Greek that warmed Skiouros to the core. He might still be in Crete and not Istanbul, but every step now brought him closer to home.

His heart suddenly thumping into accelerated life, Skiouros stopped dead, Parmenio stumbling into his back and grunting in annoyance. The young Greek held up his hand in a signal to wait, and he closed his eyes.

Lykaion?

No. It wasn't. Because Lykaion had always been one whispered voice in his mind, and this was a discordant *chorus* of shades. A cacophony of whispered thoughts.

A chill running the length of his spine, Skiouros shuddered. What was happening to him? It had never really struck him as odd that he could oft-times hear his brother's spirit and that they still conversed on occasion as though the man still lived. It was largely this fact, after all, that had led him to such great efforts to preserve what he could of Lykaion's remains and why he now robbed a church to retrieve them and take them home. But it had never occurred to him that he might one day hear the shades of others.

'What is it?' grumbled Parmenio irritably.

Skiouros shivered again. 'I… I think I heard something. Like whispered pleas.'

'You mean like all the locals whispering to God, Skiouros,' the Genoese sailor huffed, and Skiouros turned with a frown. The truth crashed on him in a mix of relief and embarrassment. He had been so intent on hearing Lykaion that he had missed the obvious. The locals whispered their prayers and pleas to God in a susurrating tide, and Skiouros smiled weakly at Parmenio, who was giving him an odd look.

'Come on.'

The side chapel – a *parekklesion* in the Greek – was covered with paintings of saints and biblical scenes, its false arches delicate and so achingly familiar. It did not escape his notice that the last arch before the dividing curtain contained an image of Saint Nikolas of Myra – the patron saint of thieves, among other groups – watching him with ironic sourness.

At least the side chapel was empty, for all the accusatory glare of the painted saint, and the pair closed on the curtain quietly and quickly. Parmenio unslung the oiled-cloth bag and held it ready, nodding for Skiouros to move.

With infinite trepidation, the former thief – falling back into his old ways only with the best of intentions – stepped up to the curtain and twitched one edge away from the wall by an inch or two, leaning close to his disapproving patron saint and peering through.

Empty.

Skiouros exhaled gratefully; he hadn't even been aware that he was holding his breath. How much he had changed over the years. Half a decade ago this sort of thing would have been so normal and simple for him that it would barely have raised his pulse. Now…

Beckoning Parmenio, he slipped through the curtain and into the main chapel. With an apsidal end beneath its own small dome, the chapel was compact and even slightly claustrophobic. Every flat surface of wall was painted with saints and holy tableaus, and from the dome the Son of God looked down holding up his fingers in a sign of blessing. Somehow that did little to comfort Skiouros.

To their right, a small, heavy and ancient door pierced the wall, a thick bar slid into sockets barring it from the outside, and a huge iron key sitting in the lock, welded to the plate with cobwebs and grime. The whole door was dusty and the crack at the bottom was not visible for debris. It had not been opened in decades – perhaps even centuries.

A small altar draped with a blue and gold cloth stood at the far end, beneath the dome. Atop the slab stood two gild wood caskets protected by a gilded metal cage that rose from the very stone of the altar, covering the caskets like protective skeletal hands. The rear of the cage was hinged, the front fastened with a heavy padlock.

Skiouros fought the urge to curse in such a sacred place and sucked in air irritably through his teeth instead. Parmenio stepped next to him.

'So which is it?'

The Greek stared at the two reliquaries. Shit! While they were clearly not the same, they were close enough to be easily mistaken by the uninitiated. Why did the damned priests not label them? A 'TITVS' beneath one and 'THEODORVS' under the other would allow the public to know which casket contained the remains of the saint they had come to venerate. But then, they were hidden from the public behind the curtain anyway. Damn it!

'*Skiouros*!' urged Parmenio.

'I don't know.'

'What?'

'I don't know which it is.'

Parmenio grabbed his shoulder and turned him into a glare filled with disbelief and ire. 'You *brought* the bloody thing here. How are we supposed to proceed now?'

Skiouros sighed. 'It's been years. I just don't know.'

'Then I suggest you look very carefully and work it out. We can't stand here forever, you idiot.'

Skiouros nodded unhappily and peered at the caskets. The one on the left was slightly more ornate. He remembered there being

41

a dent in the one he carried aboard the ship to Crete, but he couldn't remember where it was and it wasn't obvious from this angle. Probably both displayed more than one dent anyway. They were centuries old after all.

Were they of different woods? He remembered a faint cedar-like smell from the one he'd carried. He sniffed, but all he could identify was age-old dust. It was impossible to tell.

As he stood, staring at them, Parmenio stepped past him and moved to the padlock, placing his bag on the ground beside him. Lifting the padlock, the former captain examined the mechanism.

'This is a bastard of a lock. Complex.'

Skiouros ignored him, concentrating on the boxes.

Are you there, Lykaion?

Over the huffing of his friend's frustrated breath, all Skiouros could hear was the distant, almost-silent sibilance of the whispered prayers out in the main church like a gentle wind whistling through a field of wheat. No Lykaion.

Never had he felt the loss of his sibling as keenly as now. Somehow, despite not having heard his voice in so long, he had felt certain that this close to his earthly remains, they would speak once again. But the complete absence of Lykaion's ghost cut deep into his soul and he found himself staring helplessly at the two casks.

The one on the left was slightly darker, the gold more yellow and burnished. The one on the right a lighter wood, with a whiter gold...

The one on the right seemed ill-fitting somehow.

Could he hear just a whisper on the very periphery of his senses?

Had something just breathed his name with the same gentle whisper as the sound of light snow falling?

Lykaion?

Parmenio growled in frustration and let go of the padlock, stepping back.

'This is beyond me. Have you worked out which one it is?'

Skiouros nodded. 'The one on the right.'

'Are you sure?'

'Yes. It's glaring at me.'

Parmenio gave his friend another odd look and shook his head in exasperation. 'You're *absolutely* sure? I have no desire to walk away from this church with the priceless head of Saint Titus tucked under my arm.'

Skiouros nodded again. 'Definitely. It's that one.'

'Well it might all be moot. That padlock's the most complex I've ever seen.'

Skiouros stepped across to the lock and, with a frown, lifted it into the light, peering at the keyhole. He could see into the darkness. Parmenio was sharp, for sure. Not many people could spot the complexity of a padlock by sight alone. But sure enough, in that keyhole he could see at least ten pins and three grooves running the length of the mechanism. The key that opened this lock was a masterwork of labyrinthine proportions.

A suspicion stole over him and his eyes narrowed.

'Have you lost your picks?' Parmenio hissed.

'No.' Despite not having used lock-picks in an age, Skiouros had acquired some a week ago from a source in the backstreets of Heraklion – along with a tinderbox and other sundry small items – and they all sat snug in the pouch at his belt. But something was wrong with this lock. He peered into the padlock again and his suspicion deepened. Fishing out his picks, he selected the thinnest, least common tool. The chances were very small that he would ever find a situation for its use, so it was essentially disposable.

'Watch this.'

Delicately, he slid the pick into the hole and gently tapped one of the sprung pins within. With a click, a metal shutter slammed down at the near end of the keyhole, neatly snapping the pick in half.

'Booby-trapped. Clever, eh?'

Parmenio sighed. 'So no chance of picking it, then?'

'Not a chance, no. Fortunately this entire thing is a decoy.' With a grin, Skiouros stepped towards the back of the cage and felt around. A moment later there was a quiet, metallic click and the Greek lifted the cage, padlock and all, away from the altar's surface. 'Priests can be devious, but fortunately so can I.'

Parmenio retrieved his bag once again and the two moved over to the right-hand of the two caskets. 'Are you ready for this?' he asked as Skiouros joined him. The Greek gave a silent nod and his Genoese friend took a deep breath and pulled up his kerchief over his mouth and nose. Skiouros closed his eyes for a moment and took his own deep lungful of oxygen. Then, with reverence and care, he reached down and unlatched the casket, swinging the lid open.

A puff of dust rose into the air, and both men recoiled slightly from the sight of the head within. Lykaion's skull was dry and grey, tufts of hair still clinging to parchment-thin skin. Dried and partially-mummified by nature and environment, the head of Skiouros' brother still clung to much of its original flesh. Gagging involuntarily, Skiouros pulled a pair of thin leather gloves from his belt and slid them on. Trying not to breathe deeply, he reached down into the casket and gently cradled the 'relic'. Slowly, he began to lift it out, trying not to register the fragments that fell off it and the next puff of desiccated skin-dust into the air.

And then he was holding Lykaion before him. Amazingly, five years after his death, his brother still seemed to be giving him an accusatory and disapproving glare from empty sockets. Aware suddenly of the passage of time, Skiouros turned to Parmenio. The captain was breathing shallowly and the kerchief was clamped tightly between closed lips.

'Bag?'

With a nod, Parmenio lifted his oiled bag and pulled open the draw-string. It was a cumbersome and expensive thing, for a bag, but Skiouros had been insistent that it needed to be sealable to air-tight conditions. Carrying a disembodied head around might cause an odour strong enough to draw attention, no matter how desiccated it now was. As Skiouros watched with a frown, the older man dipped into the bag and lifted from it a head in an advanced state of decomposition, most of the flesh almost as dried as Lykaion's.

Skiouros stared in astounded horror.

'What the...'

Parmenio shrugged as he proffered the head. 'Have to have an exchange, don't we. Can't leave it empty. That would be inviting trouble.'

Skiouros was still staring in horror as Parmenio placed the rotten head none-too-gently into the empty casket and clicked the lid shut.

'Where,' Skiouros asked quietly and with disturbed fascination, 'did you come by a decapitated head this morning?'

'Well it wasn't easy,' Parmenio said, and Skiouros was certain that the man was grinning behind his kerchief. 'Rest assured he wasn't using it anymore.'

Skiouros continued to stare as Parmenio held up the bag, which stank of death and decay now it was open. Shaking his head in disbelief, he lowered his brother's remains into the grisly container and, while Parmenio sealed the bag once more, the Greek lowered the cage back over the two caskets, hoping the scattered dust would not attract too much attention.

Parmenio pulled the cord of the bag over his head and shoulder and settled it onto his back, and the two men shared a look. This was it. They had achieved what Skiouros had not been truly certain they could do, and all they had to do now was leave quietly and unobtrusively. With a nod, they stepped back towards the curtain, which suddenly opened before them.

The priest was clearly more surprised to find them than they were by his sudden appearance. He was not young, his face half hidden behind a grey beard still shot through with darker patches, and his rapidly thinning hair was mostly limestone-hued. The three men stared at each other in stunned silence for a moment.

Skiouros felt the panic rising, and with it came desperate, blustered words.

'I'm sorry. We... I know that... We didn't...'

Before he could string the sentence together properly, his wits were scattered as the old priest hit him on the cheek with a punch that belied his advanced years. The blow was like a mallet strike, sweeping Skiouros back and dropping him onto his posterior among the dust. The Greek stared up in shock at the priest, whose eyes blazed with fury. The old man opened his mouth to yell out a warning, and that was when Parmenio's swung oil-skin bag caught him on the jaw. The priest spun, stunned, and the Genoese captain gave him no time to recover, laying him out cold with a careful blow to the temple.

As Skiouros sat trying to regain his own wits, he watched Parmenio crouch and check that the priest was out but not critically hurt. Seemingly satisfied, the captain bunched up the hood at the back of the man's robe and nestled it under his head as a pillow before turning and reaching out to help Skiouros stand.

'You *hit* him!'

'Well, yes,' hissed Parmenio, lifting him to his feet as best he could and then returning the bag to his shoulder.

'What did you do that for?'

His friend gave him an odd look. 'He hit you and was about to shout for help. What would you *expect* me to do?'

'But he's a *priest*! You *punched a priest*!'

'Oh what do you care,' snapped Parmenio. 'You don't even *like* Catholics!'

Skiouros stared at his friend, his head still thumping and slightly woozy. 'Do you think he'll remember our faces?'

45

'What does it matter? We're not going to kill him, anyway. We'll just have to hope he can't recall too much detail and can't place us later.'

'Well there goes our unobtrusive exit. Whatever happens, soon enough they're going to know that someone was in here.'

'Then let's get going while we can.'

Skiouros nodded, but held onto Parmenio. 'Wait.'

As he fell silent, he cupped his hand to his ear and concentrated. The susurration of prayer from the naos of the church had been joined by a second murmur.

'More priests, I think, in the church itself.'

'So we're trapped?'

Quickly, sharing a look and an unspoken thought, the two men scurried back to the small door near the altar.

'How do we know it doesn't just open into another room?'

'Did you not take a blind bit of notice of all those maps we compiled at the inn? The sacristy and baptistery are both on the other side, so this has to be an exterior wall. How often have we studied the place? Besides, look at it. When was the last time this was opened? It doesn't get used, so it can't lead anywhere important.'

In order to check his theory, though, Skiouros dropped to the floor and used his hand to brush some of the debris away from the base of the door. Sure enough, the faint glow of afternoon sunlight reflected off worn-smooth paving was visible through the narrow gap at the bottom.

'Come on.'

As quietly as they could, the two men heaved the locking bar from the iron grip at one end and then slid it from the recess in the wall at the far side. While Skiouros lowered it gently to the ground at the corner of the room, partially hidden by the altar, Parmenio tried to turn the heavy, ancient key. There was an ungodly, teeth-rattling shriek from deep within the door's lock, followed by a metallic clunk and, with a grunt, the captain managed to turn it, lifting his hand and rubbing sore fingers. As he did so, Skiouros pulled the key from the lock and yanked the door inwards, where it grated noisily on the stone floor. Welcome golden light flooded into the side chapel, almost blinding the pair, but Parmenio was quick to move, dashing out into the open square beyond.

As the man exited, Skiouros listened. The murmur of the other priests was getting closer but didn't seem to sound alarmed. *That* would soon change. All the pair could do now was attempt to discourage or slow any pursuit. Stepping out, the Greek pulled the door shut once again and jammed the key into the lock, turning it with some difficulty and another metallic shriek. Giving the key a further quarter turn so that it could not easily be poked out from the other side, Skiouros spun and followed Parmenio who was sauntering across the square with a quiet, confident gait, as though he were the most innocent man in the world, and not a thief carrying the severed head of a 'saint' in the bag on his back.

Trying not to look suspicious, his heart hammering in his chest, Skiouros followed Parmenio as the Genoese sailor reached the edge of the square and ducked into one of the narrow streets that led off into the depths of the city. Skiouros was sure he could hear shouts of consternation from the church as he reached the square's periphery and his gaze roved around the visible surroundings. No one seemed to be paying him any attention. With a tense breath, he stepped into the gloom of the narrow street and, like his friend before him, ran as though the hounds of hell were nipping at his heels.

They had memorized the routes so many times in these past weeks of planning that it came automatically, every turn and crossing on the streets set out and requiring no thought. Left at the cooper's sign, across before the *Grappa* tavern, left again at the house with the stunted lemon tree, and so on. Given their relative ages, it took only four streets for him to catch up with Parmenio.

The pair descended towards the port by their snaking, convoluted path and found themselves turning into a narrow alley between whitewashed walls, only to almost fall over a seated man. Stumbling to a halt, they stared down at the ducal guardsman, who was groaning as he clutched a vicious sword wound to the leg, which had apparently crippled him. He would live, but there was little chance he would walk straight for the rest of his life.

The friends looked at one another.

'De Teba.'

Parmenio nodded, and the pair ran on, leaving the wounded guard to be found by someone else. Two streets further on, another of the Ducal Guard leaned against a downspout, blood running from his knee as he panted in pain and exhaustion.

Diego had made good account for himself, it seemed.

Again, another street or two down the hill, Skiouros found himself slipping and almost crashed to the ground, grasping a window sill to arrest his fall. As he righted himself again, he stared at the pool of blood in which he'd slipped and noted the three severed fingers scattered among it.

Skiouros shook his head. Each of these sights was an unwelcome reminder of what he'd done to Diego. There would be an accounting eventually, for this.

Parmenio gestured to him and cupped a hand to his ear. As Skiouros listened carefully, he could hear the angry sounds of the Ducal Guard searching the nearby streets, the officer yelling furiously at his men. Skiouros grinned. They'd lost Diego, then.

Slowing to a casual walk and allowing their breath to slow to a reasonable pace, the two men descended the last few streets to the port area, which was not over-busy, given the festivities back up in the town centre. As they wandered along to the spice warehouse of Dimitris Andronikos, they caught occasional glimpses of the Guard searching the narrow streets. The warehouse door was shut, but as Skiouros pushed at it, it opened easily. Shocked, he suddenly found himself staring along a gleaming blade at the narrowed eyes of Don Diego de Teba.

'Get in,' snarled the Spaniard, grabbing him by the collar and jerking him almost from his feet as he moved the sword aside.

As Parmenio closed the door behind them, Skiouros spread his hands appeasingly.

'I will apologise for what I did, Diego, but know that I'd do it again if I had to.'

'I should spit you for this.'

'But you won't.'

'No,' conceded the Spaniard. 'At least not now, anyway. Did you succeed?'

Parmenio lifted the bag from around his neck and proffered it.

'I'll take that as confirmation, then. Good. At least my involuntary sacrifice was worthwhile.'

'The Guard are searching like mad,' Skiouros said quietly. 'They've not reached the port yet – they're probably not bothering as there are Guards here already – but sooner or later they'll get to these warehouses, so we need to go straight away.'

'You think you can get me on board?'

'I'm sure of it.'

Diego narrowed his eyes, trying to determine whether Skiouros was genuine, or whether he might shortly find himself at the mercy of the port guards to facilitate some other escape.

'One last thing,' Parmenio said, and as the others turned to him he gestured to the bag at his back. 'This is supposedly air-tight, but all it would take is a pinprick, and things around us could get a little pungent. If we don't want to raise panic on board we need to drown out the smell even inside the bag.'

The others nodded their agreement and, as Diego gathered his gear from the side of the warehouse and spotted a cheap hooded cloak hanging on a peg, purloining it to replace his own lost one, Skiouros and Parmenio gathered handfuls of cinnamon, asafoetida, and expensive cloves brought from the Far East via Arabia. Quickly they stuffed the spices into the oiled-skin bag until it strained to hold the contents and then sealed it tight, knotting the cord four times for safety.

A few minutes later the trio inched the main warehouse door aside, checked for guards in the area and, seeing none, emerged into the late afternoon sun, which was rapidly sinking towards the peaks of the Rodian range to the west of the city. The port was still largely empty, just a few sailors, teamsters and merchants taking advantage of the lack of clutter to finish loading vessels or move goods from one storehouse to another. Diego pulled the hood of his cloak over his face and hunched down, but Skiouros pulled it back and shook his head.

'There's nothing as suspicious as a cloaked and hooded man. You'll be a lot less noteworthy without it. Just keep your face lowered so they can't get a good look at you. Plenty of people have a similar hairstyle.'

The warehouse had been carefully chosen, partially for its proximity to the jetty at which Kemal Reis' kadirga was moored. Even as they approached they could see that all was ready for tomorrow's departure. The vessel rode low in the water, weighed down with supplies for the journey. The entire crew would be aboard now, including the great Reis himself and his honour party. Indeed, the raised flag indicated the presence of the ship's captain. At first light, the great Turkish galley would slide out into the harbour, cutting through the water towards the heart of the Ottoman world, and they would leave Crete.

Just one small obstacle to go.

Along the jetty, Parmenio and Skiouros made sure to move slightly ahead of their friend, keeping him partially hidden behind their shoulders. As they moved, Skiouros looked up at the deck of the ship, its mast freshly painted, its oar holes empty but ready.

'Halt,' called a voice in Italian with a local twang, indicating a man born on Crete rather than one of the never-ending stream of Venetian settlers. Skiouros' eyes strayed along the sheer strake of the kadirga until he picked out the figure he was expecting, and he heaved a sigh of relief.

'Who goes there?' demanded the guard.

Without replying, Skiouros waved an arm at the man busy ordering around sailors on the deck, and he called out a stream of Turkish. Dragi moved to the edge of the ship and peered down at the three of them, then nodded and gestured to the guards to let them pass. Between the two friends, Diego kept his gaze carefully lowered as the port guards parted to allow them access to the ship.

A moment later they were climbing the boarding ramp towards the vessel and Skiouros could almost feel the waves of relief emanating from their Spanish friend.

'That's it. Say goodbye to Crete, my friend. Next, I shall show you *my* home.'

With a smile he stepped up onto the ship and smiled.

Istanbul.

Home, at last.

Chapter four – Of the greatest city in the world

The Bosphorus, May 17th

SKIOUROS stood at the gunwale of the kadirga, shading his eyes against the setting sun as the sinking golden orb cast the great city of Constantine into silhouette. The minarets added to the ancient Byzantine churches to turn them into mosques rose like slender spears stabbing at the heavens, surrounded by graceful domes and other great structures. On the wooded, grassy slopes of the south-eastern promontory the sad, neglected ruins of the ancient Roman palace complex rose among more recent Ottoman buildings. Beyond, on the highest point, the new palace of the sultan sprawled like a graceful marble lion in repose.

The young Greek wondered that his heart could contain the emotions he was feeling at the sight of this city in which he had grown to manhood, lost to him these past five years. The urge to leap over the rail and swim for shore was surprisingly strong.

Beside him, Parmenio and Diego watched the headland slip past as the Turkish galley made for the Golden Horn and the Neorion harbour. Parmenio's expression was unreadable. He had never come here as anything but the captain of his own ship with intent to trade, but the city was at least partially familiar to him. Diego, on the other hand, was staring in fascinated disbelief, as he had been since the massive walled city had first slid into view. Likely it was the largest, most urban sprawl the Spaniard had ever seen. At least it gave Diego something interesting to observe rather than stabbing his bitter gaze at Skiouros as he'd been doing periodically throughout the journey whenever the Greek wasn't looking.

As the city slipped past, the headland hiding the sun from the water and leaving it an inky purple with myriad tiny jellyfish bobbing around, Skiouros watched the Golden horn approach. His nerves were almost twanging as the vessel began to turn, the oars dipping in perfect time and driving the galley forward like a knife through soft butter, splicing the purple and sending the endless small jellyfish away from the hull in waves.

As the ship made the final turn and came into the Golden Horn, they came to face the setting sun along the water, the burnished copper of the light reflecting off the calm surface and making it abundantly clear how the inlet had acquired its famous name. The glow was almost blinding, and those not bending to their oars had to squint and shade their eyes as they watched the Neorion approaching on their left, one of several harbours before the great sea walls of Istanbul.

'What city is that?' Diego asked curiously in heavily-accented and somewhat troubled Greek. The four travellers had discovered that they could converse well enough in Italian, though all had some command of Greek from their time on Crete, and Skiouros' native tongue would be the least odd to hear among the Turk, so they had settled upon it despite it being Diego's weakest language. Parmenio and Skiouros turned to see the Spaniard pointing across to their right at the densely-packed structures that sat brooding, regarding the ancient Byzantine capital across the water.

'That's still part of the same city,' Skiouros replied. 'It's called Galata. 'Til the Turks came, it was a Genoese enclave. Now it's more of an Ottoman business quarter, though it still plays host to some foreign institutions.'

He tried not to register the bitterness that passed involuntarily across Parmenio's face, given his Genoese nationality, but Diego was already crossing the narrow bow to examine this external neighbourhood of the great city, which still sported its own defensive walls and a tall, imposing tower at the summit.

'It looks a lot like an Italian city,' he agreed, noting the belfries and grand Italianate palaces.

'But what, in the name of the Holy Mother and all the blessed saints, is *that*?' Parmenio hissed, and Skiouros frowned, trying to identify what it was to which his friend was referring, his eyes roving across the roofs and towers down to the waterline...

...where he saw it.

'Dear Lord!'

The great Imperial Ottoman Shipyards sat at the water's edge, across from the Neorion harbour and a little further along, where Galata's walls ended – a massive complex of structures, with docks and large hangar-like construction yards. Here agents of the sultan churned out the powerful navy of the Ottoman Empire, which was feared across the eastern Mediterranean.

But what had drawn both Parmenio's attention and his breath was no mere kadirga or caique of the fleet.

Skiouros stared at the leviathan languishing beneath the shade of the nearest great construction shed, his own breath catching in his throat. He had never seen any galley so large, had never even *imagined* it. The enormous hulk of a vessel was clearly designed along the same lines as the kadirga upon which they stood, though magnified to be the vessel of titans, with fore- and aft-castles. Still in dry-dock, it even seemed to loom high over those ships passing on the water. He tried to imagine what any Spanish caravel captain would think if he rounded the headland to find *that* monstrosity awaiting him. It simply didn't bear thinking about.

He could remember the trouble even the larger kadirga had in keeping steady while firing abus guns or the small cannon sometimes installed aboard. This thing lurking in the shadows of Galata would have no such issue. Skiouros could imagine it bristling with cannon and still sitting steady in the water as they battered a caravel into submission. He wondered briefly whether it could even withstand firing the great city-killer cannon of Mehmet the Conqueror that had shattered the unassailable walls four decades earlier.

He shook his head in wonder.

'Impressive, is it not?' asked a quiet, authoritative voice, and Skiouros turned in surprise to see the captain, Kemal Reis, standing by the rail a few feet away with Dragi at his side. The ship's captain had not addressed Skiouros directly throughout the voyage, so the comment came as something of a shock.

'It's *unbelievable*. Hard to imagine it floats, Reis.'

The white-bearded old sailor gave a dry chuckle. 'Her name is *Göke*. She was commissioned over five years ago, but only now is she almost complete. I have been itching to behold her in all her glory. I saw the designs when I was last here. She will be the largest ship afloat, if I am not mistaken, and certainly the most powerful. She will be the flagship of the fleet and the personal vessel of a senior admiral. I hope to still be in port when she launches, for it will be a sight – of that I am sure.'

The enormous leviathan slid from sight as the kadirga swung around and made for the Neorion harbour's reaching arms. Numerous other vessels sat at the jetties and beyond them the city rose from the waterline, marching like the advance of time up the city's Second and Third hills.

The three visitors stood and watched as their vessel moved closer to the jetty and the oars were shipped. Behind them the two other kadirga in Kemal's fleet made for their own berths, and the *emin* in control of the Neorion harbour was already stepping out along the jetty, a small army of clerks and officials at his back, while half a dozen janissaries stood guard on the dock. A tall, rangy figure with a thick, neat beard and a voluminous turban lounged close by, one slippered foot up on a crate, his expensively-tailored appearance somewhat at odds with the weathered, worn look of his skin, which suggested a sailor of many years.

As the kadirga bumped to a halt and Kemal waited for the boarding ramp to be run out, the emin of the port bowed low and welcomed the captain back to the city. The janissaries stood at attention and the mysterious sailor pulled himself upright and rose from the pile of boxes upon which he'd reclined, smiling enigmatically at the new arrivals.

'Once you deal with the bureaucracy,' Kemal advised Dragi, 'your time is your own, *Cingeneler*. I know your people have their own customs and celebrations, and I imagine you wish to visit your family. There will be no new adventures for us until after the festival, and all that is required of you in the intervening days is to check in at the Galata naval headquarters each morning until the situation changes. If I need you, you will know.'

Dragi nodded his understanding and his captain turned to Skiouros and his friends. 'Welcome to Istanbul. Thank you for causing me no trouble on our journey. Though we have spent these past few years saving refugees and ferrying them east, we have been saving good Muslims and clever Jews *from* the blight of the Catholic Church's minions, not saving those very minions. Had Dragi not vouched for you and had I not trusted him implicitly, I would never have endangered my vessel to rescue your infidel behinds. Allah works in strange ways, and I pray that what I have done is by his design. Go with peace. *Selamun aleyküm.'*

Skiouros frowned, but slid the gesture into a shrug and a wry smile. He could hardly fault the man's opinion of the western

Church, given what he had seen himself these past few seasons. 'Salām,' he replied in proper Arabic, with a perfect Turkish accent, raising an equally wry smile from the captain, who bowed respectfully to him and then to the port emin before sweeping on past them to the strange waiting sailor, who stepped forward and embraced him. Dragi nudged Skiouros.

'His nephew, *Piri Reis*. He has been harrying the Spanish every bit as much as his uncle and is rapidly making a name for himself. They even say he might become the next high admiral. I will not be surprised if that great ship across the water is given to him.'

As Dragi turned to the emin, lifting his ship's log and manifest, and began to negotiate the cumbersome business of docking in the city, Skiouros stood and watched the two captains embrace for a moment before allowing his eyes to wander on from them, past the ancient arcaded structure that had coddled the dock since the days the Romans had glorified the city, up the slope towards the neglected hospital of Irene, the seemingly endless red-tiled roofs of the grand bazaar reaching from beyond there to the crest of the hill.

Home.

'What do we do now?' Diego murmured at his side and the other two turned to him. 'I still owe you a scar or two for your trickery,' he added bitterly, 'but this place is unknown to me and potentially unfriendly. I will accompany you at least until I have found my feet.' There was an edge of iron in his voice and though Skiouros was in fact grateful for the Spaniard's continued presence, he was under no illusion that it was Don Diego's decision to accompany them, and not his own.

Skiouros huffed in the evening air. 'I would like to see my old neighbourhood in the Greek enclave. In fact, I would like to see the whole city again. I could spend hours just wandering.' He reined in his thoughts. 'I suppose the first matter of importance is to find somewhere to stay in the city. We have a little money left and, if I am honest, which these days I generally am' – he ignored the dark look from the Spaniard – 'then I have small deposits of coin secured in hidden places around the city against times of extreme desperation. Or at least, I used to have. They may not still be there. Nothing that would make us wealthy, but enough to buy a few nights' lodging, at least.'

'And what of that?' Parmenio nudged, pointing at the bag down by his feet, hermetically-sealed and knotted tight to prevent the stench of decay from spreading.

'I will have to find the best place to lay him to rest.' His mind reached back across the years to the last time he had seen his brother, staring lifeless at him in the torchlight outside a disused monastery. 'I wonder if the Saint Saviour church has been converted or whether its alterations are still ongoing? I cannot think of a more appropriate place.'

Finally, as they stood musing and peering at the city, Dragi finished dealing with the emin and passed the books over to one of the senior crew, who scuttled off in the company of several others. Skiouros watched them head to one of the numerous small ferries, preparing to take the documents for storage at the naval headquarters across in Galata where the beast, Göke, sat brooding and waiting for release, and then turned back as Dragi spoke.

'Are you ready, my friends?'

Skiouros nodded. 'I would like to head into Phanar, and perhaps Balat. And to check on the Saint Saviour church. And we need to find a place to stay. Are you planning to stay with us?'

Dragi gave him a hard look. 'Do not become so wrapped up in the drama of your sibling's remains and the culmination of your homesickness that you ignore the grand scheme of things, Skiouros the Greek. Do not forget that there is purpose in all I do. I told you that all matters of import will be revealed to you as soon as the time is right, and that time is near. It is the seventeenth of May, and the hourglass is turning. The next twelve days will change your world and mine.'

'Very cryptic,' grumbled Skiouros. 'You can tell me your folk-tales whenever you like and ruminate on the factions within your people, but for me the prime concern will still be Lykaion's burial. If the Saint Saviour church has not yet been opened as a mosque, I would like to try and inter my brother there somehow. Given his past, it seems oddly fitting that he be buried in a Christian church that will be given over to Islam, since that very much describes him, too.'

The Romani's eyes hardened again, and Skiouros felt oddly uncomfortable, as though a beloved pet had just bared its fangs at him. 'Be under no illusions, Skiouros. You owe me your life twice over, and in return I desire only your cooperation until the festival is over. After that you may do as you wish, but until then, you *will* follow my instructions.'

Skiouros found that he was involuntarily leaning back away from the man's tone, and he tried to reply in a light, confident voice. 'I understand what you're saying, Dragi, but don't treat me as a visitor here. I know this city like the back of my own hand.'

Dragi waved his fingers mysteriously, like some prestidigitator, drawing Skiouros' attention to his hands, and then delivered him a light but shocking slap to the cheek.

'See how unprepared you are? You do *not* know this city any more, Skiouros the Greek, no matter how much you *think* that you do. You have not been here in near half a decade. And for me it has been longer than that. We are not in a position to go romping around the city without first finding out how the land lies.'

'He has a point,' Parmenio urged, and Skiouros ground his teeth to see Diego nodding too. This was *his* city, and he didn't relish being treated as a tourist by a man who constantly intimated that danger and trouble lurked in their future. Still, there was no denying that Dragi *had* saved his life twice now, and no matter how infuriating and obfuscating he might be, Skiouros still owed him a great debt.

'Alright, Dragi. We'll do it your way. So what *is* your way?'

'We go to my people. There you will find sanctuary, a place to stay and local knowledge of the situation in the city at this time. We will skirt your old neighbourhoods on the way, but at the end you will be where you *need* to be,' he added with an enigmatic smile that did little to calm Skiouros. 'Come,' the Romani addressed the three of them, and marched along the jetty to the dock.

'Do we not need to fill in some sort of documentation, or present ourselves to the port bureaucracy or anything,' Skiouros frowned. 'The authorities are not commonly so easy-going with arrivals in the city.'

Dragi chuckled.

'I have registered your disembarkation with the emin, and the details will be logged appropriately. You do not need to be checked or approved in any way. You arrived under escort of a renowned Reis of the empire and have been vouched for by both he and I. Now come.'

Leaving Parmenio and Diego to share a curious glance as they slung their kit bags over their shoulders again, Dragi turned to his right and strode along the dock, parallel to the arcade, heading for the gate that gave access to the city proper, from which the sea walls marched off, bordering the golden waters.

'How far will his people be?' Parmenio murmured as they hurried along behind, rubbing his lower back, familiar with the sheer scale of the city and how much walking could be involved.

Skiouros pursed his lips. 'The bulk of the Romani peoples live by the land walls, either in Sulukule out by the Rhegion Gate or in Ayvansaray, among the Blachernae ruins. Two miles at least, and some of it at a punishing gradient.' He was unable to suppress a slight shudder as he mentioned the two regions. Throughout his time as a youth in the city, living by his wits among the streets of the Greek enclave, few folk had ever had anything good to say of the Romani. The Greek residents of the city considered the strange Roma people to be no more brothers than were the conquering Turk; less in fact. While the Turk were Muslim and held few cultural links with the conquered Greeks, they had generally been surprisingly accommodating to the erstwhile people of Byzantium. The Ottoman culture had even promoted the inclusion of former-Christians into the circles of power on a conversion basis, in just such a manner as had befallen Lykaion.

The Romani were also predominantly Muslim, though they held tight also to some of their own mystical beliefs that likely predated the wanderings of Mohammed, and rumours of their witchcraft and wicked magick had been rife throughout the Greek quarter. The fact that they were oft times insular and secretive did little to endear them to their host cultures.

Of course, to look at Dragi brought into question all those old prejudices, and despite the strange sailor's constantly shifting personae and the secrecy and mystery of his goals, it was hard to equate him with witches and seers and practisers of dark magick. Still, after years of shunning the Romani neighbourhoods as places of wickedness, it was hard to think of strolling into them without an involuntary shiver.

Strangely, his mind furnished him with a picture of that old crone he had encountered years earlier while on the run from the angry victims of his pick-pocketry. The woman sitting on the dusty ground and filleting a crow for some unknown – and seemingly ungodly – purpose. Perhaps there was *something* to the tales, after all...

Passing through the Neorion Gate from the port into the city proper, the four men entered a wide street largely cast in shadow by the late, low sun and the combination of the looming city wall and the high Ottoman-Byzantine blocks that crowded this great conurbation. The remains of a far more ancient defensive wall here marched down from the hill above, its crumbling, unused end severed to allow the passage of the street where the old defences had once met the waterline. One of the many ancient city walls that had long been outgrown by the ever-increasing metropolis. The wall of *Severus*, Skiouros seemed to remember. His sour-faced uncle had made him memorise them – had made him learn much of the fallen city to preserve its Byzantine memory in the face of the occupying Turk. The walls of Byzas, of Severus, of Constantine, Theodosius and Anastasius. The penultimate remained tall, despite their battering by Mehmet, but the rest existed now only as sad fragments here and there.

Their legs straining, unused to the steady earth and such distance after so many weeks of rolling and bucking timbers aboard the ship, the small party followed the city wall along the Golden Horn, past seven more gates piercing the defences. It all looked at the same time achingly familiar and strangely new to Skiouros. Though he knew parts of the city well, much of it had been far too dangerous for a Greek boy to wander around freely, and he had only rarely forayed to such places. Besides, he had spent some of the most earth-shaking years of his life away from the city since those days, and he was slightly dismayed at the fact that some views seemed almost alien to him now. In fact, despite the fact that he had been looking for the crumbling remains of Constantine's wall as they walked, he somehow contrived to pass the site without noticing.

But then, as the eighth wall gate came into view, he felt a wrench inside, and his gaze strayed from the fortifications to the street opposite, which ran up a steep incline lined with narrow, poor, wooden housing. If he could just see around the bend at the top, the deep red walls of the 'bloody church' awaited his gaze, etched with a decade of secret messages between Lykaion and himself. The urge to turn and climb the slope was almost impossible to resist, but Dragi was already striding ahead, along the flat land inside the walls at the water's edge, into Balat – the Jewish quarter.

Here too, as he passed, the sights were all so familiar and enticing. Shops where he'd bought… shops where he'd *made off with*… life's little essentials, sometimes with the owner's angry shouts echoing in his ears, jumping trader's carts in the street and ducking past horses, seeking a safe place to hide while he ate his hard-won bread and cheese. It raised a sad smile that had Don Diego casting him an oddly sympathetic look, though it was still infused with the distrustful bitterness that had infected the Spaniard's attitude since Skiouros' betrayal in Heraklion.

'Old neighbourhood for me,' he explained. 'A little strange being back.'

Diego looked around with a frown.

'This is a *Jewish* neighbourhood.'

'You don't feel the cultural or religious divide as keenly when you and the Jews share a common place beneath a foreign power,' Skiouros explained blandly. 'Besides, the Jews here are well-placed and can often acquire things that the poor Greeks cannot.'

His own gaze took in the newly-constructed and refurbished structures among the older, dingier ones. 'It does have to be said that it looks as though there's been something of a rebirth around here, though. It was never this densely-packed... *or* well-kept.'

Dragi turned and smiled over his shoulder. 'Kemal Reis has brought many hundreds of the cleverest and wealthiest Jews from the west to the city, and the great sultan has welcomed them. There has been an influx of deep thinkers and of thriving Jewish business into the city that promises to strengthen the empire immeasurably. The Reis *saves* the world and the sultan *embraces* it. Pray that it is always so, and when the time comes, make sure to do *your* part.'

As the man turned away and marched off again, Skiouros found he was grinding his teeth at the latest in a long line of strange half-reveals of what Dragi felt his future might contain. Had such a life debt not been held over him, Skiouros might well have walked away by now. *Despite* the debt, the Skiouros who had once live here *would* have done.

Their walk took them on tired legs in the failing light past the great 'Hunter's Gate' and the 'Palace Gate', separated by three wide arches that had once led to the Blachernae Palace harbour but had long since been blocked with hastily-cut and badly-mortared stones and bricks, the palace not having been used since before the fall of Byzantium. Skiouros could remember happy times in the few hours he managed down here – or at least on the *other* side of the walls – stealing the catches of the poor Greek and Jewish fishermen who plied their trade along the water's edge.

As they passed the gate named for the church of Saint Thekla, Skiouros watched the ruinous walls of the Blachernae looming over the tops of the buildings. They had crossed the whole city now, and those crenelated remnants marching up the slope marked the start of the ancient, once-impenetrable land walls of Theodosius that crossed two of the city's seven hills before reaching the water again at the Propontis, some four miles to the south. The four travellers were on the very edge of the Romani settlement. Indeed, the architecture had changed as they had passed, and not in a way that promoted a positive view of this strange insular people. Behind them, ancient, if often ramshackle, wooden houses rubbed shoulders with brick and stone structures as old as the empire that had created them. They had been packed together in an urban spread.

Here already the streets were wider, less crammed with buildings, filled with dust and wreckage. Here and there rose jagged pieces of ancient masonry, often sporting an arch, a once-glorious marble window, a column or tower. Some had been adapted to become places of residence, though they were clearly only a strong sneeze away from being mere rubble. This, along with the *Tekfur Sarayi* at the hill's summit, was most of what remained of the great Blachernae Palace that had been the home to generations of Byzantine emperors, including the last one – the ill-fated Constantine, whose murderous nephew now stalked the Papal palaces in Rome. Ruins, fragments and shattered sub-cellars spread out across the hillside, reminding the viewer of just how enormous this complex had once been, perhaps half a mile across, including numerous churches and basilicas, stables, gardens, residences, palaces, government halls and so much more.

But it was here that Mehmet the Conqueror's cannons had done their worst, flattening the walls and the city behind them, granting them access to the heart of Byzantium. Here the first desperate clash had taken place, from building to building, the Byzantine emperor and his Genoese general battling like lions to retain their hold on Constantinople. Blachernae had been the second casualty of the Turkish assault, after the men on the walls. Only two parts of the palace could still be truly considered intact, one of which was used as a prison and a place of pain, the other as a residence for foreigners the sultan could not countenance hosting too close to his own centre of power.

Among the great ruinous stumps of the palace, the wild had once more taken over, areas of grass and bramble and small burgeoning copses fighting for prominence with the shattered stonework. And around the whole area, new structures had sprung up that had the look of ramshackle shanty-town temporary buildings, formed from the wasted ruins of the palace, any timber that could be found – including parts of old boats and carts – scrap ironwork and the like.

It did not appear conducive to a comfortable stay in the city, and in many ways it lent support to those long-held, bred-in prejudices Skiouros held against the area and its denizens. He could quite easily picture that old crow-dismembering woman living here. She probably had.

He tried not to think of her. On the rare occasions she had slipped back into his mind, he remembered the almost supernatural premonitions of the woman, warning him to leave because a storm was coming. Well she had been right, but then he had been just as right not to heed her, for if he had, the conspirators would have eventually found a way to end both the reign and the life of the great Bayezid the Second in favour of a strict, Mamluk-supported sultan. The mystery of her knowledge and her interest in him personally was as irritating as Dragi's own inscrutability, and led him to an inescapable conclusion that no matter what he had done in this past five years, he had somehow always been influenced or even directly pushed by the Romani.

And now he was in the heart of their world.

As if to lend weight to all his fears, the sun chose that very moment to disappear completely from the horizon, and the level of light in the area deepened noticeably. He shivered again. He was gratified to note that neither Parmenio nor Diego looked any more comfortable than he, and each was walking with his hand on the hilt of his sword. Even Dragi looked a touch apprehensive, which was the most nerve-wracking thing of all. But then, how long had it been since the Romani sailor had been here? Certainly more than half a decade.

'Where now?'

Dragi simply nodded ahead and began to climb the slope, quickly stepping off the main street – though it was doing it a great kindness to give it such an appellation – and taking a narrow side alley, bordered by a low wall of ancient stones, sporting a few Greek inscriptions, and overhung by healthy young trees rooting themselves in the houses of emperors.

The alley was too narrow for a cart, and the four were forced to tread in single file, with Dragi ahead. Now, Skiouros found himself walking with hand on hilt as well, his eyes seeking out potential danger in the dimly-lit overgrown ruins. Their path took them up flights of steps formed of broken marble lintels and around sharp bends, back down into what was perhaps once a noble garden. Clearly there had been an arcade along one side, and broken marble statues rose at odd angles from the overgrown flora. The city wall loomed quite close here and, turning to face uphill once more, Skiouros could see the great ornate square bulk of the *Porphyrogenitus* Palace – the surviving residential section, crowning the hilltop.

Dragi stopped in his tracks and Skiouros' knuckles tightened automatically on his sword hilt.

The Romani tipped his head curiously to the side, and a smile crept across his face that loosened Skiouros' grip again. Then he heard it too.

Music.

Lively music played on the strings, pipes and drums of at least a dozen instruments, with an oddly pleasant discordant chorus of voices, both male and female. The music seemed to be coming from what looked like a cross between a dishevelled junk heap and an upturned boat across the lawn of the former imperial garden. Dragi called something in a language with which Skiouros was completely unfamiliar, a curtain was twitched aside, and a welcoming golden light shone from a window. Moments later the door was thrown open. The music continued in the background, though with fewer voices and instruments as their owners hurried to the door to greet the newcomers.

Skiouros peered at the dark shapes emerging. There was, in truth, little to tell them apart from their Greek or Turkish neighbours. Their clothes were perhaps poorer and more basic than Ottoman apparel, and more colourful and cheerful than the generally-drab Greeks, but in terms of their skin and hair, they could have passed for either, had they wished.

And they probably had, Skiouros found himself thinking.

Yet for the first time since he had set foot on a previously undiscovered land far to the west with a Portuguese crew, Skiouros realised that he was being genuinely welcomed by people who had never even seen him before, and that fact somehow overrode decades of prejudice and brought a smile to his face.

Three hours later, Skiouros sat back with an explosive sigh, feeling fat on a seemingly endless meal of rice, beef and chicken platters with yogurt-based sauces, pastries, stuffed vine-leaves, bread, cheese, fruit, chickpeas and beans, and continuously-refilled glasses of *ayran* and *sahlep*. His head felt slightly muzzy following a strange foray into an almost certainly lethal syrupy wine made locally which, when he'd spilled some, had taken only seconds to change the colour of the table's surface. The room was also tinted with a faintly blue-grey haze as Dragi resumed his habit of burning hemp, which was so much more headache-inducing in such a confined space than on an open ship's deck.

As the incessant cheerful music, the warm light, the inebriation and the bursting stomach did its work on him, sending him slowly towards blessed unconsciousness, Skiouros rallied one last time. One of their hosts, a smiling man with four teeth who seemed to be an elder of some sort, had come to sit close to him.

'I... I wanted...' His suddenly suspicious gaze swept the area round him, but then he remembered how he'd put Lykaion's remains in a small container outside, not wanting to offend their hosts by bringing body parts into their home.

'Is the sint... the shurrrr... the...' he concentrated, 'the *church of Saint Saviour...* now a mask? Mosque?' he corrected hurriedly, blinking to make at least one of the old men disappear.

The man laughed and shook his head.

'The vizier Hadim Ali Paşa is still set upon its conversion, but the task is slow, *kral yapımcı.*' Skiouros frowned at the unfamiliar phrase. He was familiar enough with the Turkish tongue to translate it, but not in this advanced state of inebriation. The old man was still speaking and he tried to concentrate on the words. '...so it is still a construction site. It will be years yet before it is opened to the faithful.'

Skiouros tried not to see the phrasing as a slur on his own religion, for he was sure it was not meant as such. The man nodded at him as though awaiting a further question, but Skiouros' mouth seemed to have decided that no further questions were necessary, although a small amount of drooling was clearly acceptable.

Good. He would be able to bury Lykaion there then. He would make that his first task in the city, if Dragi would allow him the freedom. Tomorrow morning, when he was bright and alert. After he'd...

Five minutes later, Parmenio crossed the room with an almost paternal smile and draped a blanket over the snoring form of his friend. It *had* been a long road home, after all.

Skiouros gripped his blade in whitened knuckles, desperation pushing the blood through his veins at break-neck pace. He shifted his footing slightly and thrust, knowing he was too slow. His foot slid on the strange, fluted surface and there was a precarious moment when he almost fell, before recovering himself and shuffling back into position.

The enemy's sword came in for two quick strikes, like a cobra, one piercing his upper arm, the other carving a hot, fiery line across his brow, above his left eye.

Skiouros struggled and lashed out again, but once more missed and almost fell. He could feel the disapproval of Don Diego, his former fencing master, at his failure, even if he couldn't quite see him, as well as the aura of desperate hope emanating from Parmenio.

And the man was moving again – the man he couldn't quite see, yet somehow felt so entirely familiar. He couldn't get away. Skiouros couldn't remember what the oh-so familiar man had done, or perhaps what it was he had threatened to do, but one thing was certain: he must not be allowed to get away with it... or possibly to do it.

Taking a breath and wiping away the blood from his eye, he stepped carefully and deliberately forward along the ancient fallen column towards the grinning medusa head at the far end, near which his quarry was already clambering.

No. He would get away. And if he got away...

What? What would happen if he got away?

Skiouros leapt. It was the only way he could possibly stop him.

But the man was too far away. The medusa head seemed to leer at him as he landed awkwardly on the horizontal column, his boots struggling to maintain his stance on the curved, fluted surface. But with the added momentum of the jump there was no chance.

His quarry turned to watch in satisfaction as he fell, but despite his desperate desire to do so, Skiouros still couldn't quite see this hauntingly recognisable quarry, for now he was tumbling, falling into the abyss below. Oddly, he seemed to be falling past a mountain top now, upon which two brothers – one a priest, the other a teacher – sat, scoring him on his failures.

Skiouros woke with a lurch, his back arching in the chair, his clothes and the blanket sodden with warm sweat.

The house was silent barring the snores of dozens of happy, replete occupants.

Apart from the old man with the four teeth, who sat close to the fire, watching him intently.

Skiouros stared in confusion and slight panic at the old Romani, the sweat running down his face in sheets and stinging his eyes. The old man nodded, once, and then closed his eyes and leaned back into sleep.

It was another hour before Skiouros' heart stopped pounding enough for him to drift once more into oblivion.

Chapter five – Of interment and deepening mysteries

May 18ᵗʰ

THE 'Country Church' of Saint Saviour, sitting atop the slope in the shadow of the city walls, did not seem to have changed a great deal from the outside. As Skiouros and his friends stood at the end of the alleyway that led towards the delicate brick structure which had upon a time been one of the most astounding churches of the Byzantine city, his eyes played across the exterior. No. *One* thing had definitely changed: the belfry had gone. And nearby, stacked in neat piles among other heaps of materials, were the graceful curved stone blocks that would be used to construct the minaret in its place.

'Are you sure the church will be empty?' Diego asked quietly, his expression suspicious. 'It displays all the signs of a building mid-construction.'

Skiouros shook his head. When would the Spaniard let go of his distrust? 'It's Friday.' He frowned. His sense of time and space was still a little twisted after so much sea travel, especially when added to the pounding of his head after the intoxicating introductions to the Romani community the previous night, and he turned his furrowed brow on Dragi. 'It *is* Friday, yes?'

The Romani nodded and Skiouros smiled at his Spanish companion. 'Part of the creed of Islam is that Friday is their holy day, like Saturday to the Jews or Sunday to us. No one will work today. No Muslim, anyway.'

'Best pray to God that the workers aren't Christians then,' Parmenio huffed.

'Come on.' Skiouros hefted the bag over his shoulder again, feeling the curiously comforting weight of the head inside, and strode towards the church. A street urchin with bare feet sat atop the boundary wall in the corner of the grassy cemetery, gnawing on a dirty crust and watching them with interest. Skiouros considered shooing him on, but decided against it. He'd been just such a boy once upon a time. The sun was already high in the clear, azure morning sky, and the city was beginning to heat up to levels Skiouros found more comfortable.

The church door was shut and a padlock hung at the latch. Diego pondered the situation and his expression shifted to a mix of concern and disapproval as Skiouros removed his new lock-pick set from his pouch and began to work at the fastener, shifting the three pins with ease until the device clicked and fell open. The Greek pocketed the padlock, unlatched the door and swung it wide, allowing a waft of dusty, powder-filled air to billow out into the open sunlight, where it glimmered in a thousand motes. Once it had cleared a little he peered inside, trying to ignore the disapproval of his newest companion as he examined the Saint Saviour church. All he seemed to get now from Diego was disapproval and suspicion and, though he knew he had brought it on himself, he would have to do something soon to reconcile himself with his former tutor.

The church of Saint Saviour echoed hollowly to his first step.

His heart felt a faint wrench of sadness.

The last time he had been here had, admittedly, been one of the worst days of his life, but he would never let that fact impact on his opinion of the building itself, which had clearly been one of the most glorious and deserving of all monuments to God. The mosaics and wall paintings covered the interior of the church, right into gilded domes, adding meticulous, exotic and complex counterpoint to the simple, marvellous marbles that formed the lower walls and the floors. Saint Saviour's was a pious maze of colour and images.

Well… *it had been.*

One of the requirements of the mosques of the new Ottoman regime was a lack of such depictions, for images of God and his prophets were not to be countenanced, in a strange cultural echo of the iconoclastic era of Byzantium when biblical personages had been covered with plain painted crosses. And so the workers had done their duty liberally with their trowels, covering all the beautiful decoration with a layer of plain plaster and then a thin coat of white paint, prior to adding the complex patterns that would give the building colour and grace without the need for 'blasphemous' images.

With a sad air of loss, Skiouros stepped into the building, his feet kicking up plaster dust from the marble floor. Behind him, Dragi mumbled quick words with the other two, and then he ducked inside with his Greek friend. 'What was that about?' Skiouros whispered.

'The others will stay outside and watch for potential interruptions.'

Skiouros' eyes narrowed. 'On a Friday? You expect interruptions?'

'Just a precaution.'

The young Greek gave his Romani companion a suspicious look and then shrugged and peered off to the right. Access from this first *exonarthex* to the side chapel where he had fought a life-and-death struggle with an assassin was impossible due to the scaffolding and boarding supporting the ceiling of the former belfry's lowest level, preparing for the minaret to go in its place. Ducking through into the inner narthex, he noted with interest that some of the mosaics had yet to be covered. Work had apparently only reached here yesterday, and there was a pervading smell of drying plaster. Passing through, into the *parekklesion*, he missed out the construction works in the corner and entered what had been the most beautiful side-chapel in the world. Now, it was a cold, echoing white space with splats of plaster and whitewash on the marble floor. But that didn't matter to the workmen. Parts of the floor were being taken up and replaced anyway.

He noted with interest that the hole where he had left a Mamluk murderer with a crushed torso five years ago was either open again, or had remained open this whole time. He wondered what the workmen had thought those years ago when they had found the body.

Dragi was watching him with interest, and the Greek cleared his throat in a business-like manner and crouched by the hole. A step-ladder led down into the gloom, and he quickly slid down it into the darkness of the substructures. The huge chambers beneath the church were no longer used as a crypt and had not been for a long time, simply remaining as vaulted supports for the building above. The workmen were clearly engaged in re-mortaring various sections of brickwork in the foundations, but that would be the grand extent of the work down here – mosques had no use for such subterranean features. The light from above was surprisingly bright, the high windows' radiance reflected in so much white wall surface as to positively glow, and a shaft of bright sunlight illuminated a circle in the crypt beneath the hole. But beyond that circle of light, only the nearest wall was visible down here – the darkness marched off oppressively in all other directions.

Skiouros downed his bag and retrieved his flint and steel from his pouch. Fishing around, he removed his tiny oil lamp, purchased back on Crete, which was a copy of the very same style oil lamps used by the Romans a thousand years ago and yet still functioned just as well. Filling the lamp from the minute oil flask in the pouch, he lay some tinder and a small taper on a piece of broken marble, striking the steel and flint until the tinder took, glowing, and then bursting into orange, fiery life. As the small, dry taper caught, he touched it to the oil at the lamp's spout and the light source bloomed slowly into a golden glow, illuminating the dark cellars. Sure enough, as he tucked away the tinderbox and oil flask once more, he could see the tell-tale signs of patchwork repairs on some walls, and other, more crumbled sections yet to be dealt with.

Snatching up the bag with his free hand, he stamped out the small conflagration on the floor and moved to one of the sections where the work was clearly complete, an entire wall and its vaulting and free-standing brick columns all newly-mortared and dry. Crouching, he examined the ground. Bedrock. There would be no digging, then, to inter his sibling. Still, the work down here was almost complete, and this particular section was already finished. The workmen would have no cause to come to this corner again, and very soon they would remove their ladder and seal in the sub-vaults again. There was probably only a day's work left here, and the crypt would need to be completed first so that the floor could be replaced to be worked upon.

Not a grave, then, but a tomb. A vast, spacious tomb, formed from the entire sub-level of the church. A tomb befitting a great man, really. Skiouros nodded his satisfaction and carefully tucked the bag containing the head and various stench-nullifying spices in the darkest corner, behind a pillar and well hidden from the centre or any part of this level where work might still be carried out.

It was done. After all this time, Lykaion was home and interred.

He felt a surprising and rather sudden sense of utter loss. Not, curiously, because he was finally burying his brother, and not simply because he had died in the first place, but because he'd become used to Lykaion's voice in his head over those years, and yet now it had been so long since he'd heard it that he was beginning to wonder whether he'd imagined it altogether. And somehow, despite the time that had passed in silence, he'd clung to the idea that at least here, at the end, Lykaion would talk to him, would say goodbye to him.

Nothing.

With a sad smile he gestured farewell to his brother, muttering a very brief prayer in an archaic form of Greek and adding a shorter one in Turkish just in case. He then extinguished his lamp and packed away his gear, turning his back on the final resting place, scurrying over to the ladder and climbing it with suddenly-tired arms.

Dragi was awaiting him at the top with a patient expression.

'He is settled?'

'Yes.'

'Good. Have you anything else to do here? We will leave shortly, but events are beginning to unfold, and you are currently where you need to be,' Dragi replied mysteriously, causing Skiouros to clench his teeth in irritation yet again. With a deep breath, he wandered over to the apse at the eastern end of the side chapel. Here, not long ago, there had been exquisitely rendered paintings of half a dozen important saints, three to each side of the window. Now the room glowed with an unearthly white brilliance, and no sad, ancient eyes peered out of the walls. In a mix of irritation at this iconoclastic destruction and sadness at the final true loss of a brother, Skiouros stepped close to the white plaster. It was still recent, probably yesterday's work, and while dry, it was also soft. Soon it would harden, but right now...

With an air of personal satisfaction, Skiouros leaned in and used his thumbnail to scratch a word into the plaster.

Λύκαιον

Stepping back, he smiled. *Lykaion.* You could see the inscription if you approached it at the correct angle and the light

71

caught the marks, though from straight on it was all-but invisible. With luck it would stay there as a grave marker, even when the decorative paints were applied.

Dragi smiled but said nothing. He was almost buzzing as though with anticipation, and Skiouros' suspicion rose a notch. He was beginning to recognise the subtle signs of the Romani's machinations at work, and expectant silence and a tension in the air were portentous around Dragi .

Silence reigned in this ancient structure, and Skiouros rolled his shoulders. 'I suppose, then, it's time to get going.'

The two men turned and walked back towards the inner narthex, exchanging glances as they heard the door to the church creak open and then shut with a click. The sounds of hurrying footsteps halted the two men in their tracks as Diego and Parmenio rounded the corner with wild eyes.

'Shit!' Parmenio explained, unhelpfully.

'We have company,' Diego elucidated, as the two men came to a halt beside their friends.

'Who?' Skiouros asked, his nerves starting to twang as he cast a sidelong glance at Dragi, who seemed totally unsurprised.

Diego shrugged, effectively reminding them with a gesture that he was a stranger here. 'No idea, but there's at least a dozen of them, including the escort.'

Parmenio pinched the bridge of his nose. 'I don't know who they are, but they're important. There are soldiers with them.'

'Janissaries?'

'I can't really be sure, since I don't know them well enough, but to me they have the look of provincial field soldiers. And a couple of high-ranking nobles among them, too. One of them has some kind of standard being carried all ceremoniously.'

Skiouros' eyes widened. 'A standard with a crescent and a horsetail hanging from it?'

'Yes.'

'More than one of each?'

Parmenio frowned. 'Yes. Three, in fact.'

Skiouros felt his panic begin to build. 'A paşa. An important one, too.'

'What is a paşa?' Diego asked quietly.

'Either a high government official or a senior military officer. Or anyone chosen directly by the sultan for merit. No one we want to meet, for sure.'

'Well that might not be your choice. They're coming here and we're trapped,' Parmenio grunted.

'The crypt,' murmured Dragi, gesturing at the hole in the floor from which Skiouros had recently emerged. The Greek nodded his agreement and the four men scurried over to the hole. As Dragi moved first down the ladder, hooking his feet around the outside of the uprights and sliding freely and swiftly into the darkness, they could hear the door being opened back at the church's main façade. Skiouros waited for Parmenio to descend as quickly as he could and Diego to slip down with the grace of an expert acrobat, and then dropped down it himself. As soon as he reached the bottom, he gestured to Dragi and the two of them lifted the ladder away from the hole in the ceiling, gently bringing it down into the darkness, taking it away from the hole and lowering it to the floor. Footsteps and murmured conversation echoed down from above, and Skiouros joined the others, lurking close by – but out of sight of – the hole, in the deep shadow.

Two men, from the distinct footsteps. One set of feet clipped on the marble and were clearly clad in fairly soft, high quality shoes. The others clunked with the heavy leather of military footwear. The two voices were as equally at odds as the footsteps: one was quiet and with an almost musical lilt, persuasive and smooth, while the other was slightly hoarse and deep – a voice of power and with a tone that suggested its owner was used to being obeyed. Skiouros would be willing to bet that the soft voice belonged to the soft shoes and likewise the deep one to the boots.

'This is your idea of a private place, Hadim?'

Skiouros frowned at the deep, hoarse voice's words. *Hadim.* The name meant 'eunuch' and suggested that its owner was a bureaucrat created by the same *devsirme* Christian draft that had torn Skiouros and Lykaion from their home. Which one of these men, then, was the paşa? There were plenty of *Hadims* in the Ottoman court, so the name did little to identify him. And a paşa might as equally be a man in military boots as a bureaucrat.

'I am having the place restructured and turned into a mosque, *Şehzade*. On a Friday, where could be more private?'

Skiouros had been trying to place the quieter man's accent and had decided on somewhere in the western Balkans, before what was actually said settled into his skull and his eyes widened again. This man was the one having the church of Saint Saviour rebuilt?

Then he was *Hadim Ali Paşa*, vizier of the Ottoman court and heroic general of the Mamluk war. *He* was the senior paşa to whom the standard outside belonged.

But that was not the revelation that was truly heart-stopping. The paşa's tone of deference suggested that even he, one of the most powerful men in the empire, felt inferior to his companion, and Skiouros could see why. *Şehzade*, he had said. The word was one to be feared, for that title was applied only to the crown princes of the empire, the sons of the sultan himself. Skiouros felt his heart skip a single beat and then begin to race dangerously. To be caught listening in on a senior paşa and a son of the sultan would most certainly buy them a slow and agonising death.

'I am still not convinced of the need for such secrecy, Hadim. I had not intended to leave the palace until the festival. Staying near to my father can only foster a closeness that will pay dividends.'

The quieter voice took on an air of strained patience. 'My Şehzade, every wall in Istanbul hides the ears of the sultan, and none more so than those of the new palace. And some things are too dangerous to discuss even with dissembling tongues.'

The prince snorted, but clearly the argument had been won by his companion.

'The time nears, Hadim. Have your emissaries met with any success?'

There was a pause. 'There are crucial groups who are with us, Şehzade Ahmet – lesser powers who will support you, including one of our most ancient enemies. But there are others who favour your brothers, too. Nothing is certain at this stage. The more time we have, the more secure your position will be. The *Khoraxané dede Babik* warns us that your brothers' champions are also moving within the city.'

Something about the way Hadim stressed the three names made Skiouros picture his face twisting sourly in disgust. The paşa clearly held no love for this person. *Khoraxané* was a name applied to the Romani of the region, and Skiouros glanced across at Dragi to see his companion chewing his cheek with narrowed eyes as he listened intently. Who was this mysterious Romani who dealt with a crown prince and a high paşa of the empire? He could almost sense the prince nodding in the silence. He glanced briefly at his other friends. Parmenio and Diego clearly had no idea what was being said or who these people were, other than that they were important. Dragi was inscrutable.

His suspicion of his Romani friend heightened again. What were the chances of them being here in this church when two such important and powerful men arrived to conspire in secrecy? "None" was the answer. There was *no* chance. Coincidences like this were *always* manufactured, and despite the fact that it had been Skiouros' choice to come here in order to bury Lykaion, what had Dragi said? *'You are currently where you need to be.'*

'I know you do not like dealing with the Alevi sect, Hadim, but I will not ignore a potentially powerful ally simply because of their heretical beliefs. So, if we seek more powerful allies, to whom do we turn? Inevitably to yet greater heretics.' Prince Ahmet murmured, a rhythmic clicking suggesting that he was tapping his toes as he thought. 'Only two powers are large enough to overcome all others. But they are mutually exclusive, so we must decide.'

'Who is this, my Şehzade?'

'Clearly Persia in the east, or the Vatican in the west.'

Skiouros blinked. He simply could not believe his ears. *Persia* – that nebulous mass to the east of the empire – was a continual war-zone of failing states and desperate khanates and provinces whose panicked leaders annually petitioned the sultan to help secure their borders against the *Turkomen* horselords from the mountains and the rising *Safavid* predators in their midst. Those powers nominally in charge of the land would be of no benefit to the empire, and those increasingly dangerous peoples threatening them would only present an ever deadlier threat to the Turks. Only an idiot or a lunatic would look to Persia for support…

But then how could a Turk of nobility and wisdom even consider climbing into the *papal* bed with its bloated, corrupt pope and his dozen painted whores either? Admittedly, Skiouros might be a little biased in his views of the papacy, but he would sooner have driven nails through his own wrists and climbed up onto a cross than place his trust in the Borgias. The Pope played games with nations as his pieces. Would a crown prince of the empire really risk the Ottoman world in such a fashion?

To his great relief, there was a calculated, negative silence, and he felt sure that neither of those options sat well with the great vizier.

'Even here, where I have brought you for safety, such names are not wise to utter. Even speaking them is to endanger us. There are *other* powers, Şehzade Ahmet. Leave my messengers to do their work. Your father is still hale and hearty. Time is not as short as you think.'

There was another pause, this one heavy with something important and unspoken, and when Hadim Ali-Paşa spoke again, it was with curiosity and suspicion. 'Time is not so short, *is it*, my prince?'

'Have me an answer before the festival, Hadim.'

An uncomfortable silence settled on this demand – a silence that was broken by the heavier footsteps moving again. Skiouros, who, until this moment had been able to see only the ceiling of the parakklesion and the very top of the east window through the hole, suddenly caught sight of a man, perhaps thirty years of age, with a neat beard and piercing eyes, the build of a great hunting cat, and the purposeful step of a soldier. The prince Ahmet skirted the hole, glancing briefly into it but noting nothing of interest, and moved to the wall, just out of sight.

'See this, Hadim?'

The paşa, remaining hidden from the listeners, simply made a noncommittal noise.

'Someone has scratched a word into the plaster. Ly – kai – on. Greek? This is wolf in Greek, yes?'

'I believe so, Şehzade.'

Şehzade Ahmet had sharp eyes!

There was the sound of furious scratching and scraping, and when the prince passed back around the hole his hands were discarding a small shower of plaster dust.

'Curse all wolves, and the one of Trabzon in particular! Secure me my support, Hadim. This empire needs steering, not just riding, and by the eyes of the Prophet, *I* am the man to steer it.'

'Of course you are, my prince. No one would doubt the Lion of Amasya to be the natural choice. You are your father's favourite. The army is with you, and I will bring you the support you desire, though I intend to do so without stretching out our neck and handing the cleaver to the Borgia devil of a Turkoman raider, Şehzade.'

The two men turned and began to move away, their voices trailing off. Skiouros hardly dared breathe until he heard the church door shut with a click, and even then the four men waited almost two minutes in silence before Dragi finally broke the spell.

'Might I ask, Skiouros of Hadrianople, what you think of the crown prince Ahmet?'

Skiouros shook his head in disbelief. 'Ahmet is said to be a lion, and an astute one – the governor who encouraged learning and cultural freedom to flourish in Amasya. Clever and untouchable, strong and proud, fierce and royal: that's what they say, yes? All *I* heard was an ambitious and short-sighted power-seeker.'

Dragi nodded, and Skiouros cleared his throat again. 'You timed this visit so that we would witness that, while making the whole visit seem to be my decision.' It was not a question, nor even an accusation. It was plain statement of fact as Skiouros saw it. Dragi gave a small smile and a half-shrug. 'I told you things would be revealed to you as and when required. The time is drawing close.'

'And what's at the end of that time, Dragi? This festival I've been hearing about? What's planned then? A coup? Is Ahmet planning to overthrow his father and take the reins of empire?'

Dragi gave him an infuriating noncommittal look, and Skiouros rolled his eyes and expelled an irritated breath. 'If he did, he wouldn't win the succession, would he? There are two other strong brothers, I remember. Both governors and generals, just like Ahmet.'

'Who can say?' shrugged Dragi. 'Şehzade Ahmet is strong. He is the eldest and the most popular with most of the higher officials in the court. He is in a strong position.'

Skiouros turned to the other two, who were staring at this Turkish exchange in complete incomprehension.

'Come on. Help me get this ladder back up. It's time to leave.

In line with Skiouros' spirits, the sun was veiled by a thin cloud that held the best of its heat at bay as the four men emerged from the church door. Once the other three were out in the open and happy that the grounds of the disused church were not filled with janissaries, paşas, princes and other worrying figures, the Greek turned and replaced the padlock on the door, clicking it closed. It was a good job he'd taken it in with him. The visitors clearly had not registered the lack of a lock altogether, but finding one there and freshly opened would have raised dangerous questions.

Dragi was being interrogated in rapidly-fired queries by the other two, he and Skiouros having briefly enlightened them as to what it was they had witnessed on their way back out through the church. Skiouros stood, adjusting to the warm light outside once again, watching the increasing disbelief in the faces of the two westerners as they learned more of the Lion of Amasya and the powerful vizier who had counselled him. It *was* hard to believe. And the more Skiouros thought on the matter, the more he realised that this encounter was not only carefully timed and prepared, but must have been so for some time. Which suggested, to his mind at least, that there were further such encounters planned.

Eleven days, Dragi had said, which would be the date of the festival. Şehzade Ahmet had also intimated that something would happen on that day. Just eleven days. Perhaps he could persuade Dragi to open up a little and give him some warning of what was actually going on? But he knew Dragi, and the chances of that were negligible. *'Things will be revealed in due course,'* he grumbled under his breath in a passable imitation of the secretive Romani.

'Pardon?' Dragi prompted, turning to Skiouros.

Sometimes he forgot how sharp the Romani's senses were.

'What is this festival on the 29th?' he asked, neatly sidestepping the issue.

Dragi pursed his lips.

'There is to be a grand festival in the city in eleven days to commemorate the Ottoman acquisition of Constantinople.' The Romani began to tap on his fingers as if counting. 'There has apparently been a feeling of heightened tension in the city recently, fed by increasing external pressures. The Pope still toys with the idea of a crusade against the east, even if that persists as little more than a dream. Moldavia and Hungary remain in a state of icy, semi-military hostility with the empire. Venice hungers for Ottoman lands despite their treaty, and the Mamluks continue to look at Istanbul and see a prize for the picking. Add to that a strong influx of Jewish refugees from Spain flooding the marketplaces, and the people of the city are beginning to feel a sense of disquiet. The sultan believes that a great festival celebrating the power, the glory and the culture of this now-Ottoman city will help alleviate some of that pressure. He may be right – Bayezid is astute, as you know.'

Skiouros nodded. Despite being victorious conquerors, the Turkish rulers had not instituted an unbending Islamic reign on the former Byzantine world, and for their pains in becoming forgiving and tolerant overlords, they had been rewarded with a state cobbled together from various peoples and religions, divided in itself as much as it was one whole.

And how could the empire hope to hold its borders against so many fierce opponents if there were cracks in the mortar at its heart? An image of Prince Ahmet embracing the Borgia pope flashed into his head, and he shuddered at the thought.

Parmenio and Diego were now strolling through the garden and back towards the alley that led into the city with Dragi at their shoulder still answering their myriad questions, and Skiouros smiled as the sun emerged from the cloud once more, blasting its furnace heat down upon his face. He paused, allowing his friends to get ahead as he angled his face to the warm glow, his eyes shut as he drank in the heat.

What it was that tipped him off he couldn't say, but something triggered his senses, and he dropped to the ground just as the arrow thudded into the brick wall of the church behind him. Heart suddenly hammering, Skiouros scrambled into the relative shelter of a large pile of sacks of plaster just as he shouted a warning to his friends. Taking a deep breath, he rose to peer over the top of the pile, seeking out the danger.

That vagrant lad was sitting atop the boundary wall again, though now a man stood next to him, wearing a domed turban of deep blue with a wide fur surround that, along with a thick dark beard, cast the owner's features in shade. His lower half was hidden by the wall, but his deep blue *yelek* waistcoat over a voluminous shirt of white suggested he was a Christian, given the close ties between blue garments and the western church throughout the empire. Most notable, though, was the small recurve bow that was the stock in trade of Turkish archers, and which he held in one hand as he fetched a fresh arrow from his quiver.

The Greek's eyes darted back to the path to see that his three friends had achieved similar positions of relative safety behind stacks of marble or of curved stonework or sacks or crates. Three more figures stood in the entrance to the alley, all armed and in a variety of clothes – including black, which was rarely worn by the Ottoman people for its association with ill-luck.

Not Turks, then.

So who?

Skiouros tried to think of a solution. There only appeared to be four of them, as well as the youth, and he was confident in the martial skills of all his friends, but they were, to a man, unarmed. Even out here at the city's edge in an area mostly given over to Greeks, Jews, Armenians and Romani, it would be dangerous for a non-Turk to walk around openly armed. All it would take was bumping into a roving janissary patrol in a bad mood, and the consequences could be dire.

Four good men, then, but unarmed and against four unknowns, three with blades and a fourth with a bow... All he could do to begin with was concentrate on the immediate danger. The archer was busy nocking his next arrow, and had turned his head, seeking one of the other targets. That would provide the tiniest of openings.

Swallowing his nerves, Skiouros continued to peer over the tip of the pile and, as soon as the archer was picking out a target among the other three, he rose to a crouch, already running. Skirting the pile, he made for a large heap of stone blocks roughly halfway between him and the wall where the man stood. The young lad hissed something to the archer as Skiouros ran, crouched, from one defensive position to the next, and the bearded man turned, the nocked arrow's tip sweeping across the grounds until it picked out the running figure.

The arrow was released in a professional, fluid move, even as the man was still turning. By God, but he was fast. Accurate, too.

The arrow tore through Skiouros' doublet arm, drawing a tiny crimson line in the flesh as it passed, and suddenly he was in the safety of the next pile. He'd never seen an archer with such instinctive skill, the arrow so accurate with virtually no aiming involved. His arm burned with sharp pain, though he knew there was no real damage other than to his garments.

There was shouting from over near the alley entrance, but Skiouros' view of that area was now too obscured by piles of workmen's gear. Besides, he didn't have the luxury of time to spend checking on his friends. As his gaze rose over the tip of the pile, he saw the archer readying a third arrow and beginning to draw back the string. He wouldn't be caught out looking elsewhere again and, given the sheer speed of the man's draw and release, Skiouros would probably be skewered before he made it three paces from cover.

He chewed his lip in frustration, his gaze roving around the surroundings. Holding his breath, he ducked down and picked up a discarded rake with two broken tines, raising its head from the ground. Hurriedly, keeping low, he shrugged out of his doublet and hung it over the rake, fastening the top button to keep it there. Hardly convincing, but then, it didn't need to be. A tight coil of rope lay nearby, knotted at the centre, and he picked it up and jammed it into the neck of the doublet, shoving some of the strands around the rake tines to hold it in place. It was the least impressive scarecrow the world had ever seen. But it might be enough. It only had to buy him a single heartbeat, after all.

Readying himself, he thrust the rake head towards the far side of the pile, just enough to poke out over the edge, as though it were checking for trouble. To his relief, the sudden appearance of the makeshift mannequin was rewarded with the *thunk* of a bowstring snapping tight and the hum of an arrow in flight. Letting the doublet-coated rake fall, he was off and running without even a glance, emerging from the other side of the pile of stones as he ran for the wall.

The man cursed in Turkish as he struggled to bring a fourth arrow up to the bow in time.

Skiouros hurtled across the intervening grass like a demon, his muscles bunching at the last moment as he leapt for the man at the wall-top. The archer brought a fresh arrow to his bow, placing it against the string and drawing back for the release, but despite his impressive speed, he hadn't quite the time to complete and the arrow discharged with a twang, hurtling harmlessly off into the air as Skiouros hit him in the chest, knocking him back from the wall and down into a dusty, reeking alleyway behind a row of low-quality wooden housing that overlooked the church grounds.

Even as the man hit the ground, the breath driven from his lungs by the weight of Skiouros landing atop him, the homeless youth was suddenly on the Greek's back, pounding at him with surprisingly heavy blows for someone his size.

Unable to do anything about the boy, Skiouros concentrated on the man beneath him. The bow was still in the man's hand and he was temporarily out of action, stunned from the fall and from Skiouros' strike. He would recover soon enough, and the curved scimitar at his belt would come into play then. Skiouros considered trying to draw that blade himself, but from this angle it was nearly impossible. Instead, he grabbed the man by the shoulders, still ignoring the painful pounding his own back was suffering as he prepared to slam the archer's head back down, hard against the ground.

However, the man was already recovering and fighting back. He was stronger than Skiouros, which came as no surprise – the young Greek had always relied upon speed and wit, not upon brute strength. Even as Skiouros realised he was losing the struggle and the man was freeing himself, one chance suddenly swam into focus. Swiftly, he let go of the archer with his left hand, fighting to keep him down with the right as his hand snaked down until it grasped feathers.

Skiouros felt his right hand being forced back and the man beginning to rise, the man's free hand moving down to the hilt of the scimitar. Skiouros' own left hand came up, gripping the arrow he had drawn from the man's quiver just beneath the head as it plunged down with every ounce of strength he could muster, driving the shaft into the neck of the man beneath him. The archer gurgled in agony, his hand shaking, the sword forgotten as the bodkin point of the arrow scythed through his windpipe and gullet and plunged on through his neck until it came to a stop, grating against his spine.

Skiouros rolled off the bucking form of the dying archer and reached for the parasite who had been sitting on his back, delivering blow after blow to his tender kidneys. The boy rolled with the movement, coming to rise a few yards away, where he immediately broke into a run. Skiouros peered after him for a moment, trying to decide whether to give chase, but his bruised torso argued against such a decision, and reluctantly he watched the boy disappear.

Turning back to the archer, who was now lying still, his legs trembling and pink froth emerging from the wound around the arrow shaft, Skiouros reached down and unfastened the scimitar from the man's belt. It was a solid, undecorated, functional blade. Gripping it tightly, Skiouros left the dying man and ran back around the church's peripheral wall until he saw his friends. He had hoped he could be of some use, coming in behind the enemy and distracting them, but it seemed he had been too late. Dragi clutched a scimitar in an arm from which dripped a steady slow flow of his own blood. Parmenio was limping and massaging his knuckles, and Diego held a broadsword up, examining the grip, as three bodies littered the floor before them.

'Where have you been?' Parmenio rolled his eyes and flashed a grin at his friend.

'I was a little preoccupied. You had no trouble then?'

'A few minor cuts. Diego here is a demon with a blade, Skiouros. You were right about going after him. He could have taught Orsini a thing or two.'

Skiouros came to a halt next to his friends. 'I think we should get back to the house. This place is starting to feel quite unsafe.'

They murmured their agreement and turned to make their way back, and Skiouros nudged Dragi. 'I don't suppose you have any idea who they were? They weren't Turks, for a start.'

'As the hourglass turns, bringing the festival ever nearer, several groups vie for position, Skiouros. You have not seen your last trouble, yet.'

'So you have no intention of telling me who they were?'

'I am not sure enough of their identity to give you a thorough answer.'

Skiouros fixed him with a suspicious, even disbelieving, glare.

'But,' Diego de Teba said, cutting in as he held up his hard-won blade to the light, '*this* is an interesting development.'

Skiouros peered at the cross embossed upon the sword's hilt, with each of its four arms an inverted 'V' giving the whole design eight individual points. It was an almost unbearably familiar symbol.

'A *Hospitaller* blade?'

Chapter six – Of poets and murderers

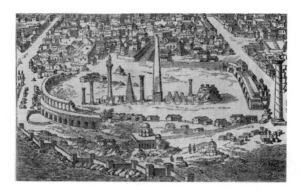

May 20th

SKIOUROS entered the open land of the sultan's grand parade ground cautiously. Despite the fact that there were but few locals here, and no one seemed to be paying the four newcomers any attention, old habits died hard. While, despite being clean shaven, he could probably pass for a Turk these days – and Dragi was something of a native anyway – quite clearly Parmenio and Diego were western foreigners, from the shape and cast of their faces to the non-Turkish cut of their clothes. In fairness, Skiouros' own clothes nodded far more in the direction of the unfashionable Greek than the fashionable Turkish, too.

And the parade ground was not a place in which to be inconspicuous. Once a grand chariot-racing circuit in the ancient city, it was still on occasion used for horse races, though now its most notable duty was for grand processions and military displays by the janissaries and the sultan's best. As such, added to its prime location at the heart of the oldest part of the city and lying directly before the great church of Haghia Sophia, it was rarely empty of visitors, from the well-to-do Ottoman residents taking a stroll, to distant travellers and academics studying the ancient pile.

Its original form was clear. Along the northern side of the former stadium, hiding the slew of recent Turkish buildings among the ancient structures, stood the tiers of seats upon which a million million Roman backsides had watched the Greens and the Blues, the Reds and the Whites racing their deadly games in pursuit of fame and riches. A similar array of seating to the southern side was in far worse condition, having been allowed to collapse into the ruins of the ancient Roman palace which it abutted. The Kathisma – the box where emperors had watched the games – was now little more than a ruinous shell. And yet there was still something about the place that summoned up spirit into the blood. For the extended platform was perfectly level between the seating, and the *spina* along the centre, around which the racers pounded, was still adorned with over a dozen columns of differing shapes and sizes, some manufactured for the purpose, others taken as spoils of war from Egypt or Greece of old.

And then there was their destination.

At the western – or more strictly speaking the *south*-western – end of the former circus, where the graceful curved seating had long gone for Turkish rebuilding, stood a curved arcade of enormously tall, delicate marble columns with an intricate architrave along the top. This stunning ancient edifice had once formed simply a structural part of the seating stands. Now it stood proud and alone like one of the graceful monuments Skiouros had witnessed in the gardens of Rome and the villas of Italy. And with the morning sun behind them the four visitors could clearly see the drop beyond for, from the heart of the hippodrome, behind those beautiful white columns naught could be seen but clear blue sky.

Skiouros eyed Dragi suspiciously as they walked west along the stadium, past the mismatched columns, towards that glorious colonnaded viewpoint. After the incident at the church two days ago, Dragi had told them that he would have the potential involvement of the Hospitaller knights investigated, and indeed a number of the seemingly endless Romani community had disappeared apparently on that very task. Yet nothing had come of it so far. And Dragi had made no further demands upon Skiouros' time, allowing him freedom of movement, accompanied by mysterious phrases like 'as necessity demands' and 'time will reveal' whenever he was pressed.

The day following their encounter at the church, the four of them had travelled around the Phanar and Balat regions, now armed against any further attacks. Those regions which were once home to Skiouros were almost solely the province of Greek and Jewish residents, and the chances of running into any authorities who might take offence at the bearing of blades were slim. Skiouros had led his friends to his old haunts, showing them the bloody church and the markets, the ruined baths and the former open air cistern, even to the house with the yellow marble columns on Zagan Paşa Caddesi, where he had found a dismembered official in a bathtub. He had also gathered up his three remaining hidden caches of coins around the city, which would give them a little finance to ease matters.

But they had not dared leave the enclaves and venture into Turkocentric areas where they could not realistically bear arms. Dragi had been insistent that it was too dangerous when Skiouros had been itching to show his friends certain other sights with personal significance around the city. And yet *this morning* the Romani had rubbed his hands together in a business-like fashion and announced that he believed they could reasonably make their way into the heart of the Ottoman city, on the condition they bore no weapons. When pressed, he had intimated that there had been progress on his investigations, though he could not detail them yet, and regardless, there were places and times that Skiouros must be.

And so here they were, ostensibly accommodating one of Skiouros' desired visits, though he was under no illusion that this outing was entirely orchestrated and executed according to the designs of the secretive Romani. Damn him.

They strode to the stunning white colonnade that curved around the hippodrome's end upon a stone lip a few feet in height and, as they came to a halt beneath the architrave, Skiouros found that he was staring in disbelief every bit as much as the foreigners.

He had seen this view a few times in his life. When he had found the courage to move through the Turkish areas, where the richest purses could be cut, and the risks so much greater, he had occasionally come here to drink in the panorama. Plus, of course, the substructures of the hippodrome on the hillside below them were a great place to hide and outwit any pursuit.

But the view had changed.

He had *expected* the change, of course, having been at least partially the architect of it. But he had not expected it to be quite so astonishing.

The curved end of the hippodrome plunged down from such a height that they were looking over the tops of trees growing close to the walls. Before them two hundred yards of land packed with red-roofed structures marched out to the sea walls and, beyond, ships plied the waters of the Propontis amid frolicking, leaping dolphins. Off to the left, though, where Skiouros' gaze had inevitably been drawn, was the familiar Bucoleon palace – one intact building abutting the water, one somewhat ruinous. But even that was not what he had fixed upon and what had drawn him.

He stared.

After a significant pause, Diego cleared his throat. 'It is a stunning view, I will grant you. Perhaps better than the view from Ronda across the gorge at the sierra beyond. But the importance of it escapes me.'

Parmenio's gaze was steadily sweeping right to left, and then his own eyes widened.

'Was that…?'

Skiouros nodded as he studied the gaping hole in the city of Constantine. Five years earlier here had stood one of the greatest churches of the Byzantine world: the Nea Ekklasia. Until a conspiracy that had threatened the life of the sultan had led Skiouros to confront his enemy there. He had barely made it away from the place alive in that dreadful Anatolian storm.

Not only was the building gone, but a large part of the neighbourhood had disappeared with it. The church of Saint John the Theologian nearby was little more than a half-standing shell. A large stretch of the solid boundary wall of the emperor Phocas was now little more than a rubble heap. The tall *pharos* – the lighthouse he and Lykaion had used to spy upon the Mamluk ambassador – had survived at less than half its full height.

Most of the houses had gone altogether. The area remained as a charred, scarred wound in the fabric of the city. The scale of the devastation was immense, as though an irate giant had rampaged across the urban landscape, tearing up some buildings and trampling others.

'What in the name of the Holy Mothe…' Diego caught his words, remembering where he was and bit down upon them. 'What happened *there*?'

Parmenio gave a small sigh and then turned an odd smile on the Spaniard. '*Skiouros the Greek* happened there. Someday, when all this is over, we'll sit down over a cup of khave or a glass of wine and I'll tell you the whole sordid, destructive tale. Suffice it to say that that large grey crater was a church five years ago.'

Diego turned an expression of disbelief on Skiouros, who simply shrugged. It was hardly worth pointing out any of the detail, including the fact that it had no longer been a church, but a gunpowder store at the time.

'Another glorious monument brought down by human foolishness,' he admitted sadly.

'Of course I never saw it,' Parmenio muttered. 'Well, I saw bits of it falling out of the sky and splashing into the sea damn close to the *Isabella*'s hull, and I certainly bloody *heard* it, but...'

'Did you hear *that*?' the Spaniard said suddenly, holding up a hand to hush them. The rest stood still and listened. The wind rushed through the trees below them and the occasional shrubbery around the periphery of the hippodrome, and the very distant murmur of conversation among the other folk formed a gentle hum of life backed by the chirruping of birds, but nothing stood out.

'What?' whispered Skiouros.

'It sounds like the music the Moors used to make in Al-Andalus. Haunting and delicate. Can you not hear it?'

And Skiouros could. Now that his companion had pointed it out, the gentle strains of music were audible as winding strands among the warp and weft of the city's aural tapestry. A *lavta* or *'ud* from the sounds of it – a pear-shaped lute common among the musical stylings of the empire. And the tune was indeed haunting. At once beautiful and mournful, sad, hollow and delicate. A thing of beauty but with a strangely menacing underlying thread. And now, almost inaudible it was so gentle, a voice was crooning along in a similarly ominous-yet-beautiful voice. Skiouros' brow creased.

'I can't quite hear what he's singing.'

Dragi cleared his throat quietly.

> *'O zealot, go become intoxicated from that cup so sweet...*
> *completely.*
> *Bow down before the Merciful in human form,*
> *for the man of God who adores the human form of the Lord*
> *is adoring*
> *faithfully.*
> *He is wise who sees his Lord; come, see your Lord,*
> *become wise:*
> *that one who before the Truth is ashamed*
> *is like a djinn in dishonesty.'*

Dragi's helpful translation into Greek, for the benefit of Diego in particular, came to a sharp end, as did the musical refrain and the poetic accompaniment as the air was riven by an ear-splitting shriek and, peering over the edge as they were, all four saw a skinny, naked figure arc out from the substructures immediately below them and plummet some fifty feet to the gravel and turf below, his limbs snapped and bent by the few tree branches as he fell. The body landed with a crack and a wet thud and, even from their height, the watchers could see the glistening pool begin to form around it.

As Skiouros, Parmenio and Diego stared at the grisly sight in shock – Dragi seemed curiously unsurprised – a calm, almost musical voice which clearly belonged to that same singer, began to speak in the manner of a preacher or an orator.

'A'ishah bought a cushion having on it images of creatures. When Allah's Apostle saw it, he stood at the door and did not enter. A'ishah noticed the sign of disapproval on his face and said, "*O Mohammed, what sin have I committed?*" Allah's Apostle said. "*What is this cushion?*" to which A'ishah said, "*I have bought it for you so that you may recline upon it.*" Allah's Apostle said, "*The makers of these pictures will be punished on the Day of Resurrection. The Angels do not enter a house in which there are such pictures.*"'

'What *is* this?' hissed Diego in disgust. Skiouros and Parmenio nodded silently by his side, and Dragi, seemingly anxious at the possibility of being discovered by the unseen orator, gestured with his thumb and began to walk away.

As they crossed the former hippodrome to an area of broken stonework where the more ruinous section of seating met the arc of columns, Skiouros deemed them far enough from the speaker for safety and laid his hand on Dragi's shoulder.

'What happened back there?'

Dragi gave him a calculating look and, as they descended the ruins to a street that ran downhill alongside the great circus, he shrugged.

'The *Eagle of Sarahun* showed his true plumage. Come. There is more to witness and to learn.'

Skiouros started slightly at the name, though found to his surprise that it had not had the impact it should. Perhaps having already witnessed Şehzade Ahmet up close had dulled the shock, though in truth, Skiouros had been half expecting some such revelation since Dragi had urged them here.

Turning left, the Romani trotted quickly downhill towards the huge curved brick substructures that supported the former hippodrome. With a nod to the others, he placed a finger over his lips to silence them, and slipped into the open doorway of a ramshackle timber house facing the great monument where the road turned away.

Skiouros frowned in concern and, noticing Dragi casting a sharp glance at the brick curve as he disappeared, followed his gaze to see an open door into the substructures. Slipping past it, the three followed Dragi into the building with some trepidation. The structure was clearly unoccupied, and dangerously unstable in places. The winding staircase up which Dragi had disappeared was missing several steps and the timbers shifted and groaned alarmingly underfoot. After a few careful moments and the odd hair-raising misplaced step, the others emerged through a ruined door into a wide room with a large window at which stood Dragi, lurking in the shade.

The others joined him and, keeping far enough back so as not to become obvious observers at the window, realised that from here they had achieved a clear view of the bricked-up arches of the hippodrome's substructures, as well as the figure seated in one of the few smaller apertures and the broken naked bodies at the foot of the great arc. For in the time it had taken them to descend from the hippodrome's top to this outer vantage point, a second broken figure had joined that first on the slope below. Their eyes slid up to the arcades.

Despite the distance, Skiouros could see that the figure seated in the opening with his legs dangling into space and the lavta on his knee, plucking the strings once more, was dressed in extremely expensive, fashionable Ottoman clothing. From here the music was audible only as a faint murmur, though.

'Who is that?' Parmenio asked quietly.

Skiouros, pursing his lips, took a deep breath. 'That, Parmenio, is the Eagle of Sarahun, Şehzade Korkut, son of Bayezid and brother of our friend Ahmet.' He turned to Dragi as the Romani began to murmur again, translating the lilting poetry that had once more begun to emanate from the hippodrome.

> 'Respect the form and recognise its content,
> for I am soul and body, but both,
> and neither can contain me.
>
> I am pearl and shell, the scales for the End of Days, the bridge to Paradise...
> and even with such riches, this world cannot contain me.
> The 'hidden treasure' that is God I am...
> eyes open...'

Without warning, a spindly, naked figure appeared at the opening next to the seated prince, the rough hands of unseen others propelling him out into space, where he fell with a piercing scream, broken by the tree branches before his life essence was ripped from him by the ground below.

Again, the poetry ended and the quiet, lilting voice spoke softly. 'Mohammed returned from a journey to find that A'ishah had placed a curtain of pictures over the door of her chamber. When Allah's Apostle saw this, he tore it down, saying, "*The people who will receive the severest punishment on the Day of Resurrection will be those who try to make the likeness of Allah's creations.*"

As Diego and Parmenio shared a stunned expression, the gentle strumming of the lavta began once more.

'*In Heaven's rose garden,
Like a sorrowful nightingale...*'

But something was happening now, and the music stopped sharply as two other figures appeared in the aperture. Another naked man, moving with desperation and panic, was grappling with a heavy-set soldier in the armour of a *ghazi* warrior. The two men came perilously close to knocking the seated prince from his perch and as the soldier finally won out and pushed the naked prisoner from the arch, the Eagle of Sarahun hooked out a leg, his face a picture of fury, and swept the ghazi's feet from under him. With a cry of surprise, the unbalanced warrior fell from the wall and joined the four naked corpses on the ground below with a crunch of metal and bone. The four observers in the damaged house watched the unfortunate soldier try to rise once, but then collapse and lie still.

'Allah despises idiots,' spat Şehzade Korkut, casting a gaze of malice down at the pile of bodies before cracking the neck of his lavta over his knee and dropping the shattered instrument down atop them.

'Will someone explain to me what's going on?'
Dragi turned to the angry, confused Diego de Teba and gave a sad smile. 'Şehzade Korkut is engaged simultaneously in two of his

favourite pursuits: musical poetry, and the violent eradication of heresy.'

'He's got some bloody nerve,' Parmenio said. 'This is hardly somewhere private to carry out so many blatant murders. There must be two dozen citizens wandering around in the hippodrome.'

'He has nothing to fear from them,' Skiouros replied. 'No one would dare confront the sons of the sultan, even his victims.' He turned to Dragi with a sour look. 'And this you brought me to see? Remember that I have faced the fanatic Etci Hassan. The fiery intolerance of certain sectors of your society is nothing new to me. Christian will likely always be persecuted by Muslim, and vice versa. And the Jew by both,' he added with a faint hint of disgust.

'Those broken bodies are not Christians, Skiouros. Nor are they Jews. In the eyes of Şehzade Korkut – in all other respects the sultan's most learned and affable son – the followers of the cross or the sons of David should be flayed and burned in public spectacle. No. These are other followers of the Qur'an, though considered heretics. Followers of Sufism or of Alevism or Hurufism. Shi'a believers. To men such as Korkut, these heretics are nothing. They are *less* than nothing. They are not even worthy of public display, but of silent, mechanical disposal.'

He gestured to the figure in the brick arches before them. 'The refrains the prince has been reciting are by *Nesimi*, an *Azeri* Turk poet and *Hurufi* teacher who was flayed alive for his heresy in Aleppo almost a century ago. They advocate the human form as the ultimate expression of God and even that God lives *within* the human form. The prince's answering verses are sacred hadith that forbid the creation of likenesses of living creatures. Misguided replies, and shot wide of the mark, but then one should never expect clarity from the extreme.'

Skiouros shook his head. Korkut was popular in the Ottoman court. He it had been who had acted as regent on the death of Mehmet the conqueror until the day Bayezid could reach the city and assume the throne. His granted governorship of Sarahun showed the clear favour of his father, for he was notably closer to the city than his brothers. And he was said to be a scholar and a poet which, it seemed, he may very well be. But he was also a devout, even radical Sunni, and there had been tales – spoken under the breath and only in the private places of the non-Turk sectors the city – that he would be a murderous opponent of the foreign enclaves if he succeeded the throne.

Skiouros felt a shiver run up his spine.

'Your point is well taken, Dragi. And I begin to see what this is all about. That night when we first arrived, our ageing host called me something, though I couldn't quite work it out at the time, what with all the wine. But it has nagged at me until the answer came just now. *Kral yapımcı,* he said. *King maker.* And you have found ways to show us two of the three crown princes of the empire, so I presume you have Şehzade Selim hiding in a closet somewhere, awaiting our viewing?'

He noted the inscrutable look on the Romani's face and sighed. 'Very well. You have me interested at the least. Something is in the wind for the coming festival, and one of these three will be ascendant, I presume? I was not aware that the sultan was in declining health?'

Again, Dragi's face was unreadable.

'And while Ahmet would be a disaster for the security of the empire, Korkut would be a disaster for its internal peace. Yet I am almost certain that Selim will be no better – he has the darkest and sourest reputation of the three. And whatever your strange tales might suggest, I have no more say in their succession than anyone. The throne will be won by the strongest and the wiliest.'

'All life is balance, Skiouros. The wise know this. And there will always be a king maker, and a king breaker. Think on the potential result if one of them refuses his role.' The Romani sighed. 'In a perfect world, I would not force such matters on people outside my own community, and it grieves me to have to involve you, but I am a servant, not a master, and such decisions are rarely mine to make.'

'Dragi, it is not my place to become involved in such things, any more than it is yours. The succession will be won by the strongest, as always.'

'And if a king-breaker is already at work, pushing one particular candidate?' the Romani replied flatly. 'What value those successional rules then? Remember what you heard of Ahmet. Already he manoeuvres and gathers to his banner groups with power. Can you recall what Hadim Ali Paşa said: an *ancient enemy* supports Ahmed – and what more ancient enemy does the Osman line have than the knights of the cross? Are you willing to sit back and do nothing if the men who killed Cem Sultan try to repeat their success in the heart of the empire? And what of the sultan? What of Bayezid

93

the Just? He is still hale and hearty. You once placed your very life on the line to protect him from assassins…'

'How do you know that?' Skiouros snapped in surprise, noting the look of astonishment on Diego's face.

'I know a great deal, Skiouros. Remember that. You risked your own life to save the sultan. Would you now sit back and let him be usurped by another, backed by powers unseen? Who would you see your precious *just* sultan replaced by? The megalomaniac or the zealot?'

Dragi was angry. Spittle was flicking from his lips as he spat the words, causing Skiouros to step back in alarm. He had never seen Dragi show such emotion, and he was suddenly acutely aware that he had no idea of what the man was truly capable. Carefully, with mollifying hands raised, he took a steadying breath.

'I gave you my word, Dragi, that I was yours until the day of the festival, and I meant it. I am just warning you that despite everything I have done over the years, I am no hero. I am no warrior or crusader for right. I am an orphaned former thief, trying to survive in a treacherous world. I will do what you ask of me as far as I am able, but do not expect great things of me. I fear I have proved time and again that greatness does not live in me.'

Dragi seemed to have calmed and when he spoke again it was as though his anger had never shown itself. 'Come, Skiouros.'

The Romani walked across the room and descended the stairs once more. As he reached the entrance hall of the large structure, he paused, and the four of them watched Korkut, the Eagle of Sarahun, leave the door in the hippodrome's substructures and, surrounded by almost a dozen heavy soldiers, climb back up to the top of the street. Once they were out of sight and earshot, Dragi led them from the house and by a snaking path to the grass and gravel slope at the bottom of the huge curve of bricked-up arches. Skiouros paused at the edge of the trees, listening to the sound of the numerous flies already at work on the bodies nearby in the early spring heat.

'Come,' Dragi urged him, somewhat forcefully, and Skiouros reluctantly did as he was bade. Parmenio and Diego shared unspoken thoughts and hung back a few paces.

Skiouros looked at the pile of men.

'What now.'

'Nothing,' Dragi answered. 'Just look.'

Skiouros peered at them with distaste. The four naked bodies had been painted with Arabic letters that Skiouros could not translate, and he peered at them.'

'Twelve phrases on each. What do they say?'

Dragi sighed. 'They are the twelve imams that the Shi'a follow. It is an expression of their heresy. *Look at them*, though. Not at their wounds, or the slogans. Look at the *people*, Skiouros.'

The Greek did so. Two were clearly bearded Turks from eastern Anatolia. He had seen plenty in the city over the years. One was a southerner – Levantine of some variety. The other... He frowned.

'I know this man. I drank Salep with him on our first night here.'

Dragi nodded. 'He was one of my people. Though most of my community are Sunni, there are Shi'a living peacefully among us. Elekchi Iusuf was one of those who went out to investigate your Hospitaller connection. He never returned, and now we know why. You see, Skiouros, how this whole matter is not some ancient Romani tale or some high conspiracy that is none of your concern. Such troubles touch all of us.'

Skiouros stared down at the body of the man he had watched engaged in a lively dance with his wife mere days ago, and something settled in him. He opened his mouth to speak but as he did so, he was surprised to see the ghazi warrior attempt to rise to his knees again, but collapse to the ground once more with a gasp and a shudder.

'Broken back,' noted Dragi with no sign of emotion.

Skiouros stared at the soldier for a moment, then reached down, drawing the sword from the unresisting ghazi's side, and plunged the blade down where he judged the heart to be, driving it deep until it met unyielding rock. The warrior spasmed twice and then went still, his foot shaking a few more times before it too became motionless.

'And what of Şehzade Selim then?' he asked quietly.

'The Wolf of Trabzon?'

'They say he is the darker of the princes.'

'And they speak true. But, Skiouros, remember that the darkest part of the night heralds the bright dawn of the new day.'

Skiouros stared down at the sword standing proud of the body. Each passing season seemed to drag his own soul down ever deeper into the darkness. Would there one day be a bright dawn for him?

Skiouros stared at the three cups on the table before him. As he watched, the street-performer placed a ball under each cup and then spun the three in and out in intersecting, snaking patterns before lining them up once again. Skiouros shook his head in bafflement.

'Choose.'

With no clear understanding, he reached out and tapped the cup on the left. The man lifted it and Skiouros was less than surprised to find no ball there. The other two cups yielded their hidden spheres easily enough.

'Now you,' the man said, pointing to Skiouros' left. He turned to see his reflection in the mirror, and boggled as that reflection acted independently, reaching out and tapping the middle cup. The game was played again, but the ball was not there for his reflection either.

'What is this?'

'This is a practice. Your only practice,' added the man. 'Now you.'

And this time, instead of a ball, he placed three intricately-carved ivory creatures beneath the cups: a wolf, an eagle and a lion. Skiouros felt panic grip him as he tried to decide which was the most important. Not the intolerant eagle, for certain, and not the dangerous lion. But even as the cup clacked down over the figure of the wolf, he couldn't help but notice that the creature was snarling at him.

Now was the time he wanted there to be nothing under the cup he chose, but he was certain he would have no such luck.

His tired eyes tried to follow the quick, snapping movements of the cups, and though he worried he had lost it twice, he believed he still had the wolf. As the man asked him to choose, he tapped the centre cup with marginal confidence.

The cup started to rise.

Skiouros awoke with a start to find Diego leaning over him with a glass of water, his habitually-hard expression softened by the faint hazy grey atmosphere of the room.

'Wha…?'

'You were almost shouting in your sleep. You sounded panicked. I thought you were having a nightmare.' He passed the glass to Skiouros, who took it gratefully and swigged the cold, clear water, still shaking and sweat-soaked.

'I was. I *was* having a nightmare, Diego. The problem is: I'm awake now, and I'm fairly sure I'm still having it.'

The Spanish swordsman gave him a look that was equal parts sympathy and suspicion, and wandered away across the Romani collective's house.

Skiouros closed his eyes again and tried to picture the three cups. He couldn't see what was under that middle one, even trying to extrapolate from the dream.

'I shouldn't be choosing,' he whispered to himself. 'It is not my job, any more than it is this king-breaker, wherever he might be.'

And in that moment he realised he had made a decision that eased at least some of his troubles. The meaning at the heart of Dragi's tale those months ago on board the ship off the coast of Sicily had been not to spend time deliberating and vying with his opposite number. If the king-maker and the king-breaker of the Romani tale had simply left the matter alone, one of the two princes would have won on his own merit in the end and the world would have been spared the cataclysmic end result of their meddling.

No. The value of the king-maker and the king-breaker was *not* in their wisdom in choosing a successor. It was in their having enough wisdom to stay out of the matter altogether.

He would do as Dragi asked until the time of the festival was up, but now he had a new goal: to persuade the Romani to his way of thinking.

And yet somehow, as he sank back to sleep picturing that snarling wolf beneath the cup, the bared fangs gradually became a smile.

Chapter seven – Of the darkest of places

May 21st

SKIOUROS looked over his shoulder at the figures of Parmenio and Diego, sitting in the shade of a yew tree and sharing a flask of ice cold water out of the sun's unforgiving glare. The pair looked more than content with their lot. And well they might, thought the young Greek, turning his face once more to the monstrosity before him.

The *Yedikule* – the fortress of the seven towers – was the most powerful and secure complex in the city. Constructed only three or four decades ago, this enormous fortification had been formed as an extension from the city walls, utilising four of its towers and adding three more and a curtain wall. In a grand show of Ottoman control the golden gate, through which so many Byzantine emperors had ridden in triumph, was now nothing more than a postern and flanking towers in this Turkish fortification.

And while it resembled nothing more than a high, powerful, unassailable fortress, that was not the purpose for which it had been built. It was constructed by the conqueror Mehmet as a powerful gaol to hold the most important and dangerous of men. In recent years, the more accommodating Sultan Bayezid had also used it to house archives, and there was talk that the mint would soon be established within its staunch walls.

But no matter how many studious men with ledgers or guard parties with chests of golden coin passed through its portal in one direction or the other, it was hard to force down the knowledge that its primary function was to see human beings pass through those gates, and corpses re-emerge. For the Yedikule was not only a place of internment, but also a place of execution.

Skiouros swore he could detect the faint tang of blood and emptied bowels even from here, some twenty five yards from the walls. At this northern approach point inside the city, the wall angled slightly inwards between two of the largest towers and was pierced partway by a well-fortified gate, where closed and barred oak doors waited under the watchful eyes of the janissaries atop.

His step faltered and Dragi cleared his throat meaningfully – a reminder to act confidently and naturally, and also to stop looking over his shoulder. He took, instead, to feeling itchy and uncomfortable in his snug outfit. The unknown tailor had delivered the ensemble to the Romani house that morning and, despite not having been measured for the fitting, Skiouros was more than a little impressed at the cut of the clothes that had been made so swiftly for him. He had argued against the deception altogether, of course, but his oath to Dragi tied him as tightly as any physical bonds and so he had sat patiently as one of the women had shaved him of his sun-bleached whiskers and tucked his hair up tight as she covered it with a white turban. A sleeveless red coat hung draped over his pale yellow shirt – through which his colourful tattoos were almost visible when the material pressed to the flesh, mustard-coloured trousers and soft brown boots completing an outfit that announced him to be an Ottoman citizen of above-modest social status, relatively well-off and a follower of Islam. He had half expected an *affluent turban* and a jewelled staff the way things were going, but impersonating a Turk of means was dangerous enough. If discovered, his punishment would be severe and most certainly final.

And to add a little extra tension to the vat of it in which he currently drowned, he was walking towards the gate of the Empire's most infamous prison under the watchful gaze of the sultan's own crack troops.

He tried not to move his head as his eyes slid to either side. Dragi, to his left, was well turned out, dressed in his naval uniform and blatantly both a local and a native. On his right, the man he'd only met this morning strolled with purpose, his red skull cap and open-chested green shirt dusty and worn, drab by comparison. *This was never going to work.*

And when it went wrong, his two close friends back across the road lounging under a tree would not be there to help, neither of them standing any chance of being able to pass as a Turk. Though they might be shaved and barbered to look like a Turk, their lack of the language nullified any real point in dressing them up. Only Skiouros, whose skin tone was close and who had a passable command of the tongue, might manage. Dragi had been insistent that such a guise would prove to be vital.

He suddenly realised in a minor panic that he couldn't actually remember a greeting in Turkish. In fact, as his eyes widened and his heart thumped ever faster, his mind seemed to be draining of every word he knew in their language. How did he even say 'yes' again? What was the word for... the word for... damn, he'd forgotten what he'd forgotten the word for!

He felt the sweat running down from the turban, and realised it was cold, trickling over his greasy forehead like a wet, icy spider. Dreadful bone-chilling fear was setting in. He almost yelped as Dragi thumped him gently on the arm and overrode the rising panic, bringing his wits back into line.

Günaydın. That was his greeting. Good morning. Or should he plump for *Selamün aleyküm*, being a good Muslim? Why hadn't he discussed such minutiae with Dragi before they left the house? What would the guards expect of him? How could he hope to survive the Yedikule, when he would mess it all up just getting to the gate? His step faltered again and another light thump from Dragi pulled him back from the edge once more.

He tried not to look up. They were closing on the heavy wooden doors now and four janissaries peered down at them from the battlements above. As they reached an invisible line only Dragi recognised, he stopped and the others fell in beside him. One of the janissaries leaned over the parapet.

'Name and business.'

Dragi stepped one pace to the side and gestured at their shorter companion. The man scratched his head around the rim of his crimson cap, stepped forward, snorting and snuffling, and held up a rolled paper document covered in scrawled script, as he grinned a grin with more gum than tooth.

'Lazari,' the guard noted, gesturing his recognition and then turning his attention to the others. The Romani sailor straightened. 'I am Dragi Abbas bin Pagoslu, first officer and pilot for the mighty Kemal Reis,' he then gestured to Skiouros as he continued, 'accompanying Aydin Reis, captain of the *Nizâmiye*, to visit a prisoner from our fleet held in the cells.'

Skiouros felt his insides lurch. When he'd asked who he was supposed to be, Dragi had hedged around the question, answering vaguely with some rubbish about a minor functionary. But... the captain of a Turkish kadirga? Was he *mad*? Skiouros had heard the name of his guise spoken during the voyage from Napoli, and had even seen the man once, upon departure from Crete. Aydin Reis had taken command of the vessel that had formerly been captained by the butcher Etci Hassan, changing its name from *Yarim Ay* to distance himself from the crimes of his predecessor. He was new to captaincy, yes, and subordinate to Kemal Reis, but still the danger of impersonating an Ottoman citizen had just intensified with the claim that he was, in fact, a reasonably important naval officer. Skiouros felt a long, low nervous fart slip out and hoped it hadn't been audible from the walls.

The janissary officer was peering at them over the parapet, now with a troublesome mix of suspicion and respect on his face. The more Skiouros dredged up fragmentary memories of Aydin Reis, the more he realised that he and the officer looked nothing alike at all. Hopefully the coat and turban would do the talking for him, though Dragi seemed to be doing a sterling job in that department, anyway.

'You have documentation?' the guard called down.

Dragi fished in the bag at his side and held forth another rolled paper, which earned a nod of acceptance from the janissary above. As the man stepped back and his face disappeared from the wall top, Skiouros hissed at Dragi from the corner of his closed mouth.

'Who forged you official documents?'

Dragi turned an appraising frown on him. 'Forged? These are entirely authentic, my Reis.'

Skiouros closed his eyes for a moment as a nervous shiver rocked him from top to bottom, and then opened them sharply as a clunk and a creak announced the unbolting of the portal before them. As the heavy wooden door crept open, revealing the dark passageway that led through to a square of light that was the courtyard, Skiouros tried to pull himself up straight as though he were some kind of dignitary and not a complete fraud. It didn't help that he was sure he was over a foot shorter than Aydin Reis and no amount of stretching himself was going to make up that deficiency.

Mind you, the last time Kemal's fleet were docked in the city that ship would have been commanded by Etci Hassan, with Aydin having been little more than a pilot or junior officer. The chances of any of the janissaries in the city having even heard of him, let alone seen him, were pretty small.

A party of three more janissaries, including another lesser officer, emerged from the gate and beckoned to the trio outside. As the dusty figure of Lazari stepped forward, he was recognised and admitted without ceremony, the officer thumbing back towards the gate and shaking his head unconcerned as the man proffered his documentation. Clearly Lazari was a regular here. Skiouros wondered in what capacity.

To Dragi, on the other hand, the officer wandered up, clicking his fingers and gesturing for the paperwork. The Romani handed it over and then settled into an attentive stance while the soldier read it. After a pause, the janissary looked up at Skiouros with dark, inscrutable eyes.

'Merhaba, Aydin Reis.'

Skiouros's mind exploded with panicked possibilities and he desperately tried to keep the expression on his face from changing. *Merhaba*? A simple hello? The expected response would be to repeat the word, but somehow it did not sound right. Yes, this man was a janissary officer – perhaps an *aşçı,* or a lower *baş karakullukçu* – but Skiouros was the reis of a naval ship. Surely he would outrank this officer? Or were rank comparisons even viable between the two different services? His panic heightened as he realised he was standing dumbstruck while he tried to reason through an impossible question for a Greek street thief.

With a monumental effort of self-control, as the janissary began to regard him more and more oddly, he twisted his expression from what probably appeared as panicked and perplexed to one that he hoped conveyed disdain and disapproval. Hoping his voice would not crack with anxiety, he fixed the soldier with a steely gaze and spoke in a deep Turkish voice, trying to emulate an Anatolian accent on the assumption that the janissary was from one of the Balkan nations, given his service's recruitment methods.

'*Günaydın,*' he replied in a stern manner. There was an uncomfortable silence, during which Skiouros kept his eyes locked on the janissary and the two men engaged in some battle of wills that the Greek could feel happening even if he didn't understand it. The tension shattered when Dragi coughed and nodded at the documentation. As the spell broke, the officer looked down at the paper in his hand, ran his eyes across it two or three times, and finally nodded, returning the documentation, stepping back and gesturing towards the gateway.

Dragi started to walk for the gate and then slowed so that Skiouros could pass through first. The Greek tried to keep his back straight and his turbaned head high as he passed the small knot of guards in the passage, and the pair emerged into the daylight once more a moment later. The guard officer's voice suddenly issued from behind Skiouros and caused him to jump slightly. He hadn't realised that the man had followed them.

'Do you know the way, Reis?'

Dragi turned to him. 'We are fine, thank you.'

The pair walked through the blistering sunshine and Skiouros marvelled at the Yedikule's interior. As a Greek in the city he had had no cause ever to enter the fortress – nor, of course, any authority to do so. It would be a fair bet that not one resident of the Greek enclave had even passed through this gate… at least not one that emerged intact again.

He wasn't sure what he'd expected. Perhaps a wide open courtyard with a couple of barrack buildings? A stable? A few civic structures to house the new records office. What he had not been prepared for was a small self-contained city. From the entrance a thoroughfare ran off through the heart of the complex to the ancient Golden Gate at the far end, and from that main road side streets ran off each lined with buildings of many different shapes and sizes. At the heart of the fortress, next to the main road, stood a recent Ottoman mosque, modelled after the more utilitarian Anatolian style than the city's former Byzantine conversions.

Dragi nudged him and walked on down the main road. Skiouros picked up the pace and fell in alongside him once again, spotting the dusty Lazari hovering at a corner some way down the street. Something nagged at Skiouros' thoughts, and he addressed Dragi in a low voice.

'I take it we're not really here to see that prisoner? I mean, we've passed the prison tower already.' He thumbed over his shoulder at the huge stone drum that was the largest of the seven towers and known infamously among the foreign enclaves as the place where those poor souls brought to this fortress languished until the angel of death took them.

103

'Oh we shall see one prisoner, and likely several more, albeit briefly. Steel yourself, Skiouros, for the execution chambers,' Drago said in an off-hand manner, causing Skiouros to shudder. 'They are kept in the old Byzantine towers. The great tower back there is where the non-Muslim prisoners are kept. Might interest you to know that it's had fewer residents than the cells of the faithful. Fewer deaths, too.'

'Charming. Why are we here to watch executions, Dragi? Is this to see Şehzade Selim? Surely you could have found us somewhere a little more forgiving?'

Dragi shook his head. 'Ahmet arranges clandestine meetings upon which we can eavesdrop, and Korkut fears not to put himself in the public eye, but Selim is more than aware of the dangers this city can hold, and astute enough not to jeopardise himself. Three times he has left his quarters in Tekfur – twice to visit his father at the new palace, both times at the heart of a small army, and now today, to come here. And it is important that you see all three princes, Skiouros.'

The Greek sagged as they closed on Lazari. He didn't like fighting. He didn't like death. He didn't even like taking a life in battle. As for the grisly business of executions...

It was then that he realised what the short, dusty man was – he'd not picked up on the red capped uniform due to the poor condition of it.

'Lazari's an executioner?'

Dragi nodded. 'One of the *Bostancı* corps. And through a miracle of organisation also one of our community by birth. Despite his allegiances to the imperial family, he still holds faith with his people, so long as there is no direct conflict. I assured him there would not be, so please be careful here.' He sighed. 'This was my only means of access to the Şehzade. I could gain us admittance to the Yedikule with permissions requested at the naval offices, but for where prince Selim will be, more surreptitious means were necessary.'

Skiouros tried to equate the figure before him – the man with the easy smile, whom he had watched drinking salep this morning while eyeing up a Romani girl – with the kind of person who could routinely – mechanically even – take a man's life. It seemed incongruous. Lazari was so harmless, so pleasant. Skiouros had heard of the Bostancı before, and even seen them in the gardens of the more important public complexes, but they had always been impeccably turned out in their red cap and green shirt, and had never been dirty and unkempt. Perhaps Lazari's state was symptomatic of the conditions in which he worked?

And now the little man was leading them on again, past the small mosque and angling off down one of the southern streets towards the old Byzantine gateway, which was flanked by twin heavy, square, white towers, each of which had been given a new, pointed Ottoman roof. Once, centuries ago, the greatest emperors in the world had ridden through the sealed-up grand arch of this Golden Gate. Now, it seemed, the towers that had watched so many emperors pass between them were witness to a whole new aspect of imperial function.

As they approached the towers, Skiouros felt his blood chilling. The Golden Gate had once been a triple-arched triumphal monument akin to the ancient ones he had seen in Rome, but since the arch had been turned into part of a larger fortification those grand, high, graceful curves had been blocked up with brick and stone, leaving only a small entrance in the central one. The left-hand of the two flanking bastions had been given additional buttressing since the conquest and it was towards this and the small, unobtrusive doorway at its base that Skiouros' eyes drifted.

'Must we do this?'

Dragi simply nodded and kept walking for the left-hand of the blocked arches and the doorway that lay just before it. As they neared, Skiouros noted that in addition to the pair of janissaries that flanked the main arch itself, the shadowy gate also held a small knot of soldiers in less ornate and much more business-like kit. *Şehzade Selim's men*, he realised, remembering the small units of provincial soldiers who had accompanied the other two crown princes. The men at the gate gestured as the three approached and demanded their papers. Lazari gave his and was directed swiftly and without ceremony to the small doorway. Dragi and Skiouros were looked up and down carefully, but once their documentation was deemed to be in order, they were saluted and admitted, with instructions to make their way to the top floor with haste and not to detour from their route.

The prince's men gave them a respectful – if suspicious – look as they passed into the gloom of the doorway and entered the main structure. Lazari led them through a larger chamber and then a smaller one, each clearly set up as a guard room though currently deserted, and emerged in a dingy corridor lit by a single blazing

105

torch. Voices in local accents echoed from their right, while the left led up an old flight of stairs into the gloom. A small door in the wall ahead had the appearance of a cell, with a small grilled hatch at eye height, and it was to this that Lazari directed them while he turned and made for the stairs.

As the executioner left them and ascended to some presumably grisly location, Dragi flashed a slightly nervous look – the first one Skiouros had ever seen on this man, and therefore in itself a worrying sight. Skiouros felt his nerves reach new heights as he and Dragi stepped to the door and the Romani reached out and tried it. The wooden portal opened with only a faint squeak on well-oiled hinges, and the room beyond was cast into gloomy, muted illumination.

Here at the lowest tier of the tower, the room was just a little over Skiouros' height, low enough that a tall man would have to stoop to enter. The floorboards of the room above – presumably that to which Lazari had ascended, creaked and groaned with unseen movement.

The feeble glow of the torch from the corridor outside would do little to permeate the gloom within, but fortunately an extra source of light illuminated the chamber, and continued to do so as Dragi closed the door behind them, putting a finger to his lips to hush his companion.

Skiouros stared at that source of light. A square hole in the ceiling – the floor of the room above – corresponded with what appeared to be a sizeable well in the floor, presumably allowing those in the room above to draw water. Or perhaps not. Skiouros frowned at the lack of ropes and buckets. And yet he could distinctly hear the sounds of running water rising from that hole.

Dragi took a few steps and sank to the floor, crossing his legs, half way between the door and the well. As Skiouros followed suit, his nerves still jumping and a sense of foreboding on the increase, he opened his mouth to speak, but the Romani simply cut him off with a motion to silence. Now, as Skiouros sat quietly, he realised that he could hear voices. Back at the edge of the room, the noises emerging through the hole from above had been drowned out by the sound of the water. Closer, the words could be picked out.

'...deserters. To my mind, such rough scum should not be executed. Their death is a waste of resources. Not only do we lose three bodies, but the executioner over there gets the pay for three more corpses from the treasury. Deserters should be punished – disciplined *severely* – but then fed back into the ranks in positions of low trust and low value. I *abhor* waste, Sefer. It should be a sin. Look at this pathetic trio.'

The voice was an odd mix of quiet grace and husky rawness. A slight scratchy tone pervading an otherwise poetic and eloquent intonation. Like being serenaded by the desiccated remains of a poet.

The sounds of new footsteps cut across the voices as three distinct pairs of bare feet entered the room and tromped across the boards, coming to a halt somewhere near the centre. Skiouros felt slightly sick as he heard one of them in a far-eastern Turkish accent begging for mercy. He turned his troubled gaze on Dragi, whose expression mirrored his distaste, though somewhat overridden with a solid determination.

A number of strange scraping and groaning sounds issued from the room above, rising to cover the pleading voices, which now made a desperate trio, and then, for a moment, everything fell silent. Skiouros was a little disturbed to hear that husky, poetic voice above humming a tune in a minor key – a Turkish children's lullaby with which Skiouros was fairly familiar.

His heart almost gave out as a hatch suddenly gave way in the floor and a pair of legs dropped into it, shaking around and shuddering. The plaintive cries above had decreased in number but risen in pitch and desperation. Skiouros watched in horrified fascination as the man's ragged, stained trousers suddenly soaked through with involuntary urine and filth and the bucking and flailing died away, leaving just a spasmodic twitch in one foot which, in turn, ended in less than a minute.

Dragi's face was bleak but accepting. Horribly – more horribly even than this first hanging that Skiouros had ever witnessed – the hummed tune above did not seem to falter or skip during the process, and warbled on pleasantly.

Skiouros tried to whisper something but his voice appeared not to want to work and his eyes remained horrified and fascinated, locked on the dangling legs until suddenly they rose a foot or so, shook a little, and then the entire body dropped through the hole to land with an unpleasant wet crunch on the flagged floor in a pool of the poor victim's own excreta.

He continued to stare in sickened intent at the body and took a while to realise what was going on above as more scraping and thudding was accompanied by a plaintive voice calling out.

'No! *No, no, no, no…*'

With a creak, the hatch was pulled back up and latched, deepening the unpleasant gloom of this chamber, which was starting to fill with the combined stink of death and faeces. Skiouros realised that he was listening to the rope being tightened now over the trilling of the last verses of that old lullaby, and turned his eyes away from the hanging site just in time as the clack, thump, scraping and rustling rang out, the gagging noises and the stink of voiding once more assailing his senses. He kept his gaze averted, concentrating on the ancient stonework of the tower's wall until a wet thump announced that the second sailor had joined the first.

Damn you, Dragi, for what you've subjected me to…

Trying not to breathe too deeply, Skiouros shut his eyes and mentally ran through each and every happening he could recall of the five years since he had stolen that fateful purse in the marketplace and set in motion the events that had carried him to the end of the Earth and back. Little of it was pleasant to remember, but his return to the city had been disjointed and complicated, leaving him with little time yet to think things through, and he felt the distinct need to try and order his thoughts, especially since *anything* was better than witnessing the third sailor's demise.

Passing over most of the events in brief, he deliberately shut out the muffled scraping and begging noises and tried to focus on every encounter he'd had with the Romani who, it seemed, had been at the centre of his woes. There were two of them he knew of for certain who had influenced – or at least *tried* to influence – events in his life. Firstly the old crone in the city who had warned him of the coming storm with an unnerving prescience, and who had urged him strongly to leave. In fact she had repeated that counsel more than once. Who was she, and why had she been so insistent that he depart the city? If he had followed her advice, the sultan Bayezid would have died at the hands of Mamluk assassins and janissary traitors. Oh, in the end the sultan had not appeared in public on the appointed date anyway, but Skiouros remembered the zeal and madness he'd witnessed in Hamza Bin Murad's eyes, and he was under no illusion that the killers would have found a way in the end, regardless. Until Skiouros had buried the main conspirator in the rubble of the Nea Ekklasia, anyway. So if the Romani woman was as prescient as she'd appeared, then she must have *wanted* the sultan dead. But why?

And then there was Dragi, who had first latched onto him in Heraklion with an eye-wateringly ridiculous accent and in the dusty drab garb of a beggar. And the man had somehow been with him throughout his journey, or at least close by, saving his life more than once and finally rescuing he and Parmenio from Napoli and bringing them back here. And all apparently because of some old Romani folk tale whose moral was horribly ambiguous anyway, as far as Skiouros could see. So again: why?

Questions. So many questions, but as yet no answers.

Then there was the current mess in which Dragi had immersed him. In eight days' time the city would revel in the sultan's great jubilee, and yet the three crown princes who had been recalled from their provincial governorships for the event seemed to be plotting for the succession as though their father lay on his death bed, and not hale and hearty and working through plans for his festival. *Something* was clearly planned at that great celebration. A coup? Certainly that was what it had sounded like. And it seemed to involve Ahmet – the Lion of Amasya – if not the other princes. And the Romani. And other, more unexpected groups?

His brain was beginning to ache a little.

He suddenly recalled a fragment of the conversation between Şehzade Ahmed and his vizier back at Saint Saviour's church a few days ago. *The Khoraxané dede Babik…*

Another Romani reference, this time in support of Ahmed's seeming push for the throne?

Only the thud of the third body landing on the hard floor drew his attention back and he realised that Dragi was looking at him intently, cupping an ear and pointing at the ceiling, where the hatch had been closed once again.

'…filthy business.' This new voice was serpentine, sibilant and entirely unpleasant to listen to. The hissing undertone sent shivers through Skiouros.

'Rule is *always* a filthy business, Sefer,' the dream-like husky tone of Şehzade Selim replied in a patient manner. 'If it is done correctly, it is more bloody than battle, more meticulous than poetry, more terrifying than nightmare and more glorious than God's own garden. Those who are not willing to wade to the waist in gore and filth – even in their own if necessary – to preserve and enhance their world do not deserve to sit upon the throne.'

'But to plot, with your noble father still so healthy, my prince…'

What occupied the tense silence that followed was all too easy to picture, given what had just been said and in such an open situation. Skiouros felt momentarily panicked for the unknown Sefer,

109

who must be quailing under the gaze of Selim. Finally, the husky melodic voice began once more.

'There *is* no plot, Sefer.'

Oh but I believe there is, Şehzade Selim...

'I have no intention of sinking a knife into my father's back,' the prince went on, 'despite any minor failings I may see in his rule. Do not misunderstand me, mind, Sefer: should he ever show himself to be unworthy of the throne upon which he sits, I will not hesitate. But for now, my father is the clear lord of the Osman line. Remember, though, that my dear brothers might not be quite so willing to hold off on such an act. Unhealthy influences plague them both.'

There was another curious silence, and then a muffled, muted voice calling out in incomprehensible stifled tones.

'Some would say that I am just such an unhealthy influence upon you, my Şehzade,' the sibilant voice replied carefully.

The prince's short, sing-song laugh echoed above the muffled desperation of the new voice in the room, and he seemed to be genuinely amused. 'How *could* you be an unhealthy influence on me, Sefer, when you have *no* influence upon me at all? I keep your counsel only because it amuses me to do so. Pray that this amusement lasts.'

Again, Skiouros could picture the nervous flick of the unknown companion's eyes, his darting tongue moistening dry lips. The young Greek could well imagine from what he had already heard that Prince Selim – the *Wolf of Trabzon* – was not a man of whom to fall foul.

Skiouros concentrated once more on the voices. The desperation in the muffled tones was clear. Why so muffled, though? Was he gagged? A bag upon his head? There was something odd about that not-quite-audible voice that he couldn't quite put his hands on while so stifled.

His heart leapt into his throat as the obstruction was removed and the voice rang out, suddenly clear, in perfect Italian with a hint of a French accent.

'...will find yourself at the mercy of the Papacy.'

The throaty harmonious voice of the prince answered in an apparently amused tone, and in remarkably good Italian.

'Please do not threaten me with that corrupt, worm-ridden fat Borgia djinn. He is too busy gathering jewels and lackeys and sharing his bed with other men's wives to concentrate on the empire. And do not for a moment think that we would be troubled by his rumoured *crusade*. I *welcome* the chance to whet my blade on his bloated skull. And before you attempt to sway me with boasts of the threat your order believes it poses to our security, please do not insult my intelligence. Your fortresses fall every month, like fleas being picked off the back of a hunting hound.'

'God will judge you for your actions today, Prince Selim, and the God of Abraham, Father of Christ, is not a forgiving God.'

The silence that followed was filled by an amused chuckle.

'You mock God, sir?'

'No, man,' Selim snapped. '*You* mock God. Let us be done with this niggling conversation and be about our true business. I am a man of action, not one given to debate, and certainly not a merciful one. Tell me for whom in the city your order is currently working, and I will see to it that you are escorted unharmed from this place and that you board a vessel bound for Rhodos. Refuse me and this room is the last thing you shall see. Decide now.'

Skiouros found that he was holding his breath. The order? Rhodos? The prisoner was a Hospitaller, clearly. Somehow, Skiouros couldn't picture Şehzade Selim taking refusal well. In the dangerous silence following the prince's ultimatum, Skiouros heard hawking and spitting, followed by a regretful sigh.

A few short shufflings echoed down through the hole, and the light that it cast into this lower chamber was suddenly blocked. There was a metallic noise and then a visceral cleaving sound, and a head, the eyes still blinking and the mouth still working silent words, dropped through the hole, passing through the lower floor in the beat of a heart before plunging on down into that well and landing with a splash.

Sickened, Skiouros now realised why the well had no rope or bucket.

'Perhaps you might have torn information from him with hot irons, my prince?' murmured the Serpentine voice of Sefer.

'He would not have broken. Or if he had, he would have lied in any case. Fanatics like him, who believe themselves so close to God, cannot be trusted to put self-preservation above martyrdom. No common sense, these zealots. Better to be done with him quickly.' The voice rose a notch. 'Thank you, executioner, for your sterling work.'

There was an embarrassed clearing of a throat, and the prince chuckled. 'Quite right. The treasury only pays the Bostancı for the

111

three sailors. The foreigner was a private commission. Sefer, pay this man for his time and his skills, and tip him well. One never knows when one might find one's own neck beneath such a blade. Always sweeten the executioner, just in case.'

Sefer gave an unconvinced, dutiful laugh. Moments later the hatch in the ceiling popped open once more and a headless body in a blood-soaked white shirt and hose was tipped through to land unceremoniously with the three sailors' corpses.

Still listening in and trying not to breathe in the mounting stink, Skiouros heard the clink of exchanged coin and the footsteps of Lazari leaving the execution room and shutting a door. In the silence that followed, booted footsteps closed on the hole above the well. Skiouros leaned back from the centre of the room, away from the figure who appeared, gazing down, though it was so dark down here that his chances of discovery were extremely small.

'See, Sefer?' The prince said in a business-like tone. 'Rule is a bloody business. And your mouth runs away with you as usual. No amount of sweetening the executioner is going to still his wagging tongue after what he heard here. Once he is done with disposal, have him followed back to his hovel and do away with him.'

'Yes, my Şehzade.'

'And be very grateful that I did not give him one last commission. Still your own tongue in future.'

'Yes, my Şehzade.'

Prince Selim crouched by the hole, looking down, and Skiouros tensed, sure he would be seen despite the gloom.

'The time may come when my brothers will have to pay a visit to this chamber, Sefer. Neither is fit to control the empire, and yet Father favours Korkut with proximity and Ahmed with titles.' He sighed as he rose. 'A bloody business, indeed.'

Skiouros jumped as the door to this lower chamber opened and Lazari entered, spattered with blood and with an easy, carefree expression. He raised a silencing finger to his lips as he glanced at them, and then began to lift the four bodies, one at a time, and carry them across to the centre of the room, where he dumped them unceremoniously into the well.

Over the noises they heard two sets of footsteps in the room above and the door opening and closing. The prince and his companion had left. Half a minute later Lazari, having finished his grisly chores, nodded at the pair of them and then left their room, patting his bulging coin-purse happily as he went. Silence reigned for a long moment in that stinking, cold, dim chamber, and Skiouros found himself trying not to gag. Finally Dragi rose stiffly to his feet and rolled his shoulders, stretching his arms.

'We should warn Lazari,' Skiouros said quietly.

'Not a clever move,' the Romani replied. 'To do so would be to risk tipping off Şehzade Selim that there were other witnesses to his conversation. Besides, remember that the Bostancı are no simple labourers. Do not be deceived by Lazari's appearance. His corps are as well trained as the janissaries, and with extra... *skills*... to boot.'

Skiouros nodded bleakly. The idea of letting the pleasant little executioner die simply for being in the room with a noble whose guard had slipped sat badly with him, but Dragi was entirely correct. Selim appeared to be a thorough and efficient man. Skiouros' life expectancy would be measured in hours if the prince discovered he had been overheard by another. The prince's guard outside would assume that the pair of them had been up on the floors that acted as cells, since that was where they had been directed. And they would not be leaving in the company of Lazari, so there was no reason suspicion would now fall upon them. Better not raise any extra misgivings among Selim's men with foolish notions of saving the poor Lazari. He would just have to hope that the little man could hold his own against the agents of the prince.

'Are we safe to talk now?'

'Quietly and quickly. Best to save dangerous discussion for when we return to the house, though I want to leave it a few more minutes before we depart.'

'Selim seems a dangerous man. Perhaps the best of the three brothers, but dangerous nonetheless...'

'And yet?' prompted Dragi, perusing from the Greek's face and waiting for him to finish his thought.

Skiouros was busy thinking back over Selim's thoughts on zealotry and fanaticism compared to common sense, and he could hardly fault the prince's stand there. 'And the Hospitallers are apparently set against him. An old adage leaps to mind.'

'That the enemy of my enemy is my friend?'

Skiouros nodded. 'I am still against interfering in this, Dragi.'

'That is because there are still things you do not know or understand and therefore you have not reasoned things through fully. Come. When we return to the house, it is time to explain all so that you can take your proper place in this drama and so that we can begin to lay our plans. Time is moving swiftly now, and so must we.'

And now, perhaps, my questions will all be answered.

Chapter eight – Of successions and divisions

SKIOUROS rose from the cushions and scurried over to the window as the old man refreshed the salep in each glass upon the table. Worryingly, another jug of that corrosive and very dangerous wine sat atop the same table, though thankfully no one had yet suggested opening it. Listening to the clinks and tinkles of the glasses, the Greek peered out through the gap in the curtains. It was late afternoon and the sun was already little more than a glow which threw the sixth hill into silhouette. Atop the crest he could see the palace of Constantine Porphyrogenitus – the most intact remnant of this ancient palace district, and the sight soured his mood. In the Turkish tongue, the structure was known as *Tekfur Sarayi* and now that Skiouros knew it to be the current residence of Şehzade Selim, it brooded with potential unpleasantness. But that was not what had caused him to rise and check the window.

That action had been born of the inescapable feeling that they were being observed, which had first tickled his spine as he and Dragi had emerged from the Yedikule and crossed the road to rejoin Parmenio and Diego. Three times as the small group had wound their way through the impoverished streets across the hills, along the line of the walls and back to the house he now knew to belong to one Mustafa, a Romani elder, he had been certain they were being followed. Once, he had seen a cloaked figure in an alleyway – a figure who had ducked into a doorway as Skiouros turned – and he had been sure that the man's cloak stood out at his waist, indicating

115

the presence of a belted sword. Two streets further on a young man was playing with a hoop, and Skiouros had harboured the sneaking suspicion – unprovable, of course – that the boy was that same urchin from Saint Saviour's churchyard. Then, as they had approached the area of Saint Saviour's church, he had felt that familiar prickle of the skin again and had just caught sight of two hulking men disappearing round a corner, both of whom appeared to be watching them. He had then led the other three, using some feeble excuse, through the sunken vegetable gardens in the ancient ruined *Aetios Cistern* in order to try and discourage pursuit. But then, as they had neared the ramshackle Romani house, he had spotted a cloaked figure on the city wall above the neighbourhood and, though the man had disappeared in a moment, he was sure it had been the same one from the other side of the city.

So they seemed to be being watched, and now, almost certainly, those watchers knew where the four of them were staying. He'd not mentioned his suspicions to the others. Somehow he felt sure that Dragi would already know and that any raising of the subject would just add more infuriating mysteries to the pile. Still, it added an extra sense of uncertainty and worry to the whole situation.

'Come away from the window,' Parmenio rolled his eyes. 'What's got you so jumpy?'

Skiouros turned an irritable look on his friend. 'Would you like a list?'

'We're safe here.'

'We're safe *nowhere*, Parmenio. Least of *all*, I fear, here.'

His friend gave him an odd look through narrowed eyes, but simply gestured to the empty seat. With a last fruitless scan of the surroundings, Skiouros returned to the table and the refreshing glass of spiced orchid-root flour, rose water and warmed milk, testing it for temperature and feeling its soothing taste working on his frayed nerves almost instantly. Sinking with a sigh into the cushioned seat, he looked at his companions around the table. Dragi. Of *course*, Dragi – *ever-present* Dragi. The old man with the few teeth, who Skiouros now knew to be Mustafa – the house's owner and most senior of the community; the leader in all but name. A woman of middle years named Lela, with kohl-rimmed eyes and a beguiling scent who, while clearly twice Skiouros' age, did something to his nethers with which he was not comfortable merely by her presence. A strange-looking gangly eastern Romani named Yayan Dimo of about Skiouros' age with a hare-lip and mismatched eyes and yet a hard look and muscles like a cart horse. And, of course, good old Diego and Parmenio.

Dragi waited for a moment, until everyone was settled, and then cleared his throat.

'I am sure, Skiouros – *Kral yapımcı* – that your companions here are more than just close friends, and they feel their bond of fellowship with you as keenly as you feel it for them. However, the next week will be a very difficult and dangerous time. *We* are prepared for it. We know what must be done. And *you* have no choice in this matter. This is your... destiny, if you will. But your friends? Need they be at risk?'

'Listen,' Parmenio snapped, leaning forwards even as Skiouros' mouth opened in reply, 'I have no intention of backing out now. You have no idea *what* we've been through.'

Dragi nodded his understanding as Diego also leaned in and spoke in low tones in his Spanish-accented Greek with a sour note. 'I believe my debts to have been paid back on Crete, when I was sacrificed to the Ducal guard in order to retrieve a piece of dead flesh. But on a purely practical level, both Parmenio and I have been seen in the company of Skiouros and yourself now for days. We have been attacked by an unknown group which seems to be linked to a crusading order. There is, as they say, safety in numbers, and I fear for my own welfare if I now leave the fold in a city I hardly know, tarred with the same brush as the rest of you. No. Prudence requires my continued involvement. Whatever this is, common sense now demands that we see it through to the bitter end.'

Again, Dragi nodded, and Skiouros echoed the motion. 'Eight more days,' the Romani sailor said, 'and this will be over. Whether we are face-down, mouldering in an unmarked grave, or free of troubles and able to enjoy an open life, we must now ride it out, as Diego says.'

Dragi looked at the other Romani at the table, each of whom nodded in turn.

'Very well. There is much to tell, Skiouros, so please listen to what we say and save your questions for afterwards.'

Skiouros nodded.

'Good.' Dragi stretched and reached for a bowl of the hemp that he had burned on board the kadirga, lighting the end from a candle and bathing his face in the heady, wisping blue smoke.

'There has, for some time, been a division among our people. You must be aware that Islam is every bit as riven with fractures and differences as your Christian faiths? Well, in this particular case, our focus falls on the Alevi sect. Not for their beliefs as such, but because of a vision that tore our community apart more than a decade ago. A *Sayyid* – a self-professed holy man who claims descent from Muhammed and holds temporal power among the Alevi Romani in Anatolia – returned from a sojourn in the wilds with an old woman he believed to speak with the voice of the prophet.'

'Slow down,' Diego said, his brow creasing. 'Remember that some of us know very little of your faith, and it's hard to see where this is going. I have enough trouble trying to work my mind around *Skiouros'* church.'

Dragi inclined his head. 'Apologies. I shall attempt to elucidate. Islam is split primarily into the Sunni and the Shi'a. Think of this as similar to your Orthodox and Catholic rift for ease. Sometimes relations between the two are good. More often they are taut or even downright hostile. We of our community here are mostly Sunni, as are the majority of the Ottoman, especially in this city. The Alevi sect that holds a small but tight minority in central Anatolia are Shi'a. Currently, the great sultan Bayezid is unusually accommodating of their sect, accepting them as equal citizens of the empire, but there are many in the court who would persuade him otherwise and it would not take much to bring about persecution of the Alevi.'

He took a deep breath. 'It is somewhat simplifying matters, but it will ease your understanding if, in current terms, you think of the Alevi as our opposition.'

Nods all round.

'Very well. The old woman in the desert had suffered a series of visions. One of these visions had involved a lion, a wolf and a double-headed eagle.'

Skiouros' eyebrows rose, and Dragi nodded. 'Precisely. In the woman's vision, she saw the eagle atop a spur of rock, watching a titanic battle between the others. Finally, after hours of fighting, the lion tore out the throat of the wolf. And then, while the victor was too tired from his struggle to feed, the eagle killed the lion and fed from both corpses.'

Skiouros held up a finger. 'I know you don't want us to interrupt, but I'm seeing a parallel of the tale of the king-maker and the king-breaker there, and Diego doesn't know that story.'

'I will enlighten him later,' Dragi noted. 'The wolf is the symbol of Ottoman heredity – it is the wolf that led the first Turks to Anatolia and therefore facilitated the birth of the empire. But the wolf is also symbolic of Selim of Trabzon, and Prince Selim, while he is no overt oppressor of sects, is no lover of the Alevi and their Shi'a beliefs. He is known to have spoken against them to his father. He is hard and unyielding, as you have learned, and a future under him could be troublesome for the Alevi.'

Dragi leaned back and inhaled his smoke once more before continuing. 'And to the Alevi, the double-headed eagle, who is Prince Korkut, is even more undesirable. His two heads – that learned poet and musician and the rabid Sunni zealot, while so disparate, are very much the same person. The Alevi sect would enter an era of hither-to unseen pain and terror under the rule of Korkut. You can, I'm sure, remember the Prince and see the truth of this?'

The four foreigners nodded their clear understanding of the matter.

'But to them,' Dragi went on, 'the lion, who is clearly Prince Ahmed, governor of Amasya, is the future. The lion is also a Shi'a symbol, going back to the early days of Persia in this region. And while Ahmed has no connection to the Alevi, he is known to have counselled his father to continued lenience. So they see Ahmed as the great hope of the Alevi sect.'

'This is all fascinating, but it doesn't illuminate much,' Diego interrupted, earning a hard glance from the Romani across the table. 'If this was all over a decade ago, what is its relevance now?'

'Can you not guess?' the largely-toothless old Mustafa interjected in thickly-accented and somewhat troubled Greek, motioning to Skiouros, who frowned in bafflement. 'Think on your own past,' the old man added.

Skiouros ran through his remembered workings from that unpleasant few minutes at the Yedikule earlier and frowned. 'The visions? The old woman in the desert? Are you suggesting that the old woman I met in the city five years ago is that same one?'

The beguiling Lela nodded. 'The dede Babik. Heretical seeress of the Alevi in the city. She is, in fact, the only one of our opposition that we know by both sight and name. If the Alevi holy man is their mind, Babik is their heart.'

119

'You see,' Dragi took up once more, 'a little over five years ago, our opposition contrived to scatter those of Mustafa's people who were in useful positions to the four winds – I ended up on Crete after a run-in they arranged with a janissary officer. Somehow, with most of us out of the way, the opposition arranged to have Şehzade Ahmed mere hours from the city at Bursa, despite the fact that he *should* have been in Amasya, much further away. By some means they had become aware of a plot between disgruntled janissaries and foreign dignitaries to assassinate the sultan. Though they were not *involved* in the plot directly, they recognised that if the sultan died, the first heir to reach the palace would almost certainly ascend the throne. And so they made sure that Ahmed was there, ready. They could not afford to have one of his Alevi-hating brothers step up, you see.'

Dragi breathed in more of the hemp smoke and tipped the last of his salep past his lips.

'And then *you* hoved into view, shattering the best-laid plans of conspirators and diplomats. The *king-breaker* had stepped onto the scene at last. You see, while to us you are the king-maker, to them you are the king-breaker, for you destroyed their hope of putting Ahmed on the throne. The Alevi mystic who leads our opposition almost exploded with rage from what I hear, and his people did whatever they could to keep the plot together. The old seer-woman Babik tried to turn you from your path, but you held fast to your destiny and stopped the assassination. I wish I had seen her face. She must have been livid!'

Skiouros shook his head in wonder. 'Five years I have carried questions about that woman and what happened back there. And you have been there lurking in the shadows for much of that. You could have warned me.'

'You were not ready,' Dragi replied. 'In some small measure, dede Babik succeeded in her secondary task. While the plot itself failed, her influence drove you from the city and into five years of wandering. And while you were gone, another claimed the credit for your deeds. Had you been in the city, we would have guided you, walked you through things in just the same manner as our opposition has guided your opposite number.'

Skiouros slumped back into the chair, a look of sheer disbelief plastered across his face. As Dragi continued, he leaned forward and, despite his best intentions, opened the jug of strong wine, tipping its glutinous, oily contents into a fresh cup and sinking two mouthfuls in quick succession.

'You see, Skiouros of Hadrianople, you were always part of this. It is not a matter of me drawing you into the affair. You have *always* been bound to it. I just had to reel you back in inch by inch. And now, at last, after five years, you are where you need to be, and at the time you need to be there. For the opposition are moving again.'

Skiouros favoured them with a sour look and the young hare-lipped easterner leaned in. 'You may not appreciate being thrust into this matter, but you are not alone, king-maker. There are many among us who would love nothing more than to take matters into our own hands, guide the future of the Ottoman sultanate, and not rely upon two semi-legendary figures from an ancient fable. But the fact remains that while neither Dragi nor I – nor many others for that matter – want to weigh everything on your shoulders, it is not our decision to make. That decision was made by God and we must live with it. While you are busy feeling sorry for yourself, your opposition is busily at work, and you are finally where you need to be at the right time.'

Skiouros threw down another gulp of the unpleasant wine and winced. 'Because your opposition are about to try a coup and put Ahmed on the throne?'

'Precisely. He is the only future they can see that ends well for the Alevi.'

'And you hate these Alevi so much that you will do anything to stop them?'

Dragi looked genuinely taken aback, but the intoxicating Lela leaned forward instead, her voice like velvet, with a shiver-drawing huskiness. Skiouros quickly began to worry that he might drool.

'There are other prophecies and tales, King-maker. Many of them. Şehzade Ahmed might be the scion of choice for the Alevi, but he would be disaster in all other ways, handing over half the empire's power to foreign nations simply for his own benefit. Korkut would be a catastrophe for *all* of us, and even the Alevi recognise that. But for the future, we must look ahead. We must look beyond Selim, whose reign might be a dark one, at the golden future that follows. He has a son, born this past winter to a princess of the line of the Khans. The boy is the empire's future. It is not for Selim that we struggle, but for his heir, in accordance with what has been revealed to us.'

'That is *utterly* ridiculous.'

'Is it?' Diego frowned, leaning across to Skiouros. 'Study your histories, Skiouros. The greatest emperors of Rome did just that. Hadrianus adopted a successor – Antoninus – simply to hold the throne until young Marcus Aurelius came of age. Sometimes a golden future can only be built upon charred base stones.'

Skiouros sloshed wine back and forth in his mouth for a short while, and finally shook his head. 'There are limits to what a person can ask of another. I said I would be your man until after the festival, Dragi, and I will do what you ask… within reason. But whatever you believe, I am no king maker. I am not wise or pious enough to select an heir, any more than this mysterious opposition is. I will not push Selim to the top. It is not my place to do so.'

The younger, eastern Romani narrowed his eyes. 'I said he would be hostile,' he sniffed in his oddly-accented Greek, thick with taints of his homeland.

'No. I am not hostile, and I appreciate all your efforts and your concerns to bring about what you think it right. Every man should strive for what he believes to be right. But I propose a different path – a compromise. I have no desire to try and raise a man to the throne. I think that the man who deserves the throne currently occupies it anyway. Five years ago I killed a senior janissary officer to save sultan Bayezid. I am not about to conspire against him now.'

This raised a surprised nod from several of the table's occupants.

'But just as I cannot realistically attempt to lift a man to the throne, I cannot in good conscience sit back and let anyone else do that either. I will not champion Selim, but I will do what I can to interrupt the designs of your opposition in any attempt to bring Ahmed to power through a coup. Let the three heirs reach for the throne when their father dies, just as the laws of succession intend. Let Bayezid live to be a happy old man, and the strongest of his progeny grasp power in your traditional manner. You see, you believe that the tale of the king maker and the king breaker is a parable urging to decisive action, and so you all scrabble around trying to promote your chosen prince and impede the others. The tale is not urging you to decision-making and urgent action. It is a warning *against* interference. And though I have no wish to meddle in this myself, you believe that my opposite number is already at work? Then it is our task to unpick the stiches in their tapestry of plots and plans.'

'By remaining impartial, of course, you risk the rise of Ahmed or Korkut even *without* the aid of the opposition,' Lela crooned.

'And if either of them rises to the top on their own merit, then God meant it to be,' Skiouros replied in an uncharacteristic fit of seeming piety. 'What do we know of the opposition and their plans, then?'

'As you know,' Dragi continued, 'we only know the dede Babik for certain. The opposition are living in Sulukule in an insular community, but we have no precise details – it is dangerous to go prying into that area if you are not one of their community. We know of this so-called 'holy-man' who came to the city with her, but his identity is a mystery. We know the king-breaker is at work but not who he is. You see we are very much in the dark as yet. They seem to be in league with Hadim Ali Paşa, and in support of Ahmed, and beyond that they likely have their talons into other groups. They have had five years of building towards this, after all, waiting for a time when all three heirs and their father would be together at the same time and in the same place. I think we can be sure that the Knights Hospitaller are involved with them – they stand to gain a great hold in the empire if the malleable Ahmed ascends to the throne with their aid. Hadim Ali Paşa mentioned to his master that other groups, including an *ancient enemy*, were already with them. He must have arranged a deputation from the knights at Rhodos some time ago. And the opposition almost certainly already have people in place across the city in positions of power and influence.'

'Why have they not done away with the other two princes already, then?' Parmenio asked, pouring some of the wine for himself.

'To kill one prince would put the other on his guard and make him almost impossible to get to. They will have to remove both at once, and even then only when they are ready to spring their coup. Only Ahmed is in a position to deal with his father – no matter how well-placed our opposition are, they will not be able to touch the sultan. We know that Ahmed has something planned for the day of the festival – on the 29th of the month – and the opposition will not risk interfering with that by removing the two brothers too long before then. Thus I believe we have until at least the 28th before any action is taken. One week to prevent the deaths of two princes and the instigation of a coup against the sultan.'

Skiouros sighed. 'From what you've said, and from what we heard from him, it seems unlikely that Şehzade Ahmed will risk the coup unless he is in an unassailable position. If we keep Korkut and Selim in the running, he has no reason to continue with a coup, and the sultan will likely remain safe.' He mused, tapping his chin. 'Though if we can identify a key figure in their scheme, we might be able to undo that likelihood, too. Do you think this nebulous enemy will already have people in place to remove the princes when the time comes?'

'Almost certainly.'

Skiouros nodded and rubbed his hands together. 'Then that must be the priority. Identify and remove those who have infiltrated the courts of Korkut and Selim, thereby saving both from being killed and foiling your opposition's plot. Ahmed is clearly in no danger from them, and I will have nothing to do with removing him from position, so we can ignore him for now. Where are the other princes staying prior to the festival?'

The woman Lela cleared her throat again, drawing all eyes at the table.

'Selim is in Tekfur Sarayi – the Porphyrogenitus palace atop this hill. It is a walled compound with solid defences, and he has a small army with him and trusts only his own people. Getting into that place will be almost impossible. They do say that old tunnels in the ruins lead to the palace, but we have never been able to verify the reality of this. Korkut is less paranoid, though equally well defended. He is residing in *Eski Sarayi* – the old palace – near the janissary barracks at the heart of the city. Proximity to that last structure might create its own problems, of course.'

'Korkut sounds like the easier of the two propositions, regardless of the janissaries.'

Dragi shook his head. 'Selim must be our priority.'

'I said I would prevent interference, Dragi, not concentrate on your favourite candidate. If Korkut is the easier to get to, then we deal with him first, with the added benefit that we might unravel more of what we do not yet understand in the process. Can you get someone into the old palace with a legitimate reason for an indefinite period?'

The young easterner nodded his head. 'I believe so. It will be you?'

Skiouros sighed. 'I suspect it will. I cannot see Diego or Parmenio blending in well and any number of lesser posts somewhere like that will be filled with servants who were taken from

Greek regions in the devsirme. I can blend in at court like no one else here. The other, entirely separate, problem we have is that we appear to know very little about the enemy. You believe that someone moves with them – my opposite number?'

'The king-breaker, yes.'

'Do we know *anything* about him?'

'No, but be sure that he is already at work, guided by the hand of the *Khoraxané dede Babik* and by other Alevi conspirators.'

Skiouros chewed his lip. 'And even if we assume that they have managed to place only one of their number among the princes' courts, what is to stop them doing so again, if we foil their plans?'

Dragi nodded seriously and Skiouros cleared his throat and straightened. 'We need to find a new place from which to work. I believe we were being observed by at least three different people on our way back to the house from Yedikule.'

'Seven, in fact,' interjected Don Diego, cleaning a fingernail with the point of his knife. 'I rather suspect they watch this place even now.'

Old Mustafa and his council showed no surprise or concern over this, though Dragi seemed a little taken aback. 'What do you suggest?'

'I know Phanar and Balat well, even after all these years. There are streets and alleyways in Phanar that few of us have ever trod, and I have friends in Balat who will help us.' He hoped to God that was true. The last time he had seen David Ben Judah and his family had been in the aftermath of his father's murder, for which Skiouros had been at least indirectly responsible. Hopefully, the old man he'd met that time would remember him and David had forgiven him. One thing of which he could be sure was that the house of Ben Isaac would be safe from the eyes and ears of this mysterious Romani opposition. The Jews of Balat were as suspicious of the Romani as were those in the Greek enclave, if not more so. 'David Ben Judah and his family will find us shelter, I'm sure. Just the four of us, though, I think. And we will have to pay them for their aid.'

'Of course.'

Parmenio drummed his fingers on his cup. 'Are you seriously talking about sneaking into an Ottoman palace and hunting an assassin on your own?'

125

Skiouros gave a bleak chuckle. 'You might recall that this isn't my first time sneaking into a palace on nefarious business.'

'Still, it's stupid to even think of doing it on your own. We're not talking about some foreign lunatic hiding out in a disused house in the city. We're talking about a well-placed, well-prepared killer in one of the most secure and monitored locations in the entire empire. For the love of the blessed Virgin, you're talking about infiltrating an *imperial palace*.'

'There's no other way we can do it. And I'm no novice. Remember the Palazzo Orsini in Rome?'

Diego nodded. 'He's right, Parmenio. But we can still be useful. If we all move location without pursuit, then you and I can turn the tables, start checking up on them, see what we can find out. Watch the watchers, so to speak.'

'Good,' Skiouros smiled, gesturing to the old man. 'We will leave for Phanar and Balat as soon as it gets dark, and I'll lead Dragi, Diego and Parmenio through some of the lesser byways. I don't care how clever or observant our watchers are, I can lose them there. And hopefully, when they realise that we four are no longer here, they will leave Mustafa's house alone. Otherwise, I fear, there is a good chance that this place will be attacked. Be prepared in any event. Arm yourselves and watch your surroundings carefully. If you need to speak to us after we leave, have someone scratch a message into the wall of the bloody church of Saint Mary. We will do the same.'

The Romani elder sucked his teeth fretfully but nodded his agreement.

'In the morning one of ours will attend the Yedikule record office and work out how to get you into the old palace. We will send you a message as soon as that is done.'

'Good.' Skiouros sat back and pushed the wine cup away. 'Clear head for the next few hours, then, I'd say.

*

'Are they still with us?'

'Two men a few hundred yards back, lurking in the doorway of a tavern. No sign of the other two, but be sure they're there somewhere.'

Skiouros nodded to himself at Diego's answer. The four of them had left the Romani house under cover of darkness not in an attempt to disappear unnoticed – he was well aware that they would never manage to exit the place unobserved. But the benefit of the hours of darkness would become clear in another minute or so, now that they were in Phanar and in streets he knew well.

'You're sure things won't have changed here?' Parmenio asked. 'It's been five years, after all.'

'The Greeks of the city stick together, my friend. Just watch.'

With just a low whistle of warning, Skiouros suddenly jinked left into a small side street, leaving the more major road. Whereas the main street had been occupied by sporadic scattered groups of locals – often drunk – this large alley was almost deserted, barring one tired whore taking the night air and a vagrant sitting on a step and hugging his knees.

'I don't like this,' Diego murmured.

'That's because you don't know the place.'

'And because it's filthy, disreputable, and an excellent place to lay an ambush.'

'That's precisely why I *do* like it, my good Don Diego.'

As the four of them reached the heart of this narrow way, Dragi, who was running at the back, his gaze repeatedly thrown over his shoulder, coughed 'here they come.'

Sure enough, as Skiouros glanced back he saw now all four of the men who had shadowed them menacingly since the Romani house turn into the alley with more haste than a careful pursuer should display. *Amateurs*! Well, they were dealing with a professional, even if he was rusty by five whole years...

'What now?' Parmenio asked as the four friends closed on the end of this narrow street.

'Now, I'm home,' Skiouros grinned and, cupping his hands around his mouth, bellowed '*Avthentis Memeti!*'

The others frowned as Skiouros suddenly burst into a jog. The Greek words echoed along the street, bouncing off house fronts and walls. *Master Mehmet* - a reference to the conqueror of the city and a phrase that carried deep seated feelings of resentment in the heart of most Greeks in the city. More importantly: a trigger from the old days...

Glancing back once more, Skiouros saw the four pursuers break into a run at the sight of their quarry fleeing, but in seconds they were lost to sight as every door in the street opened and the population of Phanar emerged en-masse into the narrow street – some of the whores still mostly naked, men in nightshirts yawning, drunks laughing and choking, children still carrying chicken legs from their evening meal. Utter chaos. In mere moments the alley had changed from a dark, deserted backstreet to one more crowded than a lunchtime market. Shouts of concern from the alley's far end were almost drowned out by the population, but not before they took on a tone of desperate fury as the four hunters struggled to push through the milling crowd. One was even flattened by an answering punch from an angry drunk.

Skiouros grinned at his friends as they rounded the corner at the end of the alley and emerged into the market place where five years ago he had cut a purse and changed his life forever. Scurrying through the now-empty square, he ducked into a narrow gap between two dilapidated wooden houses and pounded along through the filth and waste, clambering over a low wall at the end. With a deep breath he dropped down into knee-deep undergrowth surrounding the moss-coated grey-green ruins of the bathhouse where he had hidden on that fateful day five years earlier. The other three followed him down and through the shattered structure, emerging at the far side into a dusty street, breathing hard.

'They'll not find us now,' he announced in a whisper as the four of them passed from the strange, incongruous ruin and back into the streets of the city proper, though as he passed that place where he had first encountered the Romani 'witch' he half expected to see her again.

Ten minutes later, they were descending the wide street in the Jewish quarter of Balat, the moonlight gleaming on the low ripples of the Golden Horn ahead, beyond the walls. The streets here were deserted, though the shuttered and draped windows glowed with warm life. Chewing on his lip, Skiouros led his friends on toward that high stone building among the wooden ones which had once been the church of Saint Theodoros. The closer he came to the house of Ben Isaac, the less sure he now was that they would be welcome. It had seemed like such a good idea back in the comfort of the Romani elder's house, especially knowing they were becoming increasingly unsafe there, but like most great spur-of-the-moment ideas, its greatness seemed to be decreasing with every step in the real world.

He found as they approached the door that he was holding his breath, and he released it slowly and deliberately. Reaching up, he grasped the bell cord, clanging it three times, then rapped on the wood, also three times, pausing and then repeating. The old code, if it was still remembered. The worrying silence that followed dragged out for several heartbeats and Skiouros found himself in equal amounts panicking that the family of Ben Isaac had packed up and moved on, leaving the house empty, and also strangely hoping that was the case.

Once upon a time this door was never shut, for Judah Ben Isaac's business never closed.

Skiouros gave a start as the door suddenly jerked half-way open and a looming figure appeared in the gap. David looked more than five years older. His ringlets had greyed considerably and his frame seemed to have shrunk and withered, for all it was still large. He hunched as he leaned forwards, his eyes narrowing.

'Yes?'

'Shalom David. David Ben Judah? Do you remember me?'

The big man peered almost myopically at him, taking in the cut of his clothes, his sea-weathered bronzed skin, sun-bleached hair and the tips of his tattoos emerging from the collar of his shirt. No sign of recognition emerged until the man's gaze reached his eyes and settled there. A strange mix of surprise and bitterness began to fill that expression as recollection dawned.

'Skiouros of Phanar?'

'In the flesh.'

'Thought you were dead. People *said* you were. Looks like we weren't so lucky.'

'I've been away. Is your uncle home?'

'Uncle Yeshua has been in the loving *Shechinah* of God for near two years now, peace be upon him.'

Skiouros felt his spirits sag. First old Judah, and then Yeshua. Who was in charge of the business now? David? Surely not. Judah's son was no businessman. A good enforcer, but not much of a thinker. Perhaps the business had simply ended? One thing was sure: David would be unlikely to be kindly disposed towards him, since he had once suspected the Greek of being responsible in some way for the death of his father. Indeed, the big man's expression darkened as he picked out the details of the motley trio that surrounded Skiouros in the gloom.

'Shalom, David. We find ourselves in need of sanctuary and I felt that perhaps in remembrance of your father's dealings with me, you might be willing to find us a safe place to stay, in the spirit of divine compassion... and for the appropriate recompense, of course.'

The big Jew's expression faltered not a jot as he continued to glare at the four of them.

'Get you gone, storm crow.'

Skiouros' sagging spirits collapsed. This reception was exactly what he'd hoped not to find, and it made the perfect culmination of that despondency that had been building as he walked.

'Please, I…'

The door was suddenly opened wider and a second figure appeared alongside David. The woman was clearly of advanced age – greater than either Judah or Yeshua had been. Perhaps she was David's grandmother? Her long dress was midnight black, as were the *kaffiyyah* engulfing her head and the black rope wound around it. Her gnarled feet were bare in the hallway, and her face was lined as ancient parchment, the eyes a rheumy grey. But her face was a welcome sight after David's for at least it smiled.

'Invite them in, David.'

'Ama, this man is trouble, and he brings a Turk and gentiles with him.'

'Look closer, David. This is no Turk, but one of the *zigyan*. We have no quarrel with gentiles, and I told you the zigyan would come.'

David's expression darkened, which impressed Skiouros, given the unpleasantness it already conveyed. 'Ama, you should not speak of such matters. The Talmud forbids the sorcery of *ov*, and…'

'Do not concern yourself with sacred teachings, David. Just find some of the *mevushal* wine and gather some of the pastries and sweetmeats left from the evening meal and arrange them in the communal room.'

'Ama, I…'

'Just do it, David.'

With a disgruntled frown, the big man lumbered off along the passage.

'Shalom, my lady,' Skiouros said politely. 'We did not intent to intrude so. I was hoping to find master Yeshua and come to some arrangement of safe accommodation. I know that master Judah once owned at least three or four properties in Balat that he would…'

'Come in,' the woman interrupted. 'Be welcome in the house of Judah Ben Isaac.' As she waved them in and the four entered the passageway, bowing their heads respectfully as they passed, the old woman gave a smile and then reached out for the door, tapping along the wall until she found it, and then closed it and turned an unshifting gaze back onto them. *She is blind*, Skiouros realised with a start, and tried not to think too hard on how she might have recognised with unseeing eyes that one of their group was zigyan – a Jewish term for the Romani.

'I had a dream, you know?' she said amiably as she hustled them down the corridor. 'That zigyan would come. David disapproves because foretelling is forbidden in the 19th chapter of Leviticus, but to my mind, when it comes unbidden during sleep, it is the gift of the *malakim* – the angels. And if the malakim tell me to welcome the zigyan, then the zigyan will be welcome, and all who accompany them too.'

Skiouros felt himself heave a sigh of relief. The Romani opposition would be highly unlikely to track them here, and even if they did it would take long enough to buy them the time they needed. *Thank you, grandmother!* Now all Skiouros had to worry about was infiltrating an imperial Ottoman palace and wheedling out an assassin...

Skiouros was somehow aware that he was dreaming even within the dream. His lucid mind, trapped in the dreamscape of nightmare, railed against the inside of his skull, trying to wake him. But still the young Greek could see only the ruined room around him, with that impossible clarity that only dream can have, for he could see well despite the fact that this sealed room with the three ancient, charred Byzantine columns was in absolute darkness, no apertures in the walls.

He was not alone. His reasoning mind told him not to react, since this was only a dream, but regardless, he felt the beginnings of panic as he looked upon the figure that shared the ancient ruined room. It was a monster – a demon. It was a devil in the old style, though its features seemed to shift constantly such that sometimes it had one horn, or two, or three, and sometimes, none. Its face was red, and sometimes black and oily, and sometimes sickly green. And it carried an aura of evil that chilled him to the bone. Skiouros tried to back away, even though his lucid mind knew he was really lying in a comfortable bed, but in the dreamland he could not move – he was trapped. And then the demon was closing on him, between two of the fractured columns. He stared in panic while his conscious mind battered against his skull, and the demon was almost on him. The thing reached out, and Skiouros suddenly found his hands able to react. In panic, he lunged and tried to push the thing away, but the face slipped under his fingers like a badly-secured silken garment, and came off in his hand where it evaporated like dust.

He stared in horror as the bones beneath the demon mask resolved into the shape of a knight with a scarred face, his sword at his side and his white surcoat so drenched in blood that only a small cross-shape remained pristine in the middle. But even as he felt relief at the sight, the knight opened his mouth in a roar and, within, the teeth were a wolf's fangs, dripping with evil, the fires of hell glowing deep in the throat like hot coals.

Again automatically, his hand reached up and pulled away the silken face, which crumbled to dust leaving a grinning, leering priest in the robes of the inquisition. He ripped at it again...

...and his blood ran cold as he stared into the mirror of his soul, for beneath all those masks was himself, though somehow sickly and corrupt, as though his flesh displayed everything he disliked about himself in the form of an open cancer.

His hand reached up...

...and finally his eyes snapped open to reveal the low ceiling of the small room he shared with the others. He was drenched with sweat and shaking, though three different pitches of snore greeted him, so at least he had not been crying out enough to wake the others.

He lay for long moments, still twitching at the memory of his dream-self, which made him want to leap up and check himself in a mirror, and yet also left him terrified to do so.

Above the snoring, he could hear the gentle hum of life in the building, and there was a strange smell. Rolling his eyes, he realised that what was choking his senses was the remnant of Dragi's hemp, which the man had left smouldering as he went to sleep.

So *that* was what had been causing the dreams! He realised with relief that his previous awful, seemingly-prophetic nightmares had both been in rooms where Dragi had been inhaling his smouldering hemp.

With relief, he lay back in his sweat-soaked bed and vowed not to let the Romani burn his hemp in the room where they slept. At least he knew now what was responsible for the dreams and could dismiss the feeling of prescience that they brought.

They were just dreams, after all.

And yet after an hour of trying to get back to sleep, still he could not jemmy the images from his mind.

That face...

Chapter nine – Of the Eagle's eyrie

May 22nd - Seven days to the festival

SKIOUROS approached the gate of the *Eski Sarayi* with faltering step and thundering heart. Despite its name, the 'old palace' was in fact a mere four decades old, the sultans only living there for a few years before building the new palace on the headland. Since then, the old palace had housed members of the imperial family when necessary, foreign dignitaries during their visits, or just otherwise lay empty and dormant. Now, it housed Şehzade Korkut, son of Beyazid the Second and governor of Manisa in the *sanjak* of Sarahun.

The young Greek's eyes slid right, his head remaining immobile and locked on his destination. Off to the side loomed the large brooding block that was the headquarters of the janissaries in the city. Several of their number stood in guard positions around the periphery of the building and a number of flinty eyes watched him with distaste as he passed.

Skiouros tried not to feel self-conscious in his uniform, once more cursing Dragi and his companions for their choice of guise. As if entering the city's main prison masquerading as a naval officer had not been enough, their choice of pretence to get him into the old palace was almost heart-stopping in its boldness.

His head felt warm and sweaty under the red skull cap with its flowing tail, his green shirt cut so low that his chest was open to the air, plucked clean of golden hair that morning by a comely Romani girl with all the gentle medical touch of a cavalry charge on packed earth. After all, his sea-and-sun bleached hair might raise comment among the almost universally dark-haired populace otherwise. Fortunately between the red tail of his hat and the long sleeves of his shirt, the tattoos he bore were almost entirely concealed. He must finish the tattoo soon, when this was all over. But how? Not with a symbol for his brother's avenged spirit as planned, for that vengeance had turned out to be a hollow, pointless and inhuman thing. But the space needed to be filled, appropriately in some way. Seven more days and he would have time to think…

His footsteps took him inexorably on to the old palace gates.

The voluminous blue muslin trousers were a delight to wear, and the light, soft calf-skin shoes were tremendously comfortable. But it was what these clothes *meant* that chilled him. That he was one of the *Bostancı* – the corps of gardeners. And each of that five thousand strong group was knowledgeable and trained in the growing, tending and pruning of the many elegant gardens of the Imperial city. But their horticultural positions in the grounds of the palaces and imperial buildings belied their other purpose. The low cut shirt that displayed the wearer's muscular form and reminded all of their strength. The soft shoes that allowed them to move almost silent and unnoticed. The blood-red skull cap with its clear connotations.

For the corps of gardeners also formed a sultanic guard that doubled as the court's executioners. He wondered briefly, with a chill, whether the shirt and skull cap he wore had belonged to Lazari, the little man they had accompanied to the Yedikule, and whether he was still alive, hunted but healthy.

Of course, not all professional gardeners in the city were members of the Bostancı corps, but the majority that were assigned to the imperial gardens would be, so there was little doubt as to what role Skiouros was to play. The old Romani elder had assured him that ninety nine days in every hundred, the corps of gardeners performed their very mundane tasks. And then on rare occasions when someone displeased the sultan or his court, they might be called upon instead to prune the population of the palace. Somehow the odds were not encouraging, regardless.

The fact remained that, shaved, Skiouros could easily pass for a Turk, or certainly for one of the Devsirme recruits, anyway. And his Turkish language was quite reasonable, especially if he adopted a distant Balkan accent to help cover any slips. And while he knew little of gardening, if he was called on to do something distasteful, for all he might loathe doing it, he felt sure he was at least capable. He could probably get by in this role. And, as Dragi had taken pains to point out, no one bothered the Bostancı. While they were trimming shrubs they were of little interest, and any time they stopped gardening, it was wise to give them an extremely wide berth. With any luck he would be the perfect combination of tedious and dangerous to keep curiosity at bay.

The gate to the palace was manned by two soldiers in the mismatched armour and kit of the Anatolian Ghazi forces. Korkut's men, with no allegiance to the city and probably no experience of the Bostancı. Consequently, they eyed him with suspicion. *Wonderful,* damn it!

Approaching the gate and adjusting the positioning of his kit bag on his shoulder, Skiouros threw out at the pair a terse 'Iyi günler' – a *good day* that he hoped sounded aloof and superior. For all their hardness and suspicion, these men were, after all, low-paid mercenary soldiers from the borderlands, not trained imperial staff like the corps. Just as he'd hoped, the seniority with which he inflected the words shed all the confidence from the two guards like water from an oilskin, and they exchanged an uncertain glance before clearing their throats and replying to his greeting in a respectful tone.

'Hacı Sincabı bin Husnü, corps of Bostancı, assigned to the Eski Sarayi. Could you direct me to the head gardener?'

One of the men opened his mouth to request his papers, but before he could speak, Skiouros whipped a roll of paper tied with a ribbon from his belt and thrust it forcefully at the man. More could often be said with attitude than with words, and his every movement spoke of a clear seniority over these mercenaries. The ghazi scanned the documentation that had arrived that morning from the Yedikule records office, and sighed, nodding at his companion, who unlocked the palace's gate and began to swing the wide, decorative timber portal open. The first man carefully tied the ribbon once more and passed the orders back to Skiouros, who nodded. His pseudonym had been carefully chosen to allow for ease of recognition as well as to convey the best possible connotations. *Hacı* indicated that he was one of the faithful and had taken the pilgrimage to Mecca, marking him as a man to trust. *Husnü*, a name meaning excellence and goodness, carried something that augmented his position in the corps. And *Sincabı*? Unusual, for sure, but something Skiouros would automatically react to when spoken. For his own unconventional Greek name – Skiouros – meant squirrel. And his brother Lykaion had spent much of their first few years in the city calling him Sincabı – the Turkish equivalent – simply to rile him. He would not forget to react to the name.

'Take the path immediately to the right beyond the gate and follow it to the ivory pavilion. The head gardener will be there.'

Skiouros nodded his appreciation and stepped through the gate inside the high walls that surrounded the old palace. That the place should require the attention of the Bostancı corps was no surprise. The palace itself was not over-large, but was ornate and graceful, rising two storeys high above the lower wall that separated the imperial residence from the wide, beautiful garden that surrounded it, itself enclosed in a high defensive wall. An orchard lay off to one side, and numerous small pavilions, gazebos, kiosks, summer houses and sheds lay scattered about the place, their locations carefully chosen to fit perfectly in the scheme of the glorious whole.

The grounds were curiously devoid of people. Probably in the days when the sultan's court had been in residence nobles and functionaries would have inhabited every arbor and strolled every path. Now, with only Şehzade Korkut and his small travelling court present, there was little reason to exit the palace proper and stroll the beautiful grounds.

The ivory pavilion was not difficult to identify or locate, rising directly ahead at the end of the white gravel path, its glory reflected in a calm pool of green-veined marble and porphyry, the surface only disturbed by the occasional activity of the ornamental fish that lived within. The pavilion itself was beautiful enough to be counted a palace in its own right. Skiouros wondered whether possibly the head gardener might have the better residence than his master, in truth.

Skirting the pool, he spotted a man in attire matching his own, raking a white gravel-chip path flat with the care of a craftsman. The large lopping-knife sheathed at his belt would go through all but thick branches, and Skiouros wondered how many necks it had bitten into in its time. He tried not to imagine it being his own neck. He failed.

Biting his cheek, he nodded professionally to his counterpart with the rake, hoping the gesture would seem fitting – he had no idea of the proper etiquette within the corps. His only experience thus far with the gardeners was Lazari, and the little man who worked at the Yedikule prison was clearly truly atypical of his corps. To his great relief, the other gardener nodded back, never taking his attention from the careful patterns he raked into the path.

A moment later, Skiouros approached the entrance to the ivory pavilion, the doors wide open, allowing the spring breeze to refresh the otherwise stifling interior. The whole building was glorious, high-roofed and carved with ornate work, the walls inlaid with tiles of five colours in complex geometric patterns. Several doorways led off, twin staircases decorated with requisitioned Byzantine stone lions rising to the next floor, and a large window at the far end of this grand vestibule which cast ample light into the room.

At the centre of the hall stood a large circular table, curiously devoid of chairs, and a small group of men in the Bostancı uniform clustered around it. As Skiouros crossed the threshold and the soft slap of his shoes on the marble echoed around the room, the small knot looked up. One man wearing a taller, cylindrical red hat and with some sort of decorative work in gold on his green shirt stood at the centre, and Skiouros decided that this must be the head gardener. With the tense pressure under which he suddenly found himself, he felt the sweat break out in both scalp and armpits, as well as beneath the kit bag that rested against his back.

Hoping his luck would hold, he crossed halfway to the table, upon which he now saw a scale model of the palace and its grounds, and then stopped, bowing respectfully. There was a moment's silence, and then a pinched nasal voice said 'who are you?'

The Greek straightened and produced his paperwork.

'Good day, sir. I have been re-assigned from the Kabataş pleasure garden to the Eski Sarayi to replace your injured staff.' He held his breath, hoping he was right. The Romani elder had informed him that one of the palace gardeners had met with an unfortunate accident two evenings earlier and would be out of action for some time. The way he'd said it had left Skiouros in little doubt as to the cause of said accident, but the fact remained that the move had opened up a position in the palace staff – *in just the right place*, the old man had smiled.

The head Bostancı narrowed his eyes for a moment as he appraised Skiouros, and the Greek found himself self-consciously twisting a fraction to one side to help hide any possible fragments of his tattoos that might be showing between the cap-tail and the shirt. Pressed recruits to the imperial armies were traditionally tattooed, and possibly so were the Bostancı, but it would be difficult to explain the strange tribal designs of the western isles he had visited. Finally the man nodded and gestured to one of his men.

'Good. Give your orders to Iskender here. You were at Kabataş, you say?'

Skiouros nodded as he approached and passed his papers to the indicated man. 'I was, sir.'

'Good. Then you should be more than competent and we won't have to retrain you. You will take on all the duties of the man you replace, which include maintenance of the small vineyard, the arbor-maze, the *Fatih* flower garden and the half-moon pool. You can ignore all the water distribution system as it has its own maintenance staff. You can stow your gear in the half-moon kiosk, which is where you will be staying. I assume you are happy to begin work without further instruction?'

Skiouros nodded.

'Good. An evening meal for the entire staff is held in the long belvedere at sunset. Other than that you will find the kitchens in the same structure and other meals are your own affair. Do you need directing to your gardens?'

Skiouros thanked God for his observant nature, for he had spotted an ornate pool in the shape of a crescent between two hedges on the way from the gate, and behind it had been a small, grey kiosk.

'I believe I know the way.'

The head gardener seemed happy with this and nodded, waving him away dismissively before he returned to his briefing, pointing out parts of the grounds that needed extra work to his men. Skiouros heaved a hidden sigh of relief as he bowed, turned and left the pavilion.

A few minutes later he was veering off the path and heading for the secluded pool. The vineyard lay off to one side in neat, ordered rows that had been recently invaded by weeds and undergrowth, and the flower gardens were equally evident on the other. He was sure he would find the arbor-maze in due course. First thing was first: dump his kit and urinate. His bladder had been threatening to give way during his nervous time so far in the palace grounds.

As he approached the kiosk, which was large enough to hold only two reasonable-sized rooms, and was fairly plain and unadorned, he smiled with relief. Climbing the steps and taking in his surroundings, he realised that the Romani elder had not been exaggerating when he'd said 'in just the right place'. With the perfect planning of these formal grounds, the view from the kiosk was channelled by the gardens. Between two perfect box hedges he could see the front gate of the inner palace wall with its ghazi attendants. Between a narrow arcade of cypress trees, he could see the main gate in the outer wall, now shut once more. Between two rows of vines, he could just make out the ornamental pool that sat before the head gardener's pavilion, and best of all, the half-moon kiosk itself butted up against the exterior wall, utilising the high defensive perimeter as its rear wall.

His smile widened as he opened the doors to the stifled, warm and musty kiosk. The chamber that occupied the left side of the structure was a large store room, potting shed and workshop, and was lit by windows that faced the gardens for which he was responsible, but also by a small window in the perimeter wall with a view of the janissary barracks nearby. A side door stood open and he wandered through, still smiling. This small apartment was comfortable enough and reasonably appointed, with a window that looked out across the flower beds to the main gate again. Once more, a window in the outer defences gave him a pleasant view across the square including the approach to the palace gates. He could not have asked for a better place to observe everything that went on in this place.

With a sigh of relief, he cast his kit bag to the floor and dropped onto the bed. There would be a compost heap somewhere nearby he could urinate into in a few minutes. Then he would survey his new domain. He might be here for a few days – the fewer the better, but he was under no illusion how difficult his task might be. He would familiarise himself with everything this afternoon, then speak carefully to a few other lower gardeners tonight at the meal, to learn more about the palace and its occupants. Then, as he retired for the night, he could try and formulate a plan of action.

*

Parmenio and Diego sat beneath the eaves of a voluminous tree in the garden of a disused house that had been built upon a terrace which had once been a part of the Byzantine palace. The sun was now a deep orange glow silhouetting the hill to their left and the Tekfur palace atop it.

'I find myself pondering on how our young Greek is doing,' Diego sighed, knocking dried mud from the sole of his boot on a piece of ancient carved stone. 'I had assumed back in Crete that his using of me as a distraction and his insane theft from a church was some sort of crazed aberration. And now I am... fascinated... to discover that that sort of thing is, in fact, the norm for him. Do you think he is safe?'

'He's a resourceful fellow, Diego. Don't worry about him.' But Parmenio's expression suggested that he was having trouble following his own advice.

'Hello,' the Spaniard said, sitting up straight and pointing. 'We have movement.'

Parmenio, smiling at how quickly his new friend's Greek was becoming natural and easy-flowing with constant usage, followed the pointing finger. Two silhouetted figures were moving along the city walls from the south towards the Romani house where Dragi sat deep in discussion with his own people. From their vantage point, the two watchers looked from the twin figures to the shadow of the ancient tower, where another two had been observing the Romani house for the entire afternoon. There were always two on watch, the friends had soon discovered, and the pairs changed every eight hours, three times a day, just like a professional guard unit. Sometimes the relief came from the south, sometimes the north, and sometimes one from each.

The two friends sat silently, watching as the two pairs converged on the walls. Diego had initially wondered how their opposition had managed to gain position on the city walls, but it turned out on investigation that the defences were only manned in times of emergency or danger. Other than that only the city gates and the towers near the ports were staffed, and so their opposition had relatively free access to the walls.

The four men held a brief discussion in that shadowy observation point, and then the two who had finished a shift departed. One, who they had identified from his clothing and manner as Romani, turned and climbed to the south, while the other, who they could not identify due to his hooded cloak, descended the walls north towards the Golden Horn.

'North or south?' Parmenio asked, reaching to his purse to flip a coin.

'We've waited long enough. There's two of us so let's do both. I'll take the cloaked one.'

Parmenio blinked, and then broke into a grin. 'Be careful then. See you at the Jew's house.'

Diego nodded, clasped his hand, and was gone in the patter of expensive boots on cobble.

Parmenio watched his friend go, still grinning, then fixed on the shape of the tired Romani leaving his post. This morning, the captain and the Spaniard had followed the line of the city walls uphill and down, checking where to walk in order to maintain the best view. Accordingly, he kept to the streets where he had at least an intermittent view of the walls, making sure he could still see the figure each time they emerged from behind houses.

After a few minutes he neared the *Tekfur* palace of the Porphyrogenitus, where Şehzade Selim was in residence, and carefully kept an extra street back from the high grand edifice – there was no point in risking trouble now. As he passed the building and neared the walls once more, his heart skipped a beat. The figure was no longer visible on the wall top! He mentally berated himself. Of *course* he wouldn't be. Selim was serious about his security, and the palace adjoined the city walls. That section would not be free to walk along, so the Romani must have descended at the last set of wall stairs! Damn it.

Casting up a quick prayer to the mother of God and to Saint Hubert, the patron of hunters, Parmenio dithered. To pick up the trail, he would have to risk getting very close to Selim's palace and would also have to head some way back along the wall. But then the man would already be long gone and there would be little chance of Parmenio regaining the trail. Biting his cheek, he pondered. If the man had filtered into the streets around here, he would either be moving back close to Dragi's community, which seemed unlikely, or towards Greek Phanar, which seemed equally implausible. So he must still be moving south, despite having descended from the walls.

With a preparatory breath he began to run, heading for the walls and the street that ran along inside them to the south of the Tekfur, where it crested the sixth hill. He was so surprised that he almost yelped when he turned a corner onto that wide street and almost ran into a woman emptying a bucket of waste onto the filthy cobbles. Blinking and trying to calm down, his grateful gaze fell upon the Romani, who was a few hundred yards down the street, strolling unconcerned alongside the wall.

Keeping himself well back, Parmenio shadowed the figure towards the rise, pleased at how, since his days of mercantile shipping, despite still carrying a little excess around the midriff, he seemed to have become so much more lithe and quiet. But then he'd never walked – and often *run* – as much in his life as he had in Skiouros' company. Five years ago he could never have stalked someone.

Five years ago, he'd never needed to, his brain threw in sourly.

With a frown of concentration, the Genoese sailor followed his quarry up past the Hadrianople gate, the dome of the Saint Saviour church passing by on the other side as they topped the hill and began the descent to the south. With no surprise at all, Parmenio entered Sulukule on the heels of his prey. This, the oldest Romani district in the city, was a confusing mass of interconnecting streets, each little more than an alleyway, like a spider's web across the city. A man could easily become lost in there and with the increasing certainty that their enemy were based here, Parmenio began to question the wisdom of entering such a place. Dragi had told him that Sulukule would be dangerous.

Swallowing his nerves, he watched the man he'd followed turn from the main street by the walls and disappear into the sprawl. Ah well… nothing ventured, as they said.

Pausing at the corner, he stepped into the Romani community, just hoping that their opposition merely resided *within* this mass of housing, and not that they filled it *entire*. If so, this was likely to be the shortest hunt in history.

Three turnings into the mass, he had come to two conclusions: firstly that he was in no danger of being observed by his prey, since the entirety of the population seemed to have their doors open and be spilling out into the street playing games, drinking and dancing, providing excellent cover for a stealthy pursuit. Secondly, that it was going to take every ounce of his nervous brain to commit this route to memory.

Indeed, he was having trouble remembering each landmark as he turned corners when he became aware that his quarry had reached his destination. As the man stopped and broke into conversation with someone, Parmenio approached a small store selling rugs, clothing, shawls, jewellery, musical instruments and all manner of things from trestles in the street. Out of the corner of his eye, he watched the men chat and then nod and shake hands. His prey then moved down what appeared to be a cul-de-sac and into an open door. He contemplated following, but it was clear to him that the two old men sitting and playing chess on a table near the entrance to the cul-de-sac were guards, watching any who approached the short street. Satisfied that at least he had identified the place, Parmenio moved on, having bought a rather nice mug from the stall for the look of things. Once he deemed himself safely past those two gaming sentinels, he began to explore the periphery of the cul-de-sac area. The one-storey timber houses of the Romani in this area had been joined together, the narrow cut-throughs between them sealed off with heavy fencing, and each of those houses presenting no doors or windows to the rear. It was almost an enclosed fortress-like compound within the Romani neighbourhood.

With little doubt now that he had located their opposition, Parmenio pinched the bridge of his nose, tried to recall all his list of landmarks and began to make his slow, careful way back towards the main street and to the house of Ben Isaac in Balat.

A mile and a half across the ancient city and over the water, Don Diego de Teba cursed for the thousandth time as his good boots, bought at great expense in Heraklion, slipped in something foul and indescribable in the grass of the waterfront. Ahead of him, the man in the black cloak moved entirely unconcerned. Diego had begun his pursuit by shadowing in the most careful manner, but had of late begun simply following him openly. The man was either profoundly over-confident or utterly stupid. Not once since he'd descended the walls near the Golden Horn had he looked over his shoulder.

Reaching the sea walls, the cloaked man had passed through one of the old crumbling gates and down to the waterside, where a few late evening fishermen were making the most of the peace and quiet. The Spaniard had followed his prey along the waterfront until the man had reached a jetty where half a dozen small rowing boats were moored under the watchful eye of a local who seemed to control this private ferry service. There, the cloaked man had tipped the owner with a coin or two and clambered into a boat, rowing himself swiftly out and across the water. Taking a chance, Diego waited until he was some way from shore and then followed suit, paying what he considered an exorbitant price for such a vessel and then easing himself out into the almost still waters of the Golden

Horn. The current was negligible and he found he had almost no trouble keeping to course as he followed the cloaked man across the wide expanse towards the Galata shore, despite his lack of experience with boats.

The man had docked quickly, giving the boat to the man who kept the jetty at this northern side, and Diego had followed suit two minutes later, trailing the cloaked man on along the waterfront opposite the ancient city, in this almost-as-ancient suburb.

For perhaps two more miles the Spaniard followed the mysterious stranger, through a gate into rising winding streets in a district that looked so oddly Italianate compared with its master across the water. It came as little surprise to him when they rounded a high brick wall, built in what he was beginning to recognise as an old Byzantine style, and discovered that the building they had just skirted was the cloister of a large church. The building was still intact and showed all the signs of use, but was oddly dissimilar to the other Byzantine churches he had seen thus far in his days in the city. With only one small cupola visible and a tall belfry, it bore a far closer resemblance to the churches to which he was used in the west.

The cloaked man disappeared in through the church doorway and Diego followed carefully. As he approached, his suspicions were confirmed by the distinct and familiar sound of Catholic mass held in high church Latin. He had absolutely no doubt of his findings as he lurked near the door and peered inside to see a small knot of men – five in all, including his own quarry, standing in the centre of the nave discussing something in hushed voices. As the tired man removed his cloak, Diego could see that he was wearing hose and an Italian-style arming jacket, his clothing so clearly foreign. Two of the other four men were dressed similarly, in drab and sombre colours. The other two, however, confirmed everything Diego had begun to suspect. One wore a red doublet with a white cross – the everyday colours of the Knights Hospitaller. The other bore a small eight-pointed white cross on the chest of his black doublet, another common symbol for the order. Five Hospitallers.

And there could be no doubt now that they were working with the opposing Romani to put prince Ahmed in power – a man Diego knew would consider dealing with the Vatican if it put him on the throne. The knights clearly had a stake in this matter on behalf of their Borgia master.

For a moment, Diego found himself staring longingly into the church's interior. It had been a long time since he'd given confession, restricted from access to catholic churches on Crete by his fugitive status and unable to find such a place in this city. It was *his* church. And, at the most basic level, for all their current apparent status as the enemy, the Hospitallers were *his* people, warriors of the Papacy, questers for God, and not connected to the inquisition in any way. He felt he ought to be able to go in and pray, or to shake the hands of these soldiers of God, rather than steal through the city pursuing them. Why was he helping his friends undermine a plot to bring the Ottoman world close to the catholic fold? Surely he should be working *towards* that goal, not trying to *halt* it?

Shaking his head at his own confusion and the idiocy of it all, he turned from the welcome light of the blessed Virgin and scurried out into the deepening night to make his way back to the house of Ben Isaac. The damage his allegiance to Skiouros was doing to his faith was something he would have to ponder on at a later date. For now he should get back and report his findings.

But in the near future, he had a feeling that he was going to have some unpleasant soul-searching choices to make.

Chapter ten – Of crones and killers

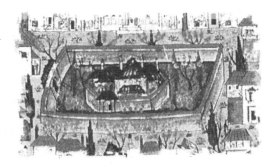

May 26th - Three days to the festival

SKIOUROS peered through the window of his small apartment, tired but as alert as he could manage. Four days of investigation and near misses in the palace had led to precisely naught. Forced to spend much of his time tending the palace grounds in order to maintain his guise, he had found fewer opportunities to spend in observation of his surroundings than he'd expected, and none of the other lesser gardeners had been particularly forthcoming during rare social moments. He was not sure whether their reticence was due to a natural unwillingness to discuss such subjects, strictures laid down by Şehzade Korkut or the head gardener, or possibly the fact that he was new and as yet unknown to the rest of the staff. Most worryingly of all, perhaps his guise was slipping – his accent too poor or his golden facial bristles putting them off. Either way, he was learning nothing, and time was thundering on towards the festival and the earth-shaking events apparently planned for that day.

But then, yesterday morning, he'd made a small breakthrough. Not enough to consider the whole thing a success, but a small breakthrough nonetheless.

Looking through this very window as he massaged aching muscles, he'd spotted something familiar and aggravating across the square opposite the main gate. The beggar who had been plying his trade there when Skiouros first arrived had moved on and in his place an old homeless person had set up stall there, a dirty blanket spread out on the ground before them selling home-made charms and the ubiquitous Turkish wards against the evil eye. Nothing unusual. Such figures were commonplace throughout the city and neither passing authorities, the ghazi at the palace gate, or the janissaries of the barracks nearby gave the figure a second glance.

But as he'd peered at the vagrant, a suspicion had quickly formed in Skiouros' mind. Half an hour's careful observation had confirmed his belief that the figure was more than a beggar or street hawker, but was in fact watching the palace gates carefully and continually. It had come as no surprise when, a short time later, the figure had stood to stretch cramped legs and he had recognised the old Romani witch who had made her presence felt so often during that dreadful week five years ago. The *Khoraxané dede Babik*, was it? What they called her? And if she was as important to the opposition as the Romani seemed to believe, then this was something entirely different to the small groups set to watching Mustafa's house.

His mind racing with the discovery, Skiouros had kept watch on the watcher. The old woman stayed in position until the *Dhuhr* call to prayer warbled out across the city from every minaret at noon. Almost as though her task was done, the old woman packed up her blanket and goods and disappeared. Skiouros, who had managed to escape the five daily prayers through his strangely solitary position, had assumed she had gone to pray, but when the rest of the population re-emerged afterwards there was no sign of her. Logging the times in his head, he had rushed out to catch up on his work, but made sure to return every quarter of an hour and have a glance through the window. Later in the afternoon, when the sun was at its highest, she reappeared and set up shop once more. On regular checking, Skiouros noted her continued presence for an hour, until the sun's shade began to tint with the orange of later afternoon, and the *Asr* prayer call rang out. Once more, she gathered her gear and was gone.

Skiouros had considered the timing and, scuttling out to continue his work, kept an eye on the sundial that stood before the half-moon pool. When he judged that an hour and a half had passed, he made his way back to his room and rushed over to the window. Sure enough, there was the old woman busy unfolding her blanket and laying out the charms for sale. One hour before each call to prayer, she was there. Nodding to himself, he watched her intently for that hour until the *Maghrib* call at sunset, and then again when she turned up for an hour in true dark before the *Isha'a* call. She was almost expectant in her manner and her body language suggested frustration each time she packed and left. She was not just observing the palace, but actively waiting for something. For what? For Şehzade Korkut's head to come rolling out of the gate? Clearly not. But there *was* one of her allies in the palace – there *had* to be, waiting to end the prince when the time came – and she had to have been waiting for something from him. Either she was waiting for news from him, or to impart some *to* him. Either way, watching her would reveal the killer in the palace.

As he'd lain in bed last night, Skiouros had decided that the Romani woman must be waiting for to given news to her fellow inside – what useful news could he pass to her? – and had begun to formulate a plan. He couldn't confront her, of course – he couldn't leave the palace grounds without ruining his guise and endangering himself, and he doubted she would willingly reveal anything anyway, even if he caught her, which he somehow doubted. But if she was as impatient as she seemed, then he was sure that her contact was overdue. The man must go to her soon. Skiouros would have to watch for him.

And so he had risen while even the owls were still rubbing their eyes with tired wings and got to work early in the pitch dark of the dead of night, rushing through his daily tasks in order to maintain his position and cover while buying himself enough free time the next day to watch the old woman when he should be working. And then he had started the observation with the crone's arrival an hour before the *Fajr* call, while the sun was still just a kiss and a promise of the day ahead. Again, nothing happened during her first or second prayer call session, and the tension in the old Romani woman seemed to be increasing exponentially with each passing visit. Her man must be *truly* overdue.

Then, as the shadows began to lengthen in the afternoon sun, the old woman thanked profusely a passing merchant who had purchased a blue and white eyeball charm from her, and then looked up in a mixture of surprise, relief and anger. To the casual observer, the man in the grey *tarbouz* skull cap simply bent at the stall, perused half a dozen charms, and then purchased one from the woman with a brief exchange of haggling. To Skiouros, prepared for the meeting, the body language was telling, and though he could not hear what the pair were saying from such a distance, he could see her berating him, see his defensive excuses, identify acceptance on both sides and a resolution reached.

The man rose again, draping the purchased charm around his neck, and then turned and strode back towards the palace gate.

Skiouros peered at him through the window. He was one of the kitchen staff, if Skiouros had identified his clothing correctly. The young Greek had not been inside the main palace itself, of course, and had seen little of the staff from within, but he was comfortable with his deduction. And who better to kill a prince than a cook, after all? He remembered with bitterness the poisoned fruit that had ended Cem Sultan's life in Napoli.

Time was now of the essence. Readying himself for what must come next, Skiouros dashed out of the kiosk... and almost fell over another of the Bostancı on the gravel path outside. Righting himself in a faint panic, the disguised Greek burbled an apology.

'In a rush, Sincabi? You look tired.'

'Working hard,' Skiouros replied, trying to sound exasperated. 'Still catching up on three days of neglect after my predecessor left.'

This seemed to satisfy the other gardener, who nodded his understanding.

'The entire corps in the palace is being called into the main building this evening. You will also be required to attend.'

Skiouros felt a knot of fear settle in him. 'Something important?'

'The Şehzade is holding a review of his palace staff. Inconvenient, I know, but who would deny a prince.'

Inconvenient, indeed. Potentially *fatally* so, in fact. But this current interruption was every bit as inconvenient. Skiouros tried to look tired and calm, and nodded his acceptance. 'What time?'

'After the Maghrib prayers, when it is dark.'

'I will be there.'

The man smiled understandingly and turned, strolling off towards the main path once more, heading for the ivory pavilion. Skiouros reached for his rake and began to drag the dirt under a hedge idly for a moment, watching as the man left, but the moment he was out of sight, he shouldered the tool and turned, running off past the decorative flower garden, between the trees and towards the main gate. As he approached the point where his arcade met the main path through the grounds, he slowed. The sound of the great decorative portal slamming shut echoed across the grass, and Skiouros prayed he wasn't too late. Ducking past the third-to-last tree in the line, he unshouldered his implement and began to gently tease the earth, his nervous eyes raking the main path instead.

149

With both relief and heightened tension, he spotted the man in the grey cap sauntering along the path back towards the palace and stopped, raising a hand. Shaping his lips, he gave a whistle which made the man in the grey hat stop in his tracks and look around in surprise. Skiouros waved and beckoned and the man frowned, pointing at his chest in question. Skiouros nodded and then stepped back behind the tree.

With a baffled expression, the kitchen worker stepped off the main path and strode along the side track between the trees, looking for the gardener who had beckoned. The surprise the man had felt at being signalled paled into comparison at the surprise he felt as the handle of a rake smashed into his forehead with enough force to catapult him from his feet and make him somersault backwards, landing awkwardly face-down on the path.

Skiouros stepped out from the tree, propping his rake against the bole. What he'd have given for his beloved macana stick instead of having to swing such a numb weapon from a hidden position... Still, it had worked as planned and, though the cook was groaning, he was far from able to struggle right now. Crouching, Skiouros rolled him over. His eyes were turned up into his head and blood trickled from his mouth where he had bitten a piece from his lip during the blow. His forehead was an impressive sight. In a matter of seconds it had grown into a huge, bulbous lump and was beginning to turn purple.

Skiouros stared at him and watched as the man's wits left him and he slid into unconsciousness. With trepidation, the Greek checked his pulse and breathing. He was still alive. The state of his head suggested that the blow had been but an angel's breath short of sending him to the netherworld. Not that such an end would be a bad thing, Skiouros reminded himself. After all, this man was no innocent. He was in position in this place to kill a prince. He *deserved* a brutal end, really. But not before a little useful information had been wheedled from him – in particular the identity of other conspirators. Straightening, Skiouros looked around cautiously. He was sure it had been quiet enough, but the gardeners could be anywhere so it was always worth checking. Fortunately he could see no one and there was no untoward sound above the gentle breeze in the leaves.

Taking a breath, he bent and picked the wounded cook up by the wrists, lifting him and dragging him over his shoulder before heaving him up and settling him into place. Now he had to move quickly. Life would be short and *very* unpleasant if he were found carrying a wounded staff member around the grounds. Praying almost continuously for solitude, Skiouros carried his burden through the gardens and back to the half-moon kiosk. As he passed inside and turned to close the doors, he heaved a sigh of relief.

Time was still of the essence. He could not keep the man restrained for long. And even with the large number of staff at the palace, Ottoman organisation was so thorough and efficient that the man's absence would swiftly be noted. The very best Skiouros could hope for was an hour before that absence began to cause alarm and the palace would become alert. Suspicion would fall on the victim at first, since he had been seen leaving the palace, but that suspicion would be short-lived, for once the ghazi at the gate were consulted it would be discovered that he had passed back through the outer wall again. A little further enquiry would reveal that he had not passed the inner gate back to the main palace complex. That would put the missing man somewhere in the gardens. And Skiouros was under no illusion that blame would quickly attach itself to the newest man.

By sundown the guards would be looking to interview him. It was possible, of course, that he could stash the cook somewhere and protest his innocence. But there was little chance of success there. His guise was good, but would hardly hold up against interrogation. Plus he had no alibi, and he was very well aware that even the *threat* of torture would be enough to make him cry like a babe. So as soon as they came looking for him, he couldn't afford to be found.

Time was short. He had to get out and had to get the unconscious cook out with him. But there was simply no hope of him doing it alone. He would have to scrawl a message for his friends and hope that they were not delayed. Either Parmenio, Dragi or Diego checked the wall outside his room four or five times a day for any messages. So far he'd had cause to leave none. Now, all of a sudden, it would be a critically urgent missive which couldn't wait.

The window in the outer wall was too small for a person to pass through – it *was* a defensive perimeter wall, after all. Half a foot wide and little more than a foot tall, the window was enough to let in light and, against the possibility that the occupant preferred darkness, it had a thick wooden shutter. Grabbing the white chalky stone he had collected from one of the nearby garden paths, Skiouros scrawled 'Help – urgent' in Italian on the dark wood, hoping that the words would not draw comment from one of the very rare passers-by. The chances of any locals having a command of Italian were miniscule, but the very presence of a foreign tongue here might raise comment.

*

Parmenio and Diego listened to the sunset prayer call echoing across the roofs of the city and shared an anxious look. 'We're running late. I don't think we can wait for him,' the Spaniard murmured.

Parmenio nodded. Dragi had been summoned to the imperial naval headquarters across the water in Galata in the early afternoon and had been gone ever since. The other two had held off the latest of their regular visits to the Eski Sarayi, waiting tensely to find out what had called the Romani away and kept him absent for so long but, as the afternoon wore on, they had become increasingly uneasy at having left Skiouros to his own devices with no contact.

'Alright. We go. But we need to be fast. Anything could be happening with Dragi.'

Quickly, the two men threw on their local-style draped coats and jammed on their heads the blue skullcaps that labelled them as Christians citizens of the empire. Dragi had reasoned that there was almost no chance of the pair being able to pass as anything but what they were, but most suspicions would be allayed by them donning the gear of Christian subjects of the sultan. Neither grabbed their sword, though both looked wistfully at the sheathed weapons in the back room before they rolled their shoulders and, bidding good evening to the matron of the house whose continued goodwill overrode the surly unhappiness of young David, they unlatched the door and stepped out into the street.

Hurrying up the street towards the crest of the hill, where Balat became Phanar and the populace shifted from Jewish to Greek, the pair pulled their coats tight against the evening breezes that seemed to be funnelled through the vertiginous streets of the city into chilling blasts of cold. Looking ahead up the cobbled slope with its detritus and murk, Parmenio cleared his throat and spoke in a low whisper. 'Do you get the feeling we're being watched?'

Diego nodded without turning his head. 'Three men, not far behind. They have been with us since we left the house.'

'What do you want to do about it?'

'I don't know how they managed it, but I can only assume that's our opposition and they have tracked us to the Jew's house. It's the knights, I believe, not the Romani. They are not subtle, not good enough at such subterfuge. The Romani, I fear, would not have been seen.'

'Can we deal with them?'

'Probably,' murmured Diego.

'Then we should, before this gets any worse.'

'Confront them, my friend. I will return in but a second.' As Parmenio opened his mouth to object, Diego slipped into a side-alley and disappeared into the gloom of evening shadows. Parmenio, suddenly alone and feeling surprisingly vulnerable in the street, swallowed nervously and turned.

'Well now, lads,' he said in a pleasant tone, in his native Italian. 'It seems that we have something of a problem.'

The two figures he could see in the street in their dark cloaks were suddenly joined by a third from a doorway, and the three came to a halt. The one at the centre pulled back his hood to reveal a bald head, with a short beard and a face like a bulldog's muzzle turned inside-out. Parmenio faltered. He'd been in enough brawls in his years to recognise the face of a born killer before, and this was one such. Some men joined the holy orders for their faith or for redemption, or for the need to serve. Others joined simply because while orders such as the Knights Hospitaller of Saint John demanded discipline, respect and piety, they also granted a license to kill in a world ever more strictly defined by codes of conduct. It was no secret that the Hospitallers were not over-choosy about the targets of their naval actions in the eastern seas, and their galleys were oared by as many Jewish and Christian slaves as Muslims. All of which meant that that even good Christians like Parmenio and Diego had no reason to feel secure around such knights.

The men to either side of the ugly brute removed their own hoods, and neither of them looked pretty or jolly, either. Parmenio felt the absence of Diego by his side keenly under that trio of gazes and noted with a speeding of the heart that each of them reached down toward swords belted tight at their side beneath the cloaks, their fingers hovering close to the hilts.

'Not subtle, that, my friends: planning to cut down a man in the street. The Ottoman authorities tend to frown on that kind of thing.' His voice rose a notch in the hope of attracting attention, but the street remained empty and silent.

'You keep poor company for a good God-fearing Italian,' sneered one with wispy facial hair and a scar that ran from nose to chin, giving his lips an odd, unpleasant shape.

'God doesn't seem to mind,' Parmenio grinned, as he spotted Diego emerging from another alleyway behind them with a short length of timber in his hand, creeping quietly up the street.

'My preceptor,' announced the third man, 'has authorised me to offer an amnesty to you and even to that half-breed Spanish *moro* you travel with on the condition that you return with us to the monastery of Saint Benoit in Galata and bend your efforts henceforth to the good of the Church, and not of your heretic friend and his sultan. I will, however, make this offer just once.'

The big bulldog-face in the centre looked less than impressed at the idea, and as Parmenio tried not to laugh, the man broke into a vicious smile at the likelihood of impending violence instead of reconciliation.

'I am, as you say, a good son of the true Church,' Parmenio smiled, 'but I have to admit that, given the choice between a Constantinople under the rule of a man like Bayezid, who lets even *your* sort roam the streets unmolested, or a Constantinople under the control of the depraved Borgia Pope and of Torquemada's black-robed murderers, I think the Turks win on a basic scale of humanity.'

He tried not to grin too broadly as behind the three men, Diego reached down with his empty hand and grasped bulldog-face's sword. As the big man felt a faint pull at his belt, his face creased into a puzzled frown and he turned to look down.

The pommel of his own sword, jerked from its scabbard, hit that hideous, confused face square on, smashing into the bridge of his nose as the Spaniard ripped the blade free. Bulldog reeled, blood exploding from his ruined nose, and the pair by his side turned in shock to find Diego behind them with a length of timber in one hand and a solid, utilitarian crusader's blade in the other.

Even as the dazed and agonised brute collapsed to the ground, Diego smacked another in the arm with the club and then drove it end-on into his stomach, causing him to explode in a gust of fetid breath and double over in pain. As he ignored the two wounded men and turned to the third, Diego threw the sword towards Parmenio.

The captain panicked for a moment and flinched away from the cast blade, which fell to the ground close to his side. Diego rolled his eyes and Parmenio dipped down and collected it even as the winded knight staggered around. With a roar of sheer fury Bulldog thrashed, trying to rise to his feet, blood still sheeting down his front, and the move distracted the Spaniard for a moment, long enough for the man he faced to draw his own sword and step back. Ignoring the rest of the scene, Diego concentrated on his fresh opponent – the one who had done most of the talking. The man's blade flicked out again and again, swiftly and accurately. He was clearly well trained and experienced with his sword. Diego, armed only with a piece of broken timber he had ripped from the rear window of a house as he ran down the narrow alleys, carefully angled each parry so that his club caught the flat of the enemy blade, turning it only slightly, but enough for the Spaniard to side-step out of danger, dancing on his toes and heels like the expert fencer he was. Indeed, twice during the flurry of blows he managed to lance out with his blunt weapon and deliver a sharp rap on his opponent, the last of which caught him on the wrist and almost caused him to drop the sword. The man recovered quickly and Diego was forced to defend himself once more.

As his struggle continued, Parmenio moved against the staggering man, his mind racing. The very idea of putting a blade through a man who'd taken holy orders seemed unthinkable. And yet he quickly reminded himself that not only were these 'holy warriors' about to do just that to him, but also their order had attempted to assassinate a guest in the Papal court, were working with Muslim Romani, and were attempting to bring about a coup in the Ottoman court which would bring down the most progressive and moderate sultan the Osman throne had ever held.

Hardening his heart, he squared up to the winded man, who was now recovering and straightening, reaching down to his weapon. Even now, Parmenio felt a momentary thrill of doubt and denial at his chosen course, but then he caught a glimpse of his enemy's eyes and saw neither pity nor reason in them. The knight's blade had slid two inches free of the scabbard's collar when Parmenio's stolen blade punched through his arming jacket, sliding through the wool and cloth garment with ease and sinking deep into the man's chest, grating on ribs as the blade widened with its passage. Parmenio winced at the sound, a noise to which he would never become accustomed. He was peering into the mortally-wounded man's panicked, staring eyes when Bulldog's ham-like hand landed on his shoulder like a collapsing bridge, causing him to stagger and panic that his shoulder had fractured under the weight. The immense grip spun him away from the dying man to face that foul, blood-drenched visage.

The sudden resurgence of the big brute caught Diego's attention, and for a moment his defence faltered. The remaining swordsman took advantage of the moment to flick one blow at him, which carved a narrow line in his arm, and then turned and ran off down the street, sword still in hand. Diego's head snapped back and forth between the fleeing knight and the beast who was now threatening Parmenio. He'd no idea how good the former sailor really was, but the way he was holding up the sword suggested that he wouldn't last long against Bulldog.

Parmenio caught sight of him past the roaring thug and bellowed 'Go! Stop him getting away!'

Diego reluctantly turned his back on the ongoing struggle and raced off after the fleeing knight. Ahead, he saw the man turn into a side alley, presumably hoping to lose his pursuer. Diego hefted his wooden club and raced on, slowing only as he reached the corner. The knight had chosen his escape route rather poorly. The alley was packed with rubble and detritus, and the Spaniard could see his quarry not far ahead, struggling to clamber over a broken crate.

Diego narrowed his eyes and steadied his breath, drawing back his hand.

With a grunt, he cast his club in an overhead arc and watched with satisfaction as the wooden baton sailed through the air and connected with the back of the knight's head, sending him sprawling into the refuse. As soon as the man disappeared to the ground, Diego was moving, and a few moments later he was behind the filthy knight as he tried to rise, covered in multi-species excrement and a rat's nest, his sword lost somewhere in the mess and his mind reeling from an almost concussive blow. Calmly, slowly, Diego reached down with distaste and retrieved the fallen sword. The stunned knight turned to face him, his expression a picture of bleak resignation.

'Even merciful God will not forgive you for this, Spaniard.'

Diego's eyes hardened and he raised the filthy sword so that the point hovered near the man's chin. 'God most certainly *will* forgive me. Whether I will forgive *myself* is in a great deal more doubt.' Heaving in a deep breath, Diego lowered the tip of the sword.

'Go.'

The man blinked in surprise.

'I have no stomach for killing crusaders over a foreign succession. Go now and do not look back.'

The knight needed no further urging, turning and scrambling away over the mess into the darkness. Diego closed his eyes for a moment, trying to decide whether he had just been unaccountably noble, or a complete fool. On balance, he decided that the best he could hope for was both. Feeling the rising tide of a faint headache, he pinched the bridge of his nose and gently rubbed his temple. With a sigh, he turned and made his slow way back out into the street.

Parmenio seemed miraculously on top of the situation further up the street. Despite being outsized and outclassed, he had a good long sword, while Bulldog brandished only a parrying dagger that he'd ripped from his other hip. While the big man was managing to turn aside most of Parmenio's blows, a couple of reasonably convincing strikes had landed and the loss of blood and constant sharp pains they caused were starting to take their toll. Even as Diego slogged his weary way up the street, he watched another blow land, and then, finally, Parmenio spotted the opening he'd sought. His last blow slid into the big man's neck and emerged beside his spine in a welter of blood.

By the time Diego reached the scene of carnage, Parmenio had already hefted the smaller body and thrown it into a side alley among the dark and the refuse. He looked up at Diego.

'Dealt with?'

Diego gave a numb nod and then helped his friend lift the huge brute and drag him off the street into the dark alley. As they stood, panting, Parmenio reached out for the sword in Diego's hand. The Spaniard gave him a questioning look.

'I don't think the old lady and her family will take kindly to the arrival of new swords. They might question their origin.'

Diego nodded and relinquished the knight's weapon, which Parmenio tossed into the alley along with his. 'I think we need to check back at the house again before we head off to see Skiouros,' the Genoese said. 'We got all three, but there might be others yet who know where we are staying. And since they somehow found out where we were staying, the place might not be safe.'

Diego ignored the swell and dip of his troubled conscience and could do nothing but nod silently and follow as Parmenio descended the blood-soaked street once more, heading for the house of Ben Isaac.

Five minutes later they crossed the threshold of their 'safe' house once more and tumbled wearily into the room they shared, only to find Dragi sitting in his best clothes on the bed.

'You're back! I have some excellent news...' he frowned as he took in the spray of blood across both of his friends and the few small marks on them. 'And it looks like you might have, too.'

'It's a grisly and slightly worrying story,' Parmenio sighed.

'Then tell it quickly,' Dragi said, sitting up. 'My business was unavoidable, but we have left our Greek friend too long.'

*

Skiouros' attention was drawn from the door of the kiosk by the sound of shuffling behind him. Turning, he saw that his prisoner had finally awakened from his head wound and was struggling against the long coils of rope with which Skiouros had tied him *very* thoroughly, a muted cry coming through the thick wad of the gag.

'Shhhh,' he said quietly, watching another small group of ghazi marching along the path at the far end of the half-moon pool and the dividing hedges. As they disappeared from sight, he turned and scurried across to the bundle on the floor. 'Five patrols so far, and they're increasing in both number and frequency. They're searching for you, my friend. And shortly they'll be searching for me too. I'm rather surprised they are not already at my door, to be honest. But any time now I am expected at a review in the palace, and when I'm not there, it will be the end of matters for me.

He smiled unpleasantly. 'But bear in mind that I know what you are, and if they come for me, I shall make sure that you are dead before they find me. Now I think we have a few minutes before the next patrol, so we are going to have a little conversation, and when I remove that gag, you are going to remain silent. If you do not – if you feel the irresistible urge to scream – I shall give you a lump on the back of your head to match the one on the front. Do you understand?'

The man continued to writhe and rage for a moment, but finally went still and nodded, his eyes hard and angry. Skiouros crouched over him and gently removed the corner of the gag. Without pause, the man cried out for help. Fortunately, Skiouros had been expecting the reaction and rather than lifting away the gag, he simply pushed it back into place, stifling the cry almost before it emerged. The sound of a man screaming would carry all too well in the night air, and it would not take the ghazi long to find the pair of them.

Giving the prisoner a hard look, he reached out, forming his thumb and middle finger into an 'O'. As the man stared in confusion, Skiouros delivered a sharp flick to the huge purple welt on the man's forehead. The prisoner screamed beneath his gag and writhed in pain, his eyes wincing shut and pouring with tears.

'That was for the shout. Would you care to try again?'

After the man slowly subsided, he managed a sickened nod and slowly, Skiouros peeled away the corner of the gag. Once again he slammed it back into place as the man cried out. This time, he grasped the wide-eyed man by the ears and gently but firmly clonked his head back against the floorboards. He was rewarded by a muffled grunt and a sigh as the man's eyes rolled up into his head again. Checking the breath and pulse to be sure, Skiouros rose. A shout echoed out across the garden and he swallowed. He was now pretty sure they were coming for him and there was not much he could do. He had perhaps minutes.

Time to put his backup plan into motion, he thought, horribly aware that his backup plan was idiotic at best. Crouching again, he grasped the end of the extra rope he had uncoiled in preparation. Glancing through the window to make sure no one had made it into his gardens yet, he swung open the door and dashed out, around the corner next to the house, and to the nearest of the large beech trees, which towered above the compost heap that also served as his personal latrine.

With a surprisingly accurate throw, he cast the end of the rope over the high, thick branch he had already decided upon for the purpose. Jogging back to the kiosk, he lifted the limp body of the prisoner and carried it from the building, pausing to gently close the door.

Sweating and grunting under the weight of the burden, and grateful that the cook/assassin was a small man and not run to fat, he carried the limp form to the tree and tied one end of the dangling rope firmly to the prisoner's bindings. Taking a deep breath, he leapt, grasped one of the lower branches and pulled himself up. Moving swiftly and lithely from branch to branch, he ascended to that high limb where he stopped, carefully positioning himself with his back to another branch and wedging his feet as best he could.

With another preparatory breath, he grasped the rope and began to haul, the tendons on his arms standing out like ropes with the effort. Slowly, jerkily, the heavy bundle lifted from the ground and began to bounce and lurch up through the air towards that high branch, the rope sliding over the bark and making a sound like a quiet saw at work.

For two minutes Skiouros hauled on the rope until the body was within reach. Heaving in exhausted breaths, he tied the other end of the coil tight to another branch, triple-knotting it for certainty, and then wound it round and round the branch to keep it high and out of sight below.

Barely had he finished when a large group of men burst out of the hedges and emerged into the open area around the pool, making for the kiosk. Half a dozen ghazi were accompanied by another half dozen gardeners, including the head Bostancı among their number. A lot of shouting ensued, with the chief gardener apparently in charge. Men burst into the kiosk and searched it roughly. Moments later they emerged with Skiouros' kit bag. Mentally he said farewell to the few personal items in there, grateful that for prudence he had left almost all his things with his friends.

More angry shouting began and two more groups turned up through the gardens – one of Bostancı and the other of ghazi. Skiouros held his breath and sat as still as possible while two ghazi with spears darted around the sparse area close to the side wall of the kiosk and then crossed to the sizeable compost heap, spending several minutes jamming their spears into the muck.

The Greek squeezed his eyes shut and prayed that his insensate companion, who swung gently back and forth on the rope, emitting the faintest of creaks that was inaudible below over the wind through the leaves, did not awake. As time passed and a second group combed this area and investigated the heap, he even panicked that the cold sweat running from his scalp and dripping from nose and chin might be loud enough as it hit the earth below to attract attention or that, God forbid, a drip might hit one of the searchers as they passed below.

But as half an hour passed and the area was searched again and again, nothing happened. Not one of the men, miraculously, looked up into the tree, the attention of anyone who approached being wholly drawn by the compost heap that would make such an obvious hiding place.

Now if only his friends would finally turn up...

Chapter eleven – Of the gardener and the cook

May 26th - Three days to the festival

SKIOUROS had lost count of the number of times the compost heap had been searched. The scouring of the grounds for the missing cook and the disappearing gardener had waned but little with the light and for the first hour of darkness Skiouros had watched, fascinated, as small parties had continued to pry under bushes and search sheds by the guttering golden light of torches. Not once in the twilight had anyone bothered to look up. And now that blackness had claimed the branches and foliage, the chances of discovery had dropped drastically, even if they started to stare upwards as they searched.

If he had dared to make a noise, he might have laughed.

Watching four torches bob along in the gloom towards the palace proper, the dancing lights flickering intermittently, often hidden by foliage, he chewed thoughtfully on his lip. One thing was clear: he couldn't stay here all night. It appeared that his friends had not come or, if they had, they had come too late and disappeared again. Either way, he would have to do this alone.

Almost as if to add impetus to his decision, the swinging body gave a muffled moan. Great. He was waking up. Wincing at the potential for discovery through noise, Skiouros reached across to a branch that hung, dead yet still attached, from the tree and snapped it off at the base with a dull crack. He held his breath for a moment but no one came running, so he slowly exhaled, and then leaned forwards.

'Sorry, but I can't have you struggling.'

With a measured swing born of years of practice with his macana stick, Skiouros gave the helpless kitchen worker a crack across the back of the head with the makeshift club. As the swaying form went limp once more, he dropped the broken branch into the soft compost heap and surveyed his surroundings for the thousandth time since he'd ascended the tree. His options were somewhat limited.

Ground level was unfeasible. The perimeter wall was simply too high and featureless. Skiouros might hope to climb it, but not dragging a rope or a body, and probably not silently enough to remain undiscovered. There was no way out of his chamber through the wall – he simply would not fit through the windows. And the wall gate was well enough secured and guarded at the best of times. With the heightened security following the vanishing of two staff it would be a veritable fortress.

It occurred to him in a moment of humour that with two of them having disappeared, the cook's quarters and movements were probably being scrutinised just as much as his. After all, the palace authorities could not know whether the gardener had taken the cook, the cook taken the gardener, or possibly even were both working in collusion? It would be a mystery for the guards to unwrap. But they would have to do it without evidence.

Because his wandering gaze had settled upon the only realistic path.

The ground was out as an option. That left him with the tree as his entire world. And the branches of the tree did not reach the perimeter wall, so he could not simply shift around the tree and drop over the side. But the outer branches of the tree *did* come close to the roof of his kiosk, which in turn butted up against that outer perimeter wall with only a seven foot climb instead of twenty-five.

He smiled. There were, of course, at least a dozen things that could go horribly, horribly wrong with the plan, but it felt good to at least *have* a plan of action, and not simply be sitting in a tree waiting for a particularly astute guard to look up.

Peering at the inclined roof of the kiosk – the slope making the whole surface visible from the ground and that being the reason the guards had not bothered climbing up to search it – he tried to estimate the height difference between the upper branch, around which he'd wound the rope, and the nearest low edge of the roof. It was perhaps a nine or ten foot drop from one to the other. But with the fact that the branch would inevitably bend beneath the weight, he could only rely on seven or eight feet.

Hoping that the cook and he between them were lighter than he suspected, he braced himself and rose to his feet, steadying himself on a higher bough. For a dizzying moment he almost plummeted head first into the wet, stinking heap below, his legs having seized up and his feet bursting into prickly paraesthesia from lack of use. He wobbled and his legs seemed to flap around uselessly, forcing him to hold up his entire body with his arms. Slowly but surely, the life returned to his legs and feet and he managed to stand steady, taking an extra minute or two to bend and stretch, limbering up. Satisfied that he was sufficiently supple and mobile once more, he began to walk out along the limb, his hands still on the higher branch that ran above and parallel to the one beneath his feet. Slowly, carefully, and with sweat pouring from his brow and dripping from his nose, he edged towards the roof and stopped, his toes perhaps four feet from it and three above, unwilling to take another step with the limb beneath his soft boots starting to creak and bend alarmingly. This was the limit, then. At best, four feet across and three feet down underfoot.

Nodding to himself and trying to picture the task ahead, he edged back along the branch and then paused by the swinging, torpid shape of the cook. A random search party of ghazi and Bostancı shuffled around the far side of the half-moon pool and scoured the vineyard, taking one row each. Skiouros waited nervously for several minutes until he saw their fruitless search move on to a small orchard some distance away, and then breathed again. Stepping up his plan, he grasped the body and with a great deal of strain and difficulty – and no few near misses with the drop to the compost heap either – managed to get the bound form over his shoulder. Gritting his teeth and breathing heavily with the effort, he unwound the coiled rope from the upper branch and, steadying himself and feeling his strength beginning to ebb, he began to edge painfully along the branch.

The journey was slow and achy, and full of trepidation, but in three minutes' time he was approaching the kiosk again, this time with his prize. Aware that his earlier calculations of weight and distance allowed only for him, he stopped several feet short of where he'd reached last time. He tried not to think of what could still go wrong and instead flooded his panicked thoughts with amazement that so far it had gone so well. Carefully, he leaned his forehead against the upper branch to keep himself steady and free his hands. His eyes took in the drop below, now with no soft heap in evidence, and he concentrated instead on the immediate task. Slowly, carefully, he threw the rope over the upper branch a yard or so further along, then adjusted it to allow six or seven feet of rope between branch and body, before looping it once around the limb and taking the weight.

Wrapping his arm around the branch, the bough beneath his armpit and hand grasping the rope tight, he braced himself and took three breaths, counting slowly. On the third, he tipped his body to the right, the unconscious cook slipping from his shoulder and plummeting into the air.

The sudden jerk on the rope as the body reached full stretch and bounced to a halt almost pulled Skiouros from the branch, and he struggled to hold onto the rope. Even then, he felt a foot of it slip through his fingers before he managed a tight grip once more.

For a heart-stopping moment he stood there, precariously balanced on the springy outer end of a branch, his captive swinging back and forth below him and the rope stinging his hands as he held it firmly. Not for the first time this week, he wondered what in the name of blessed Saint Nikolas he was doing.

A distant flicker of light announced yet another small search party doing the rounds, and the panic began to rise. He was much more open now, and anyone deciding to do another sweep of the half-moon gardens would almost certainly spot him. The pivotal point had passed, and now he had no option but to move on, and fast.

Gritting his teeth, he held onto the rope and lifted his leg, reaching out with his foot and nudging the dangling body. The swing increased, and as it came back he gave it another nudge, then another, and another, each push adding momentum to the swing. In half a minute the cook was rushing back and forth through the air like a heavy pendulum.

This was it. Skiouros cast up to the Lord the prayer of the desperate and, as the cook reached the top of his swing, released the rope. The body half flew, half fell, hitting the sloping roof of the kiosk with a dull crack. Skiouros winced. There was a very good chance that any random searcher within earshot would hear that and come to investigate. Suddenly, time was extremely pressing. Ignoring the rope altogether now, Skiouros edged quickly along the branch to where he'd tested earlier and braced himself. The limb beneath his feet gave an ominous warning creak and even as he launched himself, he felt the timber crack.

The world exploded into panic and blurred action as he fell through the air with a lot less momentum than he expected, the broken branch taking away a great deal of it, and hit the eaves of the kiosk with his chest, expelling all the air from his lungs. His eyes wide and his breath coming in gasps, Skiouros struggled for purchase, trying to climb up over the edge and onto the slope of the roof. His heart almost failed as his scrabbling hand, instead of finding a grip, dislodged a tile, which whipped past his head and hit the ground with a ceramic smash.

That had done it. If he'd miraculously remained unnoticed until now, that would attract the attention of everyone this side of the palace building. The situation went from bad to worse as the entire line of tiles, from eave to apex, started to slide down with the bottom one's support now absent. One by one the tiles hurtled past him to crash on the ground. And if he'd believed things could get no worse, the unconscious form of the cook started an inexorable slide down towards the edge of the roof.

A moment of awful dark comedy ensued, as he fought desperately and struggled up and over the eaves, using the wooden struts that had supported the now-missing tiles for handholds. And while he managed to slump face first onto the slope of the roof, the cook's body slid past him in the other direction, picking up momentum as it descended.

With wide eyes and a squeak of alarm, Skiouros reached out with his right hand, grabbing the ropes that bound the man tight, his other fingers taking the terrible strain of two bodies on the wooden strut.

His heart was thumping in his chest as fast and as hard as it could, and it was a moment before he heard the voices over the noise of it. He had been discovered! Ghazi and Bostancı were pouring across the grounds towards the half-moon kiosk with dancing torches, shouting as they came. He was about to be caught. And when that happened, he would die. Slowly. It might even take weeks. He remembered Şehzade Korkut at the hippodrome arches, merrily sending those he considered infidels to their death. He could hardly imagine what the rabid, zealous prince would do to a Christian found in his palace, masquerading as one of his staff. Vertical impalement would probably be only the start of the penalty! Even *God* could not punish him like Korkut would.

165

A fresh burst of incentive flooded through him, and Skiouros began to climb like a man possessed, his fingers reaching up and grasping the next slat. Letting go of the body for a fraction of a second, he instead grasped the rope a couple of feet from where it was attached to the cook's bindings. With a great deal of difficulty, he slung it over his shoulder and tied it so that the cook was hanging from him, a long tail of rope dangling down over the edge of the roof.

With two hands now freed and all the weight on his shoulders, he began to ascend towards the apex. The peril of the situation deepened as men started to flood into view around the half-moon pool. They were almost all shouting, the odd officers among them trying to make themselves heard over the din. Skiouros' wild eyes caught them in passing and noted among them quite a few spears that might just reach up to the roof, but more worryingly: three muskets.

His terror peaked, and, reaching the apex of the roof, he rose and staggered along it towards the boundary wall, the weight of the body dragging him down and threatening to topple him, causing him to lean precariously to the right to counterbalance as he moved.

Through the din behind him he heard the order to load muskets. These were professionals – it would not take them long. Reaching the outer wall, he was in clear view of every marksman. His fingers scrabbled up the surface but reached only two feet short of the parapet. There was no hope of him stretching far enough, and he couldn't jump with this weight dragging him down.

In a flurry of desperate action, he undid the knot around his front and let the body fall to the roof, gripping the length of rope instead. With a deep breath he jumped, the fingers of his free hand scraping the parapet for a moment until he fell back and his feet skittered on the tiles, threatening to tip him out into the air. Settling for a moment, he closed his eyes and prepared, but opened them again in sudden panic as the first gunshot cracked through the night, shards of stone from the boundary wall exploding in dust as the ball hit the surface mere inches from his arm. Spurred on, he jumped again and this time his arm hooked over the top. Grunting, he hauled himself up until he was astride the wall and turned side-on to present less of a target to the marksmen.

Willing himself extra strength and simultaneously wishing calamity and poor sight upon his enemies, he began to haul the swinging form of the cook up to the wall top.

Two more shots flashed and cracked into the night. The first seemed to go awry somewhere in the darkness, but the second took a small piece from Skiouros' shoulder and fiery white agony seared through him. Worse, the power of the ball punching into his shoulder and glancing off his shoulder blade pushed him sideways, and he found himself falling over the outer edge of the wall until he dropped four feet and then smashed into the outer face, held up by the cook's body which was wedged against the parapet at the far side on the other end of the rope.

'Never do things by half do you?' called a voice with dark humour, and Skiouros looked down to see Parmenio grinning up at him, Diego and Dragi close by.

'Agh,' was all he could manage.

'Drop down. We'll catch you.'

'Can't,' Skiouros breathed, 'got a friend up there.' For some reason he was faintly gratified by the slide from wry humour to puzzlement in Parmenio's expression. Trying to block out the agonising fire of the flesh wound in his shoulder, Skiouros climbed, panting, back up the rope to the parapet, favouring his other arm. At the top, he reached across the parapet and felt the cook wedged there. Looking down, he cleared his throat.

'Hope you lot feel strong enough to catch two.'

Without waiting for an answer, aware that the strength in his shoulder was almost gone, and he was dangerously close to blacking out, the Greek reached up with one hand, grabbing the bindings of the cook, and then let go of his rope with the other and grasped the cook with that too. Hauling with every remaining ounce of his strength, he pulled his captive over the wall and the two men fell out into space.

*

Skiouros awoke in a blur of confusion. For a moment he had absolutely no idea where he was. He was not at the bottom of the wall in a pile of his own shattered bones. Nor was he at the Romani house or Ben Isaac's in comfort. Nor, blessedly, was he in a cell in the palace with a hungry ghazi cutting open his guts and tearing at him with hooks. He was, in fact, in a small room with plain walls covered with broken plaster and peeling paint, a window with no

167

glass admitting the night breeze. Parmenio and Diego sat next to him.

'Where are we?'

'Somewhere called the Saint Irene hospital,' Parmenio murmured, 'though I'd hate to have *my* wounds tended here. There's more mould than stone.'

Skiouros gave a small smile. 'It's been disused since the conquest.'

'I'd guessed. But it seems to be safe, and it was within reach. Only three streets from the old palace, and we needed somewhere close and fast. Dragi brought us here just in time. Prince Korkut's men are flooding the streets around the palace looking for you.'

'Sooner or later they'll come here,' Skiouros said, trying to rise, but finding that he had virtually no strength in his tightly-bound shoulder.

'If they were coming they'd be here by now. We've been two hours.'

Skiouros blinked in surprise. 'I've been out that long?'

'Your head glanced off the wall as you fell,' Parmenio explained. 'I caught you, though you'll be getting an invoice for the medical work my back's going to need.'

For the first time, Skiouros realised that his head was not only thumping but tender, and the back of it felt wet. 'Am I...?'

'You'll be fine. Just a bit of a clonk. You'll be a sight better than that fellow you brought out, anyway.'

Skiouros noted the darkening of Diego's expression and sighed. 'Dragi's interrogating him?'

Parmenio nodded. 'In the next room. I'm surprised the yelps didn't wake you earlier. He's stopped making so much noise now, but you can still hear a whimper every now and then. It seems our Romani friend is displaying another hidden talent we were unaware of, though I'm less impressed by this one. All he had was a stick, a knife and a length of rope, but the noises that have been coming out of that room...' he shuddered, and again, Diego looked disgusted and turned his face away. For a fraction of a second Skiouros thought he saw something else in the Spaniard's expression.

'Mind you, the guards at the palace started the job for him,' Parmenio added, and Skiouros frowned. 'Poor bastard apparently took a stray musket ball in the leg while you were escaping,' the Genoese sailor explained.

So that was where that errant shot went...

'You were late.'

'We were unavoidably detained,' Parmenio replied, and when Skiouros shrugged in incomprehension, he added, 'the Jews' house may not be so secure any more. We got to the old palace just after true dark, but you'd obviously already had your adventure. We saw the message on the shutter, but when we looked through the window, your apartment was full of soldiers turning the place over, taking it apart looking for you. We had to duck back out of sight, but we wiped your message off first, just in case. Then we sat watching the wall until we heard all the kerfuffle and realised what was happening.'

'Who found you at Ben Isaac's?'

'Our knightly friends. Luckily Diego was with me, so we dealt with them pretty quick. None of them made it out, so hopefully the enemy are still in the dark about the place, but we can't be sure. After all they found out about it somehow in the first place. We may have to move soon.'

Again, Skiouros thought he saw something odd and indescribable pass across Diego's face, and noted it for consideration later. He was about to ask about their ongoing investigation when the door swung open and Dragi stepped in, wiping his hands with a bloodied cloth.

'Sure enough, your friend in there was positioned to do away with the prince. Two hours after the maghrib call to prayer on the 28th, apparently, the evening before the festival. He claimed not to know the details of his counterpart in Selim's court, and I am inclined to believe him, considering the pressure under which I put him. But whoever it is, he will have the same orders. Both princes were to die at the same time, so that neither would be put on guard by his sibling's demise.'

'So we're no closer to finding out what we need? We still have to get into Selim's palace somehow.'

Dragi gave an unpleasant smile. 'Not quite. I drew one critical piece of information from our friend next door: the identity of the man who gave him his instructions. No other than the king-breaker himself.'

Skiouros's eyes widened. 'You know who he is?'

'Better,' Dragi coughed, finishing wiping his hands, tossing away the cloth and then fishing something from his belt pouch. 'I know who he is *and* where he can be found. And I know how to get to him.'

169

Skiouros, ignoring the searing pain in his shoulder, sat up eagerly. 'Go on?'

'Your counterpart is a paşa of one horse-tail rank, in charge of the great Galata shipyard.' He crossed the room and dropped what he was holding into Skiouros' lap. The Greek looked down to see the blue and white eye pendant the cook had bought from the Romani witch staring up at him. 'May it bring you more luck than it brought him,' Dragi noted. 'So… to the Galata shipyard, next.'

Skiouros felt a grin slide across his face. 'And with your position in the navy…'

Parmenio chuckled. 'That's the other news. Tell him, Dragi.'

The Romani gave a modest shrug. 'Kemal Reis has been honoured personally by the sultan for his work with the refugees of Spain. He has been made *kapudan paşa* – the empire's senior admiral. He is to captain the great galley – Göke – which we saw in drydock. And with his promotion, I am to be made captain of his former ship. I am now Dragi Reis.'

'And that means no Turk is going to stand in his way at the naval shipyard, not even a paşa,' Parmenio grinned. Nothing brought out his positive side like a conversation about ships.

'So we go to take on this king-breaker, then?'

Dragi nodded. 'In the morning. He will be able to reveal the identity of the man in place in Selim's court.'

'I do find myself wondering whether we are simply delaying their plans for another day,' Parmenio mused. 'Have you given thought to marshalling your Romani, arming them, then simply heading south to Sulukule to wipe out your opposition? It seems a less elegant solution to your problem, but a lot simpler. And now we know exactly where they are based.'

Dragi shook his head. 'There are many reasons, my friend. Firstly, there will *be* no other day. This is their only chance and we only have to halt their plans this once. When the festival is over, the princes will return to their own sanjaks to govern their lands, and the next time they meet will likely be the succession on Bayezid's demise. If we stop it now, we stop it for good. And as for why we do not start a war: remember that these opposition are Romani, like myself. They may be misguided and driven by falsehoods, but that does not mean that I am willing to systematically exterminate an entire colony of my own people. Better we deal with this as a surgeon deals with disease – small, precise cuts that leave the body healthy.'

Skiouros nodded. 'The authorities in the city would take a very dim view of a civil war being prosecuted within the walls right under their nose, even if they are not threatened by it. Dragi's right. Tomorrow: the king-breaker. Then that gives us almost two days to find and remove the man in Selim's court.'

He looked at his friends and realised that Diego was half-listening to him at best, his gaze aimed through the broken panes of the window.

'See anything, Diego?'

The Spaniard turned slowly and shook his head. 'I thought I saw movement across the courtyard, but only a glimpse. It certainly wasn't Korkut's soldiers, and there were no torches. It was probably an old dark curtain flapping in the breeze.'

'Or a black cloak?' mused Parmenio darkly. 'Suddenly I'm feeling a lot less comfortable here than I was. Skiouros needs that shoulder seeing to somewhere a bit healthier than this. How's the captive.'

'Not a threat,' said Dragi with leaden finality, leaving none of them unsure as to his fate. 'Come. We will return to Balat for the night. And tomorrow we will face and defeat the keystone of the opposition.'

Chapter twelve – Of the King-breaker

May 27th - Two days to the festival

'**WHAT** *is* the matter with you, Diego? I've never seen anyone look so tense. You're like torsion artillery – wound up so tight you're positively vibrating.'

The Spaniard's head snapped around to Skiouros' comment, and his eyes were narrow, suspicious, even then. 'I can feel eyes on us, Skiouros. I thought I felt it at the hospital last night, and I never feel comfortable now in Balat. And I feel that same sensation now. I would wager my arm that we are being observed, though I fear that, that being the case, I may well need the arm soon.' As if to add weight to his words, his fingers closed around his belt where his sword hilt would be, were he armed.

Skiouros glanced round at the buildings crowding in on this wide avenue and the looming city wall on their left, behind which the Golden Horn teemed with life. There were few people around, and even with Skiouros' practiced and shrewd eye, he could identify no signs of pursuit or observation. 'There's nothing there, Diego. You're letting your nerves get the better of you.'

'Better nervous and prepared than blasé and dead,' the Spaniard replied flatly.

'I have to say,' Parmenio said in an unusually subdued tone, 'that I am feeling less than comfortable in our current surroundings myself.'

'That,' Skiouros smiled cruelly, 'is because this used to be the Venetian quarter in the days of the emperors. What you're feeling is the wraiths of all your Italian competitors trying to swipe the ducats from your purse with ghostly hands.'

Parmenio shivered. 'Stop that.'

'We should have taken one of the private boats upstream near the Romani quarter. This is too exposed.' Diego's suspicious glance raked the buildings to their right again.

'That would have been foolish. You know now that the Hospitallers are using them. And we are above-board and here on official business, so we use the ferry like good citizens.'

'Quiet, all of you,' Dragi hissed and turned to their escort. In addition to the four of them, given the potential for attacks by their enemies following the foiling of the Korkut plans, Dragi's commune had sent a small party of half a dozen of their more martial number to accompany the group, led by Dimo, the younger eastern Romani with the hare lip who had sat counsel with them each time they had planned during the week. It seemed, from what Skiouros had gleaned, that the young man had gained much vaunted military experience fighting for the empire among the voluntary *azap* troops against the Mamluk incursions of Anatolia a decade ago. As such, the community turned to him and his men when force of arms might become necessary. Despite the lack of apparent evidence that they were in any danger, Skiouros couldn't help but feel slightly more secure with the half dozen muscular fighters in their company. Dragi leaned towards the young leader.

'What do you think?'

The gangly, hare-lipped former mercenary glanced left and right. 'We are being watched by a hundred sets of eyes, but I sense no hostility among them.' He looked to the two of his men who were leading the group through the streets. 'Tigran? Kulagyoz?' Both men shook their heads, their eyes still on their surroundings.

'They're wrong,' Diego mumbled, his eyes still darting about. 'I wish we had our blades with us.' Skiouros nodded his heartfelt agreement with that sentiment. Despite Dragi being out here in an official capacity, it would have been too dangerous to wear swords or even to carry knives in public, especially given the clearly non-Turkish origin of several of the party. Skiouros had enquired anxiously as to how they intended to attack a high official, who was no doubt well-guarded, if they were unarmed and Dragi had simply answered with that usual mysterious smile. 'God will provide,' he had said. 'And if God does not, then either luck or the Turkish navy will.'

'Whether we're being observed or not,' Parmenio said quietly, drawing Skiouros back to their current worries, 'we are now in the heart of the city in plain view of hundreds of people. No one in their right mind would try an ambush here.'

'All it takes is one well-placed arrow,' the Romani replied in a menacing tone, 'and no more Genoese merchant, with precious little chance of the marksman being found. Stay alert.'

Parmenio gave a slightly nervous laugh, his eyes ranging around the windows once more, searching for hidden archers. The ten men walked on cautiously but at speed, passing the Saint John gate and finally reaching the Perama gate just before the great Neorion harbour. All walks of city life passed back and forth through this busy portal unchecked by the janissaries on watch, for the Perama gate led down to the wharf from which the ferry departed for Galata every half hour throughout the hours of daylight. The ten of them passed through the great sea walls and down towards the wide, shallow-bottomed caique that so regularly plied the calm waters of the Golden Horn. Tall fences funnelled the crowd to a narrow point, where a lesser official sat at a desk with a couple of functionaries and three evil-looking, watchful janissaries, taking coin from the citizens in return for passage, and depositing the money in a heavy iron box at the feet of the soldiers, where even the most daring thief would fear to tread.

The ordinary folk of the city milled about them uncertainly, not sure how to deal with this odd group which clearly contained foreigners among their number, yet also a man in a naval uniform and several rough looking specimens. As the party moved forward to the desk the crowd generally afforded them a little extra space, and the official at the table looked up at them in a combination of boredom and uncertainty. 'How many?' he asked tersely.

'Ten,' Dragi replied, gesturing to the entire party, and whipped from his belt a set of papers which he passed to the man. The bureaucrat peered myopically at the documents and looked up with a slightly perplexed expression. 'You and your crew are free to use all city amenities without charge, of course, Dragi Reis...' His face creased into a frown and he indicated the rest of the party. '*These* are your crew?'

Dragi gave him a hard look and collected his papers from the desk. 'Thank you for your assistance,' he replied and gestured for the others to follow. The janissaries barely registered this motley collection of sailors as they passed and boarded the caique, and the ten men were soon sitting quietly and waiting for departure.

Skiouros watched the crew going about their business and, as the ferry launched from the jetty, slopping out into the Golden Horn, he mused on what differences five years had made. Not to the city, of course. The city was little different – a few more minarets had risen since his departure, and the more crumbling, ancient ruins of the Byzantine buildings had been replaced by modern, stone Ottoman edifices, and of course, Balat had flourished with the influx of Jewish refugees. But really the city was much the same. What had changed was Skiouros, and how he perceived the city around him. In the old days Istanbul, as it was known to the bulk of the populace, had been a conquered city, ruled by a strict, if relatively just, enemy. It was a warren of streets occupied by poor, disenfranchised Greeks and smug, superior Turks. He had known of most aspects of life and authority in the city, but had seen them solely as targets for thievery or sources of punishment, considering them only ever from a personal, selfish viewpoint.

Not once in those days had he given a moment's consideration to what it was to be a citizen, be he foreigner or Turk. Living now, strangely, without fear of retribution for petty theft, was opening his eyes to the many facets of life in the city, how it all interacted and worked, despite the deep rifts in culture that should by all rights prevent such thriving. Of course, he himself had had to change to appreciate these things. In the last five years, Skiouros had faced both inner demons and real ones in several forms, and had encountered what he could only describe as both the most noble and most despicable deeds of man in the process. He had learned to trust and to give his word, knowing at last that his word was actually *worth* something.

It was a little saddening to think that after a decade of quarrelling with his uptight, authority-and-honour-obsessed sibling, now, when there was no hope of the pair of them speaking again until they sat in the presence of God, finally Skiouros had become something that Lykaion would have been proud to call brother. Indeed, five years of confrontation seemed oddly to have turned the low street thief Skiouros into a strange reflection of his janissary brother. He reached up to rub his sore shoulder, now tended and bandaged and far improved, though still sore.

I miss you, Lykaion.

'What is your plan when we reach the shipyard?' the young Romani escort enquired of Dragi, drawing Skiouros' thoughts back to the present and the approaching Galata shoreline.

175

'We must confront the king-breaker and we must pry from him the identity of the assassin in the Tekfur palace without letting him escape the complex. If he makes it out into the city streets and he is aware that we know of him, then he will disappear, and all hope of our success will vanish with him.'

The young Romani nodded. 'Then I am torn as to my course. You may have sore need of all of us in the shipyards but if his containment is that crucial then my men would perhaps be better placed outside the exits of the place to catch any fleeing personnel?'

Dragi nodded slowly. 'There are two main roads leading from the shipyard and a few minor places of egress. Between you all, you and your men could make sure no one leaves unobserved.' He bit his cheek and frowned. 'I will draw less suspicion entering the yards without a large force anyway. I can claim a tour for inspection with a few men, but ten could be viewed as a danger, so I will just take my friends here in. You create a cordon outside, and if anyone who could be a paşa makes to flee, bring him down and wait for our reappearance.'

The ferry touched the end of the jetty with a bump and then ground alongside, slowing until the sailors secured the lines and ran out the ramp. Waiting patiently for a few of the higher-class travellers to leave the vessel first, Dragi and his party strode out onto the wooden boards and made their way to the shore. Despite the ease of their journey so far, Diego seemed if anything to have *increased* in tension and suspicion as they reached this trans-fluvial district, and his eyes darted everywhere as the ten of them strode along the shore beneath the walls of Galata, which rose high and strong to match their counterparts across the water at the city proper.

The work-sheds and roofed dry-docks of the great Galata shipyards loomed like the red-tiled carapaces of a bale of titanic tortoises sunning themselves on the shoreline, all surrounded by a high perimeter wall. Further along the shore and close to the naval headquarters, as the Golden Horn narrowed slightly, the looming, brooding shapes of the new naval prison and arsenal sat, the latter still in the final stages of construction. As the group passed from the more civic area of Galata – the heart of the suburb sealed off within its ancient defensive walls which marched up the slope away from the water – the young Romani nodded to Dragi and made a number of gestures and guarded comments to his men in their own language. At the commands, the six men melted away into side alleys, leaving the four of them approaching the eastern gate to the shipyards in an almost deserted street. It struck Skiouros as odd that despite the janissaries' naval branch having two men on the gate to prevent unauthorised access, there was little in the way of actual defence, and the two leaves of the gate itself stood wide open, granting them a clear view of the organised chaos that was the empire's greatest naval installation. Within the walls, almost every inch of space that was not occupied by an actual building was filled with piles of timber and other stores, drums of ropes and even – most surprising of all – a selection of cannon of different size, recently cast and as yet unencumbered with fittings, awaiting transport to the kadirga that would bear them across the seas.

The janissaries paid a little more attention as the four men approached, their curiosity piqued by the odd makeup of the group. Despite Dragi's naval uniform, the two men demanded his papers as he came to a halt. Once more whipping out his orders, the Romani waited patiently, his hands behind him and tucked into his belt as the janissaries checked his papers. Satisfied as to his identity and authority, they welcomed Dragi Reis to the shipyard and told him that if he was seeking his new command, he would have to report to the yard-emin's office and see the secretary or one of his clerks. Skiouros nodded his understanding.

'And where would the emin himself be found?' he asked, his voice level and professional. 'As a new captain I need to make my presence known.'

The janissary shrugged, but his companion at the far side of the gate gestured to the nearest of the large buildings. 'The paşa is in the great dock, reviewing Göke, the new ship.'

'A ship I would like to take a look at.'

The janissary gave him a knowing smile. Sailors were always so sentimental about ships. 'The emin-paşa will not mind you having a look around. You are not the first to visit, nor will you be the last.'

Dragi thanked the man and gave a commanding wave to his three companions, leading them into the shipyard. As they moved towards the great dry dock, open to the sea but walled and roofed, Skiouros peered at the piles of goods all around him. Ropes and timber from Anatolia, cannon cast in the Bulgar lands to the north, local Thracian pitch and all manner of goods imported from within the empire and even beyond its bounds. The piles of goods alone were enough to make a merchant salivate and start calculating values and as Skiouros cast a sidelong glance at Parmenio, his friend seemed almost buzzing with possibility as he took in the various goods.

All around them, poor, scruffy slaves – infidels taken captive during decades of Ottoman warfare – moved about the yard, lugging goods and stacking crates alongside their free Turkish workman counterparts. Skiouros tried not to look the slaves in their hopeless, dead eyes. Slaves were a rare sight in Ottoman lands, being hard to come by legally and too much trouble for most individuals to keep. But at the oars of Turkish trade ships and in great workplaces such as these, captured Christians and even the strange men from the east of Ottoman lands were at work, helping bolster that same empire that had enslaved them in the first place. Not aboard naval ships, of course – their oarsmen needed to be able to fight in an engagement – but on a trade caique, slaves were not uncommon at the oar.

The huge building that housed Göke dominated the near end of the vast shipyard and the door that provided access stood closed but unattended. After all, with all points of access to the yard itself under the watchful eyes of the naval janissaries, and the shoreline watched and patrolled and in many places walled off, there was almost no chance of anyone being here unauthorised. Still, despite that, Skiouros kept his head down and his gaze lowered as a small detachment of janissaries trooped past them in dress uniform, their hats displaying a stylised ship on the crest identifying the *orta* to which they belonged as a naval one. Despite the fact that he had every right to be here in the entourage of a new ship's captain, old habits died hard.

The doors loomed ahead and, despite their plainness and mundanity, to Skiouros they might as well have been leaden tomb doors or the gates to hell, for he felt his pulse begin to race as he neared them, the hair standing proud on the back of his neck as shivers passed up and down his spine. Beyond that door lay his enemy. Not the unfortunate cook from the old palace, or the agents of the Papacy, or even that brutal butcher Hassan, but the *king-breaker*. Though his conscious mind dismissed any mysticism as drivel and he could only reason that this was another ordinary human who had been manoeuvred or manipulated by another group of Romani in much the same was as he himself, something about the fact that he was about to meet the man set him almost into a panic. Dragi and the other Romani from the shanty-house in Aksaray would have him believe that this man was a powerful force for the opposition and in some way just as critical to them as Skiouros was to Dragi's people.

He tried to shrug off the oddness, but it wouldn't go. At a basic conscious level, he wanted to sneer, wanted to tell Dragi and his people that they could deal with their own problems, that there was no need for him to play any part in this huge mess. But perhaps, if he thought things through, there *was*. Assuming this king-breaker was a true opposite number then the two of them would be essentially impartial third parties. Perhaps that was what they had been needed for? In the same way as the king-maker and the king-breaker of the folk tale had been approached to adjudicate a succession in which they had no part, so perhaps had Skiouros and his counterpart been sought to grant a level of impartiality that the Romani themselves were unable to achieve?

And whatever his opposite number had attempted, Skiouros had done just that. Dragi and his people believed that Selim was the future of the empire, and that neither Korkut nor Ahmet were worthy of the succession, but Skiouros had flown in the face of that, even with all Dragi's grisly presentations. He had decided that neither Korkut nor Ahmet deserved to be removed from the running. He had stated that the succession should proceed as history intended. And consequently, he had brought Dragi and his people along that path, attempting to remove the threat to *all* the princes rather than concentrating on promoting Selim and thwarting his brothers. What, though, had his counterpart for the opposition decided? Clearly he favoured Ahmet, for their agents were in place for the kill with the other two princes...

Good. He'd needed that moment of mental reasoning to prepare for what lay beyond the door. And if he'd felt a touch of uncertainty before, it had now vanished in a puff of logic. Whoever this paşa was, he needed to be stopped in order to allow the succession to run fairly.

Dragi opened the door and stepped inside.

The great dry dock was not nearly as busy as Skiouros had expected, but then it appeared that work on Göke was complete and all that remained was to launch her and raise the masts and rigging that lay waiting on deck. A small group of workers were coiling a rope and bagging a pile of unused wooden pegs near the door, and a second group with an overseer were checking the ramps that led down from the ship to the water but apart from them, the great shed was clear of workers.

Not clear of *other* occupants, though.

179

Eleven men stood atop the deck of the largest kadirga ever built, ten of them in the dress of soldiers, bearing swords at their hips, though otherwise unarmoured. One of the soldiers held tight to a standard topped by a crescent and with a limp dark-red horse tail hanging from it, signifying the presence of a paşa of the lower grade.

And amid those ten men, close to the standard, stood the paşa in charge of the Galata shipyard himself – the king-breaker at the heart of the opposition. Skiouros stared.

The king-breaker was not an imposing man, lithe and small in stature, dressed well, if conservatively, with an 'affluent turban' – a domed headpiece of white, surrounded by a bulky band of well-wrapped white linen. He could be any well-off or noble Turk in the street, but for his face.

Skiouros became aware that Parmenio and Diego were looking back and forth between Skiouros and the king-breaker, but before the paşa had noted the presence of the new arrivals, he had turned his back and descended into the bowels of Göke with half his men, leaving the other five to guard his standard on deck.

As those remaining five, their attention no longer held by their lord, turned to look at the four men, Skiouros tipped his head down, concealing his face before they could get a good look.

For gazing upon the face of the king-breaker had been like looking in a dark mirror. Had Skiouros not spent five years in the desert sun of Africa and on the decks of ships open to the elements on the wide seas, he would never have bronzed as he had and his hair would never have achieved its recent golden tint. And if that had not happened, he could have passed for the twin of the man who had just descended below deck. Shudder-inducing memories filled his mind's eye: the *dream-him*. The man at the heart of those terrible disguises that had been a darkened, somehow sick version of himself. Suddenly it was a great deal harder to dismiss those seemingly-prescient dreams as merely the product of Dragi's smouldering hemp.

Trying to ignore Parmenio and Diego's goggling expressions, Skiouros bent, wincing at the pulling in his shoulder-wound, and picked up an oddly-shaped piece of cut-and-sanded timber, pretending to examine it closely, keeping his face down. As he caught Dragi's face he was gratified to note that even the Romani seemed to have been thrown by this development.

Stepping into the strange silence before the paşa's guards could question their presence, Dragi gestured to the great ship and began to speak in Turkish, noting various aspects of its construction with the level of knowledge that only an Ottoman sailor could manage, pointing out interesting facets to the others. Despite the fact that Parmenio could understand only the occasional word and that Diego could have absolutely no idea what he was talking about, the pair of them nodded as though they were absorbing every detail, playing the part in which they had been cast with no warning. The Romani began to stroll down towards the enormous ship's bow, in the direction of the water, still opining about the ship in a clear, knowledgeable voice. His expertise, combined with his naval uniform, seemed to allay the suspicions of the paşa's guards and, though they continued to watch the four new arrivals, they made no attempt to question them or follow them down the ship. The paşa's men were, after all, just bodyguards. They would have little knowledge about the etiquette and authority of naval personnel within the shipyard, assuming them to be here with permission.

As the four of them neared the bow of the vast ship, closing on the hull so that it overhung like a towering cliff, punctured at regular intervals with huge oar holes, Dragi continued to speak about the ship intermittently, but whispered in Greek between.

'...three times the size of the bow of our last ship, but with the same angle to allow for speed, despite the bulk...'

'*That is Sincabı-paşa! The king-breaker is Sincabı-paşa!*'

'...and the scale of the bow is such that it should be able to hold twelve guns on two different firing levels, four of them facing forwards and eight arrayed in an arc...'

'*Who is Sincabı-paşa?*' hissed Skiouros, frowning at the all-too familiar part of that name.

'...you'll note how the front is built up into a massive forecastle much like the ships of the western nations...

'*Sincabı-paşa is the man the sultan rewarded for saving his life. The man who claimed credit for your deeds...*'

Skiouros stared as Dragi started to drone about the huge ram that protruded from the bow, almost as thick across as Skiouros was tall.

'*He cannot be allowed to leave the ship. This is our best chance,*' the Romani whispered between statistics.

'*How can we get to him, though?*' Skiouros mouthed. '*His men guard the deck.*'

'*There is more than one way to board this vessel.*'

*

Tigran nodded to his companion across the road. Kulagyoz sat on the grassy shore some thirty feet from the shipyard wall, idly mending a fishing net he had picked up from a pile of refuse on the way, chewing on a clove and looking for all the world like a local fisherman at work in the hot sun. Kulagyoz nodded back at him in confirmation that all was still apparently uneventful. Tigran relaxed back into the shade of the doorway of a wooden house that sat below the Galata walls with a good view of the eastern gate through which Dragi and the others had entered.

All was quiet, barring the constant sounds of sawing and hammering from within the walls of the great shipyard, and the only life in the street had been a shoeless urchin who had wandered past earlier with a slightly misshapen toy ball. All was quiet, but Tigran was prepared – he had a knife at his belt, as did all six of them, though he did not expect to have to use it. The plan would succeed or fail without them, all in the shipyard. Most *likely* fail, in fact. It was foolish of Dragi and the three foreigners to enter the shipyard, especially to face such an important personage who would be well defended. Tigran felt a little disheartened by this reckless plan of action. Dragi and his friends may succeed, but most likely they would die in the attempt and the six of them on watch would wait until dark or until the bodies were carried out, and then return to Aksaray to report to old Mustafa that Dragi had failed and had managed to get this apparently-important king-maker killed in the process.

But he would do his duty, regardless. He would watch the walls and if a paşa attempted to leave – there would only be one such important man in the shipyard – he would leap upon the man and put a knife to his spine.

He yawned.

And gagged.

The hand that slapped around his mouth and nose, cutting off his air and all sound was large and hairy, so strong and applied with such force that Tigran felt his nose crack under the pressure. He felt the prick of a needle point through his shirt and vest, the tip of a misericorde resting over his heart. Panic flooded Tigran the Romani cartwright, for even the slightest move in defence of his life would almost certainly result in that long, slender knife sliding between his ribs.

His eyes darted to Kulagyoz, but his heart sank as something hissed from the shadows of another nearby building and smacked into his friend's back with a dull thud, the man folding instantly and slumping forward over his broken net.

'What... what do you want?' Tigran managed in a desperate whisper.

His only answer was the agony of the blade sliding through the flesh, between his ribs, seeking his heart. Tigran looked up as the blade turned, speeding his passing, his disbelieving eyes meeting a cold, ice-blue gaze as his spirit fled. His pulse faltered as his last breaths gasped, mixed with blood.

Chapter thirteen – Of blades and hunters

May 27th - Two days to the festival

DRAGI stood tapping the timber of the hull, which curved up and out above them like some colossal ligneous cliff, talking low and quiet at first. Some distance away around the curve of the bow, the group of workers at the ramp began to step up their task, several men hammering rhythmically at the timbers, driving pegs into extra beams added to the ramp to take the phenomenal weight of the titan as it slid out into the Golden Horn. The noise, especially as another pair began to saw extra timbers, was immense, and echoed like the arguments of gods around the huge shed.

Dragi heaved a sigh of relief at the extra aural cover the sawing and hammering provided, which would drown out all but the loudest of noises and, from the quantity of timber they were preparing, would go on for some time.

'We have to move fast,' he said. 'The guards see nothing amiss, but if we tarry too long they will become suspicious.'

'How do we get aboard?' Skiouros murmured.

With a smile, Dragi bent his knees, crouched a little, and then sprang upwards with vigour. His fingers reached the timbers of the external housing for the oars some nine feet from the ground, and his hands wrapped around the lip, allowing the Romani captain to haul himself up into the space from where, when afloat, one of the great oars would project. As the Romani disappeared into the darkness of the interior, Skiouros caught Parmenio's look of disbelief and smiled. Then Dragi reappeared, reaching down through the hole with both hands.

Skiouros stretched, rubbed his wounded shoulder gingerly and then jumped, catching his friend's hands with his good arm and allowing Dragi to pull him up into the oar hole, almost separating his other shoulder in the process. Dragi then reached down again and clenched his teeth as Diego jumped, the Romani grabbing his wrists and hauling him up into the ship with a grunt. A moment later, and with no small amount of cursing and imprecations, Parmenio joined them in the gloomy interior of the greatest Ottoman ship ever built.

'Where now?' Skiouros whispered as he looked around the darkness in trepidation, crouched on a rowers' bench.

Dragi tapped his lip thoughtfully. 'From here and down will just be oar benches and hold space. Above us will be the main gun deck – unusually for a kadirga, Göke carries a full array of cannon inboard from bow to stern. From there we can reach the main deck, but we would be well advised to stay below and not risk bringing the other five guards down if we can avoid it. The door that *Sincabı-Paşa* took will have led him aft, and there will be steps back there that can lead us up to where he is.' He listened carefully. The sound of the workmen was a little muted by the ship's hull, but would still mask sounds like opening doors and footsteps, especially to the soldiers on deck. He smiled.

'Also: one deck up, abaft, we will likely find the armoury. If all goes well they will have stocked it and from there we move up quietly and quickly until we find them.' He smiled at Skiouros. 'I told you God would provide, and in this instance, luck and the navy both aid him.'

'And what then?' Parmenio asked.

'And then you and I and Diego silence the paşa's men as quickly as we can while Skiouros deals with the man in charge.'

'Three against five. I don't like the odds,' Parmenio grumbled.

'I could always pop up top and make it three against ten?' Dragi snapped. 'Come on.'

Without further pause, Dragi stalked off towards the rear of the ship. Skiouros looked about himself as he followed, impressed at the scale of the vessel. With three full decks and several smaller ones to fore and aft, it bore more resemblance to a western carrack or caravel than its forebears, though on this particular deck, with just

185

one huge open space lined with low benches, it still resembled the traditional galley of the Turkish navy, just hidden beneath layers of sailing ship. She really was a monster. Their footsteps echoed around the empty shell of the deck, and to Skiouros they sounded deafening, forcing him to remind himself that the workmen's racket outside would cover the sounds enough that they would only be audible in this great space and not to the enemy above.

An open stairway up into the next deck lay amidships, next to another that led down into the hold and, as they approached, Dragi motioned for quiet, slipping from a fast pace to a virtual creep. Despite the fact that the gun deck lay between the four of them and the paşa's men atop, there were no doors on the stairwell, and there was at least a small chance that sound could carry up two decks and give them away. Skiouros listened nervously, but could hear nothing over the distant sawing and hammering. Once they had passed the faint glow of light that filtered down from above and returned to the gloom heading aft, they picked up the pace again, worrying no more about the volume.

Swiftly they approached the steps at the rear and, with Dragi in the lead, began to ascend. The Romani kept to quiet, steady footfalls now, aware that they were closing on their prey. Pausing at the top to peer into the gloom of the gun room, Dragi motioned for them to follow and emerged onto that deck. The gun ports, still awaiting the cannon that lay in piles in the shipyard grouped by size, let in more light than the oar holes had, given that they faced out and not down, and consequently this wide space was slightly less dim than the lower deck.

The aft section of the deck was dominated by a huge capstan that rose through the timber above to the next deck. The steps climbed again to that upper space, and to the rear lay two doors, side by side, granting access to enclosed stern rooms.

'Too deep down for a captain's cabin,' Parmenio hissed, earning a searing glance from Dragi along with a motion to keep quiet. The Romani pointed up, and as everyone strained, they could hear the faint, muted sounds of conversation above.

Parmenio leaned close to his friends and whispered in a voice like the wafting of a cobweb in a breeze. 'Probably the armoury and the infirmary. The main magazine will be in the hold for both safety and balance.'

Dragi nodded and crept to one of the doors. Taking a breath, he grasped the door handle and turned it. Thankfully, with the newness of construction, the metalwork was well oiled and the wood had not yet picked up a creak. Drawing a breath, ready for the unknown, Dragi slowly swept the door open. This room, far enough above the waterline to allow for a few comforts, had a small window in the stern which let in enough light to see by well enough.

'My mistake,' Parmenio whispered as they took in the basic fittings of what appeared to be a galley. Though Skiouros had seen the kitchens of plenty of ships over the past few years, its presence still came as something of a surprise here. The vessels of the Ottoman navy had always been basic galleys of one sort or another and consequently their modus operandi had required them to put into port each evening. Turkish ships were not designed for extended durations at sea, and consequently were not equipped with such things as armouries and galleys. What they were witnessing with Göke was not just the launching of an outsize ship as an admiral's flagship as they had first imagined. Clearly this represented a shift in naval thinking. The Turkish world was changing, moving forward. Skiouros found himself picturing a fleet of these monsters rolling across the waves like leviathans, heading for Heraklion. They would be every bit the match for the Venetian warships, and then some.

He shivered at the image.

The four returned to the main space of the deck, Parmenio earning another sharp glance from Dragi as his boot creaked on a badly-fitted board. The Genoese sailor rolled his eyes and, stepping past the Romani, quietly opened the other door.

'Wonderful,' he whispered, pulling the door back to reveal what was clearly an infirmary – another advance for Bayezid's navy. An on-board physician to treat the inevitable sick and wounded among the crew and the rowers was new to the Turkish fleet. Skiouros slid into the room and looked around. The infirmary was already stocked, from surgical kits to blankets, towels and rags to racks of potions and salves, all carefully labelled in a neat script. The presence of a number of medical texts on a shelf, including the 'Kitab al-Tasrif' of Al-Zahrawi and the 'Cerahiyyetü 'l-Haniyya' of Serafeddin Sabuncuoglu, suggested that the ship's medic had kitted out the room himself.

In the absence of a well-appointed armoury, Skiouros crossed to the rear wall, beneath the window, and ran his hands along the boxes and cases of equipment until he found a particularly large knife, almost the length of his forearm. Wincing as his mind prompted the question as to its intended use and his imagination attempted to supply suggestions, Skiouros stepped back towards the door. It was no crusader blade, but it was far better than nothing. With a smile, he spotted a crate of splints in the corner and selected a larger one. While not as fine and well-weighted as his macana stick, it would still fetch a heavy blow to a man's head, if his shoulder would cope with the swing. Brandishing his two weapons, he stepped back out into the gloom and waited. Dragi followed suit, emerging from the physician's room with two heavy knives. Diego selected the next largest blades in the room, and Parmenio huffed irritably as he scanned the tools, realising that he was stuck with little more than scalpels or saws.

Grumbling almost silently under his breath, the Genoese sailor dipped back into the galley and emerged with one knife and a large, heavy brass ladle. He rolled his eyes again as he re-joined the group and Skiouros gave him a smile. 'Don't knock it,' he whispered. 'The janissaries use a ceremonial one of those as a weapon too.'

'Very handy when they go to war against a tureen of peppered belly-pork stew.'

Skiouros had to stifle a chuckle and the four men turned at the sound of a raised voice from above. Whoever it was, it sounded angry and, from the hint of steely command in the tone, Skiouros could only imagine it was his counterpart berating his men.

Dragi pointed upwards and then moved to the stairs, testing them carefully to make sure they didn't creak as he started to climb, staying to one side to put the least possible pressure on the boards and avoid potential noises.

Again, the group paused as the Romani reached the top and peered out into the open area beneath the quarterdeck. Cannon ports at the sides illuminated the space, and a door ahead would lead out onto the main deck – the very door through which Sincabı-Paşa had entered the ship. As he emerged, Skiouros found himself straining to hear the five soldiers out there talking, but all he could hear was the interminable battering of hammers and rasping of saws.

The stairs ended here. Above was only a small aft deck which would likely house the cabin of the reis, and that would be accessible only from the quarterdeck. There were three doors leading to rooms at the rear of this area, and the sound of the raised voice still haranguing his men came from the central one.

Not daring to speak, Skiouros pointed to the left and right doors and then gestured with his blade and stick, trying to convey the suggestion that they check the side rooms for a potential armoury, but Dragi shook his head. He was right: they were too close to the enemy now to risk alerting them through a noisy search of the adjoining rooms.

Using hand signals only, Dragi motioned to the Greek to take the door and open it, stepping back to the side and letting the other three in first. Skiouros nodded. The five soldiers would have to be taken care of fast. Dragi then gestured to Diego to move left and Parmenio right. The pair nodded their understanding and readied their makeshift weapons.

Skiouros took a steadying breath. This was it. Four men against six, and it had to be quick and as quiet as possible. Too much racket and the other soldiers out on deck would be alerted, making the odds so much less favourable.

Stepping forward, the young Greek reached out for the door handle and almost died of fright that very second as the handle turned beneath his grip. Instinct ruling him far more than conscious decision, he let go and stepped back to one side, behind the door as it began to open. Suddenly aware of the unexpected change in plans, the others reacted swiftly, stepping sharply away against the cabin walls, leaving only open space in front of the door.

The first man out, a moustachioed ghazi with a darker skin-tone that marked him as a southern Anatolian Turk from close to the border of Mamluk Syria, wore a chastened, embarrassed expression. The second man, following close on his heel, looked equally unhappy through his bearded, Balkan-hued, lined face. Further footsteps announced the approach of the others within. Skiouros watched as Dragi emerged from the shadows like some demon of ancient legend, stepping behind one of the blissfully ignorant soldiers and swiping one of his knives across the man's throat even as he pushed the other up under the ribcage, seeking his heart.

As the man died, gasping quietly, only aware of his attacker's existence as the life flooded out of him, Diego stepped with catlike grace from the far side, in front of his surprised prey, one blade jabbing out three times in quick succession and ripping into his chest while the other slid up beneath the man's chin, sliding through his mouth and deep into his brain. He shuddered and frothed for a moment before falling from the Spaniard's blades as he withdrew them.

Skiouros stared with wondrous horror at the efficient butchery perpetrated by his friends. Two heartbeats had passed and already the odds were balanced. As the two men finished off their prey, a third soldier stepped through the door, noting what had happened to his companions, and opened his mouth to shout a warning back into the room.

The man's head snapped to one side as a spray of blood and three teeth spattered and rattled against the door, his face battered and flattened by the heavy brass spoon end of the outsized ladle. Parmenio gave the man with the broken face no time to recover as he pulled back his ladle and struck again, this time bringing the weighty end down in an overhand blow and smacking the stunned soldier between the eyes.

Not even bothering with his knife, Parmenio gave the man a hefty kick in the crotch and pushed him back through the door where he fell against the other two soldiers, who were finally aware that something was wrong. The pile of men staggered back into the chamber – a navigation and chart room by the look of it – and fell to the floor. Skiouros passed the grinning Parmenio, brandishing his ladle lovingly, and stepped into the room first, the others closing in behind him.

Parmenio's victim was out of the fight. Not mortally wounded, but thoroughly stunned and disorientated, collapsed on the floor, his eyes rolled up into his head. The other two soldiers – one huge ogre of a man and one hatchet-faced northerner – were floundering on the floor, trying to pull themselves together.

At the far end of the cabin, close to the window, stood Skiouros' curious doppelganger. The paşa opened his mouth to shout for help, but then his gaze fell upon the man leading this intrusion and his eyes widened in stunned recognition. Lightly stepping around the fallen men, Skiouros advanced on the king-breaker, Sincabı-Paşa, his long knife and his makeshift cudgel held out to the sides ready for trouble.

Behind Skiouros the other three were now appearing through the doorway. The sight of the extra intruders broke the spell and the man opened his mouth again. Skiouros leapt for him, trying to silence him before he could utter a word, but Sincabı-Paşa was fast – faster by far than Skiouros was expecting. Another facet in his reflection of the former street-thief?

Even as the man bounded to the side, away from Skiouros' lunge, ripping a curved blade from his sheath, he bellowed to his guards outside for help. The men on the floor were now half-up, struggling to fight off the attacks of Skiouros' friends. Now that they had recovered from the shock of the attack their warrior training was back in control and even on the defensive, they were presenting difficulties for Dragi and Parmenio. Diego, still in the doorway, was busy requisitioning a sword from one of the fallen.

From back across the open deck there came the sound of voices raised in sharp reply to Sincabı-paşa's call, even above the workmen. The other soldiers were coming. Skiouros had little time to devote any attention to the matter, however, as he leapt once again towards the king-breaker.

Behind him, Dragi finally overcame the man with whom he'd been struggling and put his two blades into the man's sides, ripping them out in a shower of crimson and then plunging them back in for good measure. The soldier stiffened and then fell away with a gurgle of agony. Parmenio was wrestling with what looked like an angry bear in a turban, trying to bring his ladle and knife to a useful position as the man's huge arms, rippling with muscle and matted with dark hair, gradually forced the former sailor back off him.

'*Why do I... always... get the big one?*' Parmenio grumbled breathlessly as he fought. Desperately, he looked around to Dragi for help as the Romani wiped his blades on his latest victim and examined a thin cut across the back of his hand. Diego was missing, but the sound of fighting from out in the main deck confirmed that he had gone to head off the paşa's reinforcements.

'Dragi?' he managed to breathe as he struggled, his eyes flicking to the ursine bastard with the thick beard who was nearly breaking his arms, pushing him up.

The Romani nodded and said 'You have things under control,' before running out through the door to help the beleaguered Diego against five more well-prepared men. Parmenio stared for a moment, and then bent back to his titanic struggle with the big man below him.

Skiouros found himself in an unenviable position. Though he had Sincabı-Paşa backed into the corner of the navigation room, he was brandishing a knife and a stick, while his enemy held a good sword in a grip which suggested that he knew how to use it.

'Who *are* you?' breathed Sincabı-Paşa in Turkish, in a fascinated voice, his eyes narrowing. There was something odd about those eyes. Nothing clear, but...

'Can you not guess?'

The man shrugged. 'You are the supposed *king-maker*, for all this Romani superstition counts. But who *are* you?'

Skiouros felt an odd thrill to realise that this man – his opposite number among the enemy – seemed to share his sceptical opinion. He found himself wondering momentarily whether Sincabı-Paşa had considered a different path, just as he had. The fact that the man went by the familiar appellation Sincabı only added to a sudden strange feeling of kinship for which he felt unprepared.

'My name is Skiouros.'

'A Greek.' The king-breaker looked past Skiouros with his odd eyes to where Parmenio and the huge soldier were grunting and struggling on the floor. 'For the love of God, Rashid, will you finish him?'

Skiouros smiled unpleasantly and switched to Greek. If the man knew the name as a Greek word, then he likely knew the language. 'There's no need for this to end in death, Sincabı. I have had enough of killing in my few short years. If you answer my questions and agree to confinement until after the festival, you can then go free.'

'How very generous of you. I doubt your Romani friend out there would approve of the offer.'

'The Romani have pushed us into this, guiding our steps and urging us to carry out their will. But I am not here to interfere with the succession. I am here to *prevent* interference.'

Sincabı-Paşa laughed. 'You fool. I know who you are now, of course – I remember the face, so like mine, but somehow less... You are that Greek who stopped the assassins five years ago. I ought to thank you. There was I, just a street beggar in the rainy square outside the great Aya Sofya, when you ran past all covered in blood and drenched through. The old woman – *dede Babik* – said you chased the assassin down into the cistern. I had no idea what had truly happened, of course, but I spun a very plausible tale as the janissaries found me and took me to the palace. You changed my life that day. From starving beggar to one-tail paşa – favoured of the sultan – in a single day. And so in grateful thanks, I'll reverse your offer. Leave the city now and I will not pursue you. Go and live your small, insignificant life somewhere in the Morea and I will let you have it unmolested.'

Skiouros felt his jaw harden. *Good.* He had been dithering a little just now, unsure of how much he might actually have in common with this man who represented a dark reflection of himself. But the man was riling him now, bringing back the loathing he had felt at the sight of that twisted *dream-Skiouros*, and the anger that rose in response swamped any uncertainty. Still, everyone deserved one more chance...

'You don't have to do what *they* want you to do, Sincabı. Do not allow yourself to be a piece in their game. In three days this will be over and you can *choose* how you want to live.'

The king-breaker shook his head with a small, unpleasant smile.

'You don't understand, killer of Mamluks. It was *I* who persuaded *them* to direct and bloody action, you fool. The Romani favour playing slow games, positioning their pieces and waiting for the acts of others to win the match for them. Why else do you think you and I are here, now? No, Skiouros the thief. It was *I* who persuaded *them* that positioning their prince and hoping for the best was not enough. It was too much of a gamble, and my way Ahmed will rise to the throne knowing that he owes much of his advance to me. His father made me a one-tail paşa, but that is not enough. Funny thing about power: there never seems to be enough. Becoming powerful just makes you want more. It's like a drug, Skiouros. And when Ahmed is sultan, he will make me grand vizier for my efforts. And then, one day, who knows...'

Skiouros looked into the gaze of his opponent and realised suddenly that what he'd not been able to identify in the man's eyes was plain and simple madness. He'd seen it before in the terrifying gaze of the butcher pirate Etci Hassan – a specific form of madness, too, fuelled with horrifying purpose; channelled, distilled and then compacted down to a diamond. There was no hope of reasoning with the man.

'You *will* tell me who the man in Selim's court is, and anyone you have in the palace of the sultan, too. I assure you of it,' Skiouros said in a flat tone.

'Words. Empty words. My men outnumber yours. I outclass you. This will be over swiftly and then my plans will continue apace. You have saved Korkut, and congratulations for that, but he is the weakest of the three, and we will deal with him in due course. Selim will die tomorrow as planned, and then Bayezid will expire at the festival by my own fair hand – I am, after all, part of his glorious celebration, given how selflessly a Greek peasant endangered his own life to save that of his Ottoman master. I will be close to his side at the festival. And after that Ahmed will soon put an end to his remaining brother. Now, enough of these empty words. Come for me so we can end this.'

Skiouros, trying to ignore the sounds of Parmenio's desperate struggle behind him, lunged, his long knife aimed at Sincabı's heart. A predictable and basic attack – not much more he could do with a knife, really. But as the paşa stepped lightly to the side out of the way of the attack, the real purpose of the Greek's feint became clear as the wooden baton lashed out sharply, jabbing into the man's wrist. Skiouros yelped at the sharp pain in his shoulder as he thrust, but Sincabı also hissed, almost dropping the sword as his hand numbed. Quickly he flicked the blade to his other hand and brandished it ready. Skiouros sagged. *Ambidextrous too*?

There was nothing else he could do for a few moments as Sincabı took the opportunity to retaliate, his blade lancing out with breath-taking speed, causing Skiouros to dance back and left to stay out of its reach. In a panic, he bumped his back into the chart table and had to duck sharply to one side to avoid being skewered there and then. Sincabı's right hand hung down at his side, the baton-blow to his wrist having deadened his whole hand, but his left came back with the blade, twisting it ready to deliver a slash with the curved edge. At least, with both of them arm-wounded, they were a little more evenly-matched again.

Skiouros leapt back, the blade's swipe coming so near that he felt the rush of air across his throat. That was *too* close. And then suddenly Sincabı was there again like some sort of battle nightmare, his sword slashing, stabbing and lunging so fast that Skiouros had little opportunity to do anything but leap out of the way and back across the room. On came the paşa, and Skiouros staggered over the struggling bodies of Parmenio and the big man, almost falling. Reeling and skittering, on the desperate defensive, Skiouros suddenly had to raise his makeshift club to save his skin, the sword blow shearing it off just above knuckle height.

Left with just his knife now, Skiouros gained a moment's breather as Sincabı paused in his pursuit to drive his sword down swiftly through both Parmenio and the bear beneath him, ending that fight. Skiouros, his blood running cold at the sight of that steel blade rising from his friend's back as it was jerkily removed, suddenly snapped, screamed, and leapt at Sincabı, his knife aiming for the paşa's throat.

His advance halted due to his pause to dispatch the other combatants, Sincabı was now suddenly on the defensive again, his enemy close enough to use that knife effectively and to render the longer sword almost useless. Skiouros managed to sink the blade of the surgeon's knife into the man's shoulder and arm, but Sincabı was still quick and soon the space was opening up between them again and that curved sword came round, holding Skiouros at bay.

'Revenge sits well with you,' the king-breaker laughed. 'It makes you fight back.'

Skiouros felt panic rise to fill the hollowness inside. The loss of his old friend was about to be compounded by his own death. He was starting to tire a little now, and the paşa was still clearly the better warrior, still better armed and now on the offensive once again.

Desperately, Skiouros held up his knife to ward off a blow that would almost certainly end him. The sword blade grated down the knife edge, bounced on the hilt and cut a layer of skin off the top of two of Skiouros' knuckles. In pain and unintentionally, Skiouros' fingers flexed and the knife fell away. Now he was unarmed.

Sincabı-Paşa stepped in for the kill, sword pulled back for the final blow, and then suddenly he staggered, floundered and fell in a heap. Skiouros looked down in surprise to see Parmenio's ladle tangled in the man's feet. The Genoese captain was struggling to rise, clutching his belly.

'Fucking show off!'

Skiouros laughed loud as Parmenio painfully passed him the big bear-soldier's sword. Sincabı-Paşa was looking a little dazed, his head having glanced off the table as he fell. Skiouros stepped calmly over to him and kicked the man's blade away as Parmenio staggered upright behind him.

'I always said being a bit on the meatier side did you no harm,' the sailor grinned. 'Plenty of body that's not organ.'

Skiouros crouched and then, very deliberately, kneeled on his enemy's already pained wrist. Sincabı-Paşa yelped.

'Who is the man in Selim's palace?'

The king-breaker looked up at him, the madness in his eyes laced with defiance. 'I do not fear you, Skiouros Mamluk-killer. You can't finish me. If you do, your prince will die anyway.'

'But we can make you *wish* you were dead,' Parmenio grunted, pointing angrily with a finger glistening red with his own blood.

Outside the door, the sounds of fighting were dying away, though whether for good or ill they could not tell.

195

'You want to be Skiouros?' Parmenio snapped at the paşa. 'You want to be the hero-thief? Well remember what your sharia law has in store for thieves?' Gritting his teeth against the pain in his abdomen, the Genoese grabbed Skiouros' fallen knife and placed the blade over the paşa's wrist. Sincabı stared in sudden dread and tried to pull his hand away. With Skiouros still kneeling on his right wrist, Parmenio knelt on the man's left forearm with all his weight and once more placed the blade above that wrist. Slowly, he put the weight of his bloodied hand on the hilt and balled his fist, ready to bring it down above the tip. The knife would not sever the wrist in this way, of course. Not the *first* time, anyway...

'Sefer bin Yunus,' gasped Sincabı-paşa desperately. Parmenio raised his fist but left the knife threateningly in place. 'Sefer bin Yunus,' the paşa repeated, the words coming out fast and almost garbled. 'He is Selim's closest advisor and he is the man. But you will not be able to get to him!'

Skiouros heaved a sigh of relief. 'Don't be too sure about that. We're very inventive people.'

A noise drew his attention back to the door, and he felt relief flood though him to see Diego and Dragi return, though the Spaniard was limping badly and the Romani's face was so sheeted with blood it was impossible to tell whether he was wounded or not. The way he swayed as he crossed the room to this little torture-tableau suggested that he was not unharmed after the desperate fray out there.

'What has he said?' Dragi huffed as he rested against the table.

'He gave us a name. Sefer bin Yunus – I remember him from the Yedikule.'

'Is he telling the truth? I thought Sefer a little too malleable.'

'I believe so,' Skiouros replied. 'Parmenio here was about to hack his hand off.'

'Let me in,' Diego murmured and, with some difficulty on his wounded leg, lowered himself between his friends, facing the paşa. For a long moment, he looked deep into Sincabı's eyes, and finally he shook his head. 'He is stronger and cleverer than you think. That was a lie, beyond a doubt. A man can never hide a lie deep inside his eyes.'

Dragi nodded. 'Then more pressure must be applied.' He crouched with them and with no warning fetched Sincabı a heavy blow to the temple with a balled fist. As the paşa sank into unconsciousness, Dragi removed his turban and began to undo his shirt and outer garments. 'Come on. Help me undress him.'

The others frowned at him, but then Skiouros and Parmenio shared a knowing look, and the latter broke into a grin. 'We'll have to dye your hair and shave you, of course.'

'And first we need the true name.'

Dragi, finishing stripping the paşa to his underwear, nodded. 'The hair can be tucked under the turban. Use one of the doctor's sharp knives to shave. Parmenio, you get him shaved and dressed. De Teba? You and I are going to extract that name.' Leaning forward and hissing in pain, Dragi gasped the near-naked paşa and hauled him over his shoulder. 'Come, Diego.' And with no further word he left the room with the unconscious king-breaker over his shoulder and the concerned-looking Spaniard at his back.

'Will this work?' Parmenio murmured, examining the turban.

'Oddly, this is not my first time at this,' grinned Skiouros.

Chapter fourteen – Of questions and answers

May 27th - Two days to the festival

SINCABI-PAŞA slowly blinked back to consciousness, groggy and confused. His first reaction was to reach up and rub the sore spot on his head, but his arms would not move. Alerted and alarmed by this realisation, memory flooded back in and he slumped, defeated eyes taking in his surroundings. He was on the lower deck, seated against the hull, and his hands were bound tightly behind him to one of the rings next to the gun port, to which in time the gun's carriage would be attached. He was helpless, and he knew it.

Then his eyes, gradually becoming accustomed to the gloom, picked out the two figures crouched before him in the darkness of the deck. He recognised the Romani who had accompanied the Greek into the cabin. The other man was a swarthy looking fellow who somehow managed to carry an air of fineness about him despite the situation. His eyes looked haunted.

'Good,' said the Romani. 'He's awake.'

'And insensate?' suggested the other in a strange foreign accent, yet speaking reasonably good Greek. The man then wandered over and crouched in front of Sincabı. 'How many fingers am I holding up?' he asked.

The paşa frowned, blinked and shook his head. 'None.'

'At least he can see and think, then.'

The Romani nodded. 'Now, my treacherous, devious friend, we are going to have a little conversation. You are going to tell me who you have in the Tekfur Sarayi and how he intends to kill prince Selim in two days' time. And this name will be the correct one and not some random appellation plucked from the air.'

Sincabı-Paşa sneered. 'If your friend in there could not drag the name out of me under torture, what makes you think I will tell you?'

The Romani smiled, and that smile sent a chill of uncertainty through Sincabı. 'Three things, actually. Firstly, the fact that you came up with a good, convincing lie in order to save your hand tells me that your sense of self-preservation overrides your obstinacy. Secondly, that even Parmenio with a surgeon's knife still thinks like a gentleman despite his manner, while I can be most inventive and unrestrained when necessity requires...'

He rose and stepped to one side.

'And thirdly, because you know we have less than two days left and therefore nothing to lose.'

Sincabı-Paşa blinked in surprise at what was revealed when the Romani moved. Behind the man, an *abus* gun stood on its tripod, the wide barrel pointing at the floor. A small case of ammunition sat on the deck next to it, full of iron balls three inches across. He stared. The business end of the gun was facing him.

'You're insane,' the paşa breathed, staring at the gun.

The Romani shrugged. 'You're not the first person to level that accusation. You probably won't be the last.' And whistling a strangely discordant ditty, the Romani sailor walked around behind the gun, tipping it back and opening another box that contained wadding, powder flasks and other artillery accoutrements. Accompanied by the happy tune, he began to load the abus gun, shoving the components down the barrel.

The foreigner – a Spaniard by the accent – shuffled a step closer to Sincabı. His eyes were truly haunted – clearly uneasy with what he was doing. Sincabı latched on to that look with desperate hope. Perhaps this man might be his chance at escape? He opened his mouth to speak, but the Spaniard shook his head slightly.

'Shhh. Don't make him do this. For the love of *Christ*, don't force this. Give me the name.'

'If you don't want him to do it,' Sincabı whispered, 'then *you* could stop him.'

'I don't like this, but I'm no fool, Turk. I'll not let these people kill innocents or good Christians over your little war, but you're hardly an innocent. The gates of heaven would never open for you, and hell awaits your stinking behind. But it should be God that punishes you, not Dragi over there. Give me the name. I might be able to persuade him to let you live…'

Sincabı narrowed his eyes. The Spaniard seemed to be genuinely unhappy with what was going on, yet he seemed equally determined to go through with it. Odd.

'Have you any idea what that gun will do to you,' the man said quietly.

'Kill me. And the name will die with me.'

'It will not just kill you, man. It will *obliterate* you. Back in '81 I was at Zahara de la Sierra when the Emir of Granada broke the truce and took the place. I saw a small artillery piece perhaps an inch wider than this go off and saw what happened to the man it hit at close range. He had to be gathered up by three different men in order to find enough of him to bury.'

Sincabı-Paşa shuddered – not at the image this created, but at the matter-of-fact tone of the Spaniard's voice, as though he were giving a lecture on mining or some such mundanity.

'He will not do it,' he replied, though still quivering. 'I know the Romani. They are cunning, not impulsive or stupid. He knows that to kill me is to remove all hope of learning his quarry's name. And having lived the life of a beggar – beaten and torn – you would be surprised at how resistant to pain I am.'

The Spaniard shook his head, and that open sincerity was still there. 'Don't underestimate Dragi, Paşa. I've seen him do the most unbelievable – and unacceptable – things. If he says he will do it, believe that he will.'

He stopped talking, and the silence was filled with a thudding noise as Dragi rammed the barrel's contents home and shortened the tripod's legs considerably so that the gun pointed directly at the paşa's torso, all the time accompanied by a jolly old lullaby tune.

'And if you're unlikely to respond to torture,' the Spaniard went on, 'then threat is all he has left. It is a wicked thing to kill a man in such a way. Face to face, with a sword against an armed opponent, that I can live with. This…'

Sincabı-Paşa blinked as the man rose to his feet, made the sign of a cross over him, and turned away.

'Where are you going?'

'I have no interest in watching this.'

Panic crept across Sincabı as he finally began to believe that this might actually happen. Would the Romani *really* kill him?

Clearly the *Spaniard* thought so. He tried to speak but only a throaty rasp emerged. A second try came out hoarse but audible.

'If you fire that, half the shipyard will hear.'

The Romani chuckled. 'If you believe that, you've never fired an abus gun. I have done so a number of times aboard a kadirga. They are quite loud, but the hull of this ship will deaden much of the sound. In the shed outside there are men hammering and sawing. They might hear it over the noise they are making, but they are at the other end of the building and I doubt they would recognise the muted thud for a gun shot. Besides, they will not risk disturbing a paşa for the sake of their own curiosity. And no one *outside* the dry-dock will hear over their noise.'

He lifted one of the iron balls from the box, weighed it in his hand, examined it to make sure there were no imperfections in the sphere that could jam in the barrel, and then rolled it into the end of the gun. He came to the end of his lullaby, rather ominously, as he added the final wadding to the barrel and gave it two prods home with the rammer before standing back.

'I am, as you understand, rather short on time, and I have little patience for dithering, so I'm going to ask you just once more: who is the man you have in the Tekfur?'

Sincabı quailed. One part of him simply could not believe that this man would fire the gun. To do so would kill him, and that would defeat the purpose of all this. But another part of him had seen the genuine disgust and belief in the Spaniard's face and it was that part that was making his knees shake uncontrollably even though he was seated.

He tried to imagine what would happen if the gun went off. He would die... wouldn't he? He had a sudden, very unpleasant image of the iron ball passing through his gut without touching his spine or any vital organ, leaving him very much alive and in agony with a three inch hole through his middle. His panic increased again to an almost unbearable level.

'Wait...'

'A name. A genuine one.'

Sincabı felt his bladder and bowel both trying to lose their contents. Whatever *he* understood, it seemed that his *body* believed the gun could go off.

'Musa,' he blurted, and then stared at his own leaking nethers in surprise. Before he could decide whether giving the name was a good idea, he found himself elucidating on it without further consideration. 'Musa bin Ramazan'

The Romani nodded. 'Problem is: you've lied to us about the name once already, and I don't believe you. That look on your face is pure deception and calculation.'

Sincabı-Paşa stared in horror as the Romani lit a small taper and approached the gun, tipping the fine priming-powder into the touch hole.

'No. I told you the truth.'

The paşa began to struggle for the first time, the ropes that bound him rubbing his wrists raw as he tried to wriggle out of them and move out of the line of fire. He was no longer under any illusion that the Romani would do as he had threatened.

'If only I could believe that,' the sailor said, lowering the taper to the touch hole and then stepping off to the side and holding the gun steady. The recoil on these things could be quite impressive. His knuckles whitened as he gripped tight. The powder-soaked fuse in the hole hissed, and the Romani took a deep breath, closing his eyes.

'It is,' babbled Sincabı-Paşa. 'It *is* Musa. It is *Musa bin Ramazan*. He is Selim's turban wrapper!' The fuse burned down into the hole. 'I'm telling you the truuuuuuuuth!' he wailed.

As Sincabı winced and tried to withdraw into himself, there was a faint pop from the gun. The Romani opened his eyes and released his grip, allowing the barrel to drop an inch or so. He gave it a light tap and there was a metallic hollow noise as the iron ball rolled out and clonked to the timber deck, rolling off down the faint slope, leaving a small piece of wadding beneath the weapon.

The paşa stared.

'An Abus gun, like a cannon, needs both fine priming powder in the touch hole and a wad of proper powder in the barrel. Without the latter, not much happens.' He gestured to the pile of powder-packs on the floor.

Sincabı-Paşa stared in disbelief. 'You...'

The Romani turned to the darkness from which the Spaniard re-emerged with a smile.

'What do you think?'

'Absolute truth,' the Spaniard replied. 'No doubt about it.'

'You... y... y...' Sincabı stuttered, staring at the Spaniard.

'I can be every bit as convincing as you, my dear paşa,' the foreigner smiled.

'His turban wrapper,' the Romani mused. 'He would be in an excellent position. It makes sense.' He stretched. 'I think our friends outside have stopped their hammering. Good. Diego, could you check for me?'

As the Spaniard strode off towards the steps leading up to the main deck, the Romani strolled over and looked down at his captive. 'Well played, but just not quite good enough, eh?'

'You bastard,' hissed the paşa, then a thought struck him. He could still win this! If the workers out there had stopped their hammering and sawing, they might hear him now. Swishing the saliva around his dry mouth to prevent a repeat of his hoarseness, he opened his mouth to speak, and was astonished to discover that all that emerged was a faint whistle of air and some sort of tinny-tasting froth.

The pain only struck him as he saw the Romani step back and wipe his crimson surgeon's blade with a piece of gun-wadding. Sincabı-Paşa stared in horror at his killer, trying to curse him to God and the prophet, and to rattle out execrations, but all that emerged was more of that strange whistling from the new mouth beneath his chin and bloody froth from both there and his old mouth. His clothes were beginning to cling to him with the sheets of blood cascading from his neck.

'I would have preferred not to do that, Sincabı-Paşa, but expediency has its own demands, and there was more than a faint chance that the workers would hear you shout.'

Sincabı tried to move, but it seemed his strength was ebbing with his blood.

'I'm afraid that there is no viziership in your future, Sincabı-Paşa. But be consoled with the knowledge that while you die here, your *name* will go on.'

Sincabı-paşa tried to lift a leg from the murk that was a growing pool of mixed blood, urine and faeces, but his leg was cold and numb and heavy as lead. With a sigh of regret, he passed from the world.

*

Diego de Teba dropped the last few steps down the stairs and wandered over. 'They've finished and gone to...' He paused and stared. 'What happened?'

'Sincabı-Paşa has gone to whichever realm awaits him.'

'I thought we weren't going to kill him?' Diego snapped angrily.

'I said I wasn't going to kill him *with the gun*. You really should listen to the details.'

'But why?'

'Because he tried to shout out an alarm and we are still far from out of danger. Because if we let him live he would come back to cause us trouble at some point very soon. Because even on a moral level, the runt deserved to die. Pick a reason. I have more.'

As Dragi tucked his knife away into his belt he straightened. 'Don't let your squeamishness get the better of you, Diego.'

'Simple Christian mercy is not squeamishness.'

'And I am not a Christian, de Teba. I am a practical man with practical solutions. And on that note, we need to dispose of the bodies.'

'Where?'

'Into the Golden Horn. We have a ramp to the water, plenty of rope and lots of ballast we can tie to them. And as long as the bodies are stripped they will not be recognisable for who they are.' As he talked, Dragi strode aft once more, Diego hurrying to keep up. 'We can take their blades and clothes with us, and there will be no damning evidence of what happened here, barring a little blood and mess, and a bucket of water will soon solve that.'

'And what happens when they discover their paşa – the man who runs the shipyard – has vanished? A sultan's favourite? There might be questions.'

Dragi opened the door to the cabin where their fight had taken place with a grin.

'But Sincabı-Paşa is alive and well. See?'

Diego stared at Skiouros who, now wearing the paşa's clothes with the two small sword cuts neatly stitched by a sailor's expert hand, could almost have been Sincabı-Paşa had he not known otherwise. Skiouros had been adjusting the outfit and settling himself into it while Parmenio had stripped the weapons from the dead men. Dragi glanced around the room.

'Good. When I leave here in my true capacity as a newly-commissioned Reis of the Ottoman navy accompanying the shipyard's paşa, you two will need to keep your faces hidden. Parmenio, are you alright to walk?'

The Genoese sailor nodded. 'Getting weak, but I've bandaged myself quite tight. I'll make it back to the city.'

'Good. You are the closest here to the big bear one's build, so you take his clothes, and grab one of those helmets with the mail aventail – that will keep your features hidden. Diego, you can choose any of the others, but you'll have to carry the paşa's standard when we leave, since Parmenio clearly cannot. And try and find another helmet that covers your face... unless you're willing to shave your chin and just wear a moustache? You could *almost* pass for a Turk then?'

The look on the Spaniard's face made the chances of that plain, and Dragi smiled. 'Excellent. We all know what we're doing. You three make yourself look as much like a paşa and his entourage as possible. I'm going to strip the rest of the bodies and weigh them down so we can deliver them into the deep before we leave. Let's get to business, my friends.'

*

Skiouros was almost as uncomfortable and nervous as he'd ever been as he strode purposefully towards the gate of the shipyard. Behind him, Diego was muttering unhappily as the paşa's standard bobbed and dipped with each step, enhanced by the limp he had picked up in the fight, Parmenio's heavy boot steps clunking along in time, occasionally shuffling as the man tried not to succumb to the wound in his side. Despite a thorough search, it had turned out that none of the dead men – even the bear – had feet the size of Parmenio's and so he had stayed in his own boots and pulled the ankles of the trousers over the top to hide the worst of their western-appearance.

The only one who seemed remotely at ease was Dragi, who was striding alongside Skiouros, half a pace behind in deference to their relative ranks. He looked perfectly comfortable, his face serious and professional.

'The Paşa's apparel sits well on you, Skiouros.'

The young Greek answered with an anxious grunt. Would the gate guards not think this odd? The sailor had arrived an hour or so ago with three strange foreigners, and now was leaving with the paşa instead, who had apparently left most of his men behind. Dragi had shrugged off such concerns, convinced that the horn call they had heard ring out across the shipyard while they were changing had signalled a change of shifts. Skiouros had been less sure, but had to defer to his friend's knowledge. After all, Dragi was a sailor, and had been to the Galata yards several times since their arrival.

The gates still stood open and, much to Skiouros' relief, the two men attending them were unfamiliar. Better still, both guards made no attempt even to speak to the four of them, standing back and bowing low in respect for the paşa. In a matter of heartbeats, without issue, the four of them strode out into the wide dusty street that ran along the water's edge beneath the walls of Galata. Part-ruinous extra-mural houses dotted the route below the heavy fortifications and Skiouros frowned.

'Shouldn't your friends be here somewhere?'

'Keep walking. Don't look around,' Dragi replied in a hiss. 'Something is wrong.'

Diego cleared his throat behind them. 'He's right. Something is very wrong. The Romani should be on watch here. They're hardly going to have gone for a wander. And I'm fairly sure we're being watched.'

'I have that feeling too,' added Parmenio as he winced and stumbled again, quickly righting himself. 'My spine's tingling.'

'This could cause us no end of trouble,' Skiouros murmured as the four men passed a ripped fishing net that lay on the grass near the water's edge. His astute gaze picked out the fine spray of blood on both it and the grass. 'Would it be acceptable for a paşa to run?'

Diego breathed deeply. 'Here's what we're going to do. See just ahead? Fifty yards or so?'

They focused on the road ahead and spotted the jetty marching out into the Golden Horn, lined with small rowing boats. The unofficial ferry service run by enterprising locals with which the Spaniard had crossed the water a few nights earlier.

'As soon as we get there, you three pile into a boat and make for the other shore. I'm going to stay here and keep others from pursuing you. I shall meet you at ben Isaac's by nightfall.' Licking dry lips, he tossed the Paşa's standard to Dragi.

'Not ben Isaac's,' the Romani said quietly. 'The time for secrecy is past – tomorrow we move on the palace. Meanwhile our enemies close in around us, and it is no longer fair to put our hosts in any further danger. Instead, we go back to Mustafa's house in the Blachernae ruins.'

Diego nodded. 'Then I'll be there by dark.'

'You can't take them on yourself,' Parmenio breathed shallowly, holding his side again. 'Whoever they are, they've apparently dealt with six tough Romani already.'

Diego patted the purloined swords he wore on each hip. 'Meaning no affront to Dragi, but now that I'm armed, I'm a more dangerous proposition than six unarmed Romani.'

'I hope you are right,' Dragi replied, then gestured to the others and down to the jetty. 'Good luck, Diego de Teba.'

'And to you. Have some wine ready when I get back.'

Diego watched three unhappy faces – one largely hidden by mail – turn from him to the water, and placed both hands on the hilts of his swords. He wished they were good, well-balanced Spanish swords and not the strange curved eastern ones, but his level of mastery of the art would grant him a reasonable skill even with unfamiliar blade types, and he was well aware of the theory behind the scimitar's use.

As the other three hurried along the jetty, paid the owner and clambered into a boat, pushing off out into the water, Dragi rowing as fast as he could manage, Diego turned to the two dilapidated wooden houses below the Galata wall. Though he could see no sign of their pursuers, the narrow alley between the two was deep and dark and connected to a similar lane that ran along below the wall, behind the buildings, and he was certain the watching eyes lay within.

Silently he stood there, listening to the rhythmic splash of Dragi's oars pushing the others further out into the water. After a moment, he lifted the helmet from his head and dropped it to the ground. Feature-obscuring and very protective it might be, but it also seriously restricted the senses.

'Show yourselves,' he said, eventually, satisfied that the boat was now beyond reach and out of danger.

There was a pregnant pause, and finally two black-cloaked figures stepped out into the sunshine. One had his hand on the hilt of a sword at his side and the other held a light crossbow, already loaded, the quarrel trained on Diego.

Damn it. He hadn't counted on a crossbow. He was fast with a sword – faster than almost anyone he'd ever met – but no swordsman in the world was faster than a loaded crossbow.

'I don't know how you managed to get Sincabı-Paşa to leave with you, but your time for interfering is over,' the crossbowman said in a croaky Italian accent. *Of course!* For a moment, since he'd seen the crossbow, Diego had wondered why the man hadn't simply shot at them while they walked. But the Hospitallers had no idea that

Skiouros was not Sincabı. And for that matter, both he and Parmenio would have been unknown until he'd cast off his helmet just now. Only Dragi looked like himself.

'There will be no pursuit. I have no wish to pit myself against men of the Church, but I cannot allow you to kill my companions.'

'Then I'll have to settle for you instead,' the crossbowman murmured, straightening and raising his weapon. Another figure emerged from the darkness of the alley and placed a hand over the bow, gently pushing it downwards.

'Not this one. Not now, anyway.'

Diego stared into the eyes of the Hospitaller he had allowed to escape at the Jew's house a few days earlier. He nodded his recognition.

'Consider my debt paid, Spaniard. Go on your way, and know that the next time we meet, my blade will be out.'

Diego nodded again, not taking his eyes from the three black-clad men before him. For quite some time he stood watching the three Hospitallers, the one with the crossbow clearly unhappy at being refused his kill. Several minutes passed and finally Diego looked over his shoulder. His friends' boat was no longer visible. As he turned back and stood his ground, he watched the knights retreat into the darkness of the alley, their prey gone. Three men. Counting off the knights they had overcome in Balat against the number he had seen in the church, that would seem to be all there were left in the city, apart from the preceptor that one had mentioned, who was likely still at the church within Galata's walls. And yet he could have sworn that there was at least one more set of eyes watching him, unseen in the darkness. Surely the preceptor would not need to lurk in the shadows, so it had to be someone else.

Heaving in a deeply unhappy sigh, the Spaniard turned and made his way down to the jetty, still certain more eyes were on him as he went. Paying the boatman, he climbed into a vessel. As he slowly and calmly rowed back across the wide waterway, Diego pondered on his situation. It was rapidly becoming untenable. Clearly the next time the knights and he crossed paths there would be no mercy given – nor expected. And despite the threat of combat with them, he intensely disliked even the very idea of raising a blade against a soldier of Christ.

He owed nothing to anyone now. He had paid off his passage on board the Turkish ship several times over. He was not beholden to the Greek, the Romani or the Genoese sailor, though he felt that at least Parmenio – who was as caught up in this as he and without the manipulative element of the others – deserved more. And now that the Hospitallers knew he was not their most avid enemy, they would likely leave him unharmed if he stayed out of the way.

Perhaps he should simply walk away? He had no command of the language of this place, but it was a busy trade hub and vessels from all over the world docked here. Perhaps he could arrange passage on a Venetian trader, or with a Rus? Or an English one, even. He could be out of Constantinople before this damned festival even began.

His thoughts were still in turmoil as his boat slid up to the jetty on the city side of the water and in an effort to calm himself before returning to his friends, he wandered into Phanar and stopped in one of the Greek taverns he had seen there over the past few days. His strange, Turkish mode of dress and the open wearing of swords drew suspicion from the locals, but when he spoke in easy Greek, the tension slowly dissipated and things in the tavern returned to normal. Purchasing a cup and a bottle of wine, he strolled over to a table in the corner and kicked back the chair, dropping heavily into it with a jingle of fine Turkish mail and sword fittings. At least he'd left the ostentatious helm lying in the dust across the river.

Despite his better intentions, Diego found himself once more considering his problems as he poured himself a cup to the brim and began to sip it, ignoring the curious looks he was drawing from the tavern's clientele.

The Hospitallers.

As a nobleman of a good Catholic line himself – albeit with a darker smudge in his heritage – he was well aware of the uneasy dichotomy of knighthood. Not only was it *known* for those who were overtly the paragon of chivalry to harbour dark habits and prejudices, in fact it was more or less the norm. Though prior to his arrival in the Ottoman capital he had had little direct contact with the Order – given their lack of land and influence in both southern Spain and Crete – their reputation in the eastern sea was not an overwhelmingly pure one. Merchants in Heraklion feared the marauding galleys of the Hospitallers almost as much as they did the Mamluk and Ottoman vessels.

The Order had a papal mandate to disrupt Muslim shipping in the seas around their home fortress of Rhodos, and that mandate had been unofficially stretched to include Jewish merchants, Greek Orthodox captains and even catholic vessels should their nation be currently out of Papal favour. And it was these prisoners from a plethora of backgrounds who ended up rowing those same Hospitaller galleys on their seaborne crusade. The knight-clerics were 'good' Christians. But they were also fanatics. And they had a tendency to be somewhat indiscriminate.

What could have persuaded their grand master to interfere in Ottoman politics?

The answer to that was all too easy to furnish: the pope continued to murmur about the possibility of a new crusade against the Turk, and the Order owed obeisance only to Rome and to God. If there was a chance to drive a breach into the unassailable walls of the Ottoman world and open them up to Rome, the Hospitallers would see it as their duty to take it, with or without papal orders. And given their reputed history of overlooking the religious affiliation of their victims, the actions of the group in Galata seemed perfectly in keeping.

Given that, then, what could be expected of them now? They owed nothing to Diego or the other three, nor to the Jews who had harboured them. There was every chance that the family of ben Isaac would come to a bloody end regardless of Dragi's decision to move away from them. And no matter their current alliance, the knights would see the Muslim Romani as disposable at best, if not a direct enemy.

Realising he had sat for several minutes with an empty cup, Diego refilled it and sank down the warming, numbing contents gratefully.

In his heart he knew that the knights would not stop trying to complete their task until they were no more. So where did that leave him? He had no wish to take part in indiscriminate butchery in the name of Christ, though in his heart he felt the Hospitallers' cause to be right, regardless of their methods. *Exitus acta probat* – the end justified the means, in the words of Ovid. But did it?

Angrily, he drained his second cup and refilled again, surprised to find the bottle empty already. Had he poured and drunk more than he'd noticed? No. Three cups, but clearly larger cups than he'd thought.

A night of sleep on the matter was necessary, he decided. He would think on it tonight, and tomorrow morning he would decide whether to stay and face inevitable ethical difficulties, or whether to head for one of the several city ports and try to book passage away from trouble.

Three large cups of wine had eased the pain in his hastily-bound leg, but had dulled his mental anguish little, despite his decision and, by the time the light was beginning to fade and he was strolling up from the street into the narrow, winding alley that led down to the Romani house in the ancient garden, he was still uncomfortable with each and every option available to him.

Overwhelming his irritations, his skin suddenly prickled and he felt the hairs on his neck rise in alertness. Despite the extra skin of wine that coated him, his senses had kicked in once more as he approached the house, and he knew something was wrong even before he spotted the figures in the shadows.

Two men in peasant dress lurked in the shade of an ancient shattered arch, both armed with bows and largely hidden from the house, their backs to the approaching Spaniard. Shrinking back and making sure not to touch the wall in case his mail *shushed* against the stone, he concentrated on the lengthening shadows of eventide. Other watchers were in evidence here and there. An archer by a broken tree stump on the far side of the hollow in which the shack sat; two swordsmen in the shadows of an overhang that had once been the substructures of a grand building. And there, on the other path from this place, three figures in black.

Damn it.

He had not intended to make his decision so soon, and certainly not under the influence of drink. His troubled eyes turned back to look along the path he'd followed. He could easily be along it and away from this place, leaving them all to their mutual destruction.

He closed his eyes and lowered his head, sending an urgent prayer up to the almighty for guidance, though God's attention seemed to be settled elsewhere and no insight came.

There was a metallic rustle as his back rubbed on the alley's low boundary wall. Without realising it, he had inched back, robbed of his spatial awareness by the bottle of wine. He was hardly surprised when the two bowmen in the archway turned at the noise.

Damn you to hell and the pit, Skiouros, he thought viciously, already stepping forward, the swords ripping from the sheaths at his hips. The two archers, only twenty paces from him, fumbled for a moment, trying to draw an arrow from their quivers and bring them to bear and then realising they had no hope of loosing a missile before this strange figure was on them, and trying to draw their swords instead.

Diego, despite his slight fog of wine, pirouetted out of the alleyway dancing a dance of death, his swords blurred and flashing in the evening glow as he spun. Blades ripped into unprotected flesh and both men fell before they could adequately defend themselves, one dead, his neck slashed neatly across, the other crippled and staring in horror at his severed arm.

The curved sword of the Turk. Not a limb-breaker or a fencing, impaling weapon such as Diego was used to, but a slashing razor nightmare. He might not be trained with one, but the theory of their use was not difficult to comprehend. As the two men collapsed to the ground and shouts issued from the other path in Italian, Don Diego de Teba stepped into the wide grassy area, his fine mail whispering with every move.

'Skiouros! Dragi! Parmenio!' he bellowed, in case the shouts of the Hospitallers had not been warning enough.

As the garden burst into life, more men than he'd initially spotted – *damn that wine* – stepping out of the shadows, he turned and made for a tall man in a fur-wrapped turban brandishing a spear. Anything was better than heading the other way and coming up against the Hospitallers. Even now, in the midst of sudden battle, he would rather not be forced to kill them.

Diego hit the grass with a thud and cursed himself for tripping like a wine-addled idiot, but realisation quickly dawned on him and as he rose painfully and looked back, he could see the black-clad crossbowman hurriedly reloading. Agonised, clutching his side, De Teba rose and staggered off to the left, into an area of thick undergrowth close to the house, where he would present much less of a target for the ruthless Hospitaller.

As he sank down into the grass once more, he examined the wound. The bolt was lodged deep in his side at the bottom of his ribcage with little shaft jutting, displaying the flights only. Prodding around, he quickly came to the conclusion that it had passed within and wedged up against his bottom rib. He was not coughing up blood and despite the searing pain he couldn't see that it had passed through anything important. It was too low for lungs and heart, and had it been his liver, he would already be paling and feeling the effects. Slowly, gritting his teeth, he rose. The worst of the pain seemed to be being caused by the protruding shaft battering against the plates of his armour. He'd seen enough wounds in his time back in Andalucia to know that the worst possible thing to do would be to draw out the shaft, in case the head was barbed and tore him on the way out. He would have to seek proper help. The sounds of battle were now ringing out around the large garden clearing, announcing the emergence of the house's occupants. There was nothing he could do to help like this, which suited him just fine. He was at least free for now from facing other Christians blade to blade – *or even back to bow*, he added bitterly.

Painfully, he staggered to the side of the house and shuffled along the wall, hidden from the sounds of carnage by the undergrowth, until he located the rear door he knew to be there. The door was open, thankfully. Three Romani were busy stamping through the undergrowth from it, shouting to each other in their own language, and another man stood by the door with a bow, the arrow nocked ready. He almost released it at Diego before recognition dawned and the man, noting his staggering gait, waved him inside.

In the kitchen beyond, the Spaniard lurched to the table and collapsed, leaning against it and whispering in heavy breaths. He was breathing painfully for a moment, trying to call for someone to fetch him a drink, when the alluring Romani woman who'd been at their various strategy meetings appeared and hurried over to him.

'You are wounded?'

Diego nodded and pointed to the flights jutting from the mail between the small rectangular plates, now quickly soaking with blood. Without pause, the woman helped him up and began to unlace the armour, calling for someone to aid them. A young man ran in and helped strip the armour and then the clothing from him, and the woman hissed as she peered at the wound, from which gobs of blood emerged with every movement.

'It is not your liver or kidney,' the woman said in Greek, and then crouched, examining the wound. She pressed on his bottom rib and Diego screamed. 'It would have passed straight through had it not hit this rib. It is a bodkin point – very narrow and not barbed, so we will not need the *Diokles spoon*. The safest method of removal will be drawing it back out through the initial wound. But you will have to be very still, and be prepared for a great deal of pain – we do not have time to mix up a suppressant.'

'I'll manage,' Diego moaned as he was gently settled into position, leaning on the chair back, presenting his side to the woman.

'Batiya,' she said quietly, 'hold him still...'

*

Diego stirred and opened his eyes. Parmenio was sitting nearby, naked to the waist and with his trunk wrapped round liberally with bandages bearing a pink rose of blood at the side, not far from the position of Diego's own wound. The guttering lamp light was warm and calming, but the moment the Spaniard tried to move, the pain was intense and he quickly gave in and settled back, panting.

'They'll give you a nice mixture that deadens it when they know you're awake. Welcome to the small, but very exclusive, club of gut wounds.'

'You won out there?'

'Me?' Parmenio chuckled, and then clutched his side and winced. 'No. I didn't run out to fight at all. I was already bound tight in linen and drugged into a blissful fog. But your warning saved a brutal surprise attack. Dragi and his friends managed to bring down many of them and the few who remained fled into the night. Two of them were Hospitallers, too, but I suspect you already knew that.' He sighed. 'Hopefully it will all be over by the end of tomorrow. Dragi and Mustafa are convinced that the opposition will not have time now to put anything else into place. It will have taken them a very long time to get trusted people into position.'

All over by the end of tomorrow.

Diego closed his eyes, the memory of his surgery flooding back to him and the words of the woman.

Yes. Yes, it probably would.

Chapter fifteen – Of the Wolf of Trabzon

May 28th – Eve of the festival

THE four friends climbed the gently sloping street towards the wondrous yet strangely-looming complex constructed by Constantine Porphyrogenitus, in which the last Byzantine emperor had resided even as Mehmet the conqueror rolled his cannon up to the city wall. Though beautiful almost beyond comparison, there was something brooding and somehow haunted about the place, possibly through the connections with so recently deceased an empire. After all, the ghosts of Byzantium were still visible, and even the very bones of Constantinople still jutted through the new skin of the city.

The entire complex formed an extended rectangle, abutting the great city walls which formed one long axis. To the south, both side walls were occupied by plain, if somewhat dilapidated, residential and ancillary structures, sitting beneath the battlements. And between them stood the main gate into the palace courtyard. A wide staircase led up from the open space full of fruit trees and delicate gardens onto the heavy outer wall, granting access to the upper floors of the palace itself. But the north end of the rectangle was the breath-taking part. There stood the grand, red-brick and white-stone palace itself, with its delicate arcades of windows, its painted shutters and graceful balconies. This building had played host to the Şehzade Selim since he had arrived in the city – a palace fit for the crown prince, but also a fortification as strong as any castle. Its very selection – surely the choice of Selim and not his father – cried out not 'here is a prince visiting a festival', but rather 'here is a prince, untouchable and strong.'

The first issue would be getting through the gate, of course. Dragi had told them of Romani rumours and legends, born of decades living among the ruins of the Blachernae, of lost and blocked tunnels and passages that would connect the Tekfur Sarayi to other structures in the now-gone great Byzantine palace region. In preparation for this last great task, the Romani of Mustafa's community had pried carefully and conservatively around the ruins and wilderness to the south of the Tekfur, but had found nothing.

Even today, the old Romani had insisted they delay their plan until a last search had been made. But no mysterious hidden ways had come to light, and the final search had been called off in the early afternoon after the guards atop the Tekfur walls had spotted movement and threatened the Romani with execution should they come too close. As the scouts had reported back in, it had come as no surprise to any of them to learn that a black-clad figure had been spotted lurking in an alleyway nearby, watching both the palace and the Romani investigating it.

And so as the afternoon wore on and the sun began to slip down the western sky, the four friends had prepared themselves and left the house for the palace.

They must look a strange sight, Skiouros thought, as they emerged from the street into the open piazza before the palace walls under the suspicious, watchful gaze of the heavily-armoured guards spaced out along the parapet – there were more soldiers around Selim's palace than on the entire circuit of city walls, the Greek noted with interest.

Skiouros, of course, was dressed in his appropriated Paşa clothes, his hair carefully dyed this morning by a shapely Romani girl using walnut juice, his chin and neck scraped free of golden bristles. Sincabı-Paşa's original shirt had been swapped out for one with a high collar – an unfashionable style, though not unreasonably so, and with the benefit that it hid every last inch of Skiouros' colourful tattoos. With a decorative *kilij* sword slung at his side and the 'affluent turban' atop his nut-brown curls, even he had to admit that he looked every bit the Ottoman Paşa.

Dragi still wore his naval uniform with his long, flowing red hat and dark blue jacket over a bulging white shirt and white trousers. A sword and knife hung at his belt, too. The presence of a naval officer in the company of the Paşa who ran the Galata shipyard would hardly be a surprise, after all. Skiouros had wondered why the man had not yet adopted the more ostentatious dress and large turban of a reis, but Dragi had expounded on the added difficulties of such apparel if this came down to a fight.

Skiouros could only hope it *didn't* come to a fight. He was no stranger to a sword, although he was also no born warrior, but the damage to his shoulder had already made itself clear fighting Sincabı-Paşa. And while, for all his experience as a sea-trader, Parmenio could handle a blade well enough, Diego would normally be their greatest asset in a fight. But not today.

The party had moved through the city streets at a sedate, even leisurely, pace to allow for Parmenio and Diego, who both moved jerkily and winced continually through the excruciating pain in their sides. Both were thoroughly bound up and bandaged and liberally dosed with some arcane Romani potion that seemed to take the edge off their discomfort. Both men were strapped in the plate-and-mail armour of a Turkish soldier, with helmets that bore mail aventails which hid their features, and flowing red plumes, and both looked as dangerous a proposition as any man could. And yet Skiouros knew that beyond a doubt, neither would be much use in a fight now, each having enough trouble not crying out as they walked, let alone swinging a sword.

He had argued extensively against their presence, noting their discomfort and immobility and begging them to stay at the house and wait out this last great task. But neither had been willing to sit back. Though both had recognised that they stood little chance of helping on a martial basis, they had insisted that Skiouros, as a Paşa, should have adequate visible escort, and they could at least carry his one-horse-tail standard, declaring who he was.

Skiouros found himself trying to swallow a surprisingly large gulp of fear as they crossed the open space towards the gate. There was, of course, no more danger or risk involved in this particular proposition than there had been at the shipyard with Sincabı, or the old palace with Korkut's assassin. But somehow, knowing that this was the last of it seemed to escalate both the danger and importance of the task.

The prince's guards clustered on the north wall above the gate as the small party approached. Despite the clear eminence of the visitor – as announced by his standard – the door remained resolutely shut, the iron studs in its heavy oak surface presenting an unfriendly, unyielding exterior. The four men were forced to stop around a dozen paces from the gate and crane their necks to look up at the guards.

'State your name, rank and business,' called a throaty officer from the wall.

Skiouros pushed the fear down into his belly and assumed his fiercest, most unforgiving expression.

'Kasim Sincabı-Paşa, master of the Galata shipyard, seeking Musa bin Ramazan the turban wrapper with a demand for his return to my household for punishment, lest I take the matter of his misdeeds to the janissaries.'

He fell silent and held his breath.

There had been much discussion the previous evening, as the wounded were tended, about how they would gain access to the Tekfur and more specifically to bin Ramazan within the palace. There had been no simple answer and not enough time to begin investigations into the assassin's past. Besides, the name was probably a fiction anyway. In the end, the plan had been born purely of extrapolated logic.

Musa bin Ramazan was Selim's turban wrapper. However, the assassin must have been planted in the court somehow by the Romani, and the prince had only been in the city for a matter of weeks, so bin Ramazan must be new to the prince and a relatively new addition to the court in the Tekfur Sarayi. Moreover, he had likely been placed in that position specifically by the king-breaker himself, given the man's apparently central role in this entire plot, and so some history between bin Ramazan and Sincabı could be assumed.

But it was still a cobbled-together net of guesswork, for all its logic, and it would only take someone with a little more knowledge than they to unravel the whole thing. And so, Skiouros' nerves continued to play upon him, making his knee shake so that he had to concentrate on planting his foot firmly on the ground.

There was a long silence as the officer on the wall frowned in uncertainty and then consulted one of his men. Skiouros forced himself to breathe, slowly and in a measured manner. Finally, the officer opened his mouth again.

'Forgive my insolence, Sincabı-Paşa, but I must warn you that this is the residence of Şehzade Selim, governor of Trabzon and son of the great sultan Bayezid. No amount of decorative horse-tails will save your neck if the prince hears of such outspoken demands against his court.'

Damn it. Perhaps he had played the affront aspect too heavily. The last thing he wanted was for the matter to be brought to Selim's personal attention. He tried to mix outrage and contriteness on his face – suspecting he had only really succeeded in looking constipated – and cleared his throat. 'I meant no insult to the mighty Wolf of Trabzon, of course. I request your permission to confront the turban wrapper bin Ramazan?'

Please do not ask the prince...

The guard officer ruminated for a moment and then called down to the kapıcı, whose assistant opened the gate. As the heavy, near-foot-thick door swung inwards to reveal a short covered passageway out into the courtyard of the palace, Skiouros could not help but notice that the doorman was accompanied by two very heavily armoured guards and that even the minor functionary himself was scarred and wore a very practical-looking short blade at his belt. It came as no surprise to find that a man like Selim surrounded himself with only men who were also of martial use.

The kapıcı beckoned to the four men outside with the casual aloofness of a noble addressing a trader, not the deference of a doorman to a high official of the empire. Once more, Skiouros felt the nerves get the better of him, and he paused for a moment to stop his leg trembling before stepping through the late afternoon sunlight to the gate, where the man waited.

'Günaydın, Paşa. Please step inside. You and your men may wait in the courtyard by the lemon trees. I will have Nezih fetch you salep to refresh while I send for bin Ramazan.'

Skiouros fought the urge to refuse the offer, pressing the urgency of the matter, but decided against it. He had clearly almost pushed too far at the gate, and now he was being offered exactly what he had asked for, with extra hospitality besides. *Do not over-reach.*

With a grateful nod, he made his way through the gate, Dragi at his heel, followed by Parmenio carrying the standard and then Diego, who paused and turned in the doorway only long enough to convey the solid impression that his mail-veiled gaze had taken in everything of import and that he was awaiting only a single command to butcher every living thing in his presence. Even

Skiouros was impressed at the power of that single movement. The kapıcı did well not to melt under the Spaniard's gaze.

The courtyard was stiflingly warm, having caught and contained the sunlight all day, the high walls preventing a refreshing breeze from entering. Paying little heed to the structures to either side of the gate, both of which remained partially ruinous from the days of the conquest, he looked past the trees and neat gardens to the stairs that led up to the second level and to the great palace itself, two floors of grandiose habitation rising above an arcaded ground level which seemed to be home to stabling and storage. Apart from the two men at the gate and the doorman and his assistant, they were alone in the courtyard – if one ignored the numerous soldiers along the wall tops, of course.

Despite the man's horrible injury and the fact that he kept having to pause and lean on things, Skiouros was impressed to note how Diego's stance fell into that familiar 'prepared for a fight' mode. Moments wore on in tense silence and Skiouros could feel the nervous energy emanating from Parmenio close by, who had gratefully taken the opportunity to rest the butt of the standard on the floor, the crescent atop it gleaming in the sun and the horse-tail hanging limp for want of a breeze. The kapıcı had disappeared up the stairs and entered the palace and, a minute or so later, his assistant reappeared from one of the slightly ruinous ancillary buildings with salep on a tray. Two glasses, Skiouros noted. One for him and one for the naval officer, but none for the two soldiers.

He gratefully lifted the glass with a nod of thanks and took a sip, savouring the flavour, and was startled from his quiet moment by a shout from the palace. His eyes rose to the beautiful building, to see three figures making their way along the wall top towards the stairs that led down into the courtyard. The rear-most was the doorman, wearing a flustered expression. The turban-wrapper himself, however, almost stopped Skiouros' heart and a number of pieces in the great puzzle of the past week fell into place as recognition struck. He may have neatened up and now be dressed as a court official, but the young eastern Romani with the mismatched eyes and the hare-lip was unmistakable.

Dragi had told Skiouros that the Alevi sect within the Romani who constituted their opposition hailed from eastern Anatolia, and the very ethnicity of this man, whose name escaped him, had simply completely escaped Skiouros. Moreover, as another connection fired in his memory, Skiouros realised that Hadim Ali-Paşa, who aided Prince Ahmed in this great game, had been the

Victorious general of the Mamluk war, where this eastern Romani had learned to fight, possibly even under that man's very command. How had he missed that? But it explained how the Hospitallers had learned of the Jews' house. It explained what had happened to the Romani guard who had escorted them to the shipyard in Galata and vanished while they fought the Paşa – of course the young Romani couldn't afford to come face to face with the king-breaker, for they were well-acquainted! Instead he had sold his own people out to the Hospitallers and come here to carry out his mission. It even explained why the enemy had chosen last night as the time to launch an open attack on Mustafa's house – knowing from an inside source that this was their last chance.

It also created a world of problems very suddenly in the Tekfur Sarayi.

In fact, it came as such a shock to Skiouros that it took him precious moments to take proper note of the woman next to the Romani traitor. Between her bulky dark green dress and the largely-obscuring veiled hat, her features were not easily discernible, but one glance at that weathered, dark, craggy visage and Skiouros was in no doubt that he was also in the presence of the dede Babik – the old Romani crone-witch whose vision had initiated this whole nightmare and who had driven Skiouros from the city five years ago. As he stared, in the silence of his own head, he could almost imagine the clicking of bones as she dismembered birds on the paving. A chill started at his feet and shook his body all the way to the scalp repeatedly, wave after wave.

'This is not the great Sincabı-Paşa, emin of the Galata shipyard,' the young hare-lipped Romani announced loudly. 'This is an imposter and intruder. The Şehzade Selim will be infuriated that you granted admittance to this scum. These men must be apprehended and delivered to the Bostancı for execution – both the false Paşa and his pet *Romani* sailor.'

Skiouros was impressed at the level of contempt the man managed to squeeze into the word *Romani*, given his own ethnic origin and that of the witch at his side. Panic coursed through the young Greek as he failed to see any potential way out of this sudden nightmare.

'*Do something*,' hissed Dragi at his shoulder, and Skiouros' panic only increased. The very idea that for once the Romani sailor had no plan and no suggestion somehow made the situation feel a great deal more dire. His mind raced. He was an imposter, as was everyone who accompanied him...

A smile crept onto his face.

As were bin Ramazan, and his witch-friend. *They* were no more genuine than *he*, and at least Dragi was a true Ottoman officer. If it came down to a war of accusations...

The guards on the walls were moving now. Some were nocking arrows to bows and preparing for trouble, the points veering round to settle on Skiouros and his companions. Others were rushing for the stairs behind the turban-wrapper and the woman. *Time to throw in a little confusion.*

'Do not be swayed by a pair of errant Romani infiltrators!' he bellowed in good Turkish, priding himself on his inflection. He was gratified to note the young Romani's step falter, and gave the man no chance to recover. 'That man is not Musa bin Ramazan, if such a man even exists. He is...' He paused, suddenly aware that he had no idea of the man's true name.

'*Yayan Dimo,*' hissed Dragi helpfully.

'He is Yayan Dimo, a Romani of an Alevi eastern tribe who fought the Mamluks but now serves the Romani witch Babik who stands beside him.'

'Nicely put,' Dragi hissed.

Perhaps half the arrows on the walls had shifted target and were now pointing at the pair on the staircase. Confusion seemed to be reigning. Skiouros glanced back and noted that the gate had been barred, the two men stepping in front of it with weapons drawn. Whatever was about to happen, it would happen here – there would be no escape for anyone from the Tekfur.

Yayan Dimo had recovered from his initial shock at the counter-denunciation, and stormed down the last few steps, the old woman close behind, making towards Skiouros. 'How dare you, you Greek street thief! And with your pet Spaniard and Genoan hidden beneath that armour, no doubt.' He gestured to them and then expansively to the guards. 'Strip them, and you will see!' Dimo yelled to the watchers, spittle on his lips.

'What is the meaning of this?' demanded a powerful voice, carrying a curious mix of hoarseness and musical lilt. Skiouros felt his blood run cold as recognition flooded through him. Similarly, a few paces away, Dimo's face paled. Both of them turned to see the crown prince Selim standing in the doorway of the palace building, his hands on his hips and his eyes blazing and the strangely sinuous, ophidian Sefer beside him.

Skiouros opened his mouth to reply deferentially, but the kapıcı stepped in front of both he and Dimo. 'There seems to be some doubt, my Şehzade, as to the identity of both this visiting Paşa and of your own turban wrapper.'

Selim frowned, and Skiouros bit his lip in worry. A moment's unpleasant, tense silence was suddenly shattered as the old woman by Dimo's side turned and addressed Selim in thickly accented east-Anatolian Turkish. 'My prince, these men are part of a Romani conspiracy to remove you from the succession.'

Selim's only reaction to this news was to raise a quizzical eyebrow, though Yayan Dimo stared at her. 'Shut up, fool,' he hissed. Skiouros noted the hint of command rather than deference in his voice. So *he* did not serve the *witch* after all...

'It seems to me,' the prince announced from the high doorway, 'that the truth in this matter could very easily be ascertained by liberal use of *the hook*.'

Skiouros caught a faint gasp and glanced aside at Dimo, whose eyes were now wide. The hook was one of the cruellest methods of tortuous execution ever devised by man, and was saved for the worst criminals in the empire. Victims were hauled up with a rope to the top of a wall or wooden scaffold covered with huge, sharp hooks. The rope was then released, allowing the criminal to drop and catch on a hook, where he would wait to die. If he was very lucky the hook would pierce something vital and kill him fast. Skiouros had heard of a man once lasting four days...

The shaking in his leg began once more.

And suddenly Dragi was speaking from his shoulder.

'My Şehzade, your brother Ahmed would be more than able to confirm the identity of the dede Babik, since she and her cronies are allies of his, brought to him by the vizier Hadim Ali Paşa in support of a conspiracy against yourself and Şehzade Korkut.'

Selim's expression darkened at the mention of his brother's name, and Skiouros felt himself breathe for the first time in over a minute. They had the pair, now. While she seemed unconcerned, Dimo had paled again. He knew that his chance had slipped away with the revelation that Ahmed was involved.

Guards were now moving down the stairs from the wall, gestured on with a simple flick of the hand from their lord. All was still among the seven people near the lemon trees for a long, drawn-out heartbeat and then suddenly, with no warning, Yayan Dimo shoved the old woman at them and bolted. Knowing that they were sealed in the palace, Skiouros had not been prepared for such a move, and it took him a moment to recover.

The young Romani disappeared into the dark doorway of the ancillary building to the northwest, beside the great and powerful city walls even as arrows tried to track his running form. Skiouros stared, only becoming aware after precious further lost moments that the guards were now flooding down to the courtyard and that Diego, despite his wound, was moving for that doorway in the wake of the young Romani traitor at a fast hobble.

He glanced around at Parmenio, who was leaning on the standard and who shook his head like a parent despairing of a child's lack of sense. 'What are you waiting for?' he asked. 'Go!'

The Genoese sailor raised the standard almost like a weapon and grunted at the pain this caused, pointing the crescent-mounted end of it at the witch, who was spitting fury and spinning in circles looking for a means of escape as the forces of Şehzade Selim closed in on them. Skiouros and Dragi broke into a run, making for that same doorway into which Diego had just vanished, the arrows of numerous guards following them, the archers uncertain as to what was expected of them.

In the heavy, old, Byzantine building, Skiouros and Dragi entered a vaulted room, the roof supported by four pillars. The far end held two doorways, both as black as the maw of hell, and Diego, clutching his side and gasping, was lurching towards the left-hand of the two. Dragi and Skiouros raced after him but brought themselves up short in blind shock as the Spaniard stopped in the doorway and turned, his sword brandished – the point aiming at them.

'Diego, what are you doing?'

'Stop. The pair of you, just stop.'

'We have to catch the man, Diego. He is still dangerous. Can't you see? He's no lackey. The witch serves *him*. In fact, he's probably that self-professed holy man who found the witch in the first place! He won't stop. He'll do all this again somehow!'

'Yes, I know.'

Skiouros stared.

'I really didn't want to do this, Skiouros, but they're right. The Hospitallers are right. You two just can't see it. You Orthodox lot hate the true Church more than you do any Muslim, and Dragi's people are too blinded by their faith. The only hope for a settled future is for the empire to merge with Christendom. Can you not see that? Ahmed will make that happen. Selim and Korkut will prolong the world of crusades and bloodshed for centuries. It needs to end.'

'Diego...'

'No. You said you didn't want to interfere? Then don't.'

The young Greek drew his sword and took a step forward, but Diego flourished his own blade threateningly. 'Let him go, Skiouros.'

'Diego, the Şehzade will kill you for this. By the *hook!*'

'I'll be dead soon enough anyway, Skiouros. That bolt pierced my innards and I've been pissing and shitting blood for half a day now. But heaven's gate will open for me if I do one more good, righteous thing before I go.'

Skiouros closed his eyes. 'I cannot let the Borgia villains get their claws into the empire, Diego. You haven't *seen* them – they make Bayezid and his Turks seem like angels by comparison. They're *not* pious, holy men. They're *evil* men. Wickedness given human form. Now get out of my way.'

'No.'

Skiouros stepped left and flicked out with his sword. Diego easily caught the blade and turned it away, though the effort drained him and he clutched his side suddenly. Seeing his path coming clear, Skiouros dodged right and tried again. Diego again easily turned the blow, but staggered back against the archway in pain.

Skiouros looked around to see where Dragi was, suddenly realising he was fighting Diego alone, but there was no sign of the Romani sailor. Gritting his teeth, he lunged again, feinting at the last minute and coming from another angle. Despite his wound and ebbing strength, still the Spaniard was there, his sword knocking Skiouros' aside and managing to score a painful line up his forearm into the bargain.

Amazingly, he still couldn't get the better of Don Diego de Teba, even with an apparently mortal wound in his favour. He lunged again and again, trying everything he could to trick and exhaust the Spaniard, but the man's blade was always there, turning his blows aside. Sooner or later, of course, the man would collapse with the effort, but every sword blow was buying Dimo more time to escape.

Dragi reappeared suddenly from the shadows, ploughing into Diego and taking him down to the floor in a heap, his sword skittering away. The Spaniard hissed in pain, reaching to draw his knife from his belt as Dragi struggled to pin him. The Romani looked up.

    'Just go!'

    And in a heartbeat, aware that he had left a wounded Parmenio in a courtyard facing an army he could not even understand, and his other two best friends struggling to kill one another in a dark room, Skiouros took a deep breath, hefted his sword, and ran into the dark tunnel.

Chapter sixteen – Of the bones of Blachernae

May 28th – The last day

PARMENIO watched the wild-eyed Romani witch spinning in a panic as soldiers flooded down the stairs and into the courtyard, others pouring out of the ancillary buildings and cutting off any possibility of escape. The woman hissed and began shouting something at the Genoese sailor in a language that he did not know and yet was sure was not Turkish. None too gently, he pushed her with the crescent-tip of the standard, keeping her at a safe distance even though every nuance of the action sent waves of tightly-bound pain through his torso. She was likely just a mad old Romani woman, and Parmenio had had enough of a practical, prosaic life to take stories of witchcraft and magick with a pinch of salt, but everyone else seemed to consider her wicked and dangerous and only a fool ignored so much correlating opinion.

Despite the frenetic energy of the scene, there was still an odd, eerie quiet, barring the woman's curses and the jingling of armour as a large number of very experienced and professional-looking soldiers began to form a circle around them.

'Shut up, woman,' Parmenio snapped, beginning to tire of the unintelligible yet clearly virulent stream of invective. The woman merely continued her harangue unbroken and, with irritated pursed lips, Parmenio smacked her on the head with the metal crescent, interrupting her flow and dropping her to her backside, dazed, even as he had to ground the standard once more and lean on it, huffing at the agony in his side.

'*Yeter!*' bellowed the musical huskiness of Şehzade Selim as he strode out along the wall and down the stairs towards the scene in the courtyard. The word was thrown out in Turkish, and Parmenio had no idea what precisely the prince had said but, from the tone and inflection, the meaning was clear: *Enough...*

The guards parted like Moses' sea as the crown prince approached the pair at the centre of the ring and rattled out a short question aimed at Parmenio. Behind the prince, his man Sefer nodded vehemently.

The sailor swallowed nervously, and answered in Greek.

'I am afraid, Şehzade, that I have little command of Turkish. Do you know Greek?'

Selim frowned in surprise and folded his arms.

'Language of the ancients. Most of the empire was once Greek. In fact, two generations ago this city spoke little else. It would be a foolish man who could not read the words of his predecessors. You have no Turkish and yet serve as standard bearer to a paşa?' His accent was flawless – he could have been a native of the Morea – and his tone suggested that he was intrigued enough by this development that he was temporarily overlooking the urge to have his men seize them both. The oily Sefer gave Parmenio a disapproving look and opened his mouth to advise his prince, but the sailor interrupted him, coughing nervously. 'Your pardon, Şehzade, but I am the paşa's *friend*, not his guard.'

'You are wounded?'

Good lord, the man was astute. No blood had leaked out through his armour, and his hissing in pain could as easily have been arthritis at his age.

'I am, Şehzade. In the course of removing members of a conspiracy to put your brother Ahmed upon the throne.' It was blunt, but only curiosity on behalf of the prince had so far saved Parmenio from being restrained, and he needed to take every opportunity to keep Selim's good faith. Sefer was still glaring at him suspiciously, and the Genoese knew he might have a struggle there.

The old Romani woman started to rise to her feet, spitting angry curses in Turkish, but the crown prince reached out a heavily-booted leg and pushed her back down to the dirt.

'On the matter of this Greek, I am undecided. You, crone, will sing a *türkü* lullaby loud and long under the heated knife of my most inventive man until the truth of this matter is made clear.'

The woman's angry badgering changed tone in an instant, becoming desperate, wheedling and panicked. Selim gestured to two of his men and took his foot from her as the pair dragged her up and restrained her by the shoulders.

'Why did your Paşa not simply approach me about the matter?' Selim asked, puzzled.

Parmenio took a deep breath. The wrong words here could see them all condemned along with the Romani woman. With a quick prayer to almighty God and a hope that it wouldn't anger the Muslim god who might be watching with interest, he cleared his throat.

'A conspiracy of Alevi Romani exists with the intention of placing Şehzade Ahmed on the throne.' He noted impatience growing in the prince's expression, and came quickly to the point. 'Men were in place here and at Şehzade Korkut's palace with the intention of killing both of you at the same moment – tonight – in order to prevent any warning of what was to come reaching either of you. Then tomorrow, on the day of the festival, the sultan would have met with a nasty *accident*, and suddenly Şehzade Ahmed would be the only successor. We removed the threat to your brother Korkut, but if we had brought it to your attention, Şehzade, there was every chance that the plans would be brought forward and everyone would die before we could do anything about it. We chose to move carefully and nullify the threat first.'

Selim tipped his head to one side and tapped his chin. 'Why then did my turban wrapper not simply try to take my life once you had saved my brother?'

Parmenio had been wondering that himself, but believed he had the answer. 'I think, Şehzade, that the enemy were attempting a last try at carrying out the plan entire – there could be no other reason for the witch to be here at the palace, endangering herself in your presence. They were still hoping to pull the plan back from the edge of the fire.'

Selim nodded. 'You understand that I will not simply let you go, Greek. Even with the best of intentions, you broke into my house. I will have your friends found and you will await my pleasure while I have the truth of the matter uncovered in the Yedikule. If your tale rings true from the mouth of the crone, you will have your freedom. If not...'

Parmenio swallowed and hoped against hope that the woman was not tough enough to spin out lies even under torture. He caught the look on Selim's face as the prince gestured for his men to take the woman away to the dungeons of Yedikule and decided that even a rock would tell its life story if it met with what was about to happen to the Khoraxané dede Babik. He was saved having to speak as the prince's attention was suddenly drawn past him to the ancillary buildings. Parmenio turned to see Dragi half-supporting, half-dragging Diego from the doorway of the building. Etiquette forgotten, Parmenio called out to them.

'Where is Sk... where is the paşa?'

Diego opened his mouth, but simply coughed and heaved in deep breaths. Parmenio frowned as he peered at them and, despite not being able to see clearly, formed the deep suspicion that the Romani's arm behind the Spaniard was not so much supporting him, but keeping Diego's arm twisted. The Spaniard looked broken. Not physically, but hollow, somehow.

'The paşa is on the trail of the assassin.' Dragi paused and, turning, bowed respectfully to the prince before addressing him in Turkish. 'Selamun aleyküm, Şehzade Selim. It is good to see you in continued health. I am Dragi Abbas bin Pagoslu, Reis of the imperial navy. I must offer humble apologies on behalf of both myself and Sincabı-Paşa for this violent intrusion into your august presence. It would be my pleasure to explain the matter at length –'

Sefer took an angry step forward and snarled in his strange sibilant voice: 'the knives of the Yedikule will...'

Selim held up a hand, cutting him off mid-sentence. 'Your Greek friend here has explained the situation. The Romani woman is on her way to Yedikule to either confirm or deny the tale's truth.'

Dragi nodded as behind him the gate swung open and shut, ten soldiers dragging the old Romani woman away to the torturer's knives. For just the briefest of moments, the friends caught sight of two black-clothed figures out in the square beyond the gate, in the last of the sunlight. 'Then I humbly offer up myself and my friend Parmenio here for hostages,' the Romani announced, 'until the matter is resolved. If the great Sincabı-Paşa succeeds in removing the assassin, as he once did for your noble father, I remember, then I have no doubt he will return and rejoin us. I must, however, ask a boon of you.'

The prince's brow folded again at such presumption, but he nodded to continue, regardless.

'I would beg your indulgence while I deal with this man.'

Perplexed but interested, Selim motioned for Dragi to go on. The Romani turned towards the north end of the complex. 'Open the gate.'

The soldiers remained in position, having so recently closed it behind the squad accompanying the witch, but Selim, his confusion still very evident and ignoring Sefer's respectful disapproval, gestured for them to do as the sailor asked. As the door was unbarred and pulled open, Dragi turned and for the first time, the watchers could clearly see how the Romani held the other man's arm pushed tightly and painfully up behind his back. Parmenio stared.

'Dragi, what are you doing?'

'I will explain later, my friend,' the Romani replied in Greek as he shoved Diego roughly through the passage and out into the air. 'Come,' commanded the Şehzade, gesturing for Parmenio to walk with him as the large group of soldiers gave them adequate space, their weapons still readied in case of any unexpected move from this foreigner. Striding over to the gate, they paused at the inner arch of the passage and watched Dragi and Diego out in the evening light of the square, the shadows now stretching most of the way across as the last arc of sun peeked out above the city wall.

Parmenio shook his head in confusion at the change in Diego and Dragi. Though one of the men across the square was old and grey-bearded, the black cloaks identified them well enough to Parmenio. The prince's confusion simply deepened.

'Who is this?'

Parmenio huffed nervously. 'A knight of the Hospitaller order, Şehzade, who we have found ourselves pitted against this last week and, I would guess, his master.'

Across the square, Dragi came to a halt and pushed Diego roughly towards the knights, the younger of whom held out a hand to stop the staggering Spaniard, but did little to support him.

'Take him with you,' Dragi said in loud Greek. 'If I ever see his face again, I will put a blade through it.'

The Hospitaller Preceptor looked, for a moment, almost as confused as prince Selim, and the small group was still standing in the city wall's shadow, the knights watching them and the Spaniard's face lowered to the ground, as Dragi stepped back into the archway and bowed at the prince.

'All is finally as it should be, Şehzade Selim, and if the prophet is kind, then Sincabı-Paşa is even now cutting the throat of the last of our enemies.'

'Hardly,' murmured Parmenio.

'What?'

The Genoese sailor turned to the prince and cleared his throat. 'Hardly the last. The main conspirators have been removed, Şehzade, but their nest remains.'

He caught sight of the furious warning glance on Dragi's face, but straightened painfully, ignoring it. 'A small fortified community of Romani live in the Sulukule district, supporting this conspiracy. They harboured, directed, assisted, and probably even armed and trained the killers who were sent against you.'

'They have done *nothing* wrong,' Dragi snapped. 'We *have* the conspirators!'

'I beg to differ, Reis,' Parmenio replied. 'For a military man, you are not thinking very tactically. Never leave an enemy behind. In the wake of a monster's demise, all the lesser monsters start to crawl out of their holes, looking to take control.'

Dragi glared at him as Parmenio proceeded to detail the opposition's community and its location, but the former sailor let the Romani's anger bounce off him, undaunted. Finally, they were at the end of the matter, but if it *was* to end, it had to end *completely*.

There was only one loose end to take care of...

*

Skiouros staggered out of the mouth of a tunnel, clutching his still-painful shoulder that he'd bashed on a wall in the darkened passages of the complex, and looked down in the dim light. The sun was sinking fast now and tracking the fleeing Romani was becoming much harder. He could just see the footprints in the muddy ground where the ruined corridor split off into two, and turned left, following them, a heavy tower and attached complex that formed part of both the city walls and the Blachernae palace ahead, only the top of it still in the sun.

He must still be close behind the Romani. These ruinous passages that had once been substructures of the great palace complex were clearly unused and rarely, if ever, visited, and it had become instantly clear as he lurched out of the Tekfur complex and into a muddy puddle that any footprints he found would be his enemy's. The man knew this area well, having lived among

Mustafa's Romani in this district for some time, but he would have to be careful nonetheless. Dimo could not guarantee that word of his true loyalties had not already reached the old man and his people, so he would have to avoid potential contact with his former colleagues.

And that meant there was no way out for him to the north or east, down to the Golden horn or into Phanar. Which suggested that if he intended to escape this strange ruinous region that had once been the world's greatest palace, he would have to head south, back past Skiouros – a dangerous option, clearly – or to the city walls, which would grant him an easy route to freedom.

Skiouros ran on, ducking round another corner and entering a ruined room, where half a dozen fractured columns jutted up like green and grey fangs from the undergrowth, jabbing accusingly at a sky which was even now turning a shade of indigo and showing the first sign of golden ribbons lacing through it. He would have to corner the man soon. Once it got dark, his chances of success would be negligible.

Desperately, Skiouros charged to the three other doorways from the room. They had passed from the enclosed ruins now to the shattered structures left to moulder among greenery, and the grass hid any potential footprints. Squinting in the extremely dim light, he examined the grass. The doorway heading east into the city seemed to him to show signs of passage – the tips of the grass bent over – though whether by Dimo or by some animal denizen of the area, he could not tell. Still, it was the only evidence to go on.

Damn you, Diego. This is your fault. If you hadn't delayed us a good minute I'd have been right on his heels.

He pinched the bridge of his nose. In a quarter of an hour the sky would be glowing pinky-orange and all the city streets would be in murky darkness. He was almost out of time. What could Dimo be thinking of, going east? The whole area would be under the watchful eyes of Mustafa's men. Since the attack on the house, the Romani leader had become extremely vigilant. Dimo was clearly clever, so he couldn't be stupid enough to risk running into his former comrades.

Skiouros' eyes were drawn to the west as his mind replayed his earlier logic. Not north or east into Mustafa's territory. And despite the fact that he had initially thought of the south as a possibility, if Dimo went that way, he would very likely end up back at the Tekfur Sarayi, which would go badly for him.

233

No. This was a feint. Just like a swordsman. As the blade flicked out left, watch for the knife from the right…

Dimo had gone east to lead Skiouros into believing that was his goal. And while Skiouros was busy poring over the dark dusty ground there looking for prints, the man would have doubled back to the west and through the walls to safety.

With a racing heart, Skiouros realised that he'd just found a way – if there was no flaw in his logic – to catch up with his prey. The only realistic passage through the walls without straying near dangerous territory was the Kaligaria Gate off to the west. Dimo had skirted out east and would double back to the only place where he could cross the walls without going through Mustafa's territory or near the Tekfur.

Praying that he had not just deliberately abandoned the trail, and with it all hope, Skiouros ignored the signs of passage in the broken room and left through the western doorway, making directly for the Kaligaria. Moments later, he was stumbling from the shattered ruins that had formed part of the vast complex connecting Tekfur to the Imperial quarters in the Blachernae and into more open ground, with scattered orchards and gardens tended by the nearby Romani residents. Ahead, between trees and occasional ruined fangs of stone, he could see the Kaligaria gate and he jogged right and left, legs pounding on the hard compacted turf, seeking out the most major easy thoroughfare to the gate. Here and there the ramshackle wooden humps of Romani houses rose from the greenery.

The light was almost gone now and the sky had become a deep purple, decorated with golden mackerel scales, and Skiouros bit his lip as he ran, desperately clinging to the hope that he'd been right and that Dimo was not busy right now disappearing into the alleys of Phanar.

His prayers were answered and his hopes dashed in the same instant.

Rounding the corner of a wall that reached head height and was topped by thorny bushes, Skiouros found himself on a wide, well-used path, the grass pounded down by many feet and cut through with countless wheel ruts. Ahead, the Kaligaria gate stood like some dreadful ultimatum.

And halfway along the road between Skiouros and the gate, the figure of Yayan Dimo raced. He was far enough ahead that there was no doubt he would pass through that brooding archway beneath the huge heavy tower long before Skiouros. And while the Greek was well aware that he was physically fit and fast, clearly Dimo was easily his match in that, if not faster. The man was sprinting at a breath-taking pace considering how long he had already been running. Once he got through that gate he could go anywhere. He would be free.

Skiouros blinked and promised to kiss the next church altar he passed as the maghrib prayer call began to roll out across the city and, in response to the sunset call, the Kaligaria gate swiftly swung shut, a small detachment of janissaries sealing the city walls for the hours of darkness.

Thank you, God. Thank you, thank you, thank you.

The figure of Yayan Dimo, suddenly thwarted at the last moment by a matter of mere minutes, stumbled to a halt, dithering. Skiouros could imagine him weighing up the likelihood that the guards would open the gate for him and let him out. They wouldn't. Even Skiouros knew that, and clearly Dimo quickly came to the same conclusion as the uncertainty about his manner disappeared and he made for the nearest structure – a large three storey ruin that had once been some adjuvant part of the palace system, or perhaps a lone basilica.

Skiouros burst into a feral smile. He and friends had searched that very building one morning when they were checking for Romani watchers hidden in the area surrounding Mustafa's house. Only two storeys of the building were realistically visitable. The bottom floor was largely occupied by shoemakers, whose presence over the centuries had given the gate its name – Kaligaria being Greek for that very profession. The small workshops were separated from the whole by makeshift dividing walls within the large open spaces of the structure, pierced from the road by a passage with a stairwell. The middle floor was only partially occupied by the owners of some of the workshops below, other larger parts of it unstable and crumbling. The top floor was mostly unroofed, just beams and fragments covering the whole edifice, and every step a gamble. He watched with satisfaction as the Romani disappeared into the pitch black of the narrow entry corridor.

Dimo was trapped!

Skiouros slowed as he closed on the building. There was no other exit on the ground floor. Unless he was willing to jump from a higher floor, which would be risky to say the least, Dimo was going nowhere.

Narrowing his eyes and preparing himself, Skiouros drew his sword and relaxed his breathing after the strain of such a run. Better to face Dimo calm and rested, after all. Skiouros was no slacker and no stranger to the sword, but Dimo had cut his teeth on Mamluk blades in brutal warfare and could all too easily be underestimated. As he closed on the dark maw of the passage that led into the structure's heart, the young Greek paused and cocked his head, holding his breath. Sure enough, the echo of pounding feet issued from within. The tone confirmed that Dimo was busy ascending to an upper floor. Good. Searching the interior in the pitch darkness was not an appetising thought – all dingy, damp chambers with no windows, used as storerooms by the shoemakers, and often as residences by the homeless.

Skiouros hefted the curved blade. Somehow, over the years of fighting across Africa and Italy, he had become so cosmopolitan in his martial skills that it seemed as natural to be gripping a Turkish blade as it did to brandish a Spanish or Italian sword. For that matter, he had to think hard to remember that he was dressed in the easy, comfortable garb of a wealthy Turk rather than his old poor Greek gear, so natural did it feel.

Once again he wondered at the work that five years had wrought upon him.

Let's just hope there'll be a sixth, he muttered under his breath and pushed ahead into the mouldy-smelling darkness of the ancient pile. The corridor was utterly encased in darkness, the floor and walls only visible for a few paces from the entrance. Skiouros might as well have been looking into the very entrance of Hell itself, and he found himself shuddering and faltering. Chiding himself for such nerves, he forged on into the black, slowly, trying to give his eyes time to adjust but with the light outside now almost gone, there was really nothing to adjust to. It was black, and that was all there was to it. Trying to recall what he could of the building's layout, Skiouros stepped on carefully, making sure to explore with his toes so as not to crack his nose on a wall in the darkness.

The sound of pattering footsteps upstairs confirmed that the stairwell was exactly where he'd thought, and he began to climb very slowly and carefully, listening all the time. Apart from the occasional drumming of feet above, the only sounds were the last strains of the sunset prayer call and a rather enthusiastic owl somewhere close by, '*toowhit*'-ing like mad, seeking its mate.

The possibility suddenly struck him that the footsteps he was hearing above could easily be a vagrant or one of the shoemakers' families. He quickly cast aside that possibility, though, hoping he was right. Vagrants would hardly be pattering around with such a sense of urgency, and there was little chance of the shoemaking families being anything other than Muslims, which would mean they would now be at prayer, not skittering around the upper floors of dilapidated Byzantine ruins.

The footsteps had stopped. Perhaps Dimo had reached the top, or more likely found a hiding place.

Taking a nervous breath, Skiouros rounded a corner and felt for the next flight of steps, gradually ascending them until he discerned the faintest glow of light from part of the middle floor where the ceiling or wall was missing. Grateful for anything but continued darkness, Skiouros hurried up the last steps of the flight and into the middle floor.

The knife came out of nowhere, flung from some deep dark corner with the accuracy of a professional killer, and Skiouros found himself skittering back down the steps, trying not to tumble haphazardly, hissing at the pain in his leg, which was instantly far worse than the nagging soreness of his shoulder. A moment later he smashed painfully against the wall of the narrow landing where the staircase doubled back on itself, continuing on down.

The wind knocked from him, Skiouros was just grateful that his enemy had not taken the opportunity to follow up. As he staggered and tried to account for all damage, he could hear footsteps climbing to the next level. That was a miscalculation on the part of Dimo. It seemed he thought Skiouros tougher than he actually was. Had the man followed him down the stairs, the Greek would hardly have had the time, the strength, and the wherewithal to put up much of a fight.

He was wounded again – that much was clear from the excruciating pain in his thigh. The darkness had likely saved Skiouros' life, though, for he felt sure that the thrown blade was intended for somewhere much more lethal. As it happened, it seemed the knife had stuck into his thigh muscle, and a brief agonising investigation suggested that only flesh and muscle was torn – nothing that wouldn't recover eventually.

The tumble down the stairs could have been at least equally damaging, but for the miraculous fact that Skiouros had managed somehow to keep his footing as he fell. Apart from being winded and a few scrapes and bruises, there was only the leg.

Only the leg! Where had he picked up *that* attitude? He had his pick of friends to blame for that…

Tentatively, he put his weight on it, gasped, whimpered, and staggered back against the wall rather than collapse to the floor like a heap of blubber. Damn it. One thing was certain: he wouldn't be running, jumping or climbing, but until he removed the knife wedged in his leg, he wouldn't be walking, either. In fact all he'd be doing was bleeding. The handle of the knife was short and plain, and he estimated the blade at three inches, most of which was in his leg. Lucky, really. He remembered Orsini once trying to explain to him the system of blood, and one thing that had stuck was that a major, critical, blood vessel ran down the inside of the thigh, perilously close to the crotch. The dagger was not far from there!

Clamping his teeth together, he rested his sword in the corner and reached down, gripping the knife handle. Three deep breaths, two gentle nudges and one powerful prayer to Saint Nikolas, and he grasped the hilt and ripped it from his leg, along with a veritable fountain of crimson. Everything went blinding white and Skiouros was baffled for a fraction of a second by what could be the sound of a fallen angel having its wings torn away, before he realised the noise was coming from his own throat. Searing pain flooded in to fill the space left by the departing blood, and Skiouros felt the overpowering urge to collapse in a faint – or possibly vomit. Or both?. His eye twitching with the effort, he pulled himself up and tried to think straight. *Stop the blood…*

Swiftly, unwilling to lose what little advantage he had at this late stage, Skiouros reached up and removed his turban, hastily unwinding several yards of white linen from the central core. Quickly and with clenched teeth, he wound the wrapping around the leaking wound, pulling it so tight that his muscle cramped, and then bound it round again and again and again, as taut as he could manage. Half a minute later, as he tied off his makeshift bandage and noted the pink stain already beginning to blossom upon it, he tested his weight.

The first step was excruciating, but his leg held and he stayed upright. Determination overriding his agony, he collected his sword and picked up the knife, experiencing a whole new dimension of pain as he crouched, and then spent another half minute recovering. Then, slowly, but with a face that was a stony mask of resolve, he began to hobble up the stairs, leaning on the wall with his knife hand. This time, just in case, he ducked out of the stairwell and back twice, trying to avoid a repeat of the last attempt.

No knife came from the darkness.

Carefully, Skiouros turned and moved into the next stairwell, heading up to the top floor. A repeat of his duck-out-and-duck-back manoeuvre failed to produce another thrown knife, and the Greek emerged onto the upper floor tired and in pain, with a leg that seemed to be rapidly numbing. Could that be a bad thing? It *felt* better.

The near end of this level was badly floor-boarded and with many parts missing. Indeed, even the walls gave way to large areas of hole that presented views of the inky sky and fiery sunset outside, as well as the scrubland and Romani shanty homes surrounding the place below. There were precious few places a man could hide up here, as was instantly evident. Skiouros paused and concentrated, his eyes scouring the crumbled structure, his ears pricked for any giveaway movement.

The interior walls were more or less gone, just a few crumbling pillars and low tumbled piles of bricks. Only two or three could hide a human, and the floors in that area would almost certainly bow and give under the weight of a human. The few areas of outer wall did not give onto balconies or external stairs, just open air. He almost smiled as he caught sight of the heavy ancient corbels at the wall-top which once supported a decorative roofline, and his mind supplied him with an image of himself clambering through something similar at the castle of Roccabruna a couple of years ago to gain entrance to a parapet. *That* had been a life-and-death struggle, too. Of course, he'd been healthy then, not wounded in both shoulder and thigh.

As he looked at the eaves of the roof, his peripheral vision spotted movement, and he turned.

Surely not?

The figure of Yayan Dimo moved across the shattered fragments of the roof above him with catlike grace. Skiouros glanced at the corner and noticed the ladder that led up to the roof. Not an original access point – the roof would not have been reachable. Recently placed, then, and in good working order – no problem for a dextrous former thief. But for a paşa with a knife-hole in his leg...

At least Dimo was at the other end of the roof, perhaps looking for some way down, and Skiouros gritted his teeth and sheathed his sword, reaching for the ladder.

*

Yayan Dimo peered over the edge. Three storeys down to hard turf. High, old Byzantine storeys, too, not the modern low ceilings of the timber houses one saw all across the city. A fall that guaranteed broken legs if not certain death. He cursed. He had really hoped for some way out, or at least for somewhere safe from the demon that was following him. Who *was* this fake paşa? He had the build of a boy – albeit a wiry one – the face of an angel, and the eyes of an innocent, yet the tenacity of a wolf and the courage of a bear! When Dragi had first introduced him, Dimo had felt relieved that the enemy were pinning their hopes on such a poor specimen, and yet Skiouros the thief had managed to thwart them all this time, with the help of his friends. But even now, alone and wounded, facing a much tougher opponent – Dimo knew his own skills and strength – the young Greek still never gave up. Now, wounds in both shoulder and leg that would prohibit such an act for most hardened warriors, he was still managing somehow to climb the ladder. Oh he was making hard work of it, but he was still coming when most veterans Dimo knew would have long since stopped.

And the Greek was armed. Dimo had nothing now. No sword. No knives. If it came down to a fight, despite his far superior skill, Dimo would almost certainly lose to the man with the sword. He clucked and fretted, chewing his lip. He was the last of the Alevi faithful involved in the attempt, but there was plenty of new blood to draw from in the Sulukule Romani community. He had to escape and bring his people out of danger, settle them somewhere safe, away from the city, and then begin to hatch a new plan.

There was no way out, and he was outclassed. But he still had one thing – the *only* thing, in fact... he still had surprise. Bending, he reached down to the heavy roof beam upon which he trod with the sure-footedness of a mountain goat. His fingers closed on a broken tile half a foot across in each major dimension and an inch thick. His gaze fixed upon the ladder top and his eyes narrowed as he weighed up the situation, edging four paces closer to achieve a position on a cross of beams where his balance was that little bit more stable.

The Greek began to emerge through the roof, and Dimo held the tile behind his back in tight fingers, his spare hand held out for balance. The Greek paused for a moment, presumably waiting to see if Dimo threw another knife. *Would that he could...*

When no knife appeared, Skiouros the Greek heaved himself up with some difficulty until he was standing on an area of roof still relatively intact. He wobbled a little, then straightened and drew his sword, glaring menacingly at Dimo. Behind the Greek, the sky was a beautiful mackerel-skin of gold against indigo, and Dimo couldn't see much of the man's face beyond the impression of a feral scowl. But Skiouros' silhouette against the glory of God's golden creation made him appear to be some djinn from the ancient tales with a halo of flame, come for him – his own nemesis; his *qarīn* come to turn him from the righteous path...

Fuelled by sudden religious fury coupled with desperation, Dimo uncoiled like a spring, sending the tile in a deadly arc. His aim was as true as he could have hoped, given an arm that had been trained by years of slinging spears at Mamluk warriors, and the tile smashed into the Greek's good shoulder hard. The sword fell from numb fingers, clattering back down the ladder into the floor below. Good. Now they would be more even, and Dimo could fight the man.

But he wouldn't need to!

Allah was on Dimo's side this day, clearly.

Not only had the tile hurt the man's arm and forced him to drop his weapon, but it had also knocked him off balance, especially given his already-wounded leg, and Dimo stepped forward two deliberate, short steps as he watched with delight. The Greek staggered back. His leg gave way on the uneven tiles and, with a scream, he was pitched out into the air, three storeys above certain death.

Dimo thanked God and the prophets and began to inch carefully forward along the beam, back towards the intact section of roof. It was possible that the Greek had only crippled himself in the fall, but dead or not, he would certainly not be walking away from it. And Dimo would collect the man's sword from below on his way down. Killed with his own blade... that would be a fitting end for the fake Paşa.

Slowly, he crept forward, making sure not to lose his own balance on the angled tiles, and peered over the edge.

His eyes scoured the undergrowth and thick grass below, but found no body. *Impossible!* No one would walk away from that! He looked again, and then squawked as a hand closed around his ankle and pushed, hard.

In the split second his leg shot backwards and his point of balance fatally altered, Dimo's eyes caught the face of his personal devil – his qarīn – peering up over the roofline with a face that made him quail with terror, more even so than the fatal drop.

'*Corbels*,' was the last word he ever heard.

*

Skiouros watched the last of the Alevi plotters plummet past him with a disbelieving squawk. The Romani bounced off an old crumbled piece of wall just before he hit the ground, and might well have been dead before impact. The young Greek looked down at the twisted, broken shape of his enemy. If Dimo had been *lucky*, he'd already been dead. Skiouros found himself, in a fit of uncharacteristic uncharitableness, hoping the man had lived and felt each of those four limbs being bent into that unnatural shape. The rapidly-growing pool of dark liquid around the man's head confirmed even from this height that Yayan Dimo was no more.

And with him had died all the Alevi plans. Though he'd had to leave the Tekfur sharply, Skiouros had no doubt that Dragi would manage to overcome Diego and that between he and Parmenio they would put things right with the prince. The Romani witch had already been doomed even before he left. The Alevi dreamer and the holy man who had found her had both gone, and the king-breaker too. Well, *he* still *officially* existed, of course…

With a wry chuckle, Skiouros realised that not only did Sincabı-Paşa still exist, he was no longer a fake. The Sincabı who now lay at the bottom of the Golden Horn had been a greedy, opportunistic beggar, claiming to be something he was not. In the eyes of the sultan, Sincabı-Paşa was a Greek former thief who had foiled a Mamluk plot against the empire. And now, finally, Sincabı-Paşa was *indeed* that man. In a moment of odd clarity, the young Greek accepted the fact that Skiouros the low thief had finally gone. He was Sincabı the respectable citizen of the empire now.

A skitter of dust passed Skiouros' face and disappeared off into the darkness below, reminding the Greek that he was not safe yet. Two years ago he had climbed the wall at Roccabruna and found himself faced with having to pass corbels not unlike these. Today one had saved his life as he plummeted over the edge, but he'd only just made it. His right arm was slightly numb from the thrown tile and his left shoulder still burned from the musket wound. He'd hit the corbel hard and only instinct had made him pull himself to it and wrap his shot-wounded arm around it tightly, clinging on for dear life. As he'd hung there his shoulder burned with pain, but he'd heard Dimo approaching and flexed his slightly numb free arm to bring back some feeling. Grabbing the man's ankle had been surprisingly easy and, given Dimo's precarious position, it had taken hardly any force to bring him down.

But now, with two wounded arms, he was still clinging to the corbel, and his shoulder was going to sleep even as his arm strength continued to ebb. In any normal circumstance, Skiouros would have panicked, but somehow he felt that everything was going to be alright. God, luck and his own skills had seen him through plenty of predicaments in his time.

What was one more climb...?

Epilogos

Of friends and brothers…

28 years later…

8ᵗʰ November 1523, Istanbul.

SKIOUROS approached the door of the building with more than a little trepidation. Another adjustment in his thinking was required here, but one that he had been putting off for far too long. Stretching weary arms, he gestured to the small unit of janissaries that hovered protectively around him.

'Stay here. I will return presently,' he said in his long-native Turkish.

The Çorbasi in command of his personal guard gave him a hard look. He had been Skiouros' guard officer now for a number of years and had become used to the foibles and oddities of the unusual nobleman. Though he nodded his acceptance, the man made it abundantly clear that he disapproved of such recklessness.

'Yes, Sincabı-Paşa.'

Next to him, the standard bearer grounded the butt of his burden and heaved a small sigh of relief, earning him another hard look from the officer. Skiouros looked up at the standard, the crescent gleaming in the late autumn sun, which was accompanied by a cold wind that jostled the three horse-tails below and cut through no end of jackets and coats to chill Skiouros' ageing bones.

Yes. Another adjustment. Throughout his early life in the city he had known this glorious, decorative brick edifice as the church of Saint Saviour in the fields. It had been the *Kariye* mosque now for perhaps a dozen years, but it was still hard to think of it as anything other than Saint Saviour's, even with the delicate minaret soaring into the leaden-grey sky.

He had not visited the mosque.

He had even politely declined the invitation from Hadim Ali Paşa to its inauguration all those years ago. The man's involvement with Prince Ahmed and the Alevi plot had rankled long after the festival, and it had been something of a relief late in 1511 when the man had finally passed away, only weeks after his mosque's dedication.

But it had not been the rededication of the church as a mosque that had put him off coming. After all, living as a Paşa at the Ottoman court, he had adopted the appropriate religious habits long ago – since his idea of God was something nebulous and heretical anyway, it was as easy to kneel in a mosque and thank God for what had come to pass as it would have been to kneel in a church and do the same.

And it had not been Hadim Ali Paşa's involvement that had kept him away. Indeed, those sixteen long years throughout which Saint Saviour's church had undergone a slow and sporadic rebirth had passed without Sincabı-Paşa even once laying his eyes on the place.

But this morning, Skiouros had tried to rise from his bed and something had tightened and *clunked* in his ribcage. The doctor had been called quickly and had examined the ageing Paşa carefully. His prognosis was not good. Skiouros' heart was beginning to fail. There would be months at best, more likely weeks.

Naime had cried when she heard and blabbered about calling the boys back, but Skiouros had smoothed down her hair and dried her tears and smiled. Every man had his allotment of time, and few had filled it with as much as Skiouros. He was not sad. He was in fact cheerful as he looked back upon his span. And the boys' careers would suffer if they came back to the capital for their father's sake while their ships under the great Hayreddin '*Barbarossa*' Reis pressed home their advantage in the wake of the latest victory of the great Ottoman navy.

And so the time had finally come. He'd not many more days left in this world and, while the Christian priests would tell him that all loved ones are united once more in the glory of heaven, and the imams told him they would all meet again in paradise, the real uncertainness of what was to come had led to this morning's visit.

And perhaps not through chance, today was the first day of Muharram, the New Year in the Ottoman calendar and the month of remembrance. Wordlessly, he stepped inside, the old knife-wound in his leg lending him a slight limp as it had these past three decades, and hobbled through the outer narthex, all white plaster and Arabic script, the only other decoration a geometric pattern around the top of each arch. It was like walking into a different world – all those glorious mosaics and paintings gone forever. His boots clicked off the tiles as he passed around the corner of the building and into the parekklesion side chapel. So many memories...

His skin prickled a little and a chill fluttered through him.

'Lykaion?'

He didn't expect an answer, of course. Through all those years of conversing with his departed sibling, the more he had grown and gained control of himself, the less Lykaion had spoken to him. And finally, during that terrible time in Italia with poor, doomed Prince Cem, he had heard the last from his brother. He had finally come to realise that all it had ever been was his conscience playing with his imagination. But in case there was no heaven, or *Jannah*, this might be the last chance he would ever have to speak to Lykaion, reply or no.

'There are so many things I should tell you. I don't know where to begin. Perhaps at the beginning,' he smiled.

Skiouros sank with difficulty to the floor, crossing his stiff legs, and began to recount the tale of everything that had happened once Dragi, Diego, Parmenio and he had returned to the city from Crete and placed Lykaion's remains below this place. Time seemed an ethereal thing here and, though he knew that his spell alone here would be at an end when the imam came to issue the next call to prayer, in the meantime it seemed to be endless and peaceful.

He told of the saving of Korkut. He laughed aloud when he told his brother of his masquerade as one of the Bostancı. He recounted the fight in the great ship in the yard across the water. He told of the Hospitallers and of the Jews, and of the two Romani camps. He told Lykaion of the encounter at the Tekfur Sarayi and of Diego's betrayal, Parmenio's bravery and Dimo's demise.

Finally, after almost an hour of breathless narrative, he fell silent with a small smile and sat back.

'You won't know about the succession, of course,' he said, conversationally. 'And that's of prime concern, considering what we did to preserve its natural progression. It seems that the end might very well justify the means after all. The great Bayezid lived past the festival, you see. Long past, in fact. He lasted until about a decade ago and would probably have managed more years yet, but Selim had had enough by then. He had already tried for the throne once and been exiled for his pains, but a decade ago, he came back with janissary support and forced Bayezid to abdicate.'

Skiouros chuckled darkly. 'If I were being charitable, I would say that perhaps Selim had seen the end coming and moved quickly to prevent his brothers winning the day. But I think I know in my heart that Selim would have taken that throne then even without the threat of his brothers, and he was simply tired of waiting. His siblings ran to oppose him, of course. Ahmet was captured and executed the next year – 1513 that would be – and Korkut, despite pledging allegiance to Selim, was executed the same year. Selim never allowed sentimentality to overcome common sense. That, I think, was what made him strong and the best candidate in the end. Dragi's people had been right after all, you see.'

Skiouros stretched. Soon the imam would come, but there now seemed so much still to say – a veritable flood of news. Had it really been so long since he'd spoken to Lykaion?

'Selim was not a bad sultan, I suppose. He was hard. *Very* hard. He only lasted eight years but you'd have approved of him, I think. In just eight years, he put the Safavids in their place and completely overwhelmed the Mamluks. The empire now extends from Albania to Egypt and all the way to Arabia, but Selim fell ill on campaign and died early.'

His face became very serious as he remembered the harsh sultan who had become Caliph of all Islam and overlord of Egypt. 'I think he carried a grudge against the Alevi for his whole life, you know, after the festival conspiracy. Not long after he took the throne, he had forty thousand Alevi in Rum province – where the Khoraxané dede Babik and Yayan Dimo had come from – registered and put on a death list. A few of us pressured the chief cleric to intervene and he managed to persuade the sultan not to do it, but he hated them 'til the day he died.'

A smile warmed the old Greek Paşa's face 'But his son, Lykaion… if only you could have known his son Süleyman. He's only ruled for three years so far, but he is a new Bayezid, my brother, and better even than that. A *great* man! Already they are calling him the 'lawgiver', but he is so much more. He is magnificent, Lykaion. The Empire goes from strength to strength under his guidance.'

He sighed.

'But I'm wandering off course. I have limited time, and I may not get to visit again. And, of course, the events at the festival were only the start of my own story, really. From that day on, Skiouros of Hadrianople was gone, you see. And Sincabı-Paşa as he is now was born. I have served three sultans and numerous viziers. I have watched that Galata shipyard grow and change – oh, I still control it, you see. I will do until I pass on, though I think my days of striding around the sheds may be over now. The shipyard is enormous and constantly busy these days. The great Göke I mentioned earlier was one of a pair that heralded a new dawn for the navy. I had my work cut out, especially under Selim, who wanted everything instantly. Selim spent two hundred thousand ducats expanding it. We now have one hundred and sixty dry docks turning out vessels and maintaining extant ones. I have janissaries working for me – two entire orta! And we're so busy. Even without all the smaller flotillas based in troublesome areas of the empire, Barbarossa's fleet alone requires constant replacement and maintenance.'

Again the smile slid from his face, this time to be replaced by a tired melancholy. 'Of course, Barbarossa is a great admiral, but his stream of victories owes much to his predecessor. I got to know the great Kemal Reis and his nephew Piri at court, and came to greatly appreciate them. Piri Reis is an accomplished sea captain and military commander, but he's also the greatest geographer the empire has ever seen. Kemal defeated the Venetians soundly at Modon, proving our supremacy at last, and won endless smaller victories all over the middle sea until he died in a shipwreck back in 1511. Dragi Reis outlived him, having distinguished himself at Modon, and only died earlier this year at Rhodos.'

His melancholy shifted slightly, combining with a sad smile. 'Barbarossa took Rhodos from the Hospitallers back in January, and Dragi was mortally wounded in the siege. At last that black-clad, cross-wearing murdering thorn in the empire's side has been drawn, and they've retreated west across the sea. I heard stories that there were half a dozen Spaniards captured during the siege, and I often find myself wondering if one of them was Don Diego de Teba. After all, if anyone could save him from his gut wound, it would be the Knights of the Hospital.'

He chuckled. 'Parmenio never stopped telling Dragi how daft he was to let the Spaniard go, but then Dragi had little time for Parmenio after the festival, and the pair's relationship was ever cool. You see, Parmenio had led Selim's men to the Romani camp in Sulukule and the prince had every last Alevi Romani killed slowly and painfully in the dungeons of the Yedikule. They say the torrent of blood from the execution tower poured out into the Propontis for four days without pause.'

His face darkened again for a moment, but memories of the Genoese captain soon brought back his good, if melancholy, mood. 'Parmenio took a position at the Galata shipyard with me. It was his experience and knowledge that informed a lot of decisions about the way our arsenal would work and the vessels would be produced. He was, I would say, invaluable. In the end, though, I think he got sick of being on land. About five years ago, he started taking out the new ships and giving them their first run. A year or so later, he fell ill. He must have been sixty summers old by then, and he wouldn't tell me what the doctor said, but he resigned his shipyard commission, hugged me once, told me to look after myself, and then left on a Genoese merchantman. I never saw him again. I dreamed of him the night after he left, though – him and his deadly ladle – which was a shock to me, for after those dreams induced by Dragi's smoke ended, I stopped dreaming altogether. Just that once, about Parmenio. Odd, that, isn't it?'

He sat straight and rocked gently back and forth. His news had poured out in a torrent with no form, and while his mind was still sharp enough, sometimes his memory seemed as fragile as his thigh, which had never been the same since Dimo's knife, and he had to run through the years in his head to see if he'd missed anything. He smiled suddenly.

'I have a wife, Lykaion. Naime. She is a convert originally from Sofya in Bulgar-land, less than two hundred miles from Father's farm, if you could believe it. And we have two sons, both of whom are serving under Barbarossa across the north of Africa. *Hamza* is the pilot of a kadirga, and will likely make reis by this time next year. We named him that – *steadfast* – after Parmenio, you know, since that's what my Genoese friend's name means in old Greek. But *Kurt* was named for you – the wolf. Kurt is a janissary in one of the naval ortas. I tried to get him assigned to the shipyard, but he refused. He wanted to be out there on the waves.'

He chuckled. 'So far removed from their father in so many ways. They both remind me more of you: all duty and for the glory of the empire. But then I am not the sneak thief you knew once, Lykaion. It's odd, really. Once upon a time I lived in fear of ships. I'd spent a journey to Crete having to make myself sick on one. I'd been captured in battle from one and been a slave on another. I'd narrowly avoided being shot on one and sailed off into the unknown on another, drinking my own urine for survival and watching my shipmates dropping from disease. And in the end here am I, personally overseeing the construction of the navy and regularly taking ship back and forth to places like İzmit and Gelibolu.'

He sighed. A lifetime in an hour. He rose waveringly, his hip causing him a little difficulty, and hovered for a moment, steadying himself. Even with such little movement, he could feel that pulling sensation deep in his chest that reminded him that the sand was still running through his personal hourglass on its last turn. Still, he hadn't done badly for a peasant thief on the city streets. He'd done his part more than once to bring a little civilization and humanity to this corner of the earth and, under the great Süleyman it would continue in the same vein, he was sure. A thought suddenly struck him and, with some difficulty, he removed his coat and vest-jacket, and then shrugged out of his silky shirt. Was it against the law to stand half-naked in a mosque? The great Süleyman codified a dozen laws a day in his efforts to tighten the madly-sprawling legal system of the empire. What was law today might not be tomorrow, and vice versa.

Despite his age, his skin was still well-toned, if not muscular, and the tattoos his wife had long since given up trying to understand were as vivid as the day he had had them inked upon his body on a mysterious western island, by a strange tribe who had opened his eyes to the divine more than anything else in his life.

'I never got to show you these. They lay incomplete for a long time. The snarling face in the lower circle is the *guayza* – he was to represent your living spirit while I hunted Cem Sultan in the belief that somehow I'd be avenging you when I killed him. In the year following the pretender prince's death, I came to realise that your spirit had never really *been* restless and my revenge was just self-indulgence to mask my own problems. I think on some level I was always aware that the guayza was actually me – unsettled, unsatisfied and unfulfilled. Only when *Skiouros* disappeared and I became *Sincabı* did I finally realise how to finish the tattoo. My Romani friends completed the designs for me on the night of the festival.'

He looked down at his arm. Between the snarling demon in the lowest circle and the dreadful fire spirit that climbed his neck, the circle that had lain empty for three years, rather than bearing the *opia* that would be Lykaion at rest, instead held in a delicate calligraphic hand:

سلام

'Salām,' Skiouros explained, somewhat unnecessarily. 'Peace. It came at last, to the empire and to me, as well as to you.' With a sad smile, he began to pull his shirt back on and then drape his vest and coat over the top. 'And that's about it,' he added. 'I can feel my heart decaying with each passing hour, and I doubt I will have the strength to come again, so I felt I needed to say everything at once. But if the imams are right – and the old Greek priest I sometimes visit on the sly too – then I'll see you soon enough… and perhaps in the next world we won't argue.'

With that same sad smile, Skiouros walked up to the white-painted apse with the Arabic script in delicate lettering across it and reached out, brushing his hand across the heavy indentations in the plaster. It no longer said Lykaion, since Şehzade Ahmed had scratched it out for its connection to his brother the Wolf of Trabzon, but the fact remained that this was the only memorial to his brother. 'Farewell, Lykaion. In the end, I suspect we were far more alike than we were ever different.'

Straightening and blinking away a tear, Skiouros – who had been Sincabı-Paşa for three decades now – turned and wandered through the mosque without looking back, passing through the door into the steely sunlight, limping slightly on his bad leg, his janissaries rushing to aid him.

In the white-clad chapels of the church-turned-mosque, a faint breeze rippled through the air and if a man had been there to hear it, he might have sworn he heard a cracked and ancient voice whisper *'farewell, Skiouros.'*

251

The End

Author's Note

Where does one start with the contents of The Paşa's Tale? Well, since, ignoring Skiouros and his friends' personal journeys, it is a tale of the Ottoman succession, that seems a good place to begin. Throughout history there have been many methods of succession to a throne. Most common, of course, is dynastic, from the world of Ancient Egypt (and even before!) right the way up to the modern British monarchy. The eldest son takes on the role from his deceased father. Of course, gender sometimes changes, and daughters inherit before younger brothers and so on, but the principle is the same. A hierarchical dynastic approach. Most empires have advanced this way.

Occasionally it has come to a selection process, such as that adopted by the Ulpian and Antonine emperors in Rome, choosing their successor and adopting an heir appropriately. And then there is the republican and democratic method: a leader is voted in by the people (or more often by the privileged classes among that people.) There are very odd ones, where Gods are asked to choose, and similar wackiness, but the one overriding factor they all share is that there is a *system* in place.

Which is what makes the Ottoman Empire in this period so fascinating. Essentially, the throne was achieved through *survival of the fittest*. Only certain candidates could try for it, of course. Mustafa Bloggs the fishmonger was never in the running. But no son of a sultan had precedence. Relative age made no difference. In the later years of their father's reign (most sultans lived 'til around 50) their sons would begin to manoeuvre for position. One of the most important factors in the race for the throne was location. Whoever reached the city of Constantinople (the Ottoman nobles mostly still used the ancient name, while the low-born began to adopt 'Istanbul') stood a very good chance of keeping the throne, for they then had control of the shipyards, the palaces, and had immediate access to the elite janissary units. It was not a given, but likely the son who got there first would be the next sultan. And since all princes served their time as governors of provincial '*sanjaks*' under their father's reign, the location of their governorship could easily dictate their chance of succession. Thus sons would inveigle their way into their father's good books in attempts to achieve governorships that were close to the city, giving them the edge.

But political alliances and military strength also played a part. It was not good enough to reach the city and claim the throne if none of the officers and Paşas owed you any allegiance and the military had thrown their support behind your brother. And so you can see the sort of mess the succession became. It often consisted of up to a decade of jostling for position and securing power and alliances. This is what drew me to the succession as the basis for the Paşa's Tale plot. There could be few milieu in which there was more potential. And, of course, given Skiouros' prior role in keeping the sultan on the throne, it was destined to play a part in the story.

Then, of course, there are the three sons of Bayezid. My portrayals of Korkut and Ahmed are largely works of fiction. Since they failed to succeed to the throne, evidence for them is sparse. Selim, on the other hand, is well documented. He was a strong man, hard and unyielding, but undeniably good for the empire, for he expanded it and removed two of the three greatest threats it faced (the Safavids in Persia and the Mamluks in Egypt.) Like Trajan for the Romans or Alexander for the Macedonians, Selim was a conqueror who left the empire, after just a short reign, far greater and stronger than he found it. He has been somewhat damned by history for his persecution of the central Anatolian Alevi, which I have gone some way to including in the story. Indeed, extrapolating from it, it formed the backbone of the tale. But despite Selim's conquests and his strength, the greatest gift he gave the empire was his son: Süleyman 'the Magnificent'. Under Süleyman's reign, the empire reached a golden age hitherto undreamed-of and, sadly, never to be seen again.

So from here, it seems right to tackle the troublesome subject of religion. It might seem that during these four books I have rather wickedly attacked all religions. I hope it is evident that this is not so. I have endeavoured, especially in this last volume, to decry extremism in any religion, and to vaunt the ethics and morals that are the basis for them. In doing so I have made Skiouros somewhat heretical, in that he has encountered the very best and worst in all the great Abrahamic faiths, and has consequently eschewed them all as set creeds and lives with a private dogma born of them all. This is something I have seen time and again being practised, and so seems as reasonable to apply to someone in that era as in our own. And given Skiouros' outsider's viewpoint as a child born of the Greek Orthodox Church, he has a slightly more objective viewpoint than many of his contemporaries.

There is a sad tendency in the modern western world to view Islam as evil and Christianity as good. This is, of course, a rather blinkered view. I have met as many pious, peaceful and friendly

Muslims and Jews as I have Christians and equally it is quite easy to find examples of viciousness, hatred and extremism in all of them. People are people, no matter what their faith. There will always be good people and bad people.

But at this time in the world, the roles I mentioned above are very much reversed. The Islamic nations at this time are conquering, yes, but on the whole, they are busy conquering each other. It is a political expansion rather than a religious crusade. For over a hundred years the Ottoman military concentrated on overwhelming their opposition in Persia, Egypt, and all along North Africa. Yes, there were wars in the Balkans and against Venice, and particularly Rhodes and the eastern islands, but again this was largely a political, territorial push. In fact, Christians and Jews living in the empire enjoyed relative stability. They were heavily taxed and disadvantaged in comparison with their Muslim neighbours, of course, but religious intolerance-based troubles were rare.

Compare, if you will, the Papacy at this time, run by the Borgia family, which interferes in national politics, dabbles in assassinations and all manner of wickedness. The Pope himself was a womaniser with numerous mistresses. Usury was at an all-time high and almost anything was for sale if the Borgia pope gained from it. This was, in my opinion, the very lowest moment for the Catholic Church. But add to this the newly-blossoming Inquisition led by the Spaniard Tomas de Torquemada, and you're talking about a Church that is not only corrupt and wicked, but even actively deadly and murderous. Religion is always a thorny subject, but hopefully I have treated all the faiths with the objectivity of the historian, shot through with the personal opinions of my fictional character.

So what of the Romani?

Again, perhaps I might be challenged over my portrayal of them, though only the Alevi faction have been vilified, and that purely for the advancement of the plot. Indeed, they have not been turned into a wicked sect, but more of a misguided group, and even then not for their religious beliefs so much as for their own sense of self-preservation. The Romani were very much a thriving community in the empire, and in more regions than just Sulukule and Ayvansaray as mentioned in the text. They were culturally diverse and, though they had traditions that went back centuries to long before they settled in the empire, they had long been practising Muslims (just as those Romani living in Western Europe became practising Christians.) The Romani have always been an adaptable people. It is in their nature. I have attempted to make them understandable and credible in this tale, despite their active role in such a complex plot. The Romani community continues even now to thrive in Istanbul, and in the very same places they lived half a millennium ago.

In contrast to the so-human Romani, I have given the Knights Hospitaller a much harsher treatment. I have at least a passing interest in the crusading orders, though my focus is on the more obscure orders (Knights of Calatrava, Knights Teuton, etc...) I have laboured long under the impression that the Templars were victims of their own success, becoming too rich and avaricious to avoid the inevitable conflict with the State. But I had always seen the Hospitallers as more of a pious order, focusing on looking after the wellbeing of pilgrims to the Holy Land. Of course, my earlier reading focused more on the days of the high medieval period, and this is very late in the day for the crusading orders. But still I was astounded that the more I read of the Hospitallers in the eastern Mediterranean over this period, the more unpleasantness I came across. In 1530 the Ottoman navy kicked the knights out of Rhodes and they were given Malta as a new home. For centuries afterwards, Malta became a centre of slave trading as attested by numerous writers of the time. The knights were, at the very *least*, rather indiscriminate as to who they sank and captured on the seas. Many of those captives ended their days at the oars of the Hospitaller ships, and many more were sold at the markets. The knights only lost their position to the French in 1798, which means that their home was one of the last refuges of the slave trade in Europe.

Given the role of the knights in the previous book and the fact that they had been sent east by the pope, their involvement in any Ottoman successional crisis seemed a given, and they would apparently not baulk at dealing with non-Muslims who got in their way.

Much of this story revolves around the Ottoman navy, its ships and its personnel. This era was the great time of growth for the navy, which would soon pit them against Venice once more in a series of wars that only ended in the 18th century. By the time of the dreadful battle of Lepanto in 1571 the Ottoman navy seemed indestructible. Their defeat at Lepanto at the hands of a league of 8 states(!) was the first sign of naval expansion slowing.

Ottoman naval vessels were, at this time, powered by both oars and sails, and the navy was formed of the traditional galleys that still plied the seas. The great Göke was a tremendous vessel, but of as much value as new ships were the changes in organisation. Prior to Selim's reign, the centre of Ottoman naval power was still officially Gelibolu (Gallipoli), though already under Bayezid the Galata shipyards were growing in both size and importance. And over the reigns of Bayezid, Selim and Süleyman, the whole thing truly stepped up a notch. Gelibolu began to take second place and all naval functions moved to Galata, where the complex of naval headquarters, prisons, shipyards and so on stretched from the Galata walls a vast distance up the inlet's shore. It came to be known as *Tersâne-i Âmire* – the Imperial Arsenal – and rivalled that of Venice, which was famous in its own right.

And so onto my last topic for this note, which is 'locations'. We are very lucky that many of the locations I have used in The Paşa's Tale still exist and I have had the opportunity to visit them on my research trips. The walls still exist, in a bad state in many places, and with some none-too-careful reconstruction in others. But their presence makes it possible to imagine them in the late 15th century. The Tekfur palace is similar. When I first visited in 2008 it was a picturesque ruin. When I last visited in 2014, it had been glazed and reroofed and given an overhaul. It is now usable as a building in some form, but has sadly lost much of its character.

The district around it, though – Ayvansaray – is one of the most fascinating in the city. It is largely untouched by modern Turkey and bears a remarkable resemblance in some places to the region I have described in the book. It is still an overgrown area with large patches of wasteland, ancient crumbling ruins jutting out of side streets and, most interestingly, in places the very same timber shanty-houses that still belong to a Romani community. If you have an interest in experiencing this strange place, I urge you to go, and soon, for there is every chance it will soon disappear.

I had hoped to visit Sulukule and experience the Romani life there, but even in 2008 I had just missed it. This once thriving Romani district that had been famous for hospitality and dances and music, full of ramshackle timber Roma housing, had gone. In 2008 it was busy being bulldozed in its entirety. The best part of a mile of historic community had gone, leaving a dirt wasteland. Now it is full of modern, hygienic housing, in which the Romani have been resettled. The reasons are many and largely revolve around health and safety – with which even I could not in conscience argue – and I'm sure many of the resettled community are happy with their new life. But with the change died the spirit of Romani Sulukule and despite the sense in the move, viewing it in 2014 almost broke my heart. It felt the same as the clean, rebuilt Tekfur palace.

Conversely, the church of Saint Saviour (now known as the Chora church or Kariye Camii) has been beautifully preserved, as it is one of the city's greatest tourist draws, behind the Aya Sofya. Over the last century the mosque was decommissioned and converted to a museum. The plaster was carefully stripped to reveal the paintings and mosaics beneath, in their great glory. It is restored and visitable. If you should go, you will see it as a Byzantine church and your breath will be taken away. I would then recommend visiting Küçük Ayasofya Camii in the heart of the old city, which is an early Byzantine church that is now an active mosque. It is astoundingly beautiful and will allow you to imagine how the church of Saint Saviour might have looked after its conversion to a mosque.

Much of this book is set in Sulukule or Ayvansaray, or in old Balat and Fener (Phanar in the text). Fener and Balat never seem to change. They are areas of narrow, vertiginous streets where children play outside and women beat carpets in the street. The houses are old and often built of timber, and the whole feel of the place is that you have stepped a few centuries into the past. Two other book locations are now entirely gone, and only imagination and rare old paintings can help us picture them. The great Ottoman naval complex is still occupied by shipyards. Galata's Golden Horn shore is *one long* shipyard. But of course these are modern shipyards, and nothing of the old *Tersâne-i Âmire* is visible. Other than that, Istanbul's other main locations in the book are the Eski Saray (old palace) which is long gone and the site is now occupied by the university, and also the hippodrome. The general form of the hippodrome still exists as a park with three of the ancient columns in it. The curved colonnade was gone a century after this book's era, but the arc of substructures in which I had Korkut sitting still exist and are easily visible from the exterior.

One last location before I finish: The ruined church on Crete, where Diego was lurking. This is the Byzantine church of Agios Titios at the ancient site of Gortyn near Agioi Deka in the south of the island. Gortyn was once a capital city, though it has been ruined for over a thousand years. It is, if you happen to get to Crete, an astounding place to visit.

A last word, then. This series began as a standalone novel. The Thief's Tale was planned that way. But before I finished it, it became clear that Skiouros' tale could not end until Cem Sultan died. And that could not easily come about until years had passed. So the book became a trilogy. And then, again, as I sat writing The Assassin's Tale, it became clear that there was no way I could tie up all the loose ends in that volume. And so The Paşa's Tale became the planned fourth book in the trilogy (nods thanks to Douglas Adams for setting that precedent.) Lykaion had to return home, the role of the Romani had to be explained, and most of all, Skiouros had to complete his journey (geographically, emotionally and spiritually.) And so he is now home and at peace. And here the series ends. I shall be sad to say goodbye to the series, but I have enjoyed every chapter. I hope you have too. And who knows what might happen in the future. I might miss it too much and want to expand. The Spaniard's Tale? The Sailor's Tale? Who knows. But for now, farewell Skiouros.

And thank you for reading. I hope the tale satisfied.

Simon Turney, March 2015

* * *

Bibliography (for those who can't get enough Istanbul and Ottoman/Byzantine life)

Books...

Osprey publishing – Warrior 41: Knights Hospitaller (2)
Osprey publishing – New Vanguard 62: Renaissance War Galley
Osprey publishing – Men-at-arms 140: Armies of the Ottoman Turks
Osprey publishing – Elite 58: The Janissaries
Gypsies in the Ottoman Empire – Marushiakova & Popov
Constantinople: Istanbul's Historical Heritage – Stephane Yerasimos
Istanbul: The Imperial City – John Freely
Jem Sultan – John Freely
Constantinople: City of the World's Desite – Phillip Mansel
The Antiquities of Constantinople – Pierre Gilles
Walking Through Byzantium: Great Palace Region – Byzantium 1200
The Land Walls of Istanbul - Nezih Başgelen
The World Beneath Istanbul – Ersin Kalkan
The Story of the Barbary Corsairs – Stanley Lane-Poole

Academic treatises...

The Coverings of an Empire: An examination of Ottoman headgear – Connor Richardson
The rise of Ottoman Seapower – Jakob Grygiel
Medical treatment in the Ottoman navy – Miri Shefer Mossensohn

Kemal Reis: A big seaman and a hero for Al-Andalus – Prof. Dr. F.Sefa Dereköy

Websites of interest…

www.theottomans.org
www.kultur.gov.tr
www.ottomanempire.com
www.turkishculture.org
www.byzantium.ac.uk
www.byzantium1200.com

If you liked this book, why not try other titles by S.J.A. Turney

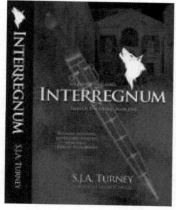

Interregnum (Tales of the Empire 1)

(2009) *

For twenty years civil war has torn the Empire apart; the Imperial line extinguished as the mad Emperor Quintus burned in his palace, betrayed by his greatest general. Against a background of war, decay, poverty and violence, men who once served in the proud Imperial army now fight as mercenaries, hiring themselves to the greediest lords. On a hopeless battlefield that same general, now a mercenary captain tortured by the events of his past, stumbles across hope in the form of a young man begging for help. Kiva is forced to face more than his dark past as he struggles to put his life and the very Empire back together. The last scion of the Imperial line will change Kiva forever.

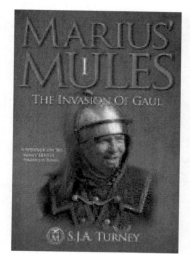

Marius' Mules I: The Invasion of Gaul

(2009) *

It is 58 BC and the mighty Tenth Legion, camped in Northern Italy, prepares for the arrival of the most notorious general in Roman history: Julius Caesar. Marcus Falerius Fronto, commander of the Tenth is a career soldier and long-time companion of Caesar's. Despite his desire for the simplicity of the military life, he cannot help but be drawn into intrigue and politics as Caesar engineers a motive to invade the lands of Gaul. Fronto is about to discover that politics can be as dangerous as battle, that old enemies can be trusted more than new friends, and that standing close to such a shining figure as Caesar, the most ethical of men risk being burned.

* Sequels in both series also available now.

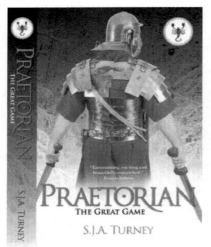

Praetorian: The Great Game

(2015)

Promoted to the elite Praetorian Guard in the thick of battle, a young legionary is thrust into a seedy world of imperial politics and corruption. Tasked with uncovering a plot against the newly-crowned emperor Commodus, his mission takes him from the cold Danubian border all the way to the heart of Rome, the villa of the emperor's scheming sister, and the great Colosseum.

What seems a straightforward, if terrifying, assignment soon descends into Machiavellian treachery and peril as everything in which young Rufinus trusts and believes is called into question and he faces warring commanders, Sarmatian cannibals, vicious dogs, mercenary killers and even a clandestine Imperial agent. In a race against time to save the Emperor, Rufinus will be introduced, willing or not, to the great game.

"Entertaining, exciting and beautifully researched" - Douglas Jackson

Other recommended works set in the Byzantine & Medieval worlds:

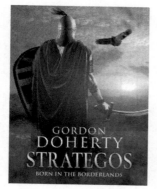

Strategos - Born in the Borderlands

by Gordon Doherty (2011)

When the falcon has flown, the mountain lion will charge from the east, and all Byzantium will quake. Only one man can save the empire . . . the Haga! 1046 AD. The Byzantine Empire teeters on full-blown war with the Seljuk Sultanate. In the borderlands of Eastern Anatolia, a land riven with bloodshed and doubt, young Apion's life is shattered in one swift and brutal Seljuk night raid. Only the benevolence of Mansur, a Seljuk farmer, offers him a second chance of happiness. Yet a hunger for revenge burns in Apion's soul, and he is drawn down a dark path that leads him right into the heart of a conflict that will echo through the ages.

Tom Swan and the Head of St George

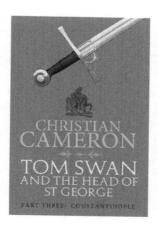

eBook series by Christian Cameron (2012 -)

1450s France. A young Englishman, Tom Swan, is kneeling in the dirt, waiting to be killed by the French who've taken him captive.

He's not a professional soldier. He's really a merchant and a scholar looking for remnants of Ancient Greece and Rome - temples, graves, pottery, fabulous animals, unicorn horns. But he also has a real talent for ending up in the midst of violence when he didn't mean to. Having used his wits to escape execution, he begins a series of adventures that take him to street duels in Italy, meetings with remarkable men - from Leonardo Da Vinci to Vlad Dracula - and from the intrigues of the War of the Roses to the fall of Constantinople.

Made in the USA
Middletown, DE
12 June 2015